John Saunders Holt

Abraham Page, esq.

A novel

John Saunders Holt

Abraham Page, esq.
A novel

ISBN/EAN: 9783337000677

Printed in Europe, USA, Canada, Australia, Japan

Cover: Foto ©Andreas Hilbeck / pixelio.de

More available books at **www.hansebooks.com**

CONTENTS.

CONTENTS.

PREFACE, BY MR. PAGE'S EXECUTOR.

I AM perfectly aware that to pretend to have found the manuscript in some unlikely place, or to have had it left to one by last will and testament, is an old and hackneyed method of introducing a story; but if it be true in any case, the fact should not be ignored for that.

The first time I ever saw Mr. Page was when he made a visit to my father, his old friend and schoolmate. It was on the occasion of his flight from the persecutions of Miss Sophia Walker, which he has mentioned in his Life; at least I judge it was at that time; for, although I never heard of Miss Walker until I saw Mr. Page's manuscript, he never made but the one visit to our part of the country. I was then a very small boy, but remember perfectly the impression made upon me by the old gentleman. He was, I suppose, forty-eight or fifty years of age, and was of medium height, very neat in his person and brisk in his movements. He had mild, benevolent, gray eyes, a rather prominent Roman nose and a broad and high forehead. But what attracted me to him was his great simplicity and fondness for children. For hours at a time he would play with me and my sisters (often at games he must have invented, for I have never seen them since) or would tell us the most comical and wonderful stories. We thought there was never such a man as he, and when he left us to return to his home our keenest desire was to see him again.

One of my first attempts at letter-writing was a letter to him, which he answered by due course of mail; and from that time, though our correspondence sometimes languished, it was kept up, when I was not with him, until the beginning of the late war.

When I became a law-student, my father, acceding to my strong desire, and to frequent and pressing invitations, allowed me to go on to Mr. Page's, where I remained nearly two years. Certainly no young man ever had a more kind, capable, and conscientious preceptor. The amount of his information upon all subjects was prodigious. He had been a hard student all his life, and seemed to forget nothing he had ever heard or read, and yet he was more free of dry scholasticisms than any man I have ever met of half his erudition. He never used a technicality when it could be avoided, and the most abstruse subjects, when explained by him, were within the comprehension of any one of ordinary mind. Every fact or system of facts seemed by some powerful process of mental digestion to be reduced by him to its simplest elements, and the most complex and dryest parts of law, theology, and politics became simple and attractive.

He appeared to be perfectly aware of this peculiar faculty of his mind, and, indeed, sometimes to indulge himself in a little self-flattery on account of it. "There now! Master John!" he would say sometimes, "consult your new lights upon that subject, and see if they are more profound, or nigh so simple."

Mr. Page had his little vanities—what man has not?—
but they were all of the most inoffensive character. It
gratified him extremely to be referred to by his neighbors
for any information, or to decide any point which seemed
to require more learning than they possessed; and such
demands were being constantly made, for he was almost as
much esteemed in his county as an oracle as he was beloved as a true philanthropist.

To tell half the good he did is impossible. I find that
he has said of his father what could equally well be said of
himself: "His knack for encountering objects of pity on his
road, and his luck for having poor orphan children thrown
upon his hands by bequest of parents, or devise of circumstances, was at all times extraordinary." I believe it to be
true that at no time from his full maturity until his death
did he have fewer than two orphans wholly dependent
upon him for support and education, while he partially
supported others, and was the providence of all the poor
widows in his neighborhood. He has omitted all this in
his Life; but some of his experience with his orphans, as I
have heard it related by his neighbors, was discouraging
enough for any man less warm-hearted than he, and some
of it was very comical. He would never admit in so many
words that gratitude was the rarest of virtues, but I feel
sure that his various experiences inclined him to believe it
so. For instances of ingratitude to himself—and from all
that I heard they were frequent—he had many excuses; as
that it ran in their blood, or that they had been so hardly
dealt with before that their souls were narrowed; but his
chief consolation was that what he did was not for their

gratitude, but for his own sake; and he insisted that he was really selfish in all his charities. His philosophy in this matter is certainly the strongest with which a man bent on doing good can fortify himself, for without it one or two ragingly or whiningly unreasonable widows, and a mean, ungrateful orphan or two, will put a stop to the warmest benevolence. The only change which could be perceived in Mr. Page's plans of benevolence was, that he, after a while, found it more pleasant to support his orphans and others away from his own house.

In the winter of 1862-3 I met Mr. Page, old as he was, at C——, very busy in his attention about the army hospitals, and know that by dint of persuasion he finally procured permission for two of the sick to go home with him to be nursed. After the surrender at Appomattox Court House I took his house on my route home, for I was sadly fagged and in want, and knew that I should get relief with him.

I arrived at a sad time. During the whole war his house had been a perfect hospital for sick and wounded soldiers, and two or three months before my arrival a raiding party of the enemy had visited the old man and had treated him most shamefully. Besides breaking up much of his furniture and robbing him of almost everything they could carry away, whether useful to them or not, they had terribly cursed and abused him as "a d—d old rebel," and had drawn their guns upon him with the intention, as they said, of shooting him; and he had borne it all like the noble old gentleman he was.

It would do no good to dwell upon the scene of wanton

mischief and cruel malice as it was truly related to me, but not by him. Such things it will do to pass over, but not to forget until a time of peace and unity shall make forgetfulness desirable. At any rate, the disasters of the war, together with these personal outrages, were too much for the enfeebled constitution of the old man—nearly eighty years of age—and I found him in a very critical state of health.

He said that my arrival was all that was wanted to make him contented again, and he insisted that I should remain with him at least a few days.

The third day of my stay I thought I perceived that in spite of his cheerful, hopeful conversation he was rapidly declining in strength, and ventured to ask him if he felt as strong as he had the previous day, "No, my son," he replied. "I do not wish to deceive you. My days will be very few, and it is principally on that account I have insisted on your remaining with me. You will find my last will in my large desk, which was fortunately among the lumber in the garret when the raiding party came, or it too might have been destroyed. I have named you my executor, for I had a strong presentiment that the war would spare you, and I find myself greatly blessed in having you with me, and being able to tell you my wishes more fully than I could possibly have written them.

"I have been a very fortunate man all my life, my son, and I wish to impress upon your mind my testimony to the goodness and power of God. I can say with perfect truth that in the checkered scenes of my life, though I have had many sorrows, I have always afterwards seen that His

A *

goodness has been manifested in them towards me. It has been invariably the case that the right thing has happened at the right time, and I have full confidence that it shall be so still, both to me and my country." (He and I had been talking a great deal about public affairs.) "We are very wise in our own conceit, and very rebellious, sometimes, towards God, but the Judge of all the earth will do right. There could be no better time than this for an old man to die, for great troubles have yet to come, and, though I feel sure they will end for the best, I am glad to escape them."

At another time the same day he said to me: "Do not be downcast about our cause, for, after all, if the principle of strict constitutional government, for which alone we contended, shall be established, is it not better that it should be over the whole than over only a part of the country? I acknowledge that I sometimes have great fears and doubts about the fate of our country; but when I reflect that the promised days of peace and true religion on earth must soon be here, and that it would in the natural course of events take ages to settle this country in peace under any other form or forms of government than that we now have—and which is perfectly feasible if the rights of the separate States and the other restrictions of the Constitution shall be strictly observed—I have great hopes that the late war and the present and prospective troubles and confusion shall end in the triumph and firm establishment of our principles as the only true basis of constitutional government. If it be so, our people shall have fought and suffered and triumphed gloriously. But, however it may be, remember at all times that it is God who rules, and that His kingdom *shall* come, and His will *shall* be done on earth as it is in heaven."

In like discourse, and in telling me his desires with regard to his property and dependants, and the proceeds of the cotton he still had on hand, which had neither been stolen nor destroyed, and the reasons why he did not make me his heir, were passed the very few days Mr. Page was able to sit up at all and converse at any length. The old gentleman was particularly concerned that I should fully appreciate his reasons for leaving Miss Bolling the bulk of his property. He said that the events of the war had rendered what she possessed almost entirely valueless; and he intimated more than once that he had long had a desire that she and some one he also loved should live in his house, the representatives of himself and his Mary; and said that he knew the property alone was not sufficiently valuable to warrant me, as I was already married, or either of my brothers, to leave our old home and our prospects there, and he could not bear to have it pass into the hands of strangers. He said, moreover, that my brothers were excellent gentlemen and brave soldiers; and he could see no reason in the word why, now that Robert Harley was dead, one of them should not come on and try for Miss Kate's hand. And as he drew nearer his end, the idea seemed to seize him more and more forcibly, and he declared that it was impossible there should be a more fit or happier match. To gratify him, I promised to use my influence to bring it about; and perhaps it may yet take place, though I doubt it. I have found that Miss Kate, though she fully justifies Mr. Page's love and admiration, has a firm will of her own, and my brothers are quite as indisposed as she to have their affections directed.

To describe the death of my good old friend would be as painful to me as it would be uninteresting to the general reader. He died peacefully, and, as he had lived, a good and loving man.

I have tried my utmost to carry out his intentions. The very considerable legacy of money to his grand-niece I have paid over, and she is spending a portion of it in contesting his will, upon the ground of his insanity. The orphan children he had in his care have been well and permanently provided for; and when the decision of the court shall allow me, I will hand over to Miss Kate her property, and thus finish my executorship, except with regard to the manuscripts left in my charge.

This "Life" of Mr. Page I publish, not only because I think it due to his memory to do so, but also because I believe that it teaches sound principles of living and of thinking, which ought to be disseminated. I have no apology to make for his style or matter, for although both could, doubtless, be improved in some respects, it is beyond my power, and I think in violation of my duty, to improve or attempt to improve them. To judge from the handwriting of the manuscript, as well as the tone of the book, I think it was written at different ages. The first chapter appears to have been written many years before the remainder, and at a time when Mr. Page was in a discontented mood with himself. I know that even so late in his life as when I went on to visit him he used sometimes to declare that he was a "Failure."   He seems afterwards to have justified himself in his own mind (as the old are prone to do) for not having reached the high public position and accumulated the large fortune his more youthful ambition declared to be his due.

As the whole book was written before and during the early part of the late war, I need not tell the reader that Mr. Page's political sentiments do not agree with those of the present ruling party.   But they are just those of the gentlemen of his class at the time they were written; and if they are now settled to be unsound, it can surely do no harm to publish, without change, an old man's opinion of them.

His ideas about the Church may also be regarded by the mass of priests, preachers, and women as very heterodox. But the subject is of so vital importance that every man should be entitled to his opinion about it; and, for my own part, I think Mr. Page's opinion worthy of serious consideration, although he has not indulged himself in a display of learning in elucidating it.

There are only two things I would ask the reader to remark about his "Life." The first is, his perfect freedom from a desire to be thought learned or over-wise; and the second is, the tone of quiet humor which pervades the whole work.   And I would say to the reader about the more pathetic parts of the book, as Mr. Page once said to me about a touching passage he was reading in another's writings: "You are fortunate if you understand that, for you could only do so by having an affectionate heart yourself."

2

The publication of Mr. Page's other manuscripts will depend upon the success of this with the public. The proceeds of the book or books are to be devoted to the support, education, and start in life of a little boy in whom Mr. Page took a great interest, though he has thought fit not to mention him in his Life.

JOHN CAPELSAY,

OF NATCHEZ,

Executor.

LIFE AND OPINIONS

OF

ABRAHAM PAGE, ESQ.

CHAPTER I.

IT is a fine sight to see an old man whose heart still beats with generous emotions, whose cares have not made him selfish, whose own vicissitudes have but made his charity more gentle and universal.

I once knew such a man, and he stands alone in my memory. By honest industry he had raised himself above the thousand evils of want, and he was revered by all the country round for his wisdom, learning, and humble piety. No excesses had wasted his powers, and though age had somewhat unstrung the high tension of his organization, his gray hairs crowned a body still erect and energetic, and covered a brain still teeming with cheerful thought. I often saw him look with a smile of tenderest love upon the trustful wife of his youth, now old and wrinkled, to whom many years before, when he first clasped her in his warm embrace, he had made vows of love he had never broken. Standing with her, and surrounded by the amiable and intelligent children with whom they had been blessed, he could look to heaven and say with deepest gratitude and love: "Behold me, and those Thou hast given me!"

The old man is dead now, and his old wife has joined him; but it seems to me he had reached a grandeur of human dignity the greatest worldly honors would but lessen. I venture to say that had his case been presented to the heathen doctors who held to the two hundred and eighty different opinions as to the principal end of human actions, all would have agreed that he had acted, at least, as though he had found the truth.

Many winters have silvered my hair, and in the course of nature I must soon lie in the cold grave, where all my rosy hopes have long since gone; and I am sometimes tempted to wish that such a destiny as his had been reserved for me. But such a wish would be both foolish and unphilosophic—foolish, because impossible of fulfillment; and unphilosophic, because everything is for the best, and because such a change would require a total reorganization of society and affairs in my own State, and consequently in America, and consequently all over the world; and Heaven alone knows what would be the upshot. In this regard every man is of the utmost importance, and he should console himself or be proud accordingly.

My life, like that of most other men, has been one of mercies and duties neglected. My youth was promising, for I was gifted with a vigorous and comely person and a sprightly mind. There are few things I could not have accomplished had I so willed. I feel convinced that I should have made a good carpenter or machinist, for to this day I am fond of tinkering; and after age had sobered my enthusiasm a little, I am pretty sure I should have made a notable archbishop—for I always had a turn for the Church. As a painter I should have suc-

ceeded finely; but not as a painter of portraits, for besides that I could not be precise long enough to paint
a portrait, my sense of the ludicrous was so strong I
would certainly have offended my patrons by carica-
turing them. I could have become a distinguished
musician, for I had a correct ear and was passionately
fond of music. I could tip off "Stay, Sweet En-
chanter," and "Robin Adair," in a manner to be ap-
plauded, and I even for awhile led the choir in the
principal church of my native village—there were three
churches there—but the young ladies of the choir got
married, or moved away, or got offended with each
other, and would no longer sit and sing together, and
the best of the two male singers died, and the other
got the bronchitis; so that I was finally left alone, and
the congregation seeming to think soon that I could
sing enough for all of us, it began to look too much
like work, and I quit it. After that, I sang only on
occasions. I should not have made a good tailor, for
the trade is too confining and laborious; but I know
of no one who could have excelled me as a cutter-out
for fancy young gentlemen. Neither should I have
made a good physician, for, besides that I abhor bad
smells, my anxiety to relieve the suffering would have
warped my judgment. Finally, I should now, as a
lawyer, be very high in my profession if I had really
desired it, and had had more perseverance.

"Much virtue in if," quoth Touchstone. Much sorrow there is in it too, Master Touchstone, although the
sorrow may be unphilosophic. There are a great many
things more desirable than high position, and even than
wealth.

2*   B

It is not from vanity that I have here detailed part of my various talents, but merely that the true nature of my life may be known. I know of no vanity more unreasonable than that which is based merely upon superior capacity or opportunities. If it produced that noble ambition which leads to true greatness—which I consider to be only superiority in the performance of duty and in conferring benefits upon our fellow-men—it could be excused, and even cultivated. But in general this feeling, known as self-conceit, is an opiate to which the poor victim has recourse when the labors of life seem too hard; and lulled into delicious repose, his imagination revels in bright visions of the future, and he satisfies himself with feverish dreams of the fame he could accomplish.

He sees himself at some future time, and on some great but indefinite occasion, mounting the rostrum to address vast multitudes. He pictures to himself how, as he warms with his subject, he is interrupted by loud huzzas. Louder and louder they increase, until at last, when he has finished, in an excess of enthusiasm they lay hands upon him and bear him on their shoulders, and hail him as the man of the people, the orator, the demigod.

Or else he heads a charge of cavalry in some great imaginary battle. He hears the roar of the artillery, the sharp fire of the riflemen, the huzzas of the soldiers. It is a critical moment. He rides in front of his men. In an ecstasy of glory he calls upon them to follow him, and with a clash and flash of sabres and a shout, amid the shrieks of the wounded and the groans of the dying, they ride in furious career through the ranks of the enemy, trampling their scattered hosts. His name, like that of David, becomes a song in the mouth of the people, and he too has a Saul over whom he triumphs by genius and virtue to arrive at supreme power.

Or, seated at the foot of some spreading beech beside a gurgling brook, his imagination is soothed by the genial warmth and the thousand beauties and pleasant odors of a day in early spring, the hum of busy insects, and the songs and twittering of birds, and he makes himself rich from the ready foundation of an "if," or a still more certain process worked out by his ingenious fancy, and he constructs and reconstructs to its minutest detail the plan of a house he will build in the shady grove, to be the abode of love and contentment to himself and some transcendent wife he has yet to see in reality— though she may, indeed, be an existing Dulcinea.

And so the poor victim dreams on, so he warms himself with his imaginings, careless of his fortune and heedless of time, till, at last, he wakes to find himself old and poor, his time and talents gone to waste; all his past confusion, all the future a blank, to be filled as the crazed fill the present.

I am an old man now, with neither wife nor child to cheer my age. Though I have many friendly acquaintances, I have few friends. Those of my youth have either died around me or removed, long years ago, to distant sections of the country, where most of them have died, and I have been left to make new friendships—as though the old vine once untwined from its support could ever adapt itself and cling to another! I am solitary, yet never lonely. God has spared me my memory, and as I travel across the desert of life I am unconscious of the burning sun and drifting sands, and have ever present with me the happy forest, with its flowers and gushing springs, its singing birds and its pleasant breezes, from which I started, the cooling shades which I have passed through here and there along the way, the dear companions who left me before the journey was half over; and, thank God! I have now at last upon the horizon the bright prospect of a happier and more beautiful country to which I am going.   I see there, even at this distance, scenes and forms which bring to mind the places where I have enjoyed myself, and the faces I have loved long ago. Ah, me! I wish to hasten my steps; and when I see so many young men and maidens, old persons and infants, gliding rapidly ahead of me, it seems that I go very slowly.   Yet all in good time! all in good time!   An old man ought not to be impatient.

I used to think it strange, and even false, that any one in his senses and free of pain should be impatient to die.   But it is not strange to me now, and I am very glad that it can be true.   I saw my old father and my blessed mother, my Mary, and my little son die, and I am sure I can pass easily through what they did.   I heard their last sighs, and saw them lie pallid before me; kissed their cold foreheads after they were laid in their coffins, and heard the cruel clods rattle down as their graves were filled, and I went with torn but hopeful heart from each spot to continue my journey.   Yet I see them now, yonder in that happy land, blooming more fresh and joyous than ever, and with smiles and outstretched arms waiting for the old man to come to them.   A little longer, my darlings!   Wait a little longer, and he will be with you.

Will not that be a happy meeting? And can any one wonder I should wish it to be hastened?

It is only when long solitary my fancy get over-charged with remembrances of the past, and my dormant affections become aroused to feel, as I imagine they once felt in my vigor, that such rhapsodies as this affect me. They warn me that, though my feelings are yet strong, they are fast becoming those of a doting old man. Falstaff, when "a babbled of green fields," showed just such an effort of energy in weakness. And yet I need not be ashamed of it and call it a rhapsody. It is surely better to look with glorious hopes and imaginings to the future than with gloom and regret upon the past.

The amount of sorrow for myself I have expended in my lifetime is past gathering up. It has been a great waste of time and feeling, for the simple reason that it has never done any good. A sorrow that leads to repentance is most wholesome; but, if you will remember it, the most contrite persons you ever saw in your life were precisely those who were the weakest, and most certain to repeat their fault upon the first temptation. I always forebode much misery to a child who too readily acknowledges a fault and is glib in his promises for the future. Where there is obstinacy before contrition there is apt to be firmness in repentance.

One other result of my observation and experience I would remark just here. It is equally as harassing and as great a waste of time to spend it in brooding over the past as in conjecturing about the future. Neither past nor future can be changed, and the present is made wretched.

CHAPTER II.

THE historians of Amadis de Gaul, King Arthur, and such like, and the monkish biographers of saints of the Middle Ages, magnified their heroes by carrying them triumphantly through desperate adventures with men, dragons, and Satan with all his hosts; and their brethren of the present day follow somewhat the same course. Even the writers of unadulterated fiction treat only of extraordinary men who have met with extraordinary fortunes or misfortunes.

I have often been vexed with shame at not being able even to understand the laughter-provoking Latin puns, or Greek conundrums, or Hebrew *jeux d'esprit* popped off, I judged by the context, at the most opportune time, by some hero of fifteen or sixteen years of age, who has already passed through more learning, loves, wars, and adventures than Methusaleh, though he lived nine hundred and sixty-nine years, and begat Lamech and other sons and daughters, ever dreamed about. It is true that these adjuncts of superiority please and excite the minds of mankind, who have a natural reverence for a superior; but I do not see how they benefit them. They can neither imitate the good, nor take warning by the mistakes, of these fictitious gentry, simply because the ordinary capacities, course, and occurrences of life are of a totally different stamp.

If this manuscript be ever read (and I hope it shall be), he who reads will find in it merely the life and opinions of an ordinary individual, who, like most of his fellow-men, felt loves and disappointments, for the most part imaginary and easy to have been prevented or overcome by a due exercise of his judgment; joys and pleasures, quite as imaginary and unreasonable; opinions, false to every one but himself and a few others; and misfortunes, caused for the most part by his own fault. And the thought that benefit may arise to any one by its perusal cheers me like the strain of the thrush, singing at midnight in the lowly thicket, delights the ear of him who wishes for the morning.

It matters little for my purpose to tell when or where I was born: these and similar matters I will hurry over. It is sufficient that I was born in one of the far Southern States, and just in the edge of the piny woods; or, to speak more picturesquely and vaguely, just where the magnolia and pine, with the other differing trees and shrubs, and soil and face of the country which accompany those two denizens of the forest, seem to be blended.

My father was a physician, by the name of Alfred Page. His circumstances were not such as to permit him to contract an early marriage, so that he did not marry until he reached the age of thirty-five, when he saw, and, with excellent taste, I think, fell in love with Miss Lucy Barnard, the daughter of a gentleman as poor as wise, and as wise as poor, whom he married, and by whom he had myself and four other children— of whom I am the only one now living. My aunt, Sarah Page, married my mother's only brother, James Barnard, so that it used to be a familiar saying with us, that "a Page married a Barnard, and a Barnard married a Page."

My Uncle James was a bustling, dapper little lawyer, with hard gray eyes, stiff and grizzled hair, thick-soled, shiny boots, and immaculate shirt-bosoms and collars. He had a good practice in the neighboring county town, Rosstown, and, as my Aunt Sarah was possessed of a very full share of that natural aristocratic feeling which belongs to woman, and he did not lack latent pride himself (though he never allowed it to interfere in his schemes), as money and popularity increased, they assumed a superior gentility to the rest of their kin, who, as they lived some distance off, were rather willing it should be so, and they were looked to by us children, and in fact by the whole family, as, *par excellence*, our genteel relations.

I remember very well a visit I once made to my aunt's house. It cast such an awful chill upon my feelings that I can never forget it. My father, having to visit Rosstown upon some business, took me with him for the expansion of my mind. My Uncle James received us with that forced cordiality so well suited to his character and purposes in life. I do not doubt but that he had a species of regard for both of us, and that if all things were otherwise equal he would, in case of a quarrel with a stranger, have taken our side—if he took either—but he was, in public, an altogether artificial personage. My father, who always showed the kindest consideration for those about him, finding he was to be detained for some hours upon his affairs, told me I had better go to my aunt's, where he intended to dine. Uncle James directed me the way, and after some search I found the house. It stood upon a rather elevated spot, just on the edge of the town, and was one of those wooden, two-story, white ephemera, with a showy portico and a stiff little garden in front, so common to pretentious villages, and so proper for pretentious people to live in.

As I knocked at the door (with a good deal of trepidation, I confess) I heard my aunt talking to one of her servants in a shrill tone, and soon was met by her. She was a tall, passionless-looking and loosely-put-together woman, with pale blue eyes; and although she had been married only some twelve years, already began to have a made-up look about her, very different from my dear mother, who was as active, cheerful a little black-eyed body as you would find. She eyed me all over, and said, without a particle of pleasure in her voice: " Is that you ? La, child, your feet are muddy. Go wipe them on the door-mat!" I did so, of course, but nervously, and feeling terribly mortified that I was about to commit such a *faux pas;* and she showed me into a frigidly decent little parlor—with the blinds all closed, and the hearth filled with evergreens and faded flowers, though it was then late in the fall, and a fire would have been very pleasant. After asking me about the family in general terms, and the potato crop, chickens and turkeys more particularly, she went out and sent in my cousins, who had been playing in the back yard, to see and entertain me. There were only two— Fitzroy, who was six months older than myself, and Anne Page.

My aunt was fond of novels and poems, and my uncle was too immersed in his projects to care about names. Fitzroy was a grand name—though I doubt if my aunt knew its origin—and "Anne Page" was a sweet name. My name is Abraham, for my father loved his Bible, and had a particular regard for the patriarch Abraham, for reasons I will give hereafter.

There was such a look of restraint about Cousin Fitzroy's black jacket, with three rows of buttons and a little peak behind, and his tight boots and curly head, and in the cold, I'm-better-than-you way he gave me his hand, that my gushing affections suddenly backed up stream. Anne was a little rosy-cheeked, brown-haired girl, with large, inquiring blue eyes, who hung behind her brother, and was as abashed as I was. We tried to play together, and Fitzroy showed me all about the place he thought worthy, but it was so evident that it was shown to excite my admiration, and such was my diffidence and his lack of heartiness, that I did not really enjoy myself at all.

I had every disposition to love him, and, in a respectful way, as towards a relation who did me honor, to make him my friend. But there are some damp people in the world who have as great a capacity for absorbing and making latent the caloric of one's affections as the vapor, in time of a thaw, has to take it out of one's body. And there are some so self-conscious as to draw undivided attention to themselves with million-magnifying microscopic power, to the rendering coarse the texture of their characters, and the detection of the voracious little dragons, crawling worms, and absurdly-acting monsters of their dispositions.

So little tact had I that I beat him jumping and climbing, and at last must needs boast of the superiority of our spacious yard at home, with its large-spreading trees, to his little inclosure, with its few dwarf shrubs and stiff rose-bushes. It was what young men of the present day would call "a flanking operation," and when he saw himself ousted from his strongholds his vanity was hurt, and of course he was in the pouts. The fact was, that by boasting he allured me to my strongest tact. I had more imagination than he, and when put upon my metal could create a Paradise with a few bushes, and all four of its rivers with a spring branch. He became sulky and pettish, and said he was tired, and chided Anne for rudeness and being too boisterous and familiar; for she soon became at ease with me, and, though what I did and said was displeasing to him, it seemed to give her pleasure.

It was a great relief to me when my father came with my uncle, for I always felt happy and at home with him. He was a man of great intelligence, but excessively single-minded and sincere; and though both my uncle and my aunt were forced to respect him, it was evident they looked with half contempt upon what they esteemed his "softness." I noticed at dinner, though I did knock over my tumbler, and could not manœuvre my knife, fork and spoon, my hands and elbows, half right, that my aunt praised the chickens, turkeys, and potatoes of our part of the country, and particularly of our place, and depreciated those brought to Rosstown, and seemed quite contented when my father suggested, in his innocence, that he would send her some by the first opportunity.

In thinking over the matter, after I had gained a little more experience, it was clear to me that my relatives had come to the singular conclusion (for persons of their blood and position) that wealth was the *sum-*

mum bonum, and had determined to get rich. An opinion of that character, like the folly of a fool, will betray itself, and is most disastrous in its effects. It naturally leads to obsequiousness to the rich because they are rich, and, among the rich, to clannish exclusiveness with those their equals in wealth. This is the thing which in our country is now-a-days called aristocracy; for, like many other mean things, it is dignified with a high-sounding, wrongly-applied name.

I can understand an aristocratic feeling arising from superior birth; for the man who derives his blood through a long line of honorable ancestors, and in whom is no mental, moral, or physical defect, has the right to regard himself entitled to a consideration superior to that bestowed upon one whose blood is muddy or tainted, however intelligent and beautiful that one may be. The chances are a thousand to one that such a man is a thorough gentleman. Even breeders of horses, cattle, and hogs act upon the known facts of hereditary qualities. But, now-a-days, people are so spiritual and so engaged in the various branches of psychology that they forget they are animals, except in their appetites, and in regard to those the large majority are governed neither by the reason of men nor the instinct of brutes. In fact, it is a recklessly extravagant declaration to say that man is governed by reason. Animals, except monkeys, are more reasonable within their sphere of action and in their indulgences.

But it certainly is amusing to see the you-tickle-me-and-I'll-tickle-you exclusiveness of our aristocracy of wealth—our snobs. A set of dirt-worshiping creatures, male and female, who, by luck, dishonesty, or meanness

—either their own or that of their predecessors—have amassed their god into piles above the average size, instantly and that with the connivance of most of their race, set themselves up as a sacred priesthood. They visit, marry, laugh, cry, have jokes and secrets among themselves, are mean to themselves and the laity, and generous to each other. In point of perversity they are only surpassed by the laity, who bow down to them; who hate each other and the rich too; who try to rob the one, and are envious of the other.

Let me not be misunderstood. It would be unbecoming to an old man, and one who hopes he has lost the wiry edge of his feelings, to have even the appearance of a want of charity or of the strictest regard for truth. I make no sweeping charges against the rich or those who move in "high circles." We have had in my beloved South an aristocracy, not soon to be altogether extinguished, thank Heaven! whatever may happen, which was by no means dependent upon wealth, though many of its members possessed it. When I call it an aristocracy I only follow the popular cant. It should rather be called a highest class of society. It was founded on hereditary virtue, intelligence, and refinement; and one of a vulgar family, however rich or accomplished he or she might be, had no part in it; because one swallow does not make a summer. In some of the vilest families I have ever known there have, phenomenally, been born daughters who were embodiments of every gentle virtue and excellence, and I have remarked that invariably their children were the copies of their precious grandparents, uncles, and aunts. As this fact was thoroughly known, the beautiful, good, rich,

3*

and accomplished Miss Scroggins, though admired and
always treated with the utmost politeness, did not belong
to the society I speak of; while poor and homely Miss
Leigh was its pride and delight, and her greatest social
trouble was how to decline those pressing kindnesses she
could not repay.   Miss Scroggins and Miss Leigh were
acquaintances, but that was all.   Miss Leigh's brother
would hardly have married Miss Scroggins, and Miss
Leigh could not by any possibility have ever married
Miss Scroggins's brother, though he was an honest man.

As I shall have frequent occasion to mention this
truly high class of society—for it is my sole source of
pride that I was born and raised and always have lived
one of its members—I will pass over any connected detail of its excellencies.   But, in connection with what I
have said of the natural obsequiousness of those who
make wealth the greatest good, I would remark that,
leaving aside dishonesty and extraordinary luck, the only
way to become rich in an ordinary lifetime is by hard
work and meanness—by selling all the large potatoes,
eating only the small ones, and toiling and conjuring to
make them all large.   This is called Prudence, Industry,
and Economy, and, when not carried to excess, it is
commendable: I only wish I had practiced it more.
But those who worship such a good, worship it with
superstitious sincerity, fear its frowns as the greatest of
evils, and strive for its blessings with groveling, self-
immolating, jealous and all-absorbing greed.

Wealth, though a good thing in itself, is very dangerous to those who overvalue it.   On the other hand, poverty is also a very good thing, for some people, and but
for it many a man would miss fame on earth, and many

more miss heaven. Wealth is like the right of suffrage — make it universal and mankind would start to the devil at lightning speed, and increase their velocity in ratio to the distance to their stopping-place.

All this disquisition about wealth and poverty is so true that it sounds trite; and to the reading and reflective it is trite, but it must be remembered that about nine-tenths of our people read very little and never reflect; memory seems to be the only intellectual gift ever exercised. Therefore, in dwelling upon the subject as I do, I am not indulging in the babble of senility. If these, my opinions, are ever read, some one who has not reflected shall be able to profit by my reflections upon these common matters, of which I have had much opportunity for observation and experience

The best state is that desired by Agur, the son of Jakeh; and a good Providence placed my father in just that condition during my early childhood, and, afterward, during the latter portion of his life. I say that a good Providence placed him in that condition, for it is certain that he himself had little to do with the planning or managing of it. He was a philosopher and a wise one; and, while he tried to do his duty in all respects, he never fretted himself about the future, put all his trust in God, and thought that everything was for the best. He laid ingenious plans for gaining wealth, because wealth was desirable and debt is terrible; yet, as each of them failed, he found many good reasons why he would have been utterly ruined had it been accomplished, and thanked God for all his mercies. His father was just like him, as I have heard, and his son has had almost daily cause for gratitude that he has inherited their spirit.

What a miserable man he must be who feels that he has to be eternally blowing and manipulating all the irons of a varied life; who has no trust but in himself, and fusses and frets about what goes best if he will only let it alone; and, will he nill he, goes its own way after all. Let him plan as cunningly as he may, he is not infallible; let him make himself as busy as a man fighting bees, he will get some stings. The affairs of one's life are like a steam-engine; and if the engineer think he has to be always on the alert to raise the levers, shut down the valves, and help on the piston, and if he live in continual dread that the wheels will stop on a center, or the whole thing smash up but for his activity, he is a poor botch at the business, is miserable whether he be in the engine-room or the cabin, and the sooner he gets off the boat the better for him and his associates. The true philosophy of life is to fear God, do our duty, and leave results with Him "who sees the end from the beginning."

"It is vain for you to rise up early, to sit up late, to eat the bread of sorrows."

CHAPTER III.

WHEN my father married, he had no property but a small frame dwelling-house, some hundred or so acres of piny-woods land, and three negroes; and in marrying he got no dowry but happiness. Though he called that "marrying rich," it took all his labor in the practice of his profession to support the land and the negroes, and the little hungry stomachs which were soon added one by one to his household. In those days the practice of medicine in our part of the country was most laborious. The settlement was new, and consequently unhealthy; the farms were far apart; there were many creeks and swamps, none of which were bridged; and the roads were generally but horse-paths through the cane. Four-wheeled vehicles less substantial than an ox wagon were almost unknown, and there were very few ox wagons. My great-niece now goes bowling along in her brette behind a spanking team over the tracks traveled by her great-grandmother riding *en croupe* behind her brother or husband, both dodging the overhanging cane or continually brushing it from their faces. In 1823, as I well remember, the tall cane over the whole country went to seed and died out, switch-cane, as we call it, in after-years coming up in its place. Before that there were bears, panthers, wild-cats, and wolves enough in the woods to make children timid about wandering from home, and to make even grown men cautious—a distinction with little difference, if you analyze it.

But neither animals nor bad roads, cold, heat, nor freshets balked my father in his duty. He had no thought of fame, nor did he harass his mind about the accumulation of wealth. If there ever was a man actuated solely by love, it was he; gentle and devoted love for his family, benevolence for his race, and reverent love for his God. My grandmother told me he was so in his childhood and youth; my mother said that because he was so, she loved him long before she married him; I know he was so from my childhood to his last hour; and in the bright visions I have of him now, a smile of ineffable sweetness glorifies his noble countenance as he stretches forth his arms to me from the outermost hill of heaven.

It is not strange that I have a high regard for good physicians and a keen appreciation of their duties, responsibilities, pleasures, troubles, and necessary characteristics, when my most tender and reverent feelings are so associated with one of their number.

Except the primary relationships of domestic life, there is not one so near as that of physician and patient. It may almost be said that the physician forms one of the domestic circle; for this abode of all man holds most dear, is his peculiar province. When invaded by disease, his aid is invoked to drive away the destroyer. The agonized husband, the helpless mother, the frightened and despairing children impatiently wait his coming, and at his approach hope revives in their breasts. They watch his boding countenance, and their hearts mark every change; their smiles wait upon his, and his anxiety makes theirs tenfold more intense. For the time, indeed, he seems to be the soul upon whose motions they all, as obedient members, wait. When peace is restored he is regarded as a conqueror, or, better still, is blessed as a dearest friend. And in the most adverse fate, if he be one whose skill and faithfulness have long been tested, his want of success is imputed to the irresistible course of nature, directed by the will of God.

To him this holy circle is always open. He comes and goes, night or day, in sorrow or in gladness. The servants are at his beck, and with eagerness and respect obey his call. From him there are no secrets; his office makes him an inquisitor to whom modesty itself must reveal its most sacred knowledge. Toward him there is no jealousy, no envy. The husband confides to his honor and skill the sanctities of the marital relation; the father, the lover, the brother, all place what they esteem most precious in his hands. But the relationship approaches closer still; "yea, all that a man hath will he give for his life," and this precious life every man must, at some time or other, place under the protection of the physician. Then his family history, their constitutions and predilections, and the vices and indiscretions of his own youth or age must be told, perhaps (and sometimes through fear he exaggerates them), and the man stands before his physician all exposed, as at the judgment bar, and finds himself utterly in the power of another. He discovers to another all his little meannesses and weaknesses, who has heretofore shrouded them almost even to himself. Yet it is without fear of consequences. He tells not only a superior but a friend, and waits with trembling hope for his judgment. Though he never before brooked direction, he now attends to counsels and obeys implicitly. No self-denial is too hard, no pain too severe for him to undergo that he may gain his precious health. Poor creature, his physician is, perhaps, to him in place of God !

No wonder the Orientals and the Indians regarded a physician as a holy favorite and friend of the gods; and Jesus, the son of Sirach, saith: "Honor a physician with the honor due unto him, for the uses which ye may have of him; for the Lord hath created him. For of the Most High cometh healing, and he shall receive honor of the king. Then give place to the physician—let him not go from thee, for thou hast need of him."

His office is the prime necessity of deranged nature, and the very capstone, next to that of the great Physician of souls, in the new order consequent upon the fall of man. It rules over all, high and low, rich and poor. From the sobs of the loneliest orphan babe that ever wailed its life out upon the midnight air, to the feeble gasps of old age, and the incoherent mutterings of the mind diseased—all fallen, suffering nature calls to him for help. And yet he is a man; alas, he is but a man! He has not been gifted with intellect superior to all others; has no familiar spirit to prompt him; has entered into no league with Hermes or Esculapius. He necessarily has doubts and waverings, half-born ideas, nervous trepidations, and bitter prejudices—more perhaps than any other professional man; and the attractions of pleasure and the enticements of idleness have often, it may be, to his bitter regret, tempted him to neglect his necessary studies. His heart beats sad pulsations with every cry of distress; and he sympathizes with every pang of anxious love. In fine, he is a man of like capacities, frailties, and tenderness with his fellows. What does not the relationship involve with him! His honor, conscience, pride, and all the noblest attributes of his intellect and affections are enlisted in his profession. Alive with all these, he is called to the bedside of the dying. Parents, children, friends, the patient, and all the affections of his own soul within him, call tumultuously to him for help. Over-whelmed by the fearful responsibility of his position, he calls hurriedly on nature, science, invention, memory, for help, but there is no help. Expiring nature stretches out no hand; science has expended its knowledge; invention has exhausted her expedients; memory tries a vain task; and he steps aside for death to do its work; and unable to scan the mysterious decrees of Providence, mistrusting his own powers, and doubting the truth of his own science, he is ready to exclaim: God alone can perfectly fill my office!

There are improvident and brutal husbands and unfaithful wives, unnatural parents and ungrateful children, cruel masters and bad servants; that with physicians and patients there should be mutual infractions of duty, is to be expected. This relationship has, like the others, been debased by many to an affair of money: the one living only to receive and spend it—the others thinking their whole duty performed when they grumblingly pay it. But the true physician undergoes labors and sufferings for which money cannot pay; and the right-minded patient receives benefits which he feels that money cannot compensate.

Much has been written about the duties of men in other relationships, and in some they have been prescribed by the State; but little has been said about medical ethics, which seem to have been left to the simple dictates of nature, while the State has abandoned its citizens to be victimized by every idle, indolent, ignorant fellow who chooses to place "Doctor" before his name. As for quacks, and careless physicians (who are little better), I cannot help but look upon

4

them as the most striking instances of the depravity of man.   Only their lack of intellect and the bluntness of their consciences prevents their regarding themselves as the most cold-blooded of murderers.   Worse than highwaymen, they take the money and the life too.

The code of medical morals involves in it, in their greatest force, all the requirements of the decalogue relating to the duties of man to man.   Its first great rule is, that the physician shall devote to his profession all his heart, soul, mind, and strength, and shall do nothing to dishonor it.   But when we look at the medical fraternity in this country, in how many instances do we find this command disobeyed!   Pleasure, business, idleness, foppery in dress and equipage, politics, the pursuit of riches and rich wives—in fine, every occupation, pursuit, and evasion have been practiced by many from their studenthood up to old age. "How can he get wisdom that holdeth the plow, and that glorieth in the goad, that driveth oxen, and is occupied in their labors, and whose talk is of bullocks?" says the son of Sirach when speaking of physicians.   When he reflects upon the variety and accuracy of the knowledge required, how can he conscientiously take under his charge the health and lives of fellow-men, who has not devoted all his time and energies to the profession? By coveting his neighbors' cotton patches and daughters, or by engaging too much in other occupations to the neglect of his profession, he is guilty of killing, stealing, and often of bearing false witness.

This fundamental rule requires, too, that the physician shall do nothing to dishonor his profession.   Yet how much dishonor is cast upon it every day by the pet nostrums, idleness, callousness, ignorance, and quarrels of many of the fraternity! Fraternity, indeed! Were it not for the respect I feel for many of its members, I should compare it to the Happy Family exhibited at the museums. Here is a snarling dog baying a vicious cat upon the bars of the cage—there, a malicious monkey is slyly engaged in pulling all the pretty feathers out of the tail of the voluble parrot—here is a canary sick with mortification that its own notes have been imitated and improved upon by a mocking-bird—there, a lusty game-cock is trying to dislodge a solemn old owl from his perch; while, on the floor, a greedy drake gobbles up all the food, crying "quack! quack!"

Many physicians are great sticklers for etiquette, but it is wonderful what crude notions they have of it. They have satisfied their delicacy when they do not call their dear brother "Ass," "Fool," "Brute," and "Quack" to his face. Behind his back they fully satisfy themselves for their restraint in his presence. And even when they do not go so far as to villify with words, they

> ' Damn with faint praise, assent with civil leer,
> And without sneering, teach the rest to sneer."

The envy, jealousy, backbiting, and quarrels of physicians have, to the dishonor of the profession, been the theme of satirists, play-writers, and novelists for ages.

If I were asked to point out the physician who performs his duties best, and who approaches nearest to what a physician should be in all his relationships—a superior and a friend—I should select the Country Doctor, as I remember my father.

The veriest slave, toiling in the galleys or in the mines, has not a more laborious task than he. Night and day, in the winter's frost and summer's heat, through mud and dust, along the highways and by-ways, through dark swamps and pleasant lanes, he toils on his mission, always intent, always cheerful. There is no pleasure but he must forego it; no obstacle but he must overcome it. By continued use all the powers of his body and mind have become doubly fortified and acute. He has pleasant little plans for keeping cool, and ingenious methods of keeping warm, and admirable devices for taking a nap in his long rides. From a broken buggy shaft to a broken leg, he is always ready, though he has neither blacksmith-shop nor apothecary-shop at the next corner to appeal to. No emergency can discompose him. Memory is always at her post, and his invention bends even science to his will. Forced to be his own cupper, bleeder, and leecher, he pulls off his coat, rolls up his sleeves, and goes at it. He blisters and glysters, pulls teeth, and gives pills himself to white and black. A sturdy philanthropist, he knows no respect of persons, and will labor and watch all night, equally in the quarter over some decrepid old negro, and in the big house over the master's son. Physician, surgeon, accoucheur, dentist, apothecary, and nurse, he travels along independently, with his saddle-bags and case of instruments, forced to make the whole science of medicine his specialty.

But there is another side to the picture. As he plys his toilsome way, there is not a negro he meets but has a ready bow and grin for him whom he looks upon as akin to the gods, as *his* doctor and special friend. At his destination he is met with the warmest kindness and deepest respect; his very presence has a charm which brings relief. He attends now, perhaps, in the families of those at whose birth he assisted, and who from their childhood have loved and had faith in him. As the first friend of the family, many are the family secrets which have been confided to him, many the anxious private consultations with him by fond mothers and doting husbands. He knows the people, and studies their very souls, and he has a place in their hearts, and cares little for the malicious jealousy of rivals. In his circuit everybody knows everybody, and he has the health of all in his charge, so that he is the cynosure of all eyes, and kind attentions accompany him everywhere. One has to tell of a mother's life he has saved; another, of a wife's; another, of his own; one tells his excellence as a surgeon, another lauds him as a nurse, while a third speaks of his integrity as a man; and blessings and praises are bestowed upon him from all sides. He is the hardest worked, the most faithful, and the least understood of all men in the high resorts of science, but he has a compensation in all worth living and laboring for, which those who frequent those resorts might well envy.

Except that the roads are better, and the appliances of science are more perfect and more attainable, the country doctor now exists, and must, for very many years to come, exist in the South as I have pictured him in my childhood and early youth; and it is for that reason, and because the most reverent love my heart can feel has always been bestowed on one of the class, and because I think that the duties of the relationship of physician and patient are better defined, and therefore better filled in the country than in the city, that I have said so much about the Country Doctor.

Just to think, a sensitive nose and a delicate stomach prevented my being a doctor! Alas, what flimsy obstructions change the currents of our lives! A dislike to discord has prevented my being a good lawyer, and a disinclination to steady labor has hindered my being a musician.

CHAPTER IV.

MY earliest recollections are of the dear old house we lived in. As I recall it, every room and every piece of furniture has associated with it something pleasing or sad in my life. From yonder back window my mother pointed out to me a great comet which bade fair to visit the earth when I was about three years old. And I remember how once, when I was even younger than that, this front window was opened to allow her to gather for me some china-berries, covered with sleet. There is my great-grandfather's chest upon which we children used to be seated for punishment. In yonder corner of the room took place the stoutly contested struggle between my mother and my eldest sister, then about five years old, who was determined that her hair should not be combed. She screamed, and mother wept, and we all cried, and it was altogether a desperate occasion—but the young lady's obstinacy was at last conquered, and peace and smiles revisited a happy household.

But if I set out to narrate all my reminiscences of the old house, I shall never have done. In its construction, I venture to say, that there is no other such house, and that there never has been, and never will be another to resemble it, even in its general appearance and situation. Houses resemble in their structure the characters and dispositions of those who build them, modified only by the builders' circumstances; and though there may have been men resembling my father, it is not probable that their circumstances, in the matter of building, should also resemble his.

His land adjoined the corporate limits of the town of Yatton, and was marvelously diversified with hills and hollows. Except in one small bottom, I do not believe there were any two adjoining acres of it level. I speak in the past tense, because, though the locality has changed but little, I am speaking of a time long since past. The soil was principally sand and gravel, with substrata of red and white ochre, or quicksand. The portions not sandy were red clay, and on all of it the pine flourished finely, springing up wherever the original growth of forest trees was cut down. A cleared field, left uncultivated, soon became a pine thicket, and then, in a few years, a pine forest. But no place could have suited my father so well. The water was excellent, and the location convenient and most healthy; there were no gnats or mosquitoes, and the poverty of the soil gave full scope to his ingenuity and hopefulness in discovering what it was best suited for, and in making it produce that. Little of it was suited for corn, but it made excellent bricks.   Neither cotton nor oats would flourish, but with a little manuring it could not be excelled for potatoes, pindars, and melons.

The great trouble was that when the timber was cut down, the thin soil would disappear the first or second year, and the hills would.wash into deep gullies through the strata of red, yellow, and white sand down to the ochre, which the water could not wear away much more readily than it could solid rock.   No hillside ditching, or horizontal plowing, or other method of culture could prevent this calamity in land so light, and so poor that it could not produce sufficient grass to hold it together; and it was about the only misfortune for which my father could not find some adequate and evident physical or moral compensation—though I believe that he increased his own stock of patience and resignation by it.   At any rate, all the philosophic appliances in the world could not keep the land from washing when it was bare of trees and bushes; and though for many years it was his hobby to clear away the pines to let the grass grow, he relinquished the plan of cultivating any but a few small, favored spots, and, in default of grass, left briers and bushes to cover the clearings, where they could do so, as better food for stock than pine straw; and to that extent, though it seemed a great waste of timber, my father's plan was wise.

In truth, I never knew him to make a plan which did not have solid wisdom for a basis, though it was generally coupled with an "if;" and, in one way or another, his plans always resulted in some good,

though seldom in that which he had designed.   If his
cider was not good as cider, it made capital vinegar;
and I remember a churning which lasted for three cold
winter days by a large fire, and which, though it produced no butter, by the addition of a little sugar and
sherry wine, made delicious syllabub.   Every child
about the house, and each of the negroes took a turn
at that churning, and, if I recollect rightly, we all had
a syllabub feast which lasted for two days longer.   The
taste of it is yet in my mouth.

At the foot of a gentle northern slope, a depression
in a ridge, my father found, when he took possession
of the 'place, a small farm-house of two rooms, raised
upon posts, about three feet from the ground.   It faced
to the south, so that the hill commenced to rise from
the front door; and as in about forty yards it joined
another ridge which ran east and west, the side of the
slope made a long and very pretty lawn.   From about
sixty feet on the east, and ten feet on the west side of
the house the ridge descended rather abruptly.   In the
rear there was a slight ascent for about seventy-five
yards, when the ridge forked northeast and northwest,
and then ran to all points of the compass.   There were
good springs of water in the bottoms east and west of
the house.   To the west the bottom and sides of the
hills were covered with pine-trees, for they had once
been cleared; on the east stood the original growth of
poplars, beeches, and oaks, interspersed with dogwood,
witch-hazels, sour-wood, sassafras, and huckleberry—
and all, both forest trees and shrubs, small of their
kind.

Why the original builder of the house placed it on

this narrow neck of the ridge between two acclivities, is more than I ever could conjecture, unless it were that he found there already the remains of an Indian wigwam, and was a hearty conservative in his feelings. But there it was, and it was for my father to take things as he found them and make the best of them. As he calculated, with his usual hopefulness, upon having in the ordinary course of nature a large family, it was evident that a house with only two rooms would in a very few years be insufficient; and, besides, to have only two rooms in his house would never have suited him had he been a hermit; for not a barefooted penitent or weary wayfarer could have presented himself without being welcomed and entertained. Indeed, his knack for encountering objects of pity on his road, and his luck for having poor orphan children thrown upon his hands by bequest of parents, or devise of circumstances, was at all times extraordinary. It seemed as though however niggardly fortune might be in her other gifts, she was determined that at all times his charity and compassion should be kept in lively exercise. It was an instance of the truth of the promise: "he that hath, to him shall be given."

Another man would most probably have contented himself with adding two or three rooms at first, and then others, if they were needed, all upon the same floor. But to have added room in that way upon the scale of my father's desire would have required either great labor to extend the level top of the ridge, or the building of some of the rooms upon tall posts resting in its side, which would have been unsafe, both from the rotting of the posts, and the caving of the sandy ground. So, as my father could not conveniently and safely spread his house out, he determined to build it upward. He therefore raised the two rooms which had a roof already on them, and built a brick story beneath them. The result was four rooms, just half enough, and to get the other four he built them in two stories by the side of the first, but on a higher level, and considerably longer and larger, and, as two roofs with the eaves joining would have been apt to leak badly, he placed one large roof over the whole, including within it the roof he found already built. This gave the structure a singular appearance, both inside and out, but a glorious garret, which is one of the most essential of rooms to such a household as ours.

Houses almost as irregular in architecture, but hardly so comfortable, may be seen here and there throughout the older inland portions of the South. They are all the results of circumstances, and not of a want of taste—for the senses of harmony and beauty in the Southern people are exceptionally acute and accurate. I speak not only of the better class of Southerners as they now exist, but of most of those who, or whose parents, in my day had so far overcome the first requirements of subduing a wilderness as to be able to indulge their fancy or talent in architecture, music, ornamental gardening, equipage, or dress. And one of the most remarkable features of their taste is that in nothing do they incline to the gaudy, or, to use a very expressive French word, the *éblouissant.* A Southern lady, however fine may be the material of her dress, is always modestly and neatly attired; and, if she follow the fashion, as indeed all ladies must and will, she deftly and quietly snips away its redundancies, and adds a little to its lack, so that modesty and fashion are blended you see but know not how. For it to be otherwise would ill suit her manners; for retiring gentleness and modesty are her glorious veil from childhood to old age. So too in architecture, the showy is generally avoided by old Southern families, and music in a minor key is most generally loved—though that, so far as my observation extends, is common to all human nature, as it well may be. I had a sister who when she was only a few weeks old would pucker up her little mouth and weep piteously when one sang to her any of the plaintive melodies so common in my young days to our religious music. She grew to be a lovely young woman, and died with all her goodness, purity, and beauty unsullied by the cares and even the knowledge of the evil in the world. I feel certain that her impressibility to sad music is not rare with children, and we know that with all races of people the earliest, uncultivated music is of that character. It is useless to try to account for it either by association, or delicacy of nervous organization. Neither the child nor the savage can have any such association, and why should B flat affect uncultivated natures more than C sharp? It would seem that the songs of the sons of God from the hills of heaven still lingered, faint and solemn by distance, in the ears of Eve's children.

CHAPTER V.

WHILE I would fain linger with the memories of my earliest days, and tell the most of them, I know that to do so would serve no purpose of good to others, and would make my life take up more room than those of all Plutarch's heroes, with Fox's Book of Martyrs thrown in. What a dreadful book, by-the-by, is the latter! With one picture (in another book) of the Last Judgment, where the angels with swords in their hands are separating a vast multitude into two parts, this, standing calm, and that, cowering or running affrighted, it was my principal sensational object when I was very young; nor, indeed, can I yet look at either of them wholly unmoved. It is, I suppose, the most effective "Tract" which has ever been published, and used to be almost as common in the country as the Bible. However short it may come of inculcating charity, its warnings of the strength and certainty of religious intolerance when a Sect becomes joined to the State, or gets greatly the upper hand in numbers and power, are most excellent. It is as common to human nature to worship the Idol of the Sect, as it is for it to be selfish; and the worship of that idol grows faster, and to a more intense enthusiasm, than the religion composed of the gentle virtues of charity and faith. With another volume, containing the Roman Catholic Martyrdoms, it would be one of the most wholesome of books for the present day—to excite terror in youth for matter of reflection in age.

My childhood was that of most eldest sons of refined and pious parents—that is, I received finer clothes and more switchings than any of my successors. I now know that my punishments were even more painful to my dear little mother, than they were to me. She used to try to impress that fact upon my mind, but I took it as an ingenious sort of excuse for doing what she secretly took a delight in. Skin and mind were both too tender to appreciate her motives, but it was certainly a sore matter to both of us. All the correction devolved upon her, for my father was too much absent from home in the practice of his profession to see my little mischiefs and note the germs of my weaknesses or viciousnesses of character. Besides, the dear little woman could not see why her son, so pure in flesh and loving in spirit, should not remain pure and loving, and be a saint, or, at least, a model. It was well enough to tell her that "boys will be boys;" she did not know what a boy's, or rather what human, nature was. The slightest deviation from truth was to her imagination the opening of the floodgates of all the torrent of *crimen falsi;* and cruelty to a fly was the very amusement Nero indulged in when he was a child. Had she punished me in passion, the effects would have been disastrous, but that she never did. Her inflictions were very often with tears, or she would make me kneel with her and would pray with me after them; and though I, in my pain and passion, often thought both tears and prayers a grim farce, it is clear to my mind that they had a more beneficial effect from the whipping, and that they made the whipping more impressive. But I thought then, and still think, that being switched so often, however lovingly done, was almost too much of a good thing.

There was a difference of two years between me and my eldest sister, Julia; and about the same between the births of the succeeding children. I do not describe each of them here because it would too much resemble a *catalogue raisonée*, and because I am not writing their lives, but my own. They came into the world bright, healthy creatures, lived bright, healthy lives, and died with fervent hopes and confidence in the future. I have often been tempted to exclaim: the most lovely die, and such as I live on! But such a sentiment is humbug. There are plenty of good and lovely men and women who live to old age, and a vast number of probable scamps who die in infancy. "Whom the gods love, die young," is a cynical old proverb, which may be more than offset by saying: (whom the gods have any use for, live till it is accomplished.) It may be a blessing to die young, and it may be a blessing to live to old age. The natural, and therefore the better preference is to live; but, after all, it is best to be ready and willing to submit to God's direction about the matter.

When I learned my alphabet, my Ableselfa and Ampezant, I do not remember; but I recall very well the first time my mother took me by the hand and led me to good old Mrs. Diggory's girls' school, and left me there, a wondering, restless, grieved little martyr. The old lady lived and kept school (I use the word kept, advisedly) not more than a quarter of a mile from our house. Her pupils were girls, from five to seventeen years of age, and I was the only boy she could be induced to take. What she taught me principally was to hold my tongue and keep still, the two most important lessons of any one's education, and the least apt to be practiced, however thoroughly learned. Her best remembered lesson, however, was how it felt to be switched before a crowd of tittering, weeping, sympathizing, and malevolent school girls. Its terror, anguish, and shame made a deep impression upon me, and though my pain, like that of a pig, bore no proportion to the noise I made, I have never yet been able to see the comical side to the scene. I had torn my geography, and the good old lady, for she was a lady if there ever was one, switched me only after solemn consultation with my parents, who themselves pronounced the sentence. (But to whip one child before other children, whether its companions or not, is wrong. It gives a shock to its self-respect from which it can never wholly recover.] It is common to repeat flippantly that early impressions are lasting; but there are few who reflect how very lasting and important they are. One night, when I was five or six years old, my father took me up in his arms, and pointing to the stars told me of the immensity of the universe, and the greatness and goodness of its Creator, and though I necessarily understood but little, the feeling of awe and sublimity was implanted in my soul never to leave it.

The next school I remember was that of young Mr. Jones, who taught for a support while he was studying law. I must have learned very little from him, as I do not even remember what I studied; but one of the larger boys introduced to me the sensation of being called a thief, and threatened with the jail, kept by his uncle, the sheriff of the county. It was all about a slate-pencil, or some such matter, which I certainly had not taken *animo furandi,* for I did not even know what such a spirit was, but my confusion and terror were great. One of the most foolish, wicked, and cruel of the exertions of power is to bring railing accusations and threats against a child.

My next school I remember perfectly well, for in it I received most of my school-book education, and gained an experience which, with a great deal of subsequent observation, qualifies me to give a respectable opinion about schools and education generally. The first teacher, or rather master, was a Mr. James Dill, or "Old Dill," as we called him, an ecclesiastical stripling, who afterward developed into a rotund parson, and after a number of shiftings from pulpit to pulpit, took up an idea that he had a call to the heathen, and so, for aught I know, got himself turned into roasts and steaks by some Cannibal Islander. The missionary spirit was extremely ardent when it began its sway in our country, and Old Dill was not really old when he obeyed its promptings — was still young enough to relish adventure and his ease beneath palms and bananas in foreign lands, where labor was little needed.

That he was the most indolent man I have ever seen, is my full conviction, and it may be well imagined that his discipline of a large "old field" school of country boys and girls of all ages, was of a lax character, and his instructions of very little permanent value. It was under his direction that I plunged (to this day) hopelessly into the mysteries of Latin and Greek. I learned the Latin grammar by heart, went through *Deus creavit cœlum et terram*, in *sex dies*, and through *Omnia Gallia* in almost as little time, to be cast with Tityrus playing on his reed *sub tegmine fagi*, which bothered me prodigiously, and I always thought a stupid operation. I learned it all, and understood none of it, for he was too lazy to explain, and seven years is not the age at which one teaches himself the reasons and niceties of a language; and as I became older I was so imbued with disgust and fear of the difficulties I encountered, that it was repulsive to me to analyze and reflect upon them. The consequence was that though I *amo*-ed and *tupto*-ed very glibly, I hated Latin and Greek, and hardly think I ever afterwards could have learned them had I tried. Mr. Dill was a good scholar, but, with all his indolence, was impatient, so that all one had to do was to balk at a word once or twice, when, lounging in his easy chair, he would give its meaning instead of making the boy refer to the dictionary; and if a great bungle were made he was almost certain to translate the whole sentence, and perhaps all the lesson, and send the boy to his seat pouting and gratified.

The school-house was in a grove of pine-trees near a field, about half a mile from the town, and a little over a mile from our house. I remember certain beech roots along the path I had to go, upon which I was constantly stumping my toes—one of which was kept sore through every warm season when I went barefooted.

The house contained only one large room, built of logs and elevated on blocks. It had a mud chimney, with a capacious fireplace, and seven windows, four of them with glazed sash, and the others closed only by board shutters, and as the floor was of heavy puncheons, not very closely joined, there was plenty of ventilation. The play-grounds varied with the seasons; that of the girls was always near the house, but during the spring and summer months the boys spent most of their recesses from twelve M. to two P.M. at or near a swimming hole in the creek about a quarter of a mile below the school-house. It was called "Bryant's hole," from the name of the owner of the surrounding land, and was the place near or in which most of the school fights were decided, and where more than one generation of boys learned to swim. They learned other things, too, which were pernicious, and I cannot think that it is ever a good plan to allow boys to expose their persons promiscuously, as must necessarily be the case where a whole school goes swimming together.

An assemblage of children of all kinds of parents at a school is about as hazardous a position as any one can place his child in. If one be vicious or filthy in manners or conversation, all run the risk of contamination, and some will certainly be contaminated—for all children are imitative, and most of them have an affinity for the lewd and vulgar, which, to say the least of it, places them in great danger. Our school was generally composed of about fifteen girls and twenty-five boys, from seven to seventeen years of age; and though I do not recollect that any one of them was particularly vicious, I do know that my own imagination was there first vitiated—not so much by hearing or seeing what was wicked in itself, as by hearing and seeing things innocent in themselves, but with secrecy, and as though they were wicked. To the pure all things are pure; but the purest facts may be made the instruments of impurity when communicated as though they were forbidden. The idea of vice which is conveyed with the fact into the child's mind can never be overcome, and what he may learn with perfect innocence by frankness, and must learn in after-life, is made a source of disquiet to his conscience and evil to his imagination. Parents should bear this in mind, and treat their children with more frankness than they usually do. If they were themselves more innocent, they would do so. If you teach your daughter that it is wrong to say "mare" or "bull," you may be certain she will find out all the possible reasons for it.

My first serious fight was with Tom Bradford, who was a little older and stouter than I was, a red-headed, freckled-faced boy, whose hair was always cut short, he told me, for safety in fighting, and who was fond of rolling his eyes and putting out his tongue at the girls both in and out of class. It was his kind of humor. He imposed upon me because I was gentle and forbearing in my disposition, and abhorred fracas of any kind. I had, too, taken up the idea that it was wrong to fight, and that I should offend my parents by doing so—but the matter of his tyranny came to my mother's knowledge, and she conjectured the reasons for it, so one day she told me sternly what she had heard, and, moreover, if she ever again heard of my being imposed upon without fighting my best, she would certainly whip me severely. The next day master Tom was rather surprised and loth when he found me eager to quarrel and fight; but fight we did, and my will was so great that I took full indemnity for the past. As he was the only bully among the small boys, I had peace thereafter from them, and from the larger bullies I was always protected by William Parker, the biggest boy in school, who had a liking for me. He was my *beau ideal.* I thought him the most amiable, bravest, and smartest boy that ever lived, and loved him just as the weak and affectionate love heroes. I remember crying heartily when he was quitting the school and came to take away his books and slate; and our friendship lasted as long as he lived, for he lived, a plain hearty planter, to dandle at least four grandchildren in his arms.

There were several of the boys who made a lasting impression on my memory. One of them was Herbert Langley, who used to wear just such multi-buttoned jackets as did my cousin Fitzroy, and who was a regular Miss Nancy, as the boys delighted to call him. He was the only child of a widow, who made some pretensions to wealth, and many to fine manners. Her boy was taught that he was too nice to play at rough games, and too genteel to play with rough boys. He was not too nice, however, to eat his own luncheon off in a corner, and yet beg from others whatever tempted a greedy appetite; nor was he too genteel to do servilely whatever a larger boy bade him, cry most contemptibly loud whenever Old Dill paddled his hand, and quarrel with the little girls upon every trivial occasion. In spite of his fine clothes and rosy cheeks, but one girl, little Jane Hopkins, liked him. Those advantages first attracted her, and her affection was rather added to than decreased by the laughter and opposition it received from the other girls. The widow, his mother, moved away from our town in a few years, and I never heard of them afterward. I believe they went to their relations in Philadelphia, where she had been raised, and had learned manners.

Another boy was Stanley Ruggles, who lived to within the last ten years, and of whom I never lost sight from our childhood. As he and his had rather more to do with the affairs of my life than was at all times agreeable, I must needs describe him as a boy. He was, I think, the handsomest and most selfish boy I ever saw. His ruddy complexion, bright blue eyes, white and even teeth, brown curls, slender and elegant form, feet and hands, were the admiration of all, myself included. He was manly enough looking, but had a great many prettinesses in his manners, and was very pettish. All his life he lacked sincerity and manliness. His affection was often almost maudlin, but it never could be depended upon. The dearest friend of the morning was, unconsciously, the meanest of human beings before night; and the bitterest enemy of one week was the most loved associate of the next, if his friendship would in any way forward master Stanley's projects, but when no longer useful, was discarded upon some trivial pretense, and discovered that the old grudge had only been concealed.

He was about two years older and much taller than I. Although he was not his mother's eldest child, he was her pet, and she always seemed to consider me as his rival, in everything but good looks, and regarded me with a jealous eye accordingly. Why it should have been so, or why she should always have pretended to be one of my mother's dearest friends, and yet have made the worst of all she or any of her children might do or say imprudently, and have depreciated all her and their excellencies, is more than I have ever been able to discover. But so it was. From the earliest time I can remember, she always professed the warmest friendship, misrepresented us with the greatest commiseration, and thwarted us when she could secretly do so.

Another schoolmate was Fred Coons; we always called him Fritz Coony. He was a heavy, Dutch-looking boy, the son of a German tanner, whose tan-yard was not far from our house, and was always to me a place for wonder and disgust. To this day I cannot eat Gruyere cheese for thinking of old Mr. Coons's tán vats. Fritz was not strong at his books, but was quite a mechanical genius, and was noted for his huge kites, his whirligigs, windmills, and cottage-like martin boxes. His father put him to no trade, and he became clerk of one of the courts, lived frugally, and died leaving a poor widow with a large family, in a small martin-box of a cottage, the very picture of neatness. Poor Fritz! his mind was narrowed by his sense of order, a mere mechanical sense, and he thought more of keeping his books neat than of collecting his fees. He might have become a fine mechanician, but was contented to be an orderly clerk, and could relieve his exacerbations of genius by the manufacture of toy windmills, running gang-saws, or miniature pumps.

CHAPTER VI.

OF course I had a sweetheart at Mr. Dill's school.
It has been one of the greatest blessings of my life
that I have never been out of love for any considerable
length of time. Some persons say that no one can
really love but once—an opinion which not only bears
unjustly upon widows and widowers who marry again,
but is, providentially, totally false. Indeed, if it were
true, there would be vastly little conjugal love in this
climate, for very few ever marry their first loves. How it
may be in some tropical countries, where marriages take
place at the age of nine years, I do not know. I suppose the same providential arrangement obtains there.
But whatever may be the general truth of the saying,
I indignantly deny its applicability to me. I have been
fervently in love at least a score of times, and it would
be a slur upon my capacity for affection, and a poor
compliment to my knowledge of myself, if I should
consider that my love was not each time real and
earnest. One love has been more holy and intense on
account of its fruition, but all were real, and for each
object I have to this day a tenderness of respect I do
not have for the memory of other girls and women.
When I see the pretty granddaughters of Molly Higgins,
who was my sweetheart at Mr. Dill's school, I feel the
more kindly to them that I loved their grandmother,
though it was but a schoolboy's passion. She was only
six years older than I, had a sweet, pretty face, and a

lithe, active figure. I thought her perfection, and when I discovered that she had a mole as large as my hand on her right shoulder just beneath where the collar of her dress came, I fancied even that to be a beauty spot, and the hairs growing in it became as precious to me as threads of gold. It matters little what may be the defects of body of those we love; even their vices are apt to be excused as marks of genius, or, at worst, assume the character of inconveniences. You revolt to see one clasp the form and kiss the lips of a dead person, and yet to him or her death has lost its loathsomeness, and is only abhorrent for depriving the dear one of the power to respond to the accents and caresses of love. The once warm living love seems still to glorify the dead flesh, as the vivid flash of lightning still lingers on the retina after darkness reigns around.

Molly married an honest tailor long before I quit school, and there would have been no great disparity had I married her eldest daughter.

When I think of the probable consequences if I had married any one of the girls I loved and who afterward married other men, I am as much astounded at the good fortune of my escape, as thankful for the blessing of having loved with all the gentle ennobling feelings a real love induces. Mary Jane Snodgrass, for instance, became a fat, frowzy, lubberly woman, who had two children—a crippled girl, and a boy who was a fool; and though to have married her would have been bad enough, it would perhaps have been far better than to have had for a wife Ann Jenkins, who had thirteen children, the most of whom were girls and lived. Then there was Lucy Ann Jones, who not only had consumption herself, but gave it to her husband, who, poor creature, driveled away his last days between coughing, and grieving for her, and whining about his poor orphans. And his fate was even better than that of the husband of Peggy Hartwell, whose tongue kept him in perpetual torment, while his neighbors were little less tormented by the five red-headed boys she bore to him.

And so I can go through the list; for it has been my fortune to see most of my young loves after they became "ageable" women, and to know the fate of all of them; and though they were all estimable in their way, when I compare my actual fate with what it might have been had I succeeded in what my soul most ardently desired in each case, I can but feel grateful. "Oh!" would I sigh to myself, "I must marry my dear Molly" (or Peggy, or whichever it might be); "I must marry her, or die broken-hearted." But she saw nothing desirable about me, and I danced, perhaps lackadaisically, at her wedding with one I (of course) knew to be my inferior, and thanked my stars when I saw my next charmer that my cherished hopes had been blasted.

And yet I do not doubt but that every one of my successful rivals who lived to see his wife an old woman thought her a very comely old lady, and, except in moments of freeze or hurricane, was perfectly contented with his lot. The fact is that when a man marries a virtuous woman, he, in a thousand cases to one, gets a wife better than himself, whatever may be her faults of temper; and in about a thousand cases to one he gets the partner who best suits the necessities of his mental and moral nature. Xantippe gave the final polish to the wisdom of Socrates; but for the thirteen children, the husband of Ann Jenkins would have been of no account; but for Peggy Hartwell's tongue, the conceit of her husband would have been unbearable; and if James Hodgson had not married Lucy Ann Jones, he would have died, long before he did, of delirium tremens.

Molly Higgins left the school about the time Old Dill quit us. We all had a notion that he was in love with her himself; and the suspicion excited my ill will, and often made me act in a captious manner, which must have puzzled him had he not been too indolent to remark it; but his taking orders and moving away dispelled every such idea, and I found myself at the same time under the necessity of changing master and mistress. Though for a few days I was disconsolate on her account, the bustle and novelty of having his place supplied distracted my pangs somewhat, and by the time we were fairly settled, Sally Selsby, a sprightly girl of nearer my own age, had aroused and pleased my fancy, and had been given possession of my heart. She was the daughter of a preacher, and therefore, no doubt, had a larger share of the attentions of the devil than other girls—for it stands to reason that the more perfect the character to be supported, the greater the difficulties and temptations. But she was an amiable, impulsive girl, who, to the end of her life, which was short, was as innocent of guile as though Eve had never heard the whispers of Satan, and conferred as much pure pleasure as though she had been an angel sent to play a little while with mortals.

She was the first, but not the last preacher's daughter I have loved, and I must say that I always remember with peculiar pleasure my experience with them, and if I had a son, would recommend his courting one or two, grown ones, to complete his assortment of studies of human nature. Satan seems to manœuvre always by taking advantage of their poverty or precision, or both, to lead them up into high mountains. If "to the hungry soul every bitter thing is sweet," how much sweeter are sweet things, and therefore the lust of the eye, in the way of dress and other finery, and the pride of life in the forms of hierarchical position, attack with double force those who either cannot, or should not indulge in finery or pride. The consequence is that they and their mothers are generally, when they try to do their duty, vastly troubled about many things; and between the feelings of " I will and I won't; I'll be damned if I do, and I'll be damned if I don't," a piquancy is added to their characters, a spiciness to their humility, and a subdued flavor to their spiciness, which is truly refreshing, but sometimes annoying. Sometimes they find that so many things in the world are wrong, they give up trying to choose only the right, but that is not often ; and I have rarely known the daughter of a really good preacher who did not turn out to be an ambitious, hard-working wife, very prim and orderly after her fashion, and with a hard temper of her own, upon occasion.

The very peculiar difficulties which beset the families of preachers may be wrought into a fair argument against the propriety of there being such a *caste* as that of clergy in the world. They constitute, for obvious reasons, no argument against the marriage of preachers, but only against their existence as a caste.

However, I may return to that subject hereafter, at a more fitting era in my life.

The character of our new master as it developed itself was not that of a preacher, as a preacher's ought to be. His name was Dagobert Q. Thomas, and he had strayed off from one of the Eastern States to make his fortune either by a rich marriage, or a profession, or as it might happen; it mattered little how so the end was gained. He had quite an expanse of rugged forehead, a long nose, and high cheek-bones, his hair was auburn and always neatly arranged in careless ringlets, and his small hazel eyes were closely set and keen; but he was by no means ill looking, and if he had only been a man of sound principles he would no doubt have accomplished his design, for there were a number of rich girls in the county, that is, rich as it was then esteemed, and some with no more sense than the law allowed, and, besides, Yankees were not then so universally distrusted, not to say detested, as they have been of late years. At any rate, he succeeded Old Dill, though I never knew by what arrangement, and took charge of the school just as it stood; and at about the same time we understood that he was studying medicine.

It may seem strange that each of my masters was a student of some profession; but in my day, unless it was a stray Scotchman, or an Irishman from Trinity College, Dublin—and it is wonderful how many peripatetic, drunken schoolmasters that college has sent abroad!—such a man as a professional teacher was

6*   E

rarely ever found with us. (School-teaching is a labor to most men, and particularly to men of learning,) compared with which mauling rails, or pulling fodder in August, is an amusement, and, besides that, until within late years, it was esteemed with us much as it was in Greece in the time of Æschines. I cannot myself understand how any one would voluntarily embrace it as a profession at any time, but, then, no one practiced it except under pressure of necessity; and those who intended entering one of the learned professions were the only class with whose necessities it fitted. It seems to me that to become a professional teacher with any hope for success would require not merely the acquisition of learning, but that one should discipline himself by mortification, fasting, and prayer, into the patience of Job; by exercise in the police, into the acuteness of a first-class Detective; and by long practice, into the perfect facility of reading countenances acquired by a successful pettifogger.

Mr. Thomas entered into his affair with a firm, assured step, throwing patience to the winds, and depending upon his natural astuteness for all the rest; and though his eye was keen and restless, and his voice harsh, he could at first have gathered all our suffrages. His first actions put our instincts at fault. His voice was that of Esau, but his hands were smooth and soft as those of Jacob. The order which commenced sometimes to blare forth like a trumpet, became a flute-like request before it was ended; and as he smiled, and smiled, and never whipped, we thought he was only a new sort of saint. But soon a ferule appeared, and then a beech switch, and then a whole fagot of switches, and we commenced to have a warm and earnest time of it. He in a month or two had taken not only the measure of every scholar's foot, as the saying is, but of the feet of all his relations, and woe to those whose feet were smallest and had least power to kick and crush! Poor little Dick Singletree—the boys called him crying Dick—was almost *apodous*, for there was besides himself only his feeble old mother, who made a living by spinning yarn and knitting socks, and he seemed to excite all the master's bile. He was stupid, in truth, and terror made him a hundredfold more so. Imagine his fate!

Another boy, Jim Holmes, a cross-eyed, wiry urchin, with stiff short hair, sallow face, and a turned-up nose with flaring nostrils, whose trowsers were always ragged by the end of the week, and held up by only one suspender, was at first the aversion and then the match of Mr. Thomas. His mother was dead, and his father was a shingle-maker, and worker at any sort of odd jobs, who spent more time in the woods with his rifle than at his work. Nothing could make the fellow have his lessons perfect, and nothing could deter him from mischief, which he always seemed to prefer to work alone. No whipping could bring a tear from his eyes, and his only manifestations of emotion under a scourging were briskly lifting one foot after the other and rubbing himself, and the occasional emission of a sharp "ay!" as though in derision, when the switch touched some unusually tender part. He intended nothing comical, but his whippings were a source of laughter to the boys out of school, and of ill-concealed amusement to the master in it. Before very long Mr.

Thomas discovered that he was a kindred spirit, and laid the rod aside, except on very extraordinary occasions when his stomach or liver was out of order, and the amusement of whipping was scarce. His second whipping was for complaining to an old aunt he lived with about his first—which was really severe and unmerited—and it gave him and us a warning we never forgot. The master placed his punishment on the high ground that it was wrong to tell tales out of school; and, though it was a novel application of the doctrine, it served his purposes. After awhile Jim found it profitable to tell tales in school, and became a despised mischief-maker and spy; a character he never lost. When he grew up, it was his delight to go on patrols, at night, pry around back-yards and quarters, and get negroes or poor whites into trouble; his highest ambition was to be the town policeman, or a sheriff's officer; not a fight occurred but he was sure to be in it, at it, or the first to know all about it, even if he himself had not brought it about. It was a passion with him to know more than any one else about every piece of rascality committed in the county, and to be very mysterious about it till called in court as a witness; and he seemed to have a bitter grudge against all thieves, though it was often suspected that he sometimes connived at and profited by their rogueries. He ended his days in a street fight he had himself incited. A pistol ball missed one of the parties and passed through his chest, killing him almost instantly.

Mr. Thomas had a sleeping-room back of a lawyer's office in a row of small one-storied offices near the court-house (for Yatton had by this time a public square and court-house), and boarded at the tavern kept by old Oberlin, a diminutive German whose head and voice were those of a giant, while his spirit was that of one of the hen-pecked. It was a strange and laughable contrast to hear Mr. Oberlin roaring submission to his shrew of a wife, or in tones of persuasive thunder soothing her exasperation. He was always busy, and seemed to do most of the cooking of his establishment, while his wife presided over the dining-room and the rest of the house. It was interesting to see him leaning with his arms folded and his feet crossed at the street door of the side entry which led to his kitchen. His woolen cap bound around with fur, pulled over his brows, his shabby black blouse and heavy soled shoes showed him to be a foreigner without the necessity of looking at his flat, sallow face, and unmistakably German eyes and mouth. As he stood there in placid repose, the smoke gently curling from the short pipe he held in one corner of his mouth, one would have thought him the most contented of men, until at the sound of his wife's shrill voice in the house over head he would cast his eye upward like a duck in a thunder-storm, and if the noise increased, would with a grunt hurriedly shake the ashes from his pipe, thrust it in his pocket, and start back to the regions of his special labors within, for fear a shower of wrath should descend upon his head if caught outside.

The study of medicine did not seem to deprive Mr. Thomas of much rest, and though he often brought a large book to school, we did not observe that he often did more than open it, apparently as a blind under cover of which to entice the wandering glances or sly

whispers of some urchin not actuated in his diligence
by real love of study.   Punishment was sure to follow
his essays at reading medicine in school.   He was,
nominally at least, the student of old Dr. Hutchins, and
consorted sometimes with one or two of the other doctors, but he was prudently reserved upon professional
matters while with them, though sometimes very diffuse and learned before a non-professional crowd.   I
have heard him in such a crowd out-talk a slow doctor
and even puzzle him in the use of hard medical terms.
With my father he was always especially polite and
reserved, and never ventured out of his depth. He was
afraid of him, and I never saw the scamp who cared
to frequent his company sufficiently to be examined
thoroughly by his penetrating blue eye, and stern sense
of right.   The only way to deceive my father was
through his affections.

I have already mentioned the care the master took
of his hair, and he took no less of his clothing, the
texture and fit of which were always unexceptionable.
His feet were long and flat, and had a knot near the
great toe of each at the head of the metatarsal bone;
but the make and polish of his boots were as fine as
sutorial art could achieve in those days and at that
place.   There was one drawback, however, to the agree-
ability of his person; he was eternally washing his
hands, which were long, cold, and clammy, and rinsing
his mouth, and, in fine, performing the same ablutions
as would a man who felt he was very filthy.   There
was also a very singular fact about his associations
which no one could understand.   He frequently visited
the local preacher, Mr. Steele, who thought him, and

proclaimed him, a promising and lovely young man whom he hoped yet to see laboring in the vineyard; for he professed to be "serious about his soul's salvation," and was punctual and devout in his attendance at church, prayer meetings, and even at class meeting. He often spoke to Mr. Steele and others, particularly devout old ladies, of the piety of his parents, of the means of grace he had enjoyed, and how he had once thought his mountain strong, but had strayed away like a lost sheep into the gins and snares of this present wicked world; until the more he proclaimed himself a sinner the more they believed him a saint incognito. Yet, Jim Cotton, and Sam Hardaway, and one or two others, men of leisure and pleasure, gorgeously dressed and glittering with rings and chains, were known to frequently visit his room at night,—with others who were strangers, passing through the town bound to the territories,—for Mississippi and Alabama had not then been admitted as States, and Texas was a savage land. He was often, too, in confab with one or more of them as though by chance at a corner or about the public square. They were noted gamblers, but it was thought that perhaps he was trying to put in the good word to turn them from their ways. He said he was, and through Mr. Steele, who somehow in the connection rung in the text about "the mouths of babes and sucklings," it got to be believed.

A few months after his advent he commenced to pay sedulous court to Miss Lucy Perkins, a fine showy girl, whose father had the reputation of being one of the richest planters then in our section, and who would, as an only child, be rich at his death. Of course, the

elegant, accomplished, and serious Mr. Thomas had the
entry of all the best society of the county in its public
sociabilities, and, to please her, he was even admitted
into many of the private parties where she was invited.
In fact, it got to be understood that it would be a
match; and as he would then be adopted into the
family of the tribe, he was treated with anticipatory
cordiality, at all hands. Whether they were ever actually engaged or not, I do not know; though I do believe
she would have married him; and if she had, her fate
could have hardly been worse than it was with the
husband she took at last. The only two differences I
can see are, that she would have had a Yankee instead
of a home-bred brute, and therefore might have been
robbed, and (because he would have been Mr. Thomas)
might have been murdered, as well. But, whatever
she might have done, it was fated Mr. Thomas should
not achieve wealth in Yatton, and the catastrophe happened in this wise.

The worldly had for some time been conjecturing
that he was not the ingenuous disciple the leading
brethren thought him to be, and they hinted malig-
nantly at his having been heard to use language of un-
godly objurgation (hints are generally vague; they did
not say he cursed outright) on several occasions when
greatly irritated, and something I did not understand,
was said about Miss Lucy's yellow servant-girl, and
various innuendoes were bandied about; but all was
looked upon by Father Steele and his stanch supporters as mere envious slander, though some of the
less enthusiastic among them began to doubt. But
the autumn came on, and with it camp meeting, at the

camp ground near Yatton. Mr. Thomas attended it regularly, always near about Miss Lucy; and he visited the altar and took his seat upon the mourner's bench with her and others two or three times, and seemed to take so great an interest in her salvation—and, poor girl, she was deeply affected!—and in securing his own, that one day Father Steele asked him to lead in prayer. I venture to say that a more beautiful and affecting prayer never was heard on that camp ground. Miss Lucy was kneeling near him, and her presence, and the "Amens!" and shouts of "glory," and groans of contrition, which greeted each sentence, seemed to inflame his memory, imagination, and devotion until one would have thought St. Chrysostom himself was speaking. He was so perfectly abstracted, however, by the strain of the purely intellectual effort he had made that he forgot himself, and where he was, and after he had pronounced his amen, he sat back on the ground and exclaimed to himself, but audibly, in a triumphant tone: "Pretty tolerably d—d well, for the first time!"

What I have here narrated is the actual fact; for though I did not hear it myself, being on the outskirts of the crowd and crying with excitement, many others did—and among them Mr. Steele himself, who cast upon him a look of surprise and sorrow, and, as did all the others, silently shunned him. He saw his error as soon as it was committed, and seemed to catch at it as though he might recall it; but his game was up on the religious deal, and he knew it. There was nothing left for him but to brazen it out, or to leave the county; and as he thought he had still a chance for Miss Lucy and a permanent and very large stake in the country, he concluded to take the first alternative; and like a wise man, he neither put on defiant airs nor apologized for his lapse.   He, on the contrary, never referred to it, and seemed humble and contrite, in hopes that it would pass over as a remnant of the old leaven; and so it no doubt would have done in time, but his misfortunes were culminating for his total overthrow.

There were at the school, as I have intimated, several boys of sixteen or seventeen years of age, stout, manly fellows, but singly no match for the master in strength.   From the first they had preserved a sort of armed neutrality, being deterred by respect for the public opinion in his favor from combining against his cruelties, notably those to Dick Singletree; but they had turned pale and gritted their teeth many a time, and vowed in their hearts what they would do if he were ever to attempt to serve them so.   The shield of public favor was gone; Mr. Steele had ceased to mention the outcast's name, and only sighed when he heard it; the class-leaders were equally as silent and evasive for fear of bringing greater scandal on the church; the worldly were loud in their jeers and scoffs, rolled the scandal like a sweet morsel under their tongues, and did not hesitate to roar with laughter at him, whom they called a hypocrite, as though he had perpetrated a merry jest; and his humility they treated as a fine stroke of policy.   With a consciousness of right, and a chivalrous feeling of benevolence, and, probably, the secret encouragements of sundry grown advisers to back them, the union of strength was formed, the command of high Justice was announced, and Sam Halliday, Phil Hartwell, and Joe Hopkins were appointed her executioners.

The occasion soon presented itself. Little Dick was called up for punishment, and advanced pale and trembling, casting pleading glances back at his champions. The master, first suppling in his hand a keen, elastic switch, was about to bring it with hissing force upon the boy's back, cowering to receive the blow, when his arm was arrested midway and his form rendered motionless by the voice of Sam, who, standing up in his place, said: "Stop, Mr. Thomas; you must not whip that boy any more." "What do you mean, sir?" exclaimed the master, in his harshest voice. "We mean," said Sam, and here Phil and Joe rose and stood by him, and most of the other scholars rose also to their feet in excitement while others shrank with terror in their seats,—"we mean that you have whipped him too much already, and that you shan't do so any more!" "You d—d scoundrel," shouted the master, "I'll whip you, too;" and he advanced switch in hand to where Sam was standing, and as his blow descended, Sam struck him with a glass inkstand on the mouth, and Phil and Joe clinched with him, and all four were almost immediately upon the floor, striking and scuffling among the desks and benches. Jim Holmes ran forward to interfere for his friend, who, he thought, must needs conquer, and would so reward; but a blow from Sam, whom he first caught hold of, sent him howling to the end of the room. The scuffle lasted but three or four minutes, when Mr. Thomas's (no longer the master's) voice was heard exclaiming, "Enough!" It was in those days the point of honor never to strike after that magic word was said; but they tied him, hands and feet, and then dictated their terms—which were neither more nor less than that he should abdicate his authority by giving up the school; terms, no doubt, from their thoroughness, the prompting of wiser heads than those of the victors; for it may be noted that boys in dealings with older persons are apt of themselves to compromise and palter, rather than go to the extremest length of right and propriety. The single article was agreed to, and signed in black and white by the teacher, after he was released from his bonds, and he walked out of the door bruised and crestfallen.

No shout of triumph broke the awfulness of the occasion. The little boys hurriedly, and the larger more deliberately gathered their slates, and books, and playthings together, amid the shuffling of feet and the slamming of desk-lids—and all went off in squads to their homes, talking over the event in subdued tones. Mr Thomas, with his handkerchief to his bruised and bloody face when about to meet any one, went across the fields to his room, and was seen no more that day in public; and the next morning he was gone from the town.

Then commenced the uproar. The boys were fully justified in their conduct by their parents; the public praised them, and little Dick worshiped them. All the story of Mr. Thomas's doings and propensities came out, greatly embellished and added to, I fear. He was a gambler. He had left between two days with all his valuables; and old Oberlin's board bill was unsettled, and the shoemaker was unpaid, and a bill against

him for perfumery, and cardamom seeds, and fancy
soap, and divers packs of cards, and bottles of brandy,
and a hymn-book, and Adams's Ruddiman's Rudiments
of the Latin Grammar, and sundry hair and tooth
brushes, and numerous prescriptions of medicine, were
charged on the books of the drug-store—for Yatton
had then a drug-store, and in it was just such a general assortment as this bill indicates. And old Oberlin swore "by damn," and his wife sneered, and up-
braided him so sorely that a year or so afterward he
refused entertainment to a man because his name was
Thomas; and would have had a fight, not a lawsuit,
about it but for the interference of his wife, who calmed
the stranger; but to her astonishment could not sub-
due the will of her lord and master. Old Wright, the
druggist, who had learned his profession in Philadelphia, comforted himself by saying that, as the fellow
was a medical student, anything was to be expected
of him; and the shoemaker forgot his loss in a roaring
drunk which lasted three days, when he returned to his
lap-stone with other feelings in his head than condemnation of his absconding debtor.

But the person most seriously injured was Miss
Lucy. She was most to be pitied and least to blame;
for the others had no business giving credit, while it
was exactly the business of her woman's nature to
give credit, and gain love and a husband—and was not
this young man handsome, accomplished, and pious, as
all thought? What more attractive could any one desire than a handsome person, fine talents, and fair
learning? and what better security than piety? Alas,
how many hundreds of thousands of Southern girls

have found the attractions, and overvalued the counterfeit security! It would seem that women will never cease taking morals and disposition upon trust. They have to do so, as do men, more or less under the most favorable opportunities, but it certainly is the most reckless of follies to trust a wandering stranger, of whose family and previous life they can have no knowledge; and even if he come highly recommended, of whose disposition they can have no experience.

If Miss Lucy had used half the discretion with regard to Thomas's morals, disposition, family, and even his present life, that he did with regard to her fortune, she would not have had to hang her head, and refuse for months to go abroad among her friends; she would not have had to reproach herself for being placed in the ridiculous position of one whose lover had been chased from her by the furies of offended justice and public scorn, and had also been the too successful lover of her maid.

Ah, it was a pitiable case; far worse than if he had discarded her. Then she might have mourned like a stricken dove; but now, like a maiden hawk whose heart has throbbed tumultuously as she has timidly answered the voice of some coming mate in the dense foliage of a neighboring tree, and who, at length, while in her tenderest pitch, discovers it is a miserable blue-jay who has imitated the gallant tones, and at the approach of danger flies screaming with affright deeper into the grove, she had to sit pondering the rude disappointment with drooping plumes, and try to persuade herself she never was deceived into a response.

CHAPTER VII.

I WAS fourteen years old when the school broke up so suddenly and dramatically, and the holiday which resulted was very delightful after my long task at books. Living out of town as we did, I was not tempted to the excitements and mischiefs of gregarious and knowing town boys, and my parents were spared the continual watching and chiding they would have had to bestow upon me. Nor did I miss the noisy crowd so much as would have been expected; for besides that I was rather a shy, thoughtful boy, my two younger sisters, and two brothers, the younger only four years old, gave me plenty of amusement. Indeed, home was always a place of delight to me, as it was to them. We loved our indulgent parents and each other tenderly, and found amusement in very simple and incongruous things. I say incongruous, because as they grew a little older, the switchings Joe received were a source of the keenest enjoyment to Eldred, unless he was himself involved; and Eldred's contortions under punishment excited as great contortions of mirth in Joe; from which facts it may be surmised that our dear little mother's discipline had lost a good deal of its vigor and wiry edge. But besides these playmates, I had Peter Hall, a son of Judge Hall, and Isaac Davis, the son of the then sheriff; both about my own age, both intelligent, noble-hearted, and gentlemanly boys, who used to visit me often, sometimes for days at a time, and whose visits I was allowed to return. Their mothers had been school-friends of my mother, and each had well-founded confidence in the other's children.

I remember how with these boys and my little brothers it was my delight of summer days to paddle about with bare feet in the spring branch, underneath the beech-trees, and build dams across it. As the current swelled in volume, our dam would break on one side, and as we patched it up, the other would break by small degrees, not noticed, until all the white sand and brilliant pebbles would rush away with grating sound, and our work would have to be begun anew. So it was, and yet I never tired of meeting the same fate. Even then, as I constructed my dam, I built air-castles too. Truly, a more hopeful, imaginative boy than I never existed. The greatest impossibilities were to me as realities. I accompanied Jack—him of the bean-stalk—in his long climb, put on the seven-leagued boots and beat the giant; I shared with the other Jack all his excitement in giant-slaying, and slew many a giant of my own. The Wonderful Lamp was among my treasures; I knew every nook and corner of Doubt-ing Castle; Ali Baba's servant was assisted by me in the disposal of the forty thieves; and the very purse of Fortunatus was in my pocket; Cinderella was no myth to me, but was one of my loves, and I had the exact match of the Marquis of Carabbas's cat. I searched for diamonds among the pebbles of the brook, and hoped to find lumps of gold among the iron py-rites in the deep wash near the house.

They were glorious days, those of my childhood.

With a halo of hopeful unreality about me, I wandered through the woods with my little single-barreled gun and dogs. There were Mingo and Beppo, poor old Juno, and half a dozen others—terriers, hounds, and curs. I knew the voice of each, and what it meant. The timid rabbit pricked up its ears, leaped stealthily from its covert, and ran for dear life, when halloo and bark announced our approach. The partridge, hide she it never so wisely, could not conceal her nest from me. The squirrel dropped his hickory-nut and chattered at us as we passed, or from 'the loftiest limb scolded me for some noisy attempt on his life. I was up to all the dodges of the woodpecker, and the red-bird was not smart enough to bite my finger as I took him from my trap. Happy days they were, and all the happier for the day-dream-land in which I lived. The rabbit was a foreign foe successfully chased away; the squirrel, some escaped malefactor against whom I vowed future vengeance; the woodpecker, a clown; the red-bird, a thief.

Because to call one a day-dreamer is intended as a reproach, and because I may have lost some time at that pleasant amusement, I will not therefore condemn what, when you analyze it, is the source of more material benefit and general content than all the surplus wealth of the world. I grant that its excess is folly, for the excess of any virtue is folly or vice, but within due bounds it is like a rosy light cast upon heavy clouds—the landscape is all the brighter for the reflection. I remember some lines I wrote when I was first grown up, which, though they may not be poetry, are applicable to the subject.

F

"Remember, too, that if in life's short day
A gloomy cloud obscure your various way,
Hope tells you that the rainbow lies concealed
In the dark thunder-cloud, and is congealed
In the smooth ice; from Heaven the light must shine
To make it seen; that in the darkest mine
The very stones have fires within them hid;
And you must be the steel at whose rough bid
They shall burst forth and light around them shed."

This hope, married to a vigorous imagination, produces day-dreams, as they are called. And the more healthy the hope and the imagination, the more lusty and brilliant the visions. But it produces also active and well-directed labor.

Imagination is not what most persons seem to consider it, or I do not understand it. Because Shakspeare and Milton had fine imaginations, it is not to be supposed that Newton and Watt possessed little or none, but were wholly absorbed in hard facts. Both were almost, or quite, as imaginative as either of the poets; their imaginations differed only in bent. Through what boundless space must not the imagination of Newton, taking charge of and up-bearing his reason, have traveled, toying with the stars, arranging and tossing the planets to and fro, enduing them with various imaginary forces, and hurling them in this or that infinite direction, until by comparing results he arrived at the great laws which govern their motions! A steam-engine is a hard fact, yet mathematics could not have invented it, however they may contribute to the perfection of its machinery. The bold and original imagination of Watt suggested that the thing could be arranged, and then, spurred on by hope, arranged it; and who can tell the brilliant dreams of future wealth and fame which kept pace with his reason, and cheered it on in its sometimes languid and discouraged flight in the clouds!

I can readily imagine some young man of talent and lively fancy imagining to write a book and give it to the world, and before he has written a line picturing to himself a glorious success. It shall be about the loves and sorrows of Araminta and Theodore, and after fifteen, nay, forty editions are exhausted, he, all unknown, shall leave his quiet home to travel. On steamboats and in rail-cars, in hotels and on doorsteps, he sees his book in hand and being eagerly read. He is jostled on the street by men reading his book; steamboat-clerks and draymen have left their work, and are seated upon boxes and bales on the wharves, reading his book; and all business is at a stand-still until his book be read. Tears trickle from young ladies' eyes as they breathe the name of Theodore, and "Ah, Araminta!" is sighed by young men and old behind counters, and at their calculations. Bridget and Dolly carry his book in their pockets, and pause in making up his bed, or, while sweeping, seat themselves upon the stairs, to finish a chapter. The players snatch all the moments between their appearances to read a little in his book behind the scenes; the call-boy is too busy with it to heed the time; and the prompter pores over it, instead of setting right the actors, who only sigh and talk, as though in dreams, of its scenes to an audience too busy reading his book to mind their vagaries.

I say that I can imagine a young man permitting all these fantastic dreams to revel in his mind, and being spurred on to exertion, and as he will do his best at his work, I think he is greatly benefited. Nor, if he should never write a line of his book, but should hammer merrily at his trade, do I see that he has received any harm. If he should permit himself to indulge the dreams to occupy his time to the exclusion of his work, or should shape his work by them, he is, in the true sense, no day-dreamer; he is crazy, an absolute lunatic, who, at best, has only lucid moments—however his friends may. think of his superior intellect, and call him only visionary. It is best to call things by their right names.

When I was a boy I could picture myself a prince, with power of life and death, wealth without parallel, and luxury without stint; but I never discovered that I obeyed my parents any the worse for it, found a two-bit piece any the smaller, or enjoyed my corn-bread and bacon, my simple pallet, or my rides in an ox-cart, any the less. Since I have been a man I have indulged myself in rhapsodies to which that I have imagined of the young would-be author is very grave, but, though I have perhaps wasted some time in them, I am not aware that the indulgence has ever warped or weakened my judgment.

There is no invention and there is little happiness without the exertions of fancy. They add savor to the dry crust, and down to the straw bed, and success to the hard toil of the laboring man; or, at least, they make those evils more bearable. It is peculiarly fit that children should have the happy faculty and a facility of day-dreaming. The occurring troubles and miseries of their inexperienced lives would be destroying without it, and it has lifted many a one from the dirt to sit in high places.

Call it day-dreaming, imagination, fancy, the creative faculty, or what you will, it is the same faculty in poets, and philosophers, and children; and is almost, if not quite, the only faculty which man possesses not also given to brutes. It is a principal moving power of man's nature, and, like the inclination to make a noise which caws with the crow, brays with the ass, or warbles with the nightingale, it manifests itself differently with different persons.

The secret of my failure in life—I mean my failure to make fame and fortune—is not that I.have been a visionary, but, perhaps, that I have been impatient. A day or two after a child has planted a cutting, he pulls it up to see if it has taken root; so have I planned the growth of many a fair scheme which I hoped should bear me pleasant fruits, and have by my impatience killed it, or made it linger long, to die at last unfruitful; and all the associations and tenor of my life tended to encourage that natural impatience the germs of which I certainly possessed in considerable vitality. In my early days I saw no one meet with any great success unless by accident, or in saving money, and as I often heard the proverb, "a fool for luck," and knew that meanness was the most certain aid to wealth, I was discouraged. During my whole life I have seen but few men who achieved a lasting fame, or one worth having, in any walk of life. However ardent he might be, and whatever his apparent chances, death stepped in, or accident, or his object lost its value in his esteem, and he never enjoyed the prize. At school I studied Latin and Greek to the pitch of irritated despair; was put through a course of algebra in about two weeks, for the purpose of hurrying me to a higher class for which I was otherwise prepared; took a-few lessons in drawing; and got a stray Frenchman to teach me the passes and guards with the foils, which I used to practice with my companions to the danger of our eyes, the scarring of our hands and arms, and by continued practice, to the complete confusion of all science in the art so slightly learned. All this tended me to be impatient; as to have seen and felt impatience would have made me patient and thorough.

Had another plausible child-tinker established himself in business after Mr. Thomas's *devastavit*, I should no doubt have been continued as at once a specimen and a subject. But for several months no eligible teacher presented himself, and in the mean time my father himself had taken to teaching me French and Spanish, and brushing me up occasionally in Latin and Greek, and my views in life, too, had altered, so that when a good school was started, I was not sent as one of the scholars.

Few men, in our part of the world at least, more thoroughly understood both Latin and Greek than my father; he was, therefore, most competent to teach, and, had not my disgust to those languages prevented, his kind explanations and assistance would have made me learn them. But his knowledge of French was very limited, and I doubt if he had ever read a page of Spanish in his life; and yet he gave me a more thorough course in

both than most teachers of modern languages in American schools have either the patience or the capacity to
give. The Spanish book he made me read, after I had
somewhat progressed in the grammar, was upon the
evidences of Christianity (I have forgotten its title), and
with his knowledge of Latin, and of what the sense
ought to be, it was impossible to impose upon him a
false translation.

I suppose that it is the quality of old age, whether
happy or miserable, to make our memories of youth
more sweet. I, at least, differ with Francesca, in hell,
who exclaims:

> "Nessun maggior dolore,
> Che ricordarsi del tempo felice
> Nella miseria."

Perhaps if I were in hell it would be so too with me.
But as it is, in my feebleness I remember with exult-
ation the strength and activity of my youth; in my
pain I laugh to see myself a child again, undergoing the
dread I had of having my first teeth pulled out with a
waxed thread; and in the long cold nights of winter,
when my hips and shoulders sometimes ache with lying
so long, and every feather I lie on feels like a stout
twig, I remember with sad but intense pleasure how I
used to snug up in my father's arms, and he would
sometimes rouse me to hear the owls hooting, or the
rain beating on the roof. So great an impression did
this last incident make upon my mind, that I to this day
feel more comfortable in a house the roof of which is
so near me as to allow the sound of every drop of rain
to be heard distinctly; and if I had to build a house
for myself, would have it of one story, without a ceiling, and with a board roof.

But among the most touching of all my memories in life is that of my father in this time of his playing teacher. Some warm summer afternoon, perhaps, he would come home, after having ridden and been worried with his patients from ten o'clock the night before, and, after first kissing my mother and hearing what news there was to tell, he would say: "Come, my son, help me off with my coat;" for all his toil and exposure had given him rheumatism in the left shoulder and back. And when I helped him doff his threadbare coat, I would notice how his pants were worn thin and white behind, and how they looked shiny at the knees, and how his shirt-collar and wristbands were frayed; and knowing that it was not my mother's fault (for no one darned, and mended, and patched equal to her), but that he had to stint himself to provide clothing and food for his family, my heart would grow very tender, as it does to this day. After lying down upon the wooden settee on the gallery, with a comfortable pillow under his head, he would tell me cheerily to get my books and come and say a lesson. Soon, as I read, his eyes would begin to close ominously, then presently he would open them sleepily and say: "Read that again!" and perhaps before it was fairly read his regular breathing would show he was sound asleep; and I would go off on tiptoe to my play, or to finish my trap, or an axe-helve, or some such pleasant occupation.

Ah, who can tell the miseries of a poor professional man—particularly of a poor country doctor! The man in commerce or the laboring man can, without carping, regulate the expenditure of his household by the amount of his income; poor profits are expected to produce

close living, and low wages may without loss of
name palliate rags and bare feet. The poor lawyer
may keep his family very private, and so escape criti-
cism; and the poor preacher is in the line of his profession when he is miserably poor. But not so the doctor.
As he, from his knowledge and position, is expected to
be a gentleman, so is his wife expected to be a lady,
and to dress as well as act like one, and to keep her
children dressed and instructed and regulated like little
gentlemen and ladies. Her visitors must be unchecked
in number or imposition, and her table must consequently be always bountiful and neatly spread, and at
least one bed must be very soft and tidy. Whether
the season be healthy or sickly, and whether good
crops insure the prompt payment of his bills, or a failure defer their settlement, it is all the same with the
country doctor. Like a candidate who stands for the
suffrages of all, he must be ready at all times to welcome all. My father was hospitable from his own
benevolence, without a thought of policy. That he
could do good, or give pleasure, was incentive enough
for him; and I doubt if it ever occurred to his mind to
make a distinction between those who employed or
might employ him, and those who should never benefit
him.

With his wife and children upon their behavior, it
is but to be expected that troubles should arise to the
poor doctor's family; for no mortals can at all times
bear such a strain—and woe the day the trouble
comes. His "Lady" must invariably—there is no
escape that I have ever heard of—have among her lady
visitors some friends, like Mrs. Ruggles, of boundless

8*

affection and great fastidiousness, who, perhaps, after receiving from a full heart some account of troubles in such general housekeeping, will remark that she was sorry to observe that Mrs. Dr. Jenkins was getting to have a great dislike of company, or that she was shocked to notice that Dr. Liffkins was either so stingy to his family, or his practice was so falling off, that poor Mrs. Liffkins is put to the saddest straits to give her children bread. All of this, except the imputation of stinginess, though but the malicious exaggeration of the friend, is strictly true; yet by just such gossip about him and his affairs the doctor receives a terrible injury; and loss of practice is followed by retrenchment, and greater loss by poverty, which comes on apace. Whatever case he may be called to see, he attends with all his alacrity and professional skill; but he finds idle time, and begins to pay more attention to his home-concerns, sees to the patching up of his fences, over-looks the garden, and soon becomes half farmer half doctor; curtails his own personal expenses even so far as to quit smoking, and yet bread is scarce, and often he is at his wit's end to know where the next shall come from

His affairs may take a turn and he may have prosperity again, but how wretched is now his case! But one thing could add to its misery. If his wife should be so unloving or so weak as to reproach him, his cup would indeed run over. The only patience which could ever stand that was Job's, and even he told his wife she spake "as one of the foolish women speaketh." Indeed, the reproaches of Job's wife were the poor man's crucial test. The loss of property and of children and of health are all in the natural and ordinary course of nature, but the reproaches of the woman one loves, and has promised, both verbally and by the very act of loving and marrying, to cherish, provide for, and protect, when added to the already unutterable wretchedness caused by disaster or failure, are too much. She must of necessity make comparisons with the success of other men; and then pride, jealousy,—in fine, his manliness,—all the combatant principles of his nature are aroused and rampant.

My father's affairs were for awhile at a low ebb, and he and his were subjected to all the troubles I have here alluded to; but fortunately his philosophy and Christian faith were not put to the test of the re-proaches of his wife. The dear little woman not only loved her husband, but was very proud of him. "The Doctor" could do no wrong; his failures were not his fault, and his successes were triumphs over unheard-of opposition Had he been sole candidate for some un-desirable office, she would have ascribed his election to his admitted superiority and the fear of others to run against him; and if he should have met with opposi-tion and defeat, she would have felt it a thousandfold more than he, and would have heartily disliked the fortunate candidate and all his supporters, though her husband and all the world should have praised them.

This was not from want of knowledge and sound discretion on her part. Few women had higher claims to be called intellectual and wise, but her intellectuality and wisdom were, like those of all true women, modi-fied by her affections. It is generally useless to argue against feeling; and, in fact, when I see one, a woman especially, allow cold reason to triumph over natural feelings, I always imagine that there is a little hypocrisy in the matter. It will not do to trust to such apparent convictions.

People are very prone to praise filial affection, as though it were a merit. (There is most generally no merit in it, though the want of it is sometimes a hideous vice.) To support and honor unworthy parents may indeed be an effort of virtue, but I cannot concede that I ever deserved praise for honoring my parents. It may be gathered from what I have already said that my father was worthy of all my love and admiration; but my mother was no less lovely and admirable, to her children and dependants, at least.

I do not recollect the minute that she was free from cares and annoyances, nor do I recollect a day when she allowed them to lessen her hope and energy. Though her frame was delicate, and from her youth up she was subject to more pains and aches than most women are, and had to be shielded from exposure like an exotic, she raised a large family through all the ailments incident to childhood, and cheered my father in all his toils and troubles as no woman less gentle, wise, and brave, however robust, could have done. From his instructions and her own observation and frequent experience, she became in a few years a really good physician herself, so far as to note and understand symptoms; and her knowledge, added to her strong and unerring sympathy, made her one of the very best of nurses. It seems to me yet that she always knew intuitively how and where one's pain was, and what was the best method of relief. Her gentle hand, I know, always soothed my racking head, and no one could arrange the pillows so softly and the cover so fittingly as she. Nor were her family the only persons to whom she was a blessing, both in sickness and in health. Old Mrs. Blodgett thought that no broth was so nourishing, and no jellies and cooling drinks were so grateful, as those she prepared; and very many persons participated in Mrs. Blodgett's belief, and were never so contented in trouble as when Mrs. Page made them a visit. It was strange how her tender frame could endure the fatigue of nursing the sick as it did, but the spirit within her was that of an archangel, and when it seemed that her aching head and weary limbs would, after days and nights of watching, hardly allow her to totter from the bedside of one of her sick children to that of another, she would always rouse to meet any new emergency. If she could not walk, she would crawl; if she could not see for blinding pain, she would feel. She was one of those who can be faithful unto death, and esteem such faithfulness the most natural of all things. "Ah," I used to think, "ah, Mr. Emperor Napoleon, if my little mother were only over there in Europe, and had the matter placed in her hands, she'd stop your career, and lug you by the ear to your seat, for all she is so gentle and loving!"

Her taste, too, and her knowledge of economy, were not less than wonderful. Those were not the days in our part of the country when young ladies were educated in all the isms and ologies, nor did they have milliners and mantua-makers in every village. A fashion was long out of date in Europe and the North before it reached Yatton, and when it did get there, it was

soon modified by good sense to the rules of good taste;
for there was little rivalry as to who should copy it the
most exactly, and a good deal of wholesome modesty,
and fear of being *outrée* even in so fantastic and irregular a thing as fashion.   My mother, with none of the
advantages of education in modern high art, had a
natural taste for simple elegance which never went
astray, and her young friends were glad to profit by
what was so rare in itself, and so kindly placed at their
service for decorating their persons, their parlors, or
their gardens.   There was a keen and unerring appreciation of the beautiful which moved like a sweet
thema through all her life, and harmonized discords as
though they were a necessary part to its melody.   Her
movements were grace itself, and all her aspirations
were induced by love.   She played upon no musical
instrument, for in her youth there were no pianos bang-
ing the life out of every echo in the land.   I myself
was a large boy before I ever saw one of those wretched
instruments, which have caused more nervous pain, and
more waste of time and money than a thirty years' war.
But my mother's voice was as sweet as that of an Indian girl, and she sang with charming correctness and
feeling the simple ballads then in vogue.   Drawing and
painting were also then, as now, almost entirely unknown in female education, yet from essays that I have
seen, and from what I know of the justness of her eye
for proportions and colors, I know that she had a talent
for both, and could have excelled in them.   Indeed,
whatever of taste in art I may have ever had, and my
passionate love for music, for flowers and perfumes,
and every other beautiful and sweet thing in nature or

art, I derived for the most part from my mother, though my father, from whom I inherited the form and constitution of my body, was by no means deficient in those things.

The darling-little woman! She was as modest and innocent after she had raised her large family of children as she was when she first became a blushing, trembling wife. Never in all my life did I hear a coarse expression from her lips, or see or hear any evidence of aught but perfect purity of mind. She was one of the very few persons I have known who was always just and ladylike even in her greatest anger; and though she could doubtless, being a woman, aggravate, and run husband and servants wild, I never knew her to indulge her natural instinct in that way.

I ascribe her innocence and amiability not to her natural disposition alone, but in a great measure to the character and conduct of my father. He was not one who indulged in broad jokes and vulgar allusions. He carried into his married life a profound respect for woman which characterized his bachelorhood. Although he could relish any conversation which had wit or humor in it, he detested what was in itself unseemly or bred unchaste ideas. ' He could see and appreciate *double entendres*, but he never explained them to her, and I verily believe that to the last day of her life she could have read Tristram Shandy and pronounced it obscure and flat. Then, too, her love for him was so intense, and so mingled with respect, that she not only could never think of scolding him, or scolding in his presence; but she could never do in his absence anything of which she thought he might disapprove. Many

women give eye-service. I will not say that most do
so, for I do not know it to be the fact; but many do,
and it shows both that they do not love with respect,
and that they are cowardly. My mother was afraid of
her husband, just as her children were always afraid
both of him and her,—not afraid of blows or harsh-
ness, but afraid of wounding his love. How could she,
by her words or acts, bring a cloud upon the countenance
of the strong and gentle man whose approval was as
the light of her life! And when he, the Bread-winner,
was absent toiling for her and their children, she was
jealous to do her part to lessen his necessity for labor
and to comfort his weariness. When he would fall
asleep hearing my lessons, her whole household talked
in whispers, and went on tip-toe lest he should lose his
rest; and when he waked the sun rose, and all was
light and life. He never waked to find her standing
near to pour upon him an account of domestic troubles,
or of our childish mischiefs. If troubles had occurred,
she chose her time to tell them when they would annoy
him least; and if any of us had been particularly good,
or deserving of praise, she related it when he most
needed to be cheered.

It will not here be out of place to mention two things
she never did, though I doubt if she ever went through
the formality of making definite rules for her conduct:
she never concealed anything from her husband, and
she never threatened her children with their father.
The consequences were that he was never suspicious,
and that they were always frank and unrestrained with
him.

CHAPTER VIII.

I WAS tired of school-books. For eight years I had been kept steadily at them, and, what with idle masters, lazy masters, and ignorant masters, and the grinding work of uninteresting lessons, I was fagged. My father's lessons were fun, and I had a great idea of getting learning by the easy plan of studying just when I felt like it—if, indeed, book-learning were worth the getting. I doubted then if it were worth the trouble, and now, in my old age, I doubt if education in books be desirable for the mass of the human race. I am sure that but for the purposes of extended commerce, it is, for the most part, not only useless, but hurtful.

Education, unless it be to greater facility in some useful employment, is a humbug. Give your son all the book-learning of which his mind is capable, and what are the consequences? Unless he make it useful to himself, and, consequently, to his fellow-men in the ways and works of life, it does not benefit; and unless it result in making him a sincere Christian, it leads to his greater eternal condemnation.

This may sound harsh, but it is certainly true. The great gloze of the devil in this day and generation of psychological nonsense, is this very cant about book education.

To understand several languages is useful, certainly; so are Algebra, and Conic Sections, and the Calculus of Variations—they are useful because they lead to higher results of utility. In themselves they are mere curiosities, and the eye-tooth of Cleopatra or the big-toe nails of Julius Cæsar would be just as useful to most men as the possession of all these results of intellectual labor. With nine hundred and ninety-nine out of every thousand, they neither lead nor can lead to any useful results to themselves or their fellows.

It is all stuff to talk about the usefulness of such studies to fit the mind for high thought, and to improve the intellectual part of man which must live throughout eternity. If a man had plenty of money, and no one dependent on him, and no earthly duties to perform, he might lead a life of purely intellectual improvement—granting, which I do not, that books, of themselves, improve the intellect. But this is a working world, and the men in it have duties toward themselves and each other to perform which are not intellectual, but muscular. They have only this life to perform them in—and it is far better to go to heaven with all duties performed, and spend eternity in improving the mind, than to go there, or into condemnation, with minds full of human learning, and the world none the better or happier for their having lived in it.

But I go further than that. To most men reading and writing are of no use except to convey or fix their plans of business, and arithmetic of no advantage except to prevent their being cheated in their transactions. When a man has those three branches of learning, he has all he can get from books essential to usefulness in any ordinary sphere of life. But, in sober truth, they do not advantage one in a hundred, either mentally or morally. They are but tools, after all; and to give a savage a jack-plane, or a screw-driver, or a watch, would do both his morals and understanding less harm than to give an ignoramus a knowledge of these items of learning. The chances are very great that in neither case will the instruments be put to a proper use. They will either be thown away, or used for injury to himself or others. To hear atheism in its most aggravated form, go to the work-shops and among the half-educated work-people of any civilized land.

My argument, rightly considered, does not tend to depriving the masses of education; but it recognizes the tremendous responsibility they incur when they learn to read, and sets forth the egregious folly of giving them educations in books at the expense of years of laborious, useless, idleness—for the time spent at colleges and schools is just that, in the vast majority of cases. If a boy be by nature cut out for a fiddler, or a doctor, or a lawyer, or an engineer, a fiddler, doctor, lawyer, or engineer, of some sort, he will become, if he have the energy of genius—and, in the name of common sense, let him have every advantage. But the mass of mankind are of the average class, and what an awful mistake is made when you attempt—as is done by the present system of education in books—to make them all, at the same time, lawyers, doctors, musicians, engineers, astronomers, chemists, geologists, and linguists! And even suppose such an education were not altogether vain, and all men could become, to a considerable degree, all of these things, who are to do the manual labors of life? Who are to do the shoe-making, and tailoring, and weaving, and rope-making, and working in iron, and. brass, and gold, to do the building, and to till the soil?

The course of reasoning seems to be this: We have here a. noble country, with a fertile soil and pleasant climate; we must make it a rich and great country, and we will import Yankees, and Dutchmen, and Irishmen, to do the work the negroes cannot do, and our sons shall be the gentlemen, to doctor, and to do justice, and to keep store, and to gouge around among strata, and to take heavenly observations for them all; or the gentlemen of elegant leisure to do the dressing and the manners, and be the high society.

No one will grant that he is such a fool as to scheme deliberately in this way, and yet the present course of education practically proves that he does so. When his son has attained all the knowledge with which it is proposed to cram him, and turns out neither doctor nor lawyer—is too openly wicked to be a preacher, and too poor to be a *gentleman*—he is so old that the shoe-maker's bristle, and the tailor's needle, and the graver's tool, and the trowel are unwieldy; and by the time he has become deft with them, more than half his life is spent. He is a bungling apprentice when he should be a master workman, is earning only the bread he eats when he should be supporting a family, and is blushing for his occupation when he should be holding his head up like a man.

At any rate, I was tired of school-books, and dreaded going back to school; and as I had a great taste for the pleasures of agriculture and horticulture, I announced my desire to be a planter. Nothing seemed to be so pleasing to my father; but he very wisely told me that I could never plant satisfactorily to myself, or manage negroes justly, unless I was practically acquainted with every kind of plantation work. I could not otherwise tell if the negroes did their work properly and industriously, and might require of them too much, or be imposed upon by them with too little. So he gave me a horse and a plow, a hoe and an axe, and I set to work and made me a maul out of the but of a small beech, well hardened in the fire.

My choice to become a planter was about the strangest I ever made in my life. I never dreamed of becoming an overseer of another's negroes; I would have starved first; and yet, suppose I became a planter, where was my land and where were my negroes to commence with? The three grown negroes my father owned were a small and most unlikely capital, even if they could all be spared from the house to the field; and his land was, as I have shown, not well calculated for extensive planting operations. With an increasing family—increasing in number and expensiveness—and with a decaying practice, it was not at all probable that my father could invest money in other negroes or in better land. But to be a planter I was determined, and I set to work bravely and hopefully at all the labors required upon a plantation.

The fact is, that though I saw and felt that my father was poor, I did not believe he was so in reality. I had an idea, or rather a suspicion (where I obtained it I cannot now tell), that he was very rich, but lived as though he were poor, for the sake of raising me to industrious habits, and prevent my becoming extravagant, or dissipated, or a fop; and I pictured to myself that some day, when he saw me fixed in principle and steady habits, he would develop his wealth and give me land and negroes, flocks and herds, without a fear that I would take a journey into a far country and there waste my substance in riotous living.

I say that I do not know where I got this idea; and yet to a boy of my disposition it was natural, and in all probability many a one has had the same idea about a father just as poor. It was certain, in the first place, that if my father were indeed poor, he did not resemble in any degree the other poor men I saw around us. He was an elegant gentleman in manners, person, and education, and was considered the superior in most respects to any of those known to be rich men in our county; whereas the other poor men that I saw were coarse in their manners, uncouth in their persons and clothing, and showed ignorance in their ideas and manner of speech. In the next place, nothing was more likely than that a father so loving and wise as he, should, for the sake of raising his children to virtue and usefulness, deny himself every luxury, and set them a good example by hard labor and close economy. My own observation showed me the danger to which the sons of those reputed rich were exposed. Examples of their idleness and vicious indulgences were constantly before me. I saw them shirk labor at books, and in any useful employment, to expend their powers on dress, fast horses, and drunken frolics; and it seemed to me but reasonable that my father should affect poverty, to avert from his children the danger of acting like them.

I wish it to be thoroughly understood that for all

this I was no fool. If I pleased my fancy with these chimeras, they were nothing more than might have been realities in the natural fitness of things. Though my father was really poor, he was one who should in all propriety have been rich; and it would very well have become the wisest of men to have acted as I conceived him to be acting. I protest that I was no fool in this matter, but was far more wise than I have been many a time since, when I had reason and probabilities stronger on my side. I was merely a healthy boy, of lively imagination, good reasoning powers, and exuberant hopefulness; and though my idea was ill founded, it rather made me strive all the harder at my labor to make myself worthy of the possible fate in store for me, and to hasten the time of its fruition in case it should be true; for I always put the case to myself with a "suppose, now," and said that if it were not true it ought to be, and was very well invented.

I take credit to myself for working as hard as I did, because I had other and more serious motives than that of fitting myself for a state of temporal beatitude—which, after all, was only a passing, pleasing idea. I saw and pitied the toils and troubles of my parents, and loved them and my brothers and sisters too well to see them want for anything I might obtain for them. Young as I was, I thought myself a man to labor, and quite a genius in some things—particularly in the matter of axe helves, of which I made a dozen from a piece of hickory I thought very choice, and sold them to a friendly merchant in the town, who was willing to encourage honest industry to the sum of two dollars and a half, which he paid me—and of which I was very proud till I saw the same axe helves, some years afterward, among his unsalable stock.   He was a very generous merchant, I thought then, more than I did when he paid me the money; and but that I considered that in our subsequent dealings he had quite made up for the price he paid, I would most certainly have returned it.

I take the more credit to myself that the work was hard. When I rose in the morning, at the dawn of day, I thought my bed the most desirable of all earthly places, and at night this thought came fresh upon me. Often when I was roused I would fall asleep again, and dream that I was up and at the stable feeding my horse and preparing him for the field, and just as I was about to tie my hame-string, whack! would come a broad band upon my back, and I would jump, to find myself in bed, and my father standing over me asking why I was not up and dressed and at my work.

Poor little fellow! I can see myself now, hilling cotton in the burning sun of June (for we planted a little cotton that year), and pausing to look upon a stump and wish that it had a soda fountain in it, and I could lie down and let it run into my mouth fresh and cold. How terribly thirsty I got! and how often I had to go to the house or the spring for water! not that I wished to shirk my work and sought any excuse, but the sun was so hot, and the labor so severe, that the only wonder is I stood it at all.

This was a great era in my life—the era of wonder. I was always finding wonderful snakes, wonderful flowers, and freaks of vegetation, seeing wonderful clouds, and sunrises, and sunsets. It was my time for possum hunts, and coon dogs; for making famous shots with my rifle—if it was an old flint-lock piece; of trying to make prodigious leaps, and to excel in strength; the time of wrestling, climbing, and rudeness. My father often gave me holiday, for he knew well that the labor was severe upon me, and, except that it was wholesome, morally and physically it could be of little other profit; and in my holidays I and the boys of my acquaintance would play at circus, and I would try to ride standing on bare-back, and was invariably the clown of the occasion.

Although I had plenty of vanity and love of admiration, and was as noisy and hopeful as ever boy was, I cannot say that this was an altogether pleasant period of my life. I can recall to this day that all the time there seemed to me there was something lacking, though what it was I neither knew, nor do I yet know. I was just entering into real thought, and into some of the realities of life, and in spite of the wondrous things I found, and the new beauties of nature, I was beginning to feel there was a something wanting, or a something foreboding which seemed to cast a veil over the real brightness of pleasure, and I used, at times, to be very melancholy. Particularly in the evening twilight, after my work was done, and before the candles were lit, I would love to get by myself upon the fence of the horse lot, and, listening to the whip-poor-wills crying on the hills and in the hollows around the house, my spirits would be overwhelmed by a vague sorrow, and often my tears would flow almost unconsciously.

Whether this arose from a mysterious foreshadowing of sorrows to come—and that such an influence is felt cannot be contradicted—or merely from that tinge of sadness which all thinking persons must have in some degree, need not be too diligently inquired into. I presume that almost every man can recollect a period in his youth when his state of mind resembled this I have attempted to describe, and I will not lengthen out my recollections of it for fear of being tiresome.

Only one thing further I would remark about it; it was a continuous state of mind, not a mere impression upon the feelings by any special cause for sorrow. For instance, it cannot be explained by such an incident as this: when I was about eight years old, one night at prayers I got to thinking of heaven and death, and imagining what a dreadful thing it would be if my father should die, and the thought set me to weeping bitterly. When we rose from our knees my father took me in his arms, and asked me tenderly what ailed me, and receiving no answer but increased sobbing, took up the idea that my stomach ached me, and feeling the waist-band of my pants that it was tight, he unbuttoned them impatiently, and jerked them off me, telling my mother that it was a shame she should make the boy's pants to bind him so. My shame for the cause of my weeping made me seize upon the excuse, and I let it pass as true, though my poor dear little mother had to bear the blame. It was, I believe, the first lie I was ever guilty of, and belonged to a very numerous class of lies—the sentimental.

These discursions from the thread of my story, though they may be uninteresting to others, afford me great pleasure. I think of myself not as myself, but as a little boy I used to know, and of whose feelings I had an intimate knowledge; and I have no doubt but that in describing him correctly I am portraying human nature —which, after all, is the most useful kind of writing.

To tell of all our disasters in planting would fill a volume. The hogs had a special spite at our garden; and one spotted ox, a famous fence-breaker, seemed to be discontented everywhere but in our field, and every morning would find him there like an enterprising eunuch, the pilot and pioneer of a bevy of placid cows and frisky yearlings. Small shot, peas, and salt bacon shot into his sides one day, were forgotten the next, or, rather, only served to stimulate him to get out of the inclosure as soon as possible after he was discovered. It would have taken a very high and strong fence to have kept him out, and ours, made of pine poles, was neither high nor strong. We would patch with infinite labor where he broke in one day, and congratulate ourselves upon future safety, but the next day would have to patch again in a different place. And so it went on, until what with the cattle, and blight, and worms, and sore-shin, and rust, and rain, the crop of cotton we gathered was a mere handful, and even our . harvest of nubbins was very small.

This was discouraging; but I went at it the second year with high hopes, to find the same fate; and then I concluded that planting was a slow business, and one in which I could never succeed. Nothing succeeds where it is done with "a lick and a promise," as the old folk used to say. The planter or farmer who is always patching his fences imperfectly, and his barns and outhouses, wagons and utensils, is in a bad way; and an impatient man will always come to that, however well fixed he may start out.

CHAPTER IX.

WHEN I concluded that manual labor was not my mission, I was seventeen years old, and as my school days were over, and my father had not yet acknowledged himself rich, it was absolutely necessary that I should choose some occupation for a livelihood, and, besides, I was ambitious to do a man's work in the world. I have already told why I did not become a doctor or a fiddler, and my reasons for not being a preacher—as my mother would have rejoiced to see me—for good women are curious creatures about that matter—were even more substantial, though they were then matters of feeling which I could not have explained, as I can now. We were a pious set of children, both by nature (for a certain degree of piety is innate) and by education—though I must say that of all exhibitions of spurious sentiment, that presented in modern Sunday-school books and modern literature, of good little children, is the most disgusting. We were not "good" in that mawkish sense, for we were healthy and natural, with strong wills, and hearty appetites and affections. But we were both pious and religious. My little sister Bel used to pray for curls with all the hope and faith with which any grown person would pray for deliverance from poverty and temptation. But I never fancied the profession of preaching, and, for reasons I will hereafter give, am now very glad that I did not.

Nor did I incline to commerce, to which Stanley Ruggles had betaken himself with an aptitude I did not envy. The principle of profit which lies at the foundation of Trade, places one in great danger—and I always thought that the man who prayed not to be led into temptation, and yet voluntarily engaged in merchandise, was very inconsistent. It sounds very harsh, but I am inclined to think that the reason why so great a proportion of merchants hold up their heads as honest men, is that custom has deprived many transactions of their odium, which in a purer age would be accounted dishonest. To have to buy for the least tempts a man to beat down the price, and to find his chances in the misfortunes and ignorance of others; and to have to sell for the most, places even greater temptations in his way. Nor can any tradesman fly these temptations. They are inseparable from his business, and though he may say "aroynt thee, Satan!" if he never, in the minutest detail, habitually deviate from charity and perfect truth, he has occasion to be thankful for a more than ordinary share of the grace of God. It would be going too far for me to say that no merchant can be honest, for I have known many so honest as to break at the business. But I can say with a fair degree of certainty, that he who has succeeded in accumulating a fortune by his business, without resorting to unfairness which is made fair only by the custom of trade, is a fortunate man.

The idea that goods are worth whatever they will fetch is one of those untruths which seem to have been made an inherent principle of trade. But I have never yet been able to see how an hundred per cent. profit is

as fair as ten per cent.   If I give two dollars for what
only cost the merchant one dollar, either I am giving
more than a fair value, or the article was purchased
and brought to the spot for less than its worth, and
therefore advantage is either taken of my necessities or
ignorance, or has been taken of the necessities or ignorance of the first seller and the carrier.   Is not this exemplified every day in the increased or diminished
prices of goods according to supply?

Possibly I am in error, owing to my own stupidity
in all matters of trade—a business for which I have
never had the hardness, coolness, patience, and shrewd-
ness necessary for success.   But such was and is my
opinion of commerce that I never would engage in it,
or suffer a son of mine, if I had one, to adopt it as his
business.

The Law was what presented itself to my mind
with all the allurements of fame as well as wealth;
and my father agreed with me that it was the best
thing I could go at.   That I should return to study
with renewed ardor had been the true reason of his
indulging my planting scheme.

Behold me then going to old Judge Jones as my
chosen preceptor, and taking home with me the first
volume of Blackstone, with all the consciousness of
one who feels that he has taken a most important step
in life.   The impression upon the spirits of one who
has just engaged himself to be married differs but little
from that I felt upon this occasion, except in degree.
In the grave consciousness of the life-long importance
of the choice are mingled bright gleams of hope.   To
compare small things with great: over the somberness

of the importance of the event is fitfully thrown a rosy light of hopefulness, which now shines steadily, and anon scintillates and flashes like the lights over the darkness of the northern sky. I knew, or rather said to myself that I knew, that to accomplish fame I must work very hard, and I repeated to myself the saying that the law was a jealous mistress, who required all the man's time and attention who would have her bestow upon him her favors. But, like many who read the Bible and pass over the precepts to seize eagerly the promises, I absorbed myself in the contemplation of my rivalry in celebrity to Coke, Bacon, and Holt, and passed over, as mere matters of course and of easy accomplishment, the labors they had used.

Nevertheless, I buckled to my book with eagerness, and in a very few days found myself reading snatches in all four volumes, with occasional digressions into Pleading and Practice, and the law of Evidence. Had it been possible, I would in a few months have had most of Judge Jones's library in my room at home. As that could not be, there were continually arising in my mind "points," upon which to satisfy myself I had, in busy loss of time, to make visits to his office, and to the other law offices of the town, where I was always welcomed, and often led into arguments in which I showed more zeal than knowledge and discretion.

It was not long till I had established in my own mind all the requisites of a good lawyer, and analyzed to my own satisfaction the capacity and quality of every lawyer who practiced at that bar. I had my model of the deep, tricky lawyer, and of the shallow, easy lawyer; of the zealous advocate who knew little, and of the quiet, office lawyer, who knew more than he could apply well.   Then, too, there was the case lawyer, old Colonel Jenks, who had started out with the profound impression that the law was an occult science, the reasons of which no man knew or could know, and who had consequently found it a mystery to himself to his old age.   If he could find a case just like his own case, it was well; if he could not, he was at sea without a compass.   He had a peculiarity,—which, however, is more common at the bar than is generally thought,—when he got a case he put it hypothetically, with other names and dates, to every lawyer in the town, except the one he knew or thought likely was to oppose him, for his opinion; and would argue over each point, and suggest difficulties to have them overcome, just as though he were a teacher of profundities and perversities, or a quiz of legal acumen.   Generally his brethren gratified his known habit, which amused them, though it was sometimes a little annoying,—but an answer he once got from Judge Pinckard rather puzzled him.   The judge was a fat, rosy-faced old fellow, who was both a profound lawyer and a persistent humorist.   One day Colonel Jenks came to his office, and narrating to him a rigmarole of supposititious facts, wound up by asking what he would advise a man to do who had such a case.   "Eh? colonel," said the judge.   "What would I advise?   I would advise—let me see—I would advise him to go to a lawyer.   Eh? colonel."

I analyzed all these men correctly, but my subsequent experience showed me that I had far underrated the power of Colonel Jenks with a jury, and exaggerated the trickiness of Squire Harkness, who never played a trick for the love of the trick, and was often generous when it would pay. A lawyer in the abstract and a lawyer in his practice are as different as an acrobat going about the streets in shabby clothes and with stupid face, and the same acrobat upon the stage turning summersets and tying himself into double bow-knots, so that you hardly know which end is uppermost and how to take him.

It was clearly perceptible wherein my seniors were defective, and I should therefore have set about making myself perfect; but I have remarked that the men who can criticise others with the greatest precision are those who are inclined to do little else than criticise. It takes an idle man to be a good amateur *cicerone* to a picture gallery, and discover to you the minute faults as well as the special beauties of the pictures. I fear that though I at all times kept myself busy doing something in the line of my future profession, I was, during all my studenthood, very idle. My hardest work, as indeed I may say of the most labored works of my life, was for naught in the end. A trivial lecture, or literary speech, or poem, or some such so-called distraction, which neither profited me nor the world, has often employed all the energies of my mind to a far more intense degree than the law of Bailments, or the Statutes of Descent and Distribution.

The gentlemen of the town, young and old, had a Debating and Literary Society, which I joined of course, and of which I was a member during the whole of its spasmodic existence. It met once every fortnight, sometimes at the court-house and sometimes at the school-house; and if the weather chanced to be good there was generally a large attendance, of young ladies especially, to hear the debates or the lectures and essays.   Like every other such association, it had its whales and its minnows; its rivals in volubility and its rivals in wisdom, who were always by universal consent pitted againt each other.   If Mr. Davis was appointed to lead in the affirmative, Mr. Smith was certain to be the leader of the negative, and wherever little Dossey (he was known as "The Count") was placed, long, gangling Joe Jenks, whose jaws seemed always hungry for talk, was certain to be found as his adversary.

Once, when I was about eighteen, I had the honor to be chosen as essayist, and I chose "Home" as my subject.   For two weeks I gave it all my thought, and the applause I received from my mother and sisters, when I had fully completed it, was very flattering. My mother suggested that if I could procure a small pocket music-box which played "Sweet Home," and would set it going at the close of the performance, it would have an electrical effect.   And indeed I think it would have added a dramatic interest to the evening.

It was my *coup d'essai*, and I had the most extravagant hopes of success.   Like most young aspirants, I thought that I would elevate the minds of my hearers by taking a high moral and philosophical view of my subject, and so I commenced with the Garden of Eden, the home of Eve; then pictured man in his fallen state, with his home left him as his only refuge from the freezing blasts and pitiless peltings of misfortune, and so forth—by which I expected to draw tears from every eye.

It is certain that every subject, moral and physical, is directly connected with the creation and the fall of man, and I am not sure but that it is the best point of departure in treating any subject; but it is apt to grow tiresome as it becomes hackneyed; and that it is hackneyed, the first efforts of most men of inquiring minds will prove. At any rate, though I have often since been tempted to date from those events I have refrained, for my success on this occasion was far more heavy than it would have been had I chosen a less lofty pinnacle from which to try my unaccustomed wings. The flying was nothing, but the alighting was the trouble; and though there was a buzz of half-approbation when I had finished, it sounded to my ears very like a pitying murmur of "poor fellow!" and I almost had to feel if some of my limbs were not broken. The Rev. Mr. Snow was president for the evening, and when I suggested that I had made a failure—with the hope that he would give me a word of consolation—he only said, "No, not a failure!" putting a pitying emphasis on the word "failure" which cut me to the quick. I cannot by words describe his tone; but I never loved him afterward, for he was cruel.

But it must not be supposed that my father abandoned me to my law studies without a thought of my deficiencies and progress. It was his opinion, and he was very right in it, that I was hardly proficient enough in mathematics to conduct a case in which a complicated patent was in controversy, or one in which it was necessary to demonstrate the area of a piece of land by a reference to field-notes; and he therefore arranged with Mr. Carden, who then taught school in the town, to supervise my mathematical studies; for which purpose I had to present myself at the school-house for a two-hours' study and recitation three times a week. I do not remember much of the mathematics, but I recall very clearly that I, being a sort of lay school-boy of superior prerogatives, had a very jolly time of it with the regular scholars, all of whom I knew well, and several of whom were about my own age. During watermelon time I kept my clique—for there are cliques everywhere, and in every congregation of men and other animals—well supplied with fine melons from my father's patch—the dear old gentleman himself often picking me out the best. One day, when we went out for recess, we discovered a large black sow in the shed at the end of the school-room, making sad havoc with my melons, which were deposited there. We instantly attacked, and pursued her for vengeance, out into the street. I being the most outraged was foremost and most forward, when my career was arrested by the sharp voices of the Misses Starbaugh exclaiming together, "You, Abraham Page!" and Miss Tabitha continued: "We little expected to see the son of Dr. Page guilty of cruelty to an animal in the public street."

Now, I was justly angry with the hog, but was even more justly afraid of the Misses Starbaugh. They were two old maids who lived in a frame house at the corner, and were noted for their precise good manners, and their rigid ideas of propriety. Both, clad in sober gray of demure cut, and with their heads surmounted with maidenly caps of snowy whiteness, stood with their half-mittened hands resting on the fence, looking at me with severe eyes, and I felt as guilty as though I had been indeed caught at some crime.

I mention this incident not because it is very interesting, or has any further connection with my story, but because it is actually the only event of my school life at Mr. Carden's which even approached the character of an adventure. In retracing the road I have traveled, I find many a quiet glade carpeted with grass and flowers, and bright with sunshine, in which scarcely a solitary shrub arrests the view. As I have said before, my life has not been one of astounding adventures, and in writing it my ambition is not to excite admiration or astonishment, but to depict it so faithfully that other ordinary individuals may avoid my errors, and may see that their sorrows are not without parallel.

But my four years of novitiate were not passed wholly in the study of law and mathematics, or the cultivation of a style of writing and speaking. I did many a day's work in garden and field, and had many a job of copying from the clerks of the courts, and from the lawyers, pressed for time, for which I got a pay even more liberal than usual for such services. Then, too, there were numerous Spanish grants of land necessary in evidence, for translating which I was paid liberally, as I had thereabouts a monopoly of understanding that language. By these means—and every dollar was a dollar—I managed to be of little expense to my father for my board, and to keep myself clothed and shod as became a young man engaged in one of the liberal professions. I would have felt it a shame for me to be a burden upon my father, when I should be an assistance; and, although I never had an inclination to be foppish, I would have been very loth to dress below my condition, which was that of a gentleman who might reasonably aspire to sit on the Supreme Bench, hold a listening Senate in admiration, or, as President, receive foreign Ambassadors.

Another strong reason for my dressing well was that my two sisters were now young ladies, and I had to be their escort to the parties and pastimes to which they were invited. They were charming girls, even to me, their brother. While they took their black eyes, and graceful forms, their elegant tastes, and pleasant sprightliness of wit, from our mother, they inherited the good health and strong common sense of our father. Although it is not my intention to dilate in this history of my own life upon their dispositions and lives, or upon those of my brothers, except in so far as they immediately affected my own, I must say here that in a sad time they made life desirable to me, and at all times made nature beautiful to me while they lived, as by their deaths they deprived death of most of its terrors to me, and added new beauty to the heaven of my desires, where I shall see them little changed from what they were on earth, and shall be freed from any fear that they shall part again from their old brother.

"Thus saith the Lord;" says Jeremiah, "A voice was heard in Ramah, lamentation and bitter weeping; Rachel weeping for her children refused to be comforted for her children, because they were not. Thus saith the Lord, refrain thy voice from weeping, and thine eyes from tears: for thy work shall be rewarded, saith the Lord; and they shall come again from the land of the enemy.   And there is hope in thine end, saith the Lord, that thy children shall come again to their own border."

This is a very precious promise to us all; to brothers and sisters, husbands and wives, and friends, as well as to parents; for it was not merely a prophecy of the restoration of the Jews to their own land, since Matthew quotes it as applicable to the parents bereaved by Herod.

My sisters were lovely girls in every respect, and their presence was eagerly sought for all the evening parties and parties of pleasure in our town and neighborhood; just as their girl companions sent for them as the most gentle and sympathizing of friends in sickness and sorrow.   As they were absolutely destitute of assumption in their manners and thoughts, their friends were of all degrees; and the rich ones were taught lessons of dignity, while the poor learned content and industry, and all saw charity exemplified by them in thought, word, and deed.

To go to evening parties was not one of my favorite pastimes, and gave me but little pleasure even at this age, when such pleasures are so becoming to a young man.   My vanity and love of approbation made me very sensitive, and I was afflicted with a painful shame-facedness which made me feel awkward in my behavior, and frequently even savage in my mirth.   Often have I for many minutes stood nervously, with cold hands and trembling limbs, outside of the door, waiting for others to come along with whom I might enter, rather than risk the embarrassment of entering alone among the company.   To this day, old as I am, I acknowledge a disagreeable sensation even in walking alone up the aisle of a church, and to bid the good evening to a party of friends without desperately shaking hands all around is beyond my ability. But to accompany my sisters was a duty, and it was often rewarded by unexpected pleasures, and what I feared would be dull or noisy proved agreeable and quiet, and a cosy chat in some corner with a fair companion before whom I was at no restraint or loss for the disposal of my unwieldy arms and protrusive knees, allowed me to go home reconciled to the high behest of society in the matter of the assemblies of young folk for pleasure.

In those days hospitality seemed to be a passion; and though it was, in some respects, a mistaken hospitality, and often one which contributed little to good habits, it was always hearty and sincere. Among the men, the first ceremony upon a visit or an introduction, was to go to the sideboard, or the grocery, for a drink; and at parties, for all to dance reels and cotilions until daybreak, was the rule. He was the best dancer who could jump the highest, and cross his feet the oftenest while in the air, and she excelled who could cut the most genteel die-away pigeon-wing—and a side-ways pigeon-wing cut with a languishing air by a pretty girl, without hoops, is as pleasant a little piece of coquetry as I ever saw. It was by no means genteel, however, to be at all rude; and out of the nursery, the games of forfeits, and other plays in which there was promiscuous kissing, were discountenanced. In fact, it was rather a dangerous business to be too loving where one had no right to be so, and a stolen kiss was sometimes resented, as it should be in every well-regulated society, by a challenge or a pistol-ball the next day. Female honor was regarded as the most sacred of all things, and manly honor was never so noble as when protecting or avenging it.

Everybody gave parties; and the enjoyment at one depended, for me, greatly upon who gave it, as well as upon who I met there. Some hosts of very small means and contracted accommodations, had the tact to place company at their perfect ease, and make them abandon themselves to the pleasures of the evening, while, with others, who had large houses, and everything in plenty at their command, the time would languish until all were glad to get away at an early hour. These last were generally very religious people, who shunned dancing, and tried to give a religious cast to mirth. There may be, and is, such a thing as pious mirth, where the soul is filled with thankfulness; but mirth and religiousness are incongruous. I have actually known the "exercises" of the evening to be closed with prayer. Oh, there has been a heap of solemn, earnest humbug in this world—however it may be now.

Twice in every year, from the time Miss Jane Carter was sixteen until it seemed almost useless, her father, the old 'Squire, gave a party. He was actuated to it by the best motives: first, it was the fashion; secondly, he was intensely hospitable; and, thirdly, old Mrs. Carter and Miss Jane thought it hard, and he thought it wrong, that some return should not be made for the many parties to which Miss Jane was invited—if the two ladies had other reasons based on hope, they kept them to themselves. But the old Squire was as poor

as a respectable man well could be. He was a justice
of the peace, and as lazy and inefficient in his own
matters as country justices of the peace usually were.
In those days, when a respectable man was very poor,
very inefficient, and very good natured, his natural
berth seemed to be that of justice of the peace. There
was responsibility enough in the office for respectability,
but not enough money to induce men of active parts to
take it, and it was too important to be given to dishonest or mean men. I used to attend Squire Carter's
court as a looker-on in the occasional criminal examinations which came before him, as well as at the regular
civil terms he held, and his careful helplessness, as he
sat with spectacles upon his nose, now taking a note of
evidence, now referring to a statute which was hard to
find, and now, with many a hem and haw, asking a
witness some question of pitiable irrelevancy, used to
enrage me; while the weak but important tone with
which he dawdled over foreign "ifs" and "buts" before
he rendered his decision, and the nervous, pleading
smile with which he glanced around to see how his
decision was taken, completely extinguished any disposition I might feel for laughter. But the old Squire
was a good man, who loved his fellow-men, and his
dogs, and his old horse, Blaze; had an intense respect
for his wife, and fairly worshiped his daughter.

To see him perform a marriage ceremony was worth
the while of any student of character. Just before the
hour arrived, he could be seen with a copy of the
statutes under his arm, walking with dignified brisk-
ness up to the front door of the house, his shirt collar
showing a redundancy of snowy well-starched linen,

his old black coat and pants well brushed, and his shoes well blacked with soot, and tied with buckskin strings. After gravely saluting the company on the porch or gallery, and depositing his book and hat, he would manage in whispers, and with much pointing, to learn from his host the exact door at which the couple would enter, and where they would stand, and he should stand, and how many bridesmaids there were, and with the information he would retire within himself without a word for any one, and only acknowledging, with a most courtly bow, the salutations of the comers; a nervous twitch of the upper lip, and a rest-lessness of his hands, increasing as the time drew nearer, alone showing that his mind was on sublunary affairs. When, in response to the whispered summons of the host, he entered the room, book in hand, happy if he stumbled over no chair, or tread upon no intrusive dog, he took his stand as though the elements could not make him move, and the awfulness and tenderness of the occasion strove for mastery in the expression of his good-natured countenance. As a magistrate, he was important; as a father, he was gentle and paternal; and as a husband who knew what was what, he seemed to be a little jolly, and very respectful. He appeared to wish it particularly understood that it was a State, and not a religious or personal affair with him, and he always ended by saying: "In the name of God, and by the authority of the State of ——, I declare you man and wife." And, when the cast of his office was over, he blushed like any school-boy if the bride offered to kiss him, and retired to a corner, looking on till the feast was ready, when he tucked in a fair supply of good things, and made his way home, fingering his fee of a silver dollar, or whatever more the generosity and means of the bridegroom may have bestowed; and Mrs. Carter had, no doubt, a faithful account of all that was said and done—if, indeed, Mrs. Carter and Miss Jane had not been there, and, all be-shawled and be-tucked up, had not accompanied him home.

Squire Carter's parties were as delightful to his guests as the preparations for them were harassing to his wife and daughter. He, good man, felt all the delight of preparation, was great at makeshifts, and was insensible to inconveniences for himself. He could never understand what in the plague (that was his nearest approach to blasphemy) Mrs. Carter and Jane made such a fuss about. "The room is clean enough to dance in without all that scrubbing, and if the table is not long enough there are plenty of plank in the back yard. And chairs! What do you want with more chairs? The people are coming here to dance, not to sit down and twirl their thumbs; a good long plank and three chairs will make a bench the whole length of the room, and if it is too rough for the ladies' dresses, cover it with a couple of sheets!" When he saw the piles of odd cups and saucers, plates, knives and forks, and tumblers, Mrs. Carter had borrowed from all the neighbors around, he would tell her that her crockery lasted very well, and he thought from the looks of the table every day she must have it put away very carefully—for the Squire delighted in a mild joke.

If, when night came, his makeshift sconces against the wall broke down, he seemed unconscious of the mortification of his poor wearied wife, and was ready to make sticks of empty bottles for flaring, guttering tallow candles—people did not have to see their legs to dance, he would say jocularly. If a sponge-cake cut heavy, or the white sugar gave out, or the syllabub tasted salty, or the coffee-pot leaked over a lady's dress, or the brindled dog got to howling outside of the window, or the lemonade was diluted particularly weak to make it last, or the patch he had put in the floor in front of the hearth got displaced, he appeared entirely unaware of the agony of Mrs. Carter, and the misery of Miss Jane; saw neither their paleness nor flushes, their bitten lips nor their sickened smiles, as they tried to pass over the disaster; and in all the apparent stupid innocence of his head and heart would press a little more of the cake or syllabub or lemonade upon his guests; while the howling of Beauty he said was evidence that she was interested in the fun.

Oh, yes! The Squire would have a party every night if he could, and his dear Jane should dance and enjoy herself, with the best of them, to her heart's content, until after awhile she got a husband, and then she would give parties at her house.

Bah! The old gentleman noted every incident as keenly as did his wife; his misery far exceeded hers; and though his good nature was too kindly to show it, his heart sank within him when he helplessly ruminated over the cost in money, trouble, and mortification, which a little firmness and exercise of common sense in the veto power might have prevented. But his guests were gratified—that was the great thing after all. They knew what they were to expect before they came. He entreated them to use no ceremony, but make themselves at home, and they did so. It was his trouble, and that of his wife and daughter, but it was their party, and they could not help liking their hosts, if they did pity the effort which had been made to do things up in fine style. The Squire's parties were vastly more popular than those of Judge Vance, where the cakes and creams, and syllabubs and ices were expensive and perfect, and a devout blessing dismissed the guests—but they cost a great deal more.

There is nothing in the world more pitiable than the efforts of good people to keep up appearances, and nothing more extravagant than a poor man's emulation of the rich.

Perhaps it is because at this period of my life I was put to great perplexities and contrivances to keep up my own appearance and ruffle it with the best, that these ideas have so impressed themselves upon my mind. One pair of boots I got from Haick, the shoemaker, gave me almost as much uneasiness as if they had been the boots of torture, and Haick had been the executioner, mallet and wedges in hand. For three months did their price rest upon my spirits as though each of the eight dollars had weighed a ton, and I had to pay for them at last by the dollar at a time, on account, as I could get and spare it. The party for which I got those boots cost me a great deal.

What with parties and barbacues, and the camp-meeting, which was still kept up as when Mr. Thomas immortalized himself, and the Debating Club, and occasional political assemblages, and the courts, which I diligently attended and puzzled over, for my public amusements, and law, natural philosophy, mathematics, copying court papers, collecting notes and accounts by hand—as it was called to distinguish it from their collection by the machinery of the law—an occasional dip into the science of engineering, gratifying an insatiable curiosity by studying Lord Bacon, and Locke, and an old Latin book in my father's library entitled *Johannes de Vacuo*, a few attempts at poetry, and two or three desperate attacks of love, for my labors, my time sped on apace, and I found myself twenty-one, was examined, and received my license to practice law.

CHAPTER X.

IT is strange in how little space the labors, pleasures, and troubles of four years of life may be narrated. The lives of men so nearly resemble each other in their main features, that the fact of any incident being stated it is rarely considered necessary to amplify the particulars; and yet it is in the variation of those particulars that a man's immortal soul is affected for good or ill; and, in truth, it is only this effect upon the soul that makes one's life of more importance than that of a coral insect, the catching by which of a larger or smaller animalcule than usual is a momentous event in life.

We say that John was born, had a vigorous constitution, received a good education, became a lawyer, fell in love with four different girls, the last of whom married him, and bore him five children; that he became a Judge of the Probate Court, and held that office till he died, at the age of forty-five ; and we have an outline of John's life, which any one can fill up with more or less correctness by the exercise of a fancy educated by experience and observation. But how little does one know of the real internal life of John, which may have been blasted by a struggle for office, or made vigorous and beautified by a happy marriage ! In the last paragraph of the preceding chapter I have given the events and occupations of my life for four years, and from them it may be gathered that I was a brisk young fellow, with a restless mind, and considerable capacity for enjoyment; but that is all. You cannot tell if I was an amiable companion, how far my honesty could be trusted, or whether I had my passions and appetites sufficiently under control to be worthy of being called virtuous; for I take it that the greater part of man's moral nature is included in these three points.

It would ill become me to praise myself, though, for what existed so long ago, even if I could honestly do so; and I could not, for shame, admit that I was obnoxious to censure in these particulars. No man who knows himself, and has any self-respect, can make a perfectly candid confession of his thoughts, desires, and actions. There must always be some reserve, and it is well if he try to conceal nothing even from his God. These candid confessions of sins or peccadilloes made by some people, are a sentimental humbug, and amount in effect only to acknowledging that they are men and women. Even though you were to confess that appetite had more to do with your love for Miss Betty than calm reason, no opinion could be formed to your prejudice or in your favor; for, besides that you would, perhaps, at the time have been horror-struck.at such a suggestion, it may be that she was as tempting a bit of Eve's flesh, and as insipid a little soul as you ever saw, and it was the most natural of all things that you should have longed for her, and not really have loved her. And Tom, who afterward married her with doubtless the same kind of love you had, would, perhaps, have cut any one's throat who had presumed to lay the exact quality of his love before him. Possibly the poor fellow died before he found it out himself.

Do you not perceive, then, that these confessions are nonsense?—or, worse than that, are confessing a little in order to hide a great deal? God alone knows the heart, and, consequently, can alone know wherein a man has sinned, can alone absolve him from his sin, and can alone help him to sin no more; and I think that the less a man has to say to his fellow-man in the way of confession of sins, the better for both parties. I'll warrant, too, from my own experience, as well as observation, that in nearly all such confessions more stress is laid upon the efforts of the soul to resist and overcome the sin, than upon the sin itself—so that the penitent has vastly the appearance of an angel who has been surprised or conquered by a whole host of irresistible devils.

The fact is, that in these four years of my life, little, almost unnoticed, incidents occurred which shaped my destiny, and it would be difficult to place them before a reader either in proper order, or in such a manner as

to make them entertaining. The little pebble which
first deflects the current of a river at its source is but
an insignificant object, though it has rendered a mighty
stream tortuous throughout its length. I can only present my life as it is, with all its sinuosities and eddies,
without pretending to discover the moving causes for
either.

If the Rev. Theobald Snow and his wife were alive,
and had the writing of my history, I doubt not but that
I should be dissected up to seventeenthly, with most
orthodox energy and acumen. Although the parson
and I preserved a sort of armed truce, Mrs. Snow was
not quite so placable.   .

She had come of such a long line of Puritanic
preachers, that it was almost a pity there were ever
any girls born to the family; at least, I suspect that
the Rev. Theobald sometimes thought so. As she
could not be a preacher herself, she came as near it as
she could, and took it as her mission to regulate a
preacher, which she did, zealously. He was an amiable, well-meaning man, and, I doubt not, was a sincere
Christian, but his intellect was rather ordinary and
slow in its motions, and the energetic limb of the hierarchy he had made part of himself was continually running away with him, or getting him into all sorts of
disagreeable muddles. To change the figure, his yoke-
fellow was too lively for him, and was always running
ahead and turning him from the smooth road he wished
to travel; and not content with carrying him forward,
she tried to press and drag the whole team and load,
and, of course, he got the blame, which was unjust.

(It is a mere conventional joke to say that a man is

really accountable for what his wife does;)especially if she be a Mrs. Snow. It was but a small matter with her to lecture an elder, or an old deacon, and as for his wife and family, she could spiritually spank them with an earnestness and authority too astonishing to be resisted while the operation was going on. She demanded implicit submission. The spirit of command had been concentrated in her by nature and education. The ceremony of ordination was the first lesson her lisping tongue could pronounce by rote, and the communion cups were her childish play-things. Such familiarity with church arrangements, and church phraseology, and church pains and penalties, and church gossip, and church enterprises, was never, in our part of the country, dreamed of in a woman before; and the pertness with which her answers came to any questioning of church dogmas could only have been inherited from high officers in the church militant.

It was not to be expected that such a Deinologian in petticoats should be either a neat or careful housekeeper; though her zeal in bearing little Snowbirds to be provided for was quite as wonderful to every one as it was astounding to the poor parson, whose salary could ill afford the increased outlay. But, bless you, thought Mrs. Snow, it costs nothing for doctor or nurses, and even the sparrows are provided for. The fact was, Mrs. Snow, as the daughter of a preacher so zealous that he swapped, or was called from pulpit to pulpit, from Maine to Georgia, had been accustomed, like a good traveler, to live from hand to mouth all her life; and though she could relish the creams, and cram in the cakes and the turkey and other good things with

an infinite gusto, it had always been at the tables and
expense of others, who would kill their last hen, and
break up its nest, if the eggs were not too far gone, to
provide delicacies for the palates of a preacher and his
family who came upon a visit, or as a visitation.   She
therefore had no idea of going to the expense of such
niceties herself, and if her husband or children wished
them, all they had to do was to go somewhere and
spend the evening, or send word they were coming to
dinner.   She could do so, and she did.   Consequently,
the poor parson was but a sorry host, and with the
bedclothes topsy-turvy till night, and the chairs filled
with clothes and bandboxes, and the floor littered with
soiled clothes and old shoes, and his shaving-brush and
razors not to be found, and the wash-basin straying off
into the back yard, and the towels all wet or soiled,
and his books and papers piled pell-mell with baby
linen and old petticoats in the corners, the misguided
man was often as puzzled to know which end was uppermost, as were his little brats when they were jerked
up to be spanked, either by hand or with their mamma's
slipper, which, as she went slip-shod, came off in a
twinkling.

Mrs. Snow was a nervous woman.   I do not mean
that she was puny or had weak nerves; on the contrary, her nerves were very strong, and she had an
extra number of them, to judge by her motions.   She
was lean, but not at all emaciated, and in her spanking
showed plenty of bone and muscle.   Her nose was long
and sharp—indeed, it was notably prominent, and often
was red and swollen at the tip—and her eyes were
gray and keen.   Behold her, with her bonnet on awry,

and her mantle streaming behind, exposing, when a sudden gust would take it, two or three hooks of the back of her dress unfastened sailing out on one of her corrective expeditions. Holding her antepenultimate hope by the hand, and vigorously calling in or hieing away a couple of brace of the others, or sometimes stopping to blow a little in the friendly shade of a tree, and perform the operation of tying the little one's shoes, and wiping all their noses, she makes her way—say, to our house. Scarcely pausing to make the compliments of the day, after she has had a snack provided for her "poor fatigued children," she opens with a vim upon my mother:

"Mrs. Page, don't you think we are very slack in the Lord's work? We must have a sewing society. Here are you and your two daughters, Mrs. Jones and her two, Mrs. Carter and Jane, and sixteen other ladies of Mr. Snow's congregation, who are actually doing nothing for the church abroad. We are told to go into all lands and preach the gospel; and how shall preaching be done without a preacher? and how shall they preach unless they be sent? and how can they preach with any hope of being attended to by a set of naked heathen? We are told to clothe the naked; but here we are spending all our time and money in clothing ourselves with finery——"

"But, Mrs. Snow——"

"Don't interrupt me, Mrs. Page, if you please, until I tell you what I came for. We must have a sewing society as an adjunct to our branch of the Tract, and Foreign Missions. The Rev. Mr. Dill, who used to live here, I believe, writes that there are hundreds at his mission who would attend his ministrations if they had decent clothing to appear in. The North is sending forth her strength, and it is a shame that we, in this favored part of the vineyard, should fold our hands in spiritual sleep."

"But, Mrs. Snow," said my mother, "I am sure we are all willing to assist in any good work. Only a day or two ago, Mrs. Vance and I were planning an association for the relief of the destitute families in the county, and we agreed that the best mode of action was to procure sewing for the women and girls. There is a great deal of plantation clothing to be made up, and if we could get it for them to do, it would assist them to make a living; besides——"

"Of course, Mrs. Page," retorts Mrs. Snow, with a smile of pitying dissent, "we cannot expect Mrs. Vance to take part in our work, as she belongs to a different denomination."

"Why, madam," interrupts my mother, "we were not thinking of denominations at all. It was——"

"It was taking you from your duty to your own church," says Mrs. Snow, emphatically. "The poor people about here have the gospel preached unto them when they choose to come and hear Mr. Snow, which they don't often do; and it will be their own fault if they remain in heathen darkness. But we owe a duty to the propagation of gospel light in lands in which there is no light, and we can perform it no better than by making use of our moments of leisure to meet together and sew for them."

"The Doctor," hazards my mother, "says that such meetings are rather for the purpose of comparing uncharitable ideas, than——"

"Allow me to say, madam," interrupted Mrs. Snow, with rigid dignity, "with all due respect to the Doctor, that he is not a good judge of the case. At any rate, the plan has been settled, and Mr. Snow will announce from the pulpit, next Sunday, a call for a meeting for organization at my house on Thursday. Mrs. McIntyre will be vice-president, and Mrs. Holywell, secretary. The ladies will have to choose their president, and should choose a lady of energy, who has her heart in the work. Of course, in so important a matter, I did not like to put any one's name down for the position. Mrs. McIntyre, and Lucy and Sarah, and even Mary, volatile as she is——"

"Mary is not volatile, Mrs. Snow," spoke up my mother; "she is only light-hearted and spirited——"

"Well, well; it makes no difference. I ought to have been more cautious in speaking of one of your favorites. Volatile or light-hearted, she was at first inclined to laugh at Mr. Dill's letter; but when she heard the scheme of the society, even she favored it, and said she would do her best for it."

And so, after announcing her high purpose, and overbearing all opposition, Mrs. Snow gathers her children together with much calling and bustle, washes from Master James's countenance a mustache and divers other marks placed upon it with a burnt cork by one of my mischievous little brothers, and marches off to some other neighbor's, where she enacts a like laying down of the law; and persuading herself that Mrs. Page and her daughters are converts to her scheme, uses their names to give it additional weight.

"Ma," says my sister Bel, starting up, "isn't it a

shame that your plan for doing so much good right here at home should be so thwarted?   I don't blame Mary for laughing at Mr. Dill's letter—I had to laugh myself; and then to call her volatile, and think she reasoned her into submission—for that was her idea. She doesn't know Mary at all.   With all her sprightliness, Mary has more common-sense and sense of propriety than Mrs. Snow can even appreciate."

"Don't say that, my daughter," interposed my mother. "Mrs. Snow is a very good woman, and has very good sense—only she is sometimes too rigid and too ultra in her ideas.   If the ladies wish to form this society, we must do what we can."

"I don't believe the ladies do wish the society, Ma," said Bel; "and Mrs. Snow may have good sense, but she is not nice, and she doesn't see what is judicious and what is extravagant in any church scheme. Mary is nice, and she sees also what is ridiculous in a very strong light, and is too young not to show what she thinks and feels.   Lucy and Sarah, I know, don't approve this scheme any more than Mary does, but they are older, and, like their mother, seem to have a sort of superstitious respect for preachers and their wives.   If Mary does go into this affair it will be because she anticipates fun at the meetings."

"Yes, miss," says my mother, "and you and she will go off to yourselves to giggle, and turn everything Mrs. Snow and the other ladies say or do into ridicule to each other, and will not do a stitch of work."

And Miss Bel went off smiling, and her mother turned to work on a pair of Master Eldred's pants which he had made very practicable in climbing.

The meeting was held, as per order, and Mrs. Snow announced, in effect, that it was projected to make up baby caps and slips, fancy aprons and pincushions, ornamented shirts and underclothing for gentlemen, cigar cases, tobacco bags, lamp mats, and all sorts of footy pretty things, and when enough were made, either to send them on to the parent society at Philadelphia, or to hold a fair in Yatton and dispose of them at preposterous prices. And Miss Mary and Miss Bel found plenty of amusement in the disappointment of the reverend lady when old Mrs. Diggory was chosen President instead of herself, and the sudden way in which she found that objections might be raised to parts of the plan. It was a fund of amusement for them for a long time afterward, and " Oh, Mrs. Diggory, I greatly fear you overrate our means !" was almost a cant phrase with them whenever they met and happened to differ about the practicability of anything.

CHAPTER XI.

THE society was formed, and I bless it to this day, because it was the means of my first realizing, as though a veil had been drawn from my eyes, the gentle and lovable nature of Mary McIntyre. True, I had known her well before, as the dear friend of my sisters, —she was about a year younger than Bel,—and had perceived she was a pretty and pleasant girl; but I, in my manliness, had been passing her over as a sort of bread-and-butter Miss, who would make some man a good wife at a future, distant day, and had been looking far away for some princess worthy of my fealty.

Have you not noticed how you may be the companion for years of some man, woman, or child, and yet find all of a sudden that you never appreciated the sprightliness, purity, or perfections you now see in every action? So it was with me; as though my pleasant little Miss had been suddenly taken up into the clouds, transformed, and, before I had remarked her absence, placed before my sight a beautiful creature made to love and to be worshiped. But a moment before I could not have told whether her eyes were blue or gray—now I saw they were a deep-melting blue, sparkling with mirthfulness, or, in her thoughtful moods, beaming with the diamond light of dawn. Only yesterday I could not have decided whether her hair was sandy or reddish—now I discovered that its abundant tresses were a deep glossy brown. I knew that she had a small and beautifully-shaped hand, and had heard my sisters say that her feet were also models of beauty; but now I could see that she was perfection in all of her slender and flexible proportions. And when this lovely vision, almost penitent of her beauty, stood modestly before me, beaming with the halo of her own goodness and purity, I was for the moment entranced, and then cast my life and soul at her feet, to be taken up and cherished, or, as in my humility I thought most likely, to be spurned. After this I would have cheerfully undergone a life of toil and misery to gain her love, and often wished the old times of romance were here again, so that I could by chivalrous emprise, or some doughty deed, have beguiled her of her love, or taken it by storm. Willingly would I have died in the attempt, so that she would at least have loved my memory and dropped a pitying tear upon my grave.

My love came upon me like enchantment, and I walked hereafter like one in a dream. The spell was but a foretaste of heaven's reality, and from the dream I never yet have waked.

CHAPTER XII.

I HAD now commenced the practice of my profession, and was beginning to learn not to despise any antagonist. Col. Jenks had taught me to be wary. Mr. Harkness had shown me that there were deeps within the depths of the law which I must approfound (that word is not English, but it ought to be), and that the law was in reality a science; and Judge Carswell, who presided in court with placid dignity until a time for him to speak arrived, when his square jaws moved, and his nervous lips seemed to bite off his words as though it were Fate which spake, taught me the propriety of being respectful. His decisions were as irreversible as the procession of the equinoxes, and were as quick as lightning. Woe to the wight who gave cause for a fine or an imprisonment for contempt—no excuses could save him. I venture to say that during the fourteen years he was upon the bench, not one remission of a fine, unless one upon some juryman who had been detained by high water, was ever recorded; and as for fine or imprisonment for a contempt, I seldom saw one hardy enough to seek to evade it. He was a rare judge; one of a class which was then common in our country when the right of choice was not exercised by so many, and the number to choose from was not so great as it is fast becoming. He was absolutely and relatively impartial, and as for fear, it was well known that he rather enjoyed a fight.

His knowledge of the practice of law was very great, and the Superior Court rarely reversed one of his decisions. It was a great advantage to me, and to the other young members of the bar, that our Gamaliel was one who had Rhadamanthus for a model. Carelessness was never overlooked, and the statute of Jeofails was most rigidly interpreted. Justice never went slipshod in his court as she did before Squire Carter, but tread firmly in boots with long spurs.

One of the best qualities of a judge is to preserve order. I do not mean quiet and silence in the courtroom, for that is the business of the Sheriff and his officers—but order in the proceedings; and only a judge who thoroughly understands practice as well as law, can do that. It was in this, as well as in his inflexibility, that Judge Carswell excelled. When a case went to one of his juries it had its beginning, its middle, and its end, all clearly defined before them, and they were never in confusion—except with that confusion which naturally exists in the heads of about eleven out of every twelve of an ordinary jury. If the decisions of civil cases tried by jury were not always right, it was certainly the fault of the system, under Judge Carswell's rule. He had a contemptuous fear of the system, as has every good lawyer who knows he has the right side of a case to be decided. Not one client in ten can make a plain and correct statement of his own case, and not one in twenty can come to a correct judgment of it with any certainty. How then is it possible that they can understand more clearly and judge more infallibly the cases of others?

The truth is that the trial by jury has been carried to an excess both in this country and in England. Magna Charta was such a glorious triumph that it has sentimentalized two nations, and ruined vast numbers in every generation of men for six centuries. Because it gives a criminal a better chance for escape—for juries almost never err to the side of severity, even in that best of all courts, in its proper place, the Court of Judge Lynch; and because it is more agreeable to divide the responsibility of punishing between twelve men rather than impose it upon one,—*therefore* twelve men can decide more *ex aëquo et bono*, and with less burden of responsibility, upon the most abstruse and confused questions of law and fact involved in civil affairs! The *non sequitur* is apparent, and yet for twenty generations, in two hemispheres, men have followed it.

There were two reasons why the grant of the trial by jury to the English people was a great boon, neither of which is to any degree applicable to this country, so far; what it would be under a different form of civil government, or under a military despotism, we need not concern ourselves about. In England the judges were the creatures of the court, and were wholly under court influence, to imprison and kill at its command, and therefore trial by jury, and the writ of Habeas Corpus, were absolutely essential for the lives and liberties of the subject. But the trial by jury was also a political measure. The king governed by divine right; his acts could not be questioned or reversed, and his courts were wholly under his influence and that of his nobles; the people had no protection except by revolution, which was then impossible with them, and the right to try and decide their own civil causes was justly considered a triumph, and a protection and elevation of the people.

In this country the people have everything their own way. They have liberty, which, but for the restrictions of a mere paper constitution, would soon be developed into licentiousness, or the frenzy of a mob, which is no better, or, rather, is the same thing.* Their judges are either directly elected, or are appointed by those who are elected for very short terms, and the right of impeachment is very clear, and its exercise is unobstructed. If they have not good judges, it is their own fault; so that by continuing the trial by jury in civil cases, they virtually declare that they have little confidence in their own discretion to elect honest and capable men—and, therefore, that the right of suffrage is a questionable excellence in human government. The idea of leaving a man's fortune or honor to depend upon the agreement in a verdict of twelve men taken at random, without regard to knowledge, honor, or discretion, rather than to a judge who at least knows some law, and who is subject

---

* It must be remembered that Mr. Page wrote this in 1861, or before that time, and died just at the close of the late war.

to prosecution for misfeasance or malfeasance, and whose decision is subject to revision by a higher tribunal (why is that not also a random jury?), is simply preposterous, and can be the choice of only a set of idiots, or ignoramuses, or sentimentalists,—and the mass of the English and American people are not idiots, whatever else may be said of them.

If I express myself strongly upon this matter it is because I feel strongly; because I have in my long practice actually seen so much folly and injustice committed without blame, and borne without a murmur, by two generations of men educated to a superstitious reverence of Magna Charta, which, considered as a panacea for civil ills, I now in my old age pronounce to be a humbug. There is no panacea for wrong and injustice except divine love and divine knowledge united in divine wisdom. There is no human cure-all for any species of derangement, and the man who pretends to have found a system or a maxim in politics, law, or medicine, of universally strict application and virtue, is a quack. The only perfect institution is divine—the Christian religion—and even that must be taken in its simplicity, or it becomes itself a fruitful cause of sad derangement and destruction in the hands of men.

The world has been governed by sentimental maxims long enough, and the man who invents a maxim, or a popular saying, should publish it in the position of a Locrian who proposed a law, or an amendment to a law—with a rope around his neck to strangle him the moment it is decided unsound.

One of the most false and pernicious of all modern political maxims is this: " The best government is that which governs least." Let a man try it in his family or on his plantation, and he will soon find out his error.

All this, however, is by-the-by. I find as I get older that I am more and more apt to wander into by-paths, which branch with never-ending succession from the main arteries and veins of my subject, and unfailingly run into them again if followed far enough. At some more appropriate era in this history (and many will doubtless occur) I will expose the falsity of this maxim, and the folly of its kindred dogma, universal suffrage, both of which are based on sentiment, unsupported by reason and experience. I could do so now, and if my reader would go quietly along with me, could, by the plainest paths, lead him again naturally, while always progressing, into my experience at the bar, from which we have wandered thus far; but there is no call for a display of my skill as a pilot. I would only have him remark that violence in going from a digression back into the main line of discourse is rarely necessary except for brevity—which was a quality upon which Judge Carswell always insisted in all the pleadings, oral or written, and in the examination of all witnesses in his court.

CHAPTER XIII.

AN occurrence which took place during this time of my life I will relate, as illustrating the state of the society in which I lived.

It was then the fashion to give gentlemen's dinner parties, at which no ladies were present—even the mistress of the mansion taking the opportunity to spend the day abroad with all her children, if she had any, or, if she remained at home to superintend the service of the meal, remaining secluded, invisible to the guests. As was to be supposed, on these occasions great quantities of wines and liquors were consumed, and though there was rarely actual stupid or frenzied drunkenness, the gentlemen became very mellow and jovial.

One day there was a large dinner party at Dr. Luckett's, and among the guests were Mr. Charles Burruss, Dr. Colburn Sandys, and Colonel James Morton, three gentlemen well acquainted with each other, as indeed were all the others present. It will be necessary to describe these gentlemen, in order for the reader to appreciate the catastrophe.

Mr. Charles Burruss was a stout, florid young lawyer, about twenty-seven years of age, who, though he had the reputation of a rising man in a grave profession, was yet a most incorrigible practical joker. His jokes were never ill-natured in the sense of an intention to seriously injure the subjects of them, but were the results of a keen sense of the ridiculous, united to high animal spirits, and a considerable degree of selfish disregard to the feelings and comfort of others. As the number of his subjects was of course limited, and the laughers were many, he was very popular, and was therefore rather petted and screened from the odium and punishment his pranks sometimes deserved.

Dr. Colburn Sandys was rather a personage than a person. He was a tall, lank, dark-faced man of thirty-three or four years of age, who wore spectacles, and abroad was always seen walking with a gold-headed ebony cane. His dress and manners were very precise, and he assumed a grave aristocratic bearing, which did not ill become him. He was a Marylander—one of the Eastern Shore Sandyses, as he insisted, to distinguish them, I suppose, from the Baltimore Sandyses, and, again, from those from Frederick, with whom he seemed still more anxious not to be confounded. As a Marylander, he was of course a *gastronome* of the first order; and his taste in terrapin-soup and stews was certainly undeniable, while his knowledge of wines showed much observation, and great practice in distinguishing their ages, qualities, and kinds. He was therefore in great request on these occasions, when the very best viands and most skillful art of the county were displayed upon the board; and his opinion was oracular. His profession—or trade, which is it?—was that of dentistry, of which he was one of the pioneers in our part of the country, and the number, variety, and beauty of his instruments of torture were the wonder of town and county. Having the bearing of a gentleman, and bringing favorable letters of introduction to one or two gentlemen of note—Colonel Morton being one of them—he had been received from the outset, about two years before, into our best society, and had so conducted himself as to be highly respected by all, if a little disliked by some for a slight narrow-minded haughtiness and fire they thought they perceived, and which they thought hardly became one of his profession, or trade, of "tooth-carpentry." Though his education had been neither very varied nor profound, he had evidently been well raised; and though his aristocratic gravity and punctilio were somewhat offensive to the very familiar acquaintanceship which exists in country villages and neighborhoods, he was undoubtedly a well-meaning and honorable man, and was so esteemed.

Of Colonel Morton, his earliest friend and patron, I need say but little. His father, James Morton, the elder, had removed from Maryland while the colonel was still a lad, and had opened a plantation near Yatton, upon which the colonel now lived. Nothing could be breathed against his probity; but he was vain, choleric, and unreasonable; and had unfortunately married a wife who resembled him, and was, if anything, an instigator rather than a soother of his unreasonable whims and prejudices.

The dinner had progressed most harmoniously; the dessert and decanters were upon the table, and the jest and laugh were in full tide, when Dr. Sandys was heard to say, in an excited tone, "Sir, allow me to tell you that I do not admire your wit or your jokes; the one is vulgar and the others brutal, and unless you wish your jaws slapped——"

Every one looked up astonished, and saw that the doctor was standing up and shaking his finger at Mr. Burruss, who, as he rose from the opposite side of the table at the word "slapped," threw the contents of his wineglass in his face. No one knew the beginning of the altercation—nor do I know it to this day—but every one rose instantly, and those on either side of the table rushed to the nearest party to prevent their getting together in conflict. That end being apparently accomplished, all was silence for a brief moment, when Mr. Burruss turned to the host and said: "Dr. Luckett, I regret extremely that this should have occurred at your table; but you heard the gross insult offered me by Dr. Sandys, and I could not have acted otherwise than I did. I was perhaps wrong in attempting a joke with Dr. Sandys, whom I know to be sensitive, and but for his folly I would have apologized; but now there is no question of whether I was wrong or right, and I shall hold myself ready to give him, or any one of his friends, any satisfaction desired."

This was rather a long speech for such an occasion, but it was made by a man who in danger was as cool as death; and he was not interrupted even by the doctor, who stood glaring at him, livid and speechless with passion.

Mr. Markham and Captain White then advanced to Burruss, and they went out of the room and house together, after first bowing politely to Dr. Luckett, and bidding him good evening.

This was every word spoken on the occasion after the attack by Dr. Sandys, except this—which could not be related in the order in which it occurred: The moment Burruss threw the wine in the doctor's face,

Morton, who was sitting near him, rushed at him, exclaiming, "Burruss, God d—n your soul! what do you mean? You d—d brute!"

In his remarks to Dr. Luckett, Burruss did not once look at Morton until he came to the words "or any one of his friends," which he uttered looking and slightly bowing meaningly at Morton, who, however, answered not a word.

There is actually all that occurred in the room—except the provocation which Burruss gave, which was some remark no one heard or knew—although there were a thousand reports, each differing and exaggerated. Some had it that Burruss had given the lie to both Sandys and Morton; others that he had given the lie to Sandys, and that Morton had taken it up and retorted it; some this, others that; and, in fact, the tragic end of the quarrel could have warranted the worst provocations to be ascribed.

It was in the latter part of June—Wednesday, the 24th, I think—that the dinner was given, and the affair I am relating took place about an hour by sun—say, at six o'clock P.M. About half-past six, Burruss, who was standing on Main Street talking with Captain White, was informed that Dr. Sandys had armed himself and was looking for him. He instantly remarked, "I am sorry for that, White; for I hoped that if the matter had to come to the worst, it should have been in the regular way. At any rate, the man is a fool, and I don't wish to kill him; so I will keep out of his way if possible." With that he started off to his room, which was the one formerly occupied by Dagobert Q. Thomas, where he put a pair of small pistols in his pocket; and thinking that perhaps that would be the first place to which Sandys would come, he went out, closed the front door, and started leisurely down toward the drug-store.

Just as he reached the corner he saw Sandys on the opposite side of the cross street advancing toward him, and then about forty feet off. The doctor had a pistol in each hand, and the moment he saw Burruss halt, he exclaimed: "Defend yourself, you d—d rascal!" and raised the pistol in his right hand and fired. Before he could change hands and fire his other pistol, Burruss fired—and the ball passed through Sandys's head, and he fell dead without a groan. As Burrows raised his pistol to fire, he said: "Well, if you will have it, take it!"

Hardly had Sandys's body touched the ground when Morton was noticed about forty yards off running to the spot with a pistol in his hand, to take part in the fray; but before he could come near enough to fire at Burruss with any certainty, a crowd of their mutual friends had gathered around both, and Morton, finding himself thwarted, shook his fist at Burruss, exclaiming, "You d—d murdering scoundrel, I'll pay you yet!"

Burruss immediately surrendered himself to the sheriff, who by that time had reached the spot, and was examined at once and discharged by Squire Carter, who had not yet left his office for home, upon the ground that he had acted in self-defense.

Morton had the body of Dr. Sandys tenderly removed, coffined, and laid in-state in the parlor of the tavern in which he had boarded, and, as I was told, manifested a kind of morbid concern over it, as much grief, in fact, as would have been natural had it been the body of a beloved brother. He talked over and over again about their having come from the same State, and remarked that he had been the one to introduce Sandys into society, and it was his duty to see his murderer punished.

The next day, Thursday, at 4 P.M., the funeral took place, Col. Morton and his wife acting as chief mourners. There was a large escort of ladies and gentlemen, in carriages and on horseback, and the body was conveyed out to Col. Morton's family burying-ground, about four miles from town, where it was interred.

Friday afternoon it was rumored over town that Col. Stewart, who was a noted fire-eater, acting on the part of Morton, had waited upon Mr. Burruss with a peremptory challenge, which had been accepted; and that Col. Stewart had been referred to Capt. White as Burruss's friend.

But this was not all true. Stewart had been sent for by Morton, and after hearing his statement of the case had decided that Burruss had neither done nor said anything for which he, Morton, could call upon him to apologize, and certainly had neither done nor said anything he could retract with honor, or even retract at all, and that therefore if Morton was determined to fight him, he must either do so upon the first opportunity of their meeting, after giving due notice, or must send a peremptory challenge assigning no cause. And thereupon the peremptory challenge was drawn up and was presented, as was said, but Burruss had referred the bearer to Capt. White, without accepting it.

And here is what followed—or, rather, the important part of it; for the negotiation was long and involved.

Capt. White asked Col. Stewart a delay of twenty-four hours that he might consult his principal; which was granted. Before the time had elapsed he returned a written answer, the points of which were that Mr. Burruss had always from boyhood been on the most friendly terms with Col. Morton; that Burruss was a bachelor while Morton had a wife and child; that Morton had assigned no cause for his challenge, and that Burruss could neither consent to kill him nor to expose himself to death without a valid reason being shown.

In answer to this, Morton replied that Burruss knew very well the causes of the challenge, but that, to be more definite, he, Morton, would assign for sufficient reason the insulting looks, gestures, and threats used toward him by Burruss at Dr. Luckett's dinner table on the 24th inst.

To this, Capt. White, under the instructions of his principal, replied that if Col. Morton would withdraw and apologize for the abusive language used by him at Dr. Luckett's table, Burruss was perfectly willing to withdraw what he had said on that occasion in the heat and excitement of the moment.

This, Col. Morton absolutely refused to do. He said that what he had then said he now repeated, and that if he, Burruss, did not accept his challenge he would post him as a coward, and would cane him upon the street, and shoot him if he resisted.

This estopped Burruss from every objection, and he accepted the challenge, choosing rifles as the weapons, and generously leaving the day, place, and distance to be fixed by his adversary. In this matter he was moved, I suppose, by consideration of the family, and business arrangements which Morton would necessarily have to make, and the known fact that his, Morton's, eyes were weak.

Never in all my life, in which I have known of many and been concerned in two or three affairs, which, however, it could do no possible good to speak of in this history—have I known so much generosity as was displayed by Burruss in all the preliminaries of this duel.

On the other hand, it will hardly be believed when I say that Mrs. Morton was consulted by her husband in the whole affair, and was even urged on by her to take the course he did. Much less can I expect full credence when I say that after the time (the 26th of July) was fixed, she accompanied her husband every day to the orchard where a target (upon which the outlines of a full-grown man were marked, with a straight line running from the crown of his head to his feet) was prepared, and that she gave him the word, and exhorted or instructed him how to make his shots, whether at the hips, the breast, or the head. But this is actually the fact. How it should be accounted for I do not know. Though she was high tempered, and narrow minded, she was not a bad woman in any sense. One more hospitable and ladylike in her own house will rarely be seen, and she was well known to be an impulsively charitable woman to the poor.

Perhaps the secret lies in that very word "impulsive," which does not, when rightly used, denote merely a kind of spasmodic action, but an action which, however sudden in its commencement, may be continuous for years. Some of the most impulsive persons I have ever known have been the most obstinate when once the impulse was allowed to act.   Besides this, impulse is used as an antithesis to calculation or reflection, and many impulsive persons never make use of sober second thought, but have their pride aroused to persevere blindly in what they have undertaken.   It is possible that some secret personal spite to Burruss as well as a natural espousal of the anger of her husband gave rise to her conduct; but I never heard such a fact mentioned, or any reason for its existence, nor do I believe that she could be willing to gratify a feeling so murderous at the risk of her husband's life, for she undoubtedly loved him devotedly.

But whatever may have been her reasons she had to drink the gall of sorrow to its dregs.   Before ten years rolled over, her only child, a son, was killed by his own knife in a fight with a young cousin of Burruss's, about this very duel.   As he cut upward at the boy, running after him, he stumbled and fell forward on the knife, which penetrated his neck, and killed him on the spot.

Col. Morton knew that Burruss was a splendid rifle-shot, nor could he, under the circumstances, blame him for choosing that weapon on the ground that it gave him the advantage.   It was, according to the "Code" as interpreted in the South, a strictly legal weapon, and as by his own terms the duel was to the death, Burruss could have been censured if he had not chosen the legal weapon which gave him the best chance. The colonel, therefore, practiced diligently up to the very morning before the fatal day, by which time he had arrived at a degree of quickness and precision from which both he and his wife augured the safest results. Burruss, on the contrary, positively refused to practice, and incurred a great deal of blame from his friends by his refusal. But he told them from the first that if Morton persisted in fighting, he would kill him; and he was so impressed with the certainty of the event that he seemed to take up a morbid dislike to his rifle, as though it were going to inflict upon him some great sorrow, the black shadow of which already began to throw a crepuscular shade upon his life; and he implored several of his friends, who were also friends to Morton, to use their influence to arrange the difficulty amicably. He told them that he was yet a young man; that he had already been forced to take the life of a fellow-creature, and though his conscience justified the act, he could never shake off the regret such an occurrence naturally caused; that Morton was insanely unreasonable, for he had no real cause of quarrel with him who had never done him a wrong, but on the contrary, had always felt and shown a warm friendship for him in spite of his oddities and overbearing touchiness.

"Gentlemen," said he, "you know that I am no coward; but I would be almost willing to incur some appearance of cowardice to avoid killing Morton, as I certainly shall do" (he did not say "will do") "if he persist in fighting me. It has always been the great wish of my life to live at peace and love with my fellow-men, and it seems hard that I should be forced to bear the sorrows that my soul most hates. But you know, gentlemen, that if Morton persist in it, I must fight him. What choice have I? To flee the country; or, if I remain in it, to have every dog lifting his leg upon me, and all my hopes for usefulness and happiness de-

stroyed!   Why, that would be worse than murder;
and my life and the lives of a dozen men would not
be worth the sacrifice. My God! my God!" exclaimed
he, clasping his hands, and walking hurriedly up and
down the room, "why should I have to suffer this terrible alternative! Save me, gentlemen, from having
the brightness of my life all extinguished, and save
Morton from his death!"

And so he would talk at times when foreboding of
the anguish to come was too heavy upon him for quiet.
And the friends did try earnestly to turn Morton from
his purpose; but he and his wife had made themselves
like stones.

It may be asked why, as all this was going on so
publicly as to be in every man's mouth, even to its details, the officers of the law did not interfere, and put
the parties under bonds to keep the peace?

To this I answer that there were several good reasons why such a course was not pursued: First, that
no amount of bond could have accomplished the object. Secondly, that the grand jury was not in session,
and by the law no magistrate could issue his warrant
unless for an offense committed in his view (though I
knew an ambitious young magistrate to decide that
"view" meant "jurisdiction"), except upon affidavit
made by some credible person, and no man, who
thought he knew the fact sufficiently well to take an
oath about it, was willing to interfere. Thirdly, duels
which originated in the county were fought out of the
jurisdiction of the officers, just across the river in the
adjoining State; and, lastly, not to be diffuse, the officers of the law and all good citizens knew that a duel,

bad as it was, was the way in which the affair could be settled with least harm to individuals, and with most benefit to the community; that it was far better for the parties to meet under the restraints of the laws of the Duello, and finally end the quarrel though at the expense of one or both lives, than have them continue the quarrel and meet in conflict, in defiance of all law, and not only endanger their own lives, but the peace and lives of others who would almost inevitably be drawn into it, as they would be present at it.

Old as I am, or rather (as perhaps I should begin the sentence) with my experience, I do not hesitate to say that, within just bounds, the practice of dueling is the best preventive for many infinitely worse evils with which society is necessarily afflicted, and the arguments against it are in a human point of view namby-pambily sentimental. Shaving was invented for men who had no beards, and the wholesale talk against dueling was invented for men who had no stomach for being jerked up to answer for wrongs they wished to commit with impunity or to answer for only under legal process, with all the chances to escape afforded by the law's delay and uncertainties.

There are very great errors lying at the bottom of all the transcendental theories of law which are erroneously called Christian. One is, that they are too literal. Because it is taught that men should be meek and forbearing, if a man, Christian or sinner, does not literally turn his cheek to be smitten on the other side, he must be read out, and punished, thus ignoring the very nature God has given us. Another error is that they are laws for Christians alone—as Christians—and the fact is not recognized that evils exist which cannot be prevented, and can only be regulated. But law must be adapted, as well as made, for the unrighteous (the righteous need neither law nor repentance; they are a law unto themselves), and I do not doubt but that if the duel were legalized, or, at any rate, suffered, under proper restrictions, it would be the means of preventing a vast deal of bloodshed, and worse crime, which now goes unpunished—and prevention is better than punishment.

At any rate, where the duel is recognized as proper *ex necessitate*, seduction, slander, and all other offenses which affect the honor, are very rare, gossip has a law it recognizes, and even assaults, assaults and batteries, and quarrels are resorted to only on great provocation. It is a great promoter of charity and peace.

I am now seventy-six years of age, and I have never seen a suit for breach of promise of marriage, and have heard of but three or four cases of seduction in our county (where such things could not possibly be concealed), and they took place among the lowest class of society in the "rural district," of which I will speak after awhile, perhaps, and two of them ended in murder. Moreover, Mr. Carey's school for boys, which closed only some ten years ago, was the most orderly ever known in the county; and it was because if two boys of about the same age and size commenced a quarrel, he made them fight it out, and if a larger boy commenced a quarrel with a smaller, he made the smaller and a sufficient number of other small boys thrash him.

The reasons, then, I have given, and the spirit I

have described prevented any legal interference with this duel, and the day arrived.

The place fixed upon was a small pasture in the river bottom near a mile below Holman's Ferry, about nine miles east of Yatton. Colonel Morton, as had been agreed by the seconds, had crossed the river the afternoon before, and with Colonel Stewart, Dr. Cannon, and one or two others, stayed all night at General Archer's, about a mile and a half from the place. Mr. Burruss, with Captain White and Dr. Holt—he objected to others going—stopped at Mr. Holman's residence about three-quarters of a mile above the ferry, which was attended to by an old negro man named Jerry, who had formerly belonged to Burruss's father. Each party had therefore about the same distance to ride to the scene, and there could be no advantage on either side from fatigue.

The precise spot selected was on the eastern side of the pasture at the edge of the woods. It was a beautiful place, as level as a floor, and the forest of pines, oaks, beeches, and magnolias—which are often found growing together in such localities—looked cool and inviting in its shady depths, and the dewy grass sparkled in the rays of the rising sun like myriads of rubies and diamonds set in emerald

A slight delay at the ferry, caused by old Jerry's slowness and agitation, allowed Colonel Morton's party to arrive first by about five minutes. Old Jerry had evidently heard of what was going on, and as Mr. Burruss led his horse into the boat, he said: "See here, Mass Charley, I'm afeard you ain't gwine arter no good this mornin'. Colonel Morton an' dem crossed here yesterday evenin', an' I hearn 'em say as how you'd be along early."

"Oh, never mind, Uncle Jerry," said Mr. Burruss; "I am only going over to meet some friends."

The old man had by this time got hold of the pole he used for shoving off, and was nervously fumbling with it as he looked up at Burruss, with tears in his eyes, and said:

"I's knowed you, Mass Charley, sence you was a little shaver, so high, an' for de Lord's sake take care of yourself. What would old mis-tuss say, if she knowed what you was gwine for! If you will do it, you mus', an' de Lord help you. But you mus' shoot quick, Mass Charley, quicker'n you did when dat——"

"Oh pshaw! Uncle Jerry," interrupted Burruss; "you've got notions in your head this morning. You must have had bad dreams last night. I'm afraid Aunt Sukey has been giving you a piece of her mind again. Come, old fellow, we are in a hurry."

As they rode up the farther bank, old Jerry shouted out, "Good-by, Mass Charley, an' de Lord pertect you! I'll keep the boat over this side till breakfus time!"

There were two pairs of draw-bars to be let down in order to pass through a field which lay between the road and the pasture, and Colonel Morton's party had left them partly down as they saw by the absence of horsetracks that they were first. Burruss rode in perfect silence and seemed melancholy but determined. What his thoughts were, as he rode along between the rows of corn, now beginning to tassel and with its tender silks gemmed with dew, I can imagine; but my reader can do so quite as well. The tripping of his horse at some clod in the road, or the sprinkle of the dew in his face as the horse's foot struck some tall weed all wet with crystal drops, caused not a single gesture or murmur of impatience. His mind was far ahead of him, on the ground of the duel—and then stretched far ahead of that, through the long, dim vista of the future, overshadowed by a cloud which was coming on fast and black.

Colonel Morton's party had hitched their horses at a beech-tree about forty yards north of the chosen ground, and when Burruss saw that, he rode on, the captain and doctor following, to about an equal distance beyond and dismounted at a wide-spreading Spanish oak, whose willowy limbs hung low, and after they had fastened their bridles to the pendant branches and had adjusted their dresses, somewhat disordered by the ride, they walked up to near where the other party were seated, and halted; Colonel Stewart advanced to meet Captain White, who walked on toward him, and after a few words they commenced to mark off the ground. Captain White took his stand at a certain spot, which they marked with a short cane, and Colonel Stewart stepped thence due north twenty steps, and planted another piece of cane. Captain White then stepped it off and verified it, and they went aside to load, in the presence of each other, each his friend's weapon.

Hardly had they finished that operation, when Burruss—who was standing near Dr. Holt seated at the root of a tree, and had been steadily looking at Morton, who was likewise standing up, but sideways to him—suddenly left his position and advanced up to Morton, who turned and looked at him as he said:

"Colonel Morton, withdraw your challenge!"

"I will not, Mr. Burruss," replied the colonel.

"Do, for God's sake, colonel. I do not wish to kill you!" exclaimed Burruss.

"Do not be so certain that you will do that, Mr. Burruss," replied the colonel, with a cold smile.

Just then the seconds, having heard the conversation, advanced, and each took his principal by the arm and led him to his position, which had been previously determined; and when he had delivered him his loaded weapon, stepped to a position to one side and about midway the line between them. Colonel Stewart had been, by lot, chosen to give the word, and he asked:

"Are you ready?"

"Ready!" replied Colonel Morton, raising his rifle from his side.

"Stop a moment!" said Mr. Burruss, without moving; "I again ask you, Colonel Morton, to withdraw your challenge."

"Such conduct is unheard-of, sir! You have already had my answer. If you are afraid, I am not; and I will kill you if I can!" exclaimed Colonel Morton, somewhat excitedly.

"Very well," replied Mr. Burruss

After a moment's pause, Colonel Stewart again asked, "Are you ready?" "Ready!" answered both, bringing their rifles up from their sides, and cocking them. "Fire! One! T——" Before the word "two" was pronounced, Mr. Burruss, who had leveled his gun apparently with a jerk, so sudden was his motion, fired—and hardly had its smoke sped from its muzzle when Colonel Morton's rifle was also fired, and the reports of both went blended to the echoes in the forest. Colonel Morton, as his gun went off, wilted down, and, when his second and surgeon reached him, one gasp of life was all that remained—and with that his soul left his body. Burruss brought his rifle again to an order, and remained in his tracks, with his right hand resting upon it. Captain White and Dr. Holt went up to the other party, and, as by that time all was over, they only looked to see, where Dr. Cannon pointed, where the ball had entered,—just above the left hip, fracturing the top of the pelvis and crashing on through the backbone,—and they turned, taking Burruss with them, and mounted their horses and rode off.

Though I omitted to state it, General Archer's carriage and quite a number of the mutual friends of both parties were in the field, though out of sight in the edge of the woods, and came up on hearing the firing; so that the proffered assistance of Captain White and Dr. Holt was not needed.

Such was the course and event of this duel, which created a great sensation all over the country. All regretted it; but with Colonel Morton's determination, it could not be averted. The seconds, who were both gentlemen in every sense, and men who thoroughly understood their own responsibility to the parties and to the community, used every means of settling it— but in vain.

When Burruss rode off, the cloud had come down upon him; and though his conscience could not prick him,—and though he afterward married a lovely lady, and had a large family of fine children,—his high spirits were gone; and he went his way to the end, a grave, sober citizen, unwearyingly charitable to the widow and orphan—particularly if their protector had come to a violent end.

CHAPTER XIV.

ONE of my first profitable clients was old Captain Nesbitt. And here I would remark that it must not be thought strange that I have rarely mentioned a male character, so far, who had not either been a doctor or had a military title. That fancy for giving titles was not peculiar to our section, but it was certainly carried to an excess. Yet several good reasons may be given for it, and among them, that it saved a great deal of the trouble of remembering names. It is much easier to say, "How are you general?" than to say, "How are you Mister Higginbotham?" particularly if you have only just been introduced to him, and do not think you have heard his right name distinctly; and it is much easier to remember that the gentleman approaching you is a colonel, major, captain, or doctor, than to remember the name he inherited from his father.

Captain Nesbitt, then, was one of my first profitable clients; and I remember the fact the more distinctly that my obtaining a fee from him was regarded by my professional brethren as a hopeful sign of my future success.

He was an old revolutionary veteran, who had amassed a very large estate by hard work, judicious speculations, always exacting what was due him, and never paying anything when he could avoid it. The consequence was that he was always at law, and had been engaged at that amusement for so many years that he never seemed contented unless he had one or two suits on hand. But of late years it had been so difficult to get a fee from him that the members of the bar shunned his business. In one particular case every lawyer had been at one time or another engaged, and had been discharged from it, or had relinquished it for non-payment of fees. A term of court was coming on at which a demurrer in the case had to be tried, and as the old gentleman regarded me with favor, and, m re particularly, as for good causes no other lawyer could be got to appear for him, he came to my office, and placed the matter in my hands.

He began by saying that he had a case in court of such great importance that if it were ably handled it would establish the reputation of any lawyer, and as he liked me he would place it in my hands, and it would be a splendid chance for me to appear my best, as I was young and aspiring; and that he supposed I would require no fee, or, if any, a very small one, under the circumstances. I told him that if he would pay me one hundred dollars cash, as a retainer, I would take charge of his case. After a great deal of chaffering, he actually pulled out the money and paid it. I studied the case thoroughly—a full hundred dollars worth—but, alas for the demurrer, it had two disadvantages, intrinsic worthlessness, and Mr. Harkness, to contend against, and I lost it. The captain was in court at the time, and came up to me hurriedly and told me to move for a rehearing, and if that were not granted, to take a Bill of Exceptions. I answered him that it was useless, as the demurrer was untenable. He said I must do as he said. I told him I could not consent to make myself ridiculous by doing so; and he discharged me from the case on the spot. As he had a term to answer over, he managed to persuade, or paid cash, some other lawyer; but the case came to an ignominious defeat after living eight years.

Most of my first cases were mere collection suits, but the first year of my practice I made eight hundred dollars. This was doing very well I was told, but still it seemed to me a very slow business. The second year my collected fees amounted to fifteen hundred dollars, and it was in the latter part of this second year, or the very beginning of the third, that the sewing society was formed, and Mary McIntyre first attracted my special attention.

When Mary became so dear to me, I, of course, began to take great interest in her family, to study their dispositions, and to calculate what would be my chances among them for opposition or assistance in my suit.

Mr. McIntyre was a tall and large Scotchman, about fifty years of age, with a heavy suit of sandy hair and sandy whiskers well sprinkled with gray, keen blue eyes, and a large, florid countenance. He was by no means an ugly man, but was rough, and a little gruff at times, when he would "dawm!" and storm at everything in reach. He was highly esteemed as an honest, sensible man, who was already rich, and would be very wealthy if he lived a few years. The peculiarities I noticed most particularly about him were, his reticence about his own affairs, and his never interfering with his wife and daughters in their dress, their outgoings and incomings, their company, church-matters, or preacher-blindness.

He had a profound respect for his wife, who was a second cousin of Mrs. Ruggles, and had been a dark-haired beauty in her youth. She was an excellent woman, of more than average piety, though her religion was of that character which fears to differ with church authority. As a wife, she was respectful, and was allowed to have her own way in her domestic concerns. As a mother, she was tender, judicious, and firm—except with Mary, the youngest, who could wheedle her to do as she pleased. As a friend, she was undemonstrative, and rather taciturn, but never wanting in the offices of friendship.

Of the two eldest daughters, Sarah, the elder, was tall, had black eyes and hair, a fine figure, delicate hands and feet, and, to strangers, seemed haughty. Lucy was more like her father in appearance, had fair hair, blue eyes, and a fine complexion, though somewhat freckled, and was a very sweet girl in her disposition. Both of them were intelligent, refined, and good, and treated with profound deference whatever their mother believed in. At the time I am speaking of, Miss Sarah had as an aspirant the Rev. Walter Hopkins, a slender young minister who had strayed South for the cure of the Preacher's sore-throat, or to have the disease confirmed by marrying comfortably. He was a funny gentleman, who evidently thought he could pun and pray himself into Miss Sarah's good graces. But, though she had every reason to believe (as I still believe) that he was at heart a good man, and would have made an indulgent husband, and though her mother was not at all opposed to the match, and though she could laugh heartily at his puns and jokes, she had already refused him several times, and it was becoming a habit, and almost a joke, for him to pop the question about every three months, and be refused.

Miss Lucy's lover, Tom Merriweather, to whom she was already engaged, was a heavy-set young planter, with a frank, handsome countenance, and a genial smile, but very much out of place among ladies, and particularly uncomfortable when Mr. Hopkins was along with his gay gambols of wit and words. He would sit in the parlor bolt upright for a half hour at a time, and never utter a word unless spoken to. How he ever did his courting was more than I knew, though I suspected that when he and Miss Lucy got off to themselves he fully made up for his awkward silence and shame-facedness in company. At any rate, she treated him as though she understood him thoroughly, and he was already quite as domestic an animal as the house cat, came and went unquestioned, and was sometimes petted when his chosen could slyly place her hand on his head, or pat his cheek.

These, with Miss Mary, were all the family, for the only son, the old man's pride, had died about three years before.

No gambler ever calculated his chances more narrowly and earnestly than I did, so far as the influences of these elder and beloved ones were concerned. Every day I would take apart and put together again with fresh complications, my grounds for fear and hope. I had no fear of the old gentleman, for although I had no special acquaintance with him, I knew that so far as family, morals, and prospects were concerned he could not object to me, and that Mary was his darling to whom he would grant anything which might contribute to her happiness. I even hoped that he might speak favorably of me as a fine young man, if nothing more, some day when by chance my name was mentioned in the family.

With regard to Mrs. McIntyre I had some assurance of hope, for although I was no preacher nor the son of a preacher, I was raised in the church—of which I was a sort of floating member—and my father was more learned in matters religious and ecclesiastical, and even more certainly pious than most preachers, and was an influential member of her own church. I felt certain that she would say nothing against me, and would allow Mary to love me or not, as she might choose.

But I was afraid of the elder sisters, and of the Rev. Mr. Hopkins—not that they would work against me purposely, but that they might find the weak part of my armor and turn me into ridicule before Mary. The weak part of my armor was my sensitiveness, which was acute at all times, and, when in love, was almost morbid. Though my head is gray and I am beginning to totter when I walk, I am yet afraid of the laughter of girls unless I know exactly what it is about, and if I hear it when my back is turned I instinctively fear it is directed to me.

All these calculations of mine were preparatory to the assault I was about to make; for my fair and beloved enemy, as Don Quixotte termed his lady-love, had as yet no idea that my ambitious and avaricious eyes were directed to the citadel of her affections. But the deployment of my forces and my cautious advance, under cover, when it could be so, soon revealed to her my design, and she began to call in the pleasure parties of friendly wit and mirthful smiles which had been in innocent security disporting themselves before my covetous eyes, and to sometimes hang out the crimson banner of her modest blushes, which when I saw my soul rejoiced at, for I knew it was the signal of alarm in the fortress. But beyond this there were no signs that I could detect of consciousness or of fear of the impending storm.

Sometimes in my company she was thoughtful; often just as frank and gay as she ever was before; sometimes she seemed to avoid me with perhaps a little scorn, as I thought, in her regard. How anxiously I scanned each look and syllable! From her thoughtfulness I augured well; her gayety forboded ill to me; and her avoiding me I interpreted well or ill, according to my mood. It might be that she was determined to drive me away from her, and then, again, it might be that she had discovered and wished to conceal the weakness of her defense. And often when in my ambition I imagined I was so blessed, as I thought of bringing my fate to the test, my hands grew cold, and I was seized with trembling, and as I sat alone in my room with my eyes shut, and my head bent down, I made in my imagination the most beautiful speeches, and received the most loving answers. With what rapture did I dwell upon each imagined sigh, each gentle tear! I sometimes even felt the warm embrace of her soft arms around my neck, and had her head pillowed fondly on my breast. I made myself a great name for my Mary, toiled on to wealth, and in our old age looked upon her wrinkled brow and gray hairs with tender love, and thanked God for all his mercies.

More than that, my imagination would become intoxicated and crown itself with love, clothe itself with rapture as a garment, and with the scepter of hope in hand would stalk through the future a glorious monarch to whom possibilities and probabilities were alike subject, and create for me the most cherubic children which were to be brought without fear, and pain, and danger, to make us happy.

There were always two of them, David and Juliet, and with the two I was content. Juliet, with the large hazel eyes and dark curls, with the pearly teeth and balmy breath, with her baby-talk and animated smile, standing in my lap with one dimpled hand patting my cheek and the other thrown around my neck, loving me with love inexpressible; and David, the precious little humbug, as his father was before him, always finding something wonderful as he paraded around in his first boots—David, to whom every sparrow was as large as an eagle, and every rat a wild-cat at least, who frightened his little sister with stories of snakes and Indians, whose brain was teeming with imagination and wonder and curiosity, whose little heart was brimful of affection and sensitiveness. I could see him attending, with all the impressiveness and gallantry of one of his most courtly ancestors, his little sweetheart, the daughter of my neighbor. And see Juliet, with her tiny shoes neatly laced to her delicate round ankles, and her little stockings held up by pink-silk garters, and her short lace pantalets, and blue gown with white sprigs in it, and broad-brimmed hat, holding her mother by the hand as they went from church, and looking at Davy, who walked ahead of her, with as much serious confidence in his abilities and worth, his bravery and honor, as though she were eighteen and he twenty-one. How I nursed those children in their infancy, played with them when well, and walked the room with them almost the live-long night when they were fretful. I guarded with the most vigilant anxiety their traits of character as they were developed; and both grew up comely, and intelligent, and virtuous. I directed their studies. Juliet married happily, and I trotted grandchildren on my knees. David rose to distinction, and I rejoiced that when I died I would leave some one like me, but a great deal more intelligent and noble than I in my youth, to take my place and protect his dear old mother.

All this was the frenzy of a young and ardent lover whose imagination toyed with his judgment as a plaything. Yet there is no sweeter madness, and as I recall it—for my imagination can never grow forgetful —feelings of bitterness will intrude themselves that my scepter of earthly hope is broken. But though I be old, and fading like a leaf soon to fall, in looking back I find nothing to regret of all the joys of my life. The past is past, and I would not live it over again if I could. I would not have Mary alive to die again, nor have my father again at his toil, nor my mother to feel again her pain in giving life to her children, and her agony at seeing them die. I would not recall again my brothers and sisters and friends to hope and suffer, to rejoice and be shrouded and buried again. Nor do I regret that they lived, nor, though the silent tears roll down my withered cheeks, regret that they died. All my appointed time shall I live to thank God for his goodness in giving me so many to love, so many for whose love I have only loving thoughts, for whose lives I have no regrets; and when my time to die shall come, if my mind be free of confusion or of sleep, I shall still be certain that I shall live, and love, and be loved by them again where there is no sorrow and no parting.

The happiness of my life is now in the past and with the future, but at the time of which I write it was in the present as it was and as I wished it to be. Surely no heart could be more troubled with its love than mine was. Disquiet seemed to have seized me; and, like a blind man who has just received sight, I found things that were upright all awry or upside down, and obstacles in my path that did not exist, or were really too remote from it to impede me.

Except for the excitement of a pleasant visit, to go to Mr. McIntyre's had never been with me a matter of any moment, and I had often gone alone, or with my sisters, in the most natural way in the world. But now I was troubled to find an excuse for going there. What should I say I came for? It would hardly do to call and say I came to see Miss Mary, and yet when I should see the ladies in the parlor, it would be to expose me to suspicion if I had no other excuse than to say that, as I was riding out, I thought I would call; for though the distance was only six miles, and was a pleasant ride, it was too far for the mere afternoon or morning ride for pleasure of a man who had his office and business to attend to. And even if the first visit should pass off unremarked, the second, or third, or fourth would inevitably betray me as Miss Mary's beau to the wondering smiles of Miss Sarah, and the snickering puns and jokes of Mr. Hopkins—not that I would have cared so much for myself, though the position was awkward, but it might be disagreeable to Mary; and Hopkins was such a confounded fool that he never knew when to stop.

What should I do? To wait for a special invitation would be to wait six months, till Miss Lucy and Tom Merriweather were married—and I might almost as well have consented to content myself with six years. I must go on that general invitation I had by right of birth and friendship, and how to do that and save appearances annoyed me for several weeks. My sister Bel was inexorable, and Julia would put forth no hand. "Why should we go with you?" said Bel. "We see Mary every week at church, and at the Sewing Society; and we know that Lucy has not commenced to prepare for her wedding, and does not need our assistance. And even if we should go with you once, don't you see, goosey, that you would be, for your next visit, just as embarrassed? We love Mary, and would be glad to have her for a sister; but you must do your own courting, Master Abraham. We will have nothing to do with it, but to wish you success."

"Yes, but you dear little sisters—how I do love you! —you might go with me just once, to open the way, as it were,—as Mrs. Snow says,—and then may be something will turn up by which I can go again without suspicion "

"No, sir," said Miss Bel. "We will have nothing to do with it. Do you suppose that they do not all know you are in love with Mary? What do you think they have been doing with their eyes and ears for the last three months that you have been paying what you call your modest, unobtrusive attentions to Mary? going always at her side, directing your conversation to her as though there were no one else in the world, being silent and uneasy when she goes out, and brightening up when she comes in? Why, Mrs. Snow laughed, and told Mary she had caught a beau at the third meeting of the Society——"

"Confound Mrs. Snow and her sharp eyes and long tongue!" I commenced, impatiently. "But say, little sister, what did Mary answer and how did she look?"

"Oh, ho!" replied my sister. "Then Mrs. Snow's sharp eyes and long tongue may have done you a service, you think? Well, Mary did not answer at all, nor did she blush; but she sat silent, and turned a little pale "

"Heaven bless Mrs. Snow, for once! But I do hope she will not keep up her observations and remarks," was my reply.

But Mrs. Snow did keep up her observations, and her remarks were, I learned, made not only to Mary, but to her mother and sisters, and to my mother and sisters, and, for aught I know, to the whole county.

Hang the woman ! She seemed to think that my courting Mary McIntyre was a church matter, to be talked over in session and meeting, to be discussed with elders and ministers, and regulated by church discipline. Mary was a rather too precious and profitable lamb to be handed over out of the fold of the ministry, or, at any rate, to a willful limb of the law like Abraham Page, who would be pretty apt to rule his own house in his own way. But if poor Hopkins would give up his vain pursuit of Sarah, and try and capture Mary, with what ardor would she not have assisted his plans ! It came to my ears that she had so advised the man, but he had sense enough to know that Mary did not like to be bothered---at any rate, more than once.

The fact is that Mrs. Snow did not more than half like me. She thought me rather an irreverent stripling; first, because she had heard that I had condemned her husband's sermons for their length, and, secondly, on account of an answer I once made her. I had been absent from home about four weeks attending the circuit, and a day or two after I returned I found her at old Mrs. Diggory's, upon whom I had called to pay my respects. She seemed rather dignified, and presently told me that she was surprised to see I had called on Mrs. Diggory before I had upon Mr. Snow. I told her I thought my visit to Mrs. Diggory, who had taught me to read, was the most natural thing in the world. "Yes," said Mrs. Snow, "but you owe a superior duty to your Pastor !" The tone and assumption so irritated me that it was on my lips to say, "The devil I do !" but I restrained myself, and told her that I could not recognize the obligation—and so the matter ended. But it put a little black spot in Mrs. Snow's heart, and she recalled to mind and magnified a very natural incident which had occurred to me about six years before, and which every one else, even I myself, had forgotten.

I had attended a large party at Colonel Stewart's, and between the dancing, and the champagne, and sherry at the supper, I was in a pleasantly jolly mood when I went out with four or five others to mount our horses and go home. I had, no doubt, been talking rather more glibly than usual to the young ladies in the dancing-room, and it had been noticed by some who were willing to get a joke on "sober-sides," as they called me, and when I had found my way in the dark to my horse, I found that some one had, as I thought, removed my left stirrup, and I hailed my neighbor in a pretty loud tone, and told him of the fact; but upon feeling I found that the stirrup had only been crossed over the seat of the saddle, and I mounted and we rode on without further incident. The next day I heard that I had been too drunk to distinguish my horse. Others said that when he was brought to me I mounted with my head to his tail; others, still, said that about two hours after I had left the house, two gentlemen were driving into town, and met me going toward Colonel Stewart's, and that I told them I was going home but had been riding for hours in the dark to find it, and was lost.

Mrs. Snow had got hold of this story with all its variations, and had argued that where there was so much smoke there must be some fire—a favorite way of destroying reputation effectually and without appeal

—and that I must, at all events, have been very drunk; and though it happened when Mary was only eleven or twelve years old, and though if it had been true, the offense had never been repeated, she referred to it, and expressed her fears that I was inclined by nature to intemperance, but she would hope for the best, and dear Mary must not place her confidence in the morality of this world, or in human strength, etc. etc. etc.—just what Mrs. Snow would say upon such an occasion, and with such an object.

For all this I was afraid of Mrs. Snow; but my fear of her was as nothing to compare with the dread I had of Mrs. Ruggles, who, as a relative, would naturally have a much greater influence.

Mrs. Ruggles was what was termed in our part of the world, a smart woman. What I have heretofore said of her will give a pretty good idea of her character, though not of her habits and customs. She was a notable housekeeper, and had her servants in excellent training, both to do their work well, and to make speedy and correct reports of whatever they saw or heard of the neighbors' sayings and doings. Not only so, but not a servant or child could visit her house but she would in a few minutes get the most precise information of what was going on and being said on any subject in their respective houses, and even of how they lived. The consequence was that Mrs. Ruggles was a self-constituted depot for all the scandal, and trouble, hopes and fears and arrangements and intentions of the people of the town, and, as far as possible, of the county also. It used to seem to me that she had a spy at the little market-house to report what each purchased for dinner, for she asked me one day, when I was a very small boy, how I liked cow-heel; and I knew we had had some the day before.

But when Mrs. Ruggles made a discovery she did not go blabbing it about over the country. She kept it to herself, made her reflections upon it, and imparted it to others, or intimated to the person concerned that she knew it, only when it would subserve some object she had in view.

Her son Stanley was, as I have said, in the commercial line; and he dressed more finely than would have become any other young man I ever saw, but he was a "young buck" who, adorned or unadorned, was always handsome. It had been the dearest wish of his mother's heart to see him married to one of her second-cousin's daughters, but he had hung back from Sarah's dignity, had been cut out from Lucy by Tom Merriweather, and now was being urged by his mother to try his chance with Mary—particularly as I might be thwarted in that quarter by his success. I will do Master Stanley the justice to say that he behaved very well, and when he found that he had no hope, and that I was too seriously concerned to put up with nonsense or underhanded interference by a man, he remained perfectly neutral, and tried to get his mother to do so. She knew that her attempts to thwart me must be indirect and covert, for it was of material service to her comfort that she should be on good terms with Dr. and Mrs. Page, who were very kind and useful in sickness and trouble, of which she and hers had a full share. So she would talk at Mr. McIntyre's of how poor so good a family as ours was, and to what straits they should be driven if the doctor were to die. "Abraham," she would say, "would in that case have to support them all, and though the girls and Mrs. Page are economical, the two boys have to be sent to school, and he would find his hands as full as they could be all his life." If Mrs. McIntyre should reply that she hoped it would be very many years before the doctor was taken away, the good lady would be ready to say that life was very uncertain, and that the doctor was very much exposed to disease, and in the ordinary course of nature it was to be expected that Abraham would have to provide for the family.

My darling wife told me afterward of these conversations, and she said that when she thought of the possibility of my having such a burden upon me, her heart warmed with the desire to assist me by her means, and comfort me in my labor and trials.

CHAPTER XV.

HOW to get to pay a visit to Mr. McIntyre's without an express invitation, or the excuse of business, was a great embarrassment, but I at last hit upon a plan to overcome the difficulty. The next sewing society day I found that the two elder young ladies had come into town early, and were in Mr. Youngblood's store shopping. I went in there, as though upon business, was of course surprised and gratified to see them, and soon entered into conversation. After a little, I told Miss Lucy that I understood there was good fishing in Baker's Creek, back of her father's field. She said she had not heard of it, but supposed it might be so. "Oh, yes," said I, "it is so, and I have a mind to try it in a day or two, and will be able to report fully upon the subject." My cheeks burned, and my eye wandered everywhere but to her face as I said this, for it seemed to me that my ruse was so evident she would see through it at once; and I have little doubt but that she did understand it, for she said she supposed they would see me when I came out, and they would be very happy to do so. I had indeed heard that there were two or three tolerably good perch holes in the creek, but I cared no more for fishing than I did for hunting phœnixes.

The trouble was over, and I felt great relief and lightness of spirits. I impatiently fixed my visit, in my own mind, for the next day but one, but on that day it rained. On the following day, however, it was fair, and though I knew the creek was muddy, and catching fish almost impossible, I mounted my horse, and with fishing rod in hand started, about two o'clock in the afternoon, expecting to try the creek, for the sake of appearances, and then to make a good long visit, and ride home by moonlight. For a wonder, my programme was carried out to the letter; I caught no fish, but passed a most delightful evening. Even Hopkins, who was there, made himself agreeable, and Miss Mary's quiet attempts at nonchalance and unconsciousness before her sisters, who evidently were highly amused at this first declaratory visit of her beau, did not annoy me in the least. The muddy water was a fair excuse for coming again to try it when it should be clean, and I appointed the next Wednesday (it was then Saturday) as a day certain when I would come. "But suppose," said Miss Sarah mischievously, "that it should rain on Tuesday—the creek will be muddy again." "Never mind, Miss Sarah," I answered, "I will come and see." And I rode home happy.

And so I did go and see, and found an excuse to go again at an early day; and when my visits, though always on some particular excuse, became so frequent that Hopkins, who was there nearly every day, began to perceive their design, he began to be witty and most thoroughly disagreeable. I fairly hated him, and but that he was a non-combatant, would sometimes have insulted him.

He was not the only fool of his peculiar kind I have ever seen. He had a large amount of solid learning, both civil and ecclesiastical, had studied hard with many advantages, was quite a musician, and often really witty, and yet, with all his learning, and polish, and intellect, he was totally lacking in dignity. A volatile demon seemed to possess him, and neither time, nor place, nor occasion could restrain it. (He would whisper a pun at a funeral, and look one in a sermon.

My visits had not been very numerous, however, when I was called away from home by business which detained me nearly two months. The lands in Alabama, which State was now being settled very fast, were a source of wild speculation such as I have never since seen. The land excitement now going on in Minnesota and the far northwest may be a parallel, but hardly its equal. A company of planters who had made large purchases of adjoining lands from speculators, and who intended removing a portion of their negroes upon them early in the next winter, for the purpose of opening plantations, solicited me to go and locate their places precisely by having them surveyed and marked out. As after the spring term of court was over there would be little law business until the fall term approached near, and as the amount to be paid me was considerable, and, besides, as I was young and adventurous, I consented to go so soon as the weather and my business permitted.

It was now early in June, the heavy spring rains were over, and I made my preparations and started on horseback. A pair of saddle-bags contained my clothing and papers, and a bag of heavy homespun cotton cloth was across my saddle, to be used for carrying provisions for myself and horse when I should get to the wild country where settlements were far apart. A quart tin-cup, a small frying-pan, and my rifle completed my outfit. My horse was a cross between the Indian pony and the old "Black Creek" breed, and was hardy, docile, and strong. His name was Bango; his color a rusty dun. He had a fashion of traveling with one ear pointed forward and the other pointed back, and to rest the muscles, he would sometimes change ears. His gait was easy, but indescribable by any word or words in the jockey language. It was neither a rack, pace, nor gallop; but as he held his neck sideways, as though he thought it all fine and himself handsome, and put it down in a leisurely and earnest style in all those gaits at once, he was as affected a piece of serviceable and comical ugliness as you shall ever see.

My parting with Miss Mary, or, as I had then got to calling her, Little Lady, the evening before was such as would, at least, not weigh upon my spirits while I was gone. She was embroidering a pair of slippers, which I had good reason to hope were for me, though she would not acknowledge it (I have them yet among my treasures), and manifested a concern about the exposures and dangers of my journey, which, though very maidenly and quiet, showed that she took some interest in it.

It was necessary for me to pass through Rosstown, and remain there two days for some papers I had to use, to be completed and signed. Fitzroy wished me to stay at his house, but I preferred, as I always do, my liberty at the tavern. To be intruding on a family when there is public accommodation convenient, I have always thought very selfish, and, unless under peculiar circumstances, I have never done so yet. Even had I been inclined to accede to my cousin's invitation, it would have been perhaps a little embarrassing under the circumstances. He had but recently got married, and had just commenced housekeeping, and I neither knew his wife nor the quality nor capacity of his domestic arrangements, and, besides, this thing of being alone in a house with a young married couple is never pleasant.

Fitzroy had now been practicing law nearly five years. My Uncle James, who had been dead about two years, had left his family a sufficient estate, if it had been kept together, to make them comfortable; but Anne Page had married a cantankerous sort of creature who must certainly have frightened the poor child into loving him, and her husband must needs have her share divided off, and that broke up the unity of the family as well as of the estate. Fitzroy and his mother preserved their portions in joint ownership, but the old lady insisted upon its being also, under joint management, and Fitzroy had abandoned it into her hands, and contented himself with the law business, and influence for other law business, he had inherited. He, too, had gone fishing for a wife—but in a different way from that I had adopted and hoped would succeed.

About eighteen months before my visit, a very fine gentleman, who called himself Captain Cartwright, had come to Rosstown with his wife and daughter, and announced himself as an architect and civil engineer. He was very polite, very pompous, and very fat and fussy, and from the way he talked and lived it was generally supposed that he lived upon the interest of a considerable fortune in Richmond, Va., and had come out to the new country for the purpose of investing in the best lands he might discover in the pursuit of his scientific investigations. Mrs. Cartwright was a quiet, meek little woman, who dressed neatly, and showed most ladylike manners. Miss Sallie (I wonder if I shall live long enough to see Johnny spelt with an *i e*?) Cartwright, who was about twenty-two, was a fine dashing girl, not very beautiful, but amiable looking, spirited, a fine talker and dancer, and with a rare knowledge of the toilet. She had soon talked, danced, and dressed herself into Fitzroy's particular notice, and one day at a fishing party she had fallen into a deep hole in the creek, and Fitzroy had at some risk to his clothes and comfort, if not to his life, got her out. Hence the courtship and marriage. His mother had opposed it warmly; had told him that perhaps Miss Sallie was as good as she appeared to be, but that no one knew her family antecedents; her father had come without letters of introduction, etc. etc. etc., to which he answered that he was not going to marry Miss Sallie's family, or her father, but herself, and as long as she suited him the others made no difference.

In this matter Fitzroy was wrong, and he found himself so. I have heard numbers make the same remark, but with the exception of Anne Page's husband—who seemed to constitute himself a sort of step-husband, so far as making the family discontented and miserable was concerned—and one or two others, I have never yet known a man of whom it could not be said that so far as his comfort and usefulness in life were concerned, he had more or less married his wife's family in marrying her. At any rate, when a man marries, he unites to himself the temper, proclivities, and constitution of another family, and he finds in his children that he did actually marry his wife's family.

About ten years after this I was again in Rosstown, and Fitzroy insisted so strongly upon my staying at his house that I consented, much against my will and to my subsequent regret. He looked worn and haggard, and, though he was well dressed, had a shabby appearance I cannot describe. His wife did not come at once to welcome me in the parlor—the very picture in neatness and discomfort of that I had entered in my Uncle James's house twenty-five years before—and when, in about a half hour, she did make her appearance, the marks of haste about her entrance and dress, and the fretful discontented expression upon her countenance, confirmed my foreboding that Fitzroy did not have a happy home. She was very polite and kind, but the meals were ill served, and there was a general appearance of slovenliness about the table which indicated that she was a poor housekeeper, and also that, most likely, their fortunes were not prosperous. The four small children and the baby were prim in their best clothes, their faces were clean, and their hair was carefully combed, but they were noisy and quarrelsome, and seemed to pay little respect to their father, who generally remained silent and depressed, though he sometimes joined volubly and excitedly in the talk, and would lead it at random to a different subject.

The second morning of my stay, as I lay awake in my bed, separated from their room by a thin partition, I heard their voices for some time and paid no attention to them, but presently I heard him say in a raised tone, "I do not care, madam, if my cousin does hear what I say, for he is a man of sense and discretion. But why should he not hear and speak of what all the world knows and speaks of already? Are you, perhaps, ignorant that I am the laughing-stock of the county, or the most pitied object in it?"

"Go on," said she, "I'm used to your brutality!"

"Brutality!" he exclaimed bitterly. "Because when you have put me to the rack and torture I cry out, I am to be called brutal! You have made my life miserable. Though I work hard, and deny myself every pleasure, you reproach me continually, because I have not the money for all your occasions. If I propose any

scheme, you throw cold water upon it. If I do anything and think it excellent, you tell me it will come to
nothing, and you teach my children to despise me as a
poor, inefficient, and ill-tempered creature. I actually
stand alone in the world, without encouragement at
home or abroad; for you have separated me from my
mother and sister by your vile temper and unreason-
ableness. I am alone, desolate, and wretched. For
my joys I have to depend upon myself, for counsel I
have to depend upon my own unaided judgment. You
seem to think that you perform the whole duty of a
wife when you keep my clothes and those of your children clean, and in good order, but I could hire a woman
to do that for thirty dollars a month, and never be
troubled by her tongue or sour looks. Though you
know that I need consolation in my troubles in the
world, and am faint for love, you scatter firebrands,
arrows, and death, like a madman, and when a little
access of repentance comes, you tell me you did not
mean any harm. I tell you, madam, that your re-
proaches and ill humors must stop. One would think
you had plenty of beauty and charms to squander my
love as you do, and have done, but you must know that
when you have squandered it all you will find that
your beauty and charms are too faded to regain it
again!"

The last part of the tirade was so loud that my
coughs and hems, which I had been using from the
first, could not be heard. It was a dreadful talk from
a husband to a wife, and he must have been either an
outrageous scoundrel, or a good man driven to des-
peration who uttered it. His gloom and his wife's pla-

cidity at the breakfast table showed the fault was hers, and I thought to myself with horror what would be my fate should my gentle Mary, after ten years of marriage, torment me thus.

How he and his wife got along afterward I had no means of knowing. They never formally separated, though I heard that they became husband and wife only in name, until in a drunken fit he shot himself. She then sold out, and removed with her children to Baltimore, where her mother, then a widow, was living, and they all passed out of my ken. I wish the painful recollections of his condition and talk would also pass from my memory, but the impression was too deep, and as I pursued my journey after breakfast, a gloom hung upon my spirits until the new scenes I was passing through displaced it.

My long ride was without notable incident. The country became gradually more wild, and, but for the road, seemed for many miles at a time never to have been visited by man. Through the Nation I passed unmolested. Bango once or twice accomplished two stations, about fifty miles, in a day, but I generally rode only from station to station, as I was in no hurry. Strawberries were just out of season, but the Indians brought in plenty of blackberries for sale at the taverns. After leaving the Nation, the road was even worse and less defined than before, but at last I reached the Land Office at Fort Claiborne, and obtained the surveyors and their party, who had been engaged, and we started on our expedition.

It would be too long and uninteresting to tell my adventures, none of which, except as connected with .

Bango, have the slightest interest even for me. He was a great horse, and before our trip was over I could have sold him for a large sum, or swapped him for any other two horses in the party. He could travel all day upon what he browsed at night, seemed unconscious of thirst, was always to be found when wanted—for he seemed to realize the fact that it wouldn't do to stray off—could swim like an otter, and travel through the dark like a panther. The comical old fellow actually won for himself the admiration he seemed always to be challenging, and I overheard a little Englishman we had along designate me as "Mr. Page, the gentleman what owns the horse which his name is Bango."

Poor Bango, when you died, years afterward, I felt like one in the circle of whose friends a great void had been made, and the thought kept recurring to my mind: And shall he never live again? I can easily understand the Indian superstition. Man is instinctively unwilling to admit that what he has loved is dead forever.

My return home was much the most wearisome part of my absence. The way was long, and though Bango was kept at his best rate of traveling, the miles lengthened as I approached Yatton, until the last three miles seemed as long as any ten I had previously traveled. Besides this, a day or two before our survey was over I had unwittingly handled a vine of poisoned oak (*Rhus Toxicodendron*), and being peculiarly sensitive to its effects, the poison spread over my whole body. Behold me then late one warm afternoon in August riding through Yatton to my father's house. My hat and clothes were in such disorder as to seem of antique cut; my unshaven face was splotched up with hair, and sores from poison oak; Bango, gaunt with his journey, and tired, but with spirit unbroken, sidled along the street, and I looked little like one whose mind was filled with the joyful idea of seeing his sweetheart.

But in the state I was how could I go to see her? It was enraging! I could not shave without flaying myself, and if I could, my face was too swollen for me to hope to excite even pity for a figure so ridiculous. Nature this time stepped in to relieve me from my embarrassment by throwing me that night into a fever, which confined me to my bed and the house for about two weeks, by which time the effects of the poison had worn off, and my power for impatience was somewhat weakened.

One day, about ten days after my arrival at home, my sister Bel came into my room, and I saw by her looks she had something important to tell me; so I said, without preface, "Well, out with it!"

"Who do you think has just left the house?" said she.

"Mrs. Ruggles," said I. "She is very kind. I suppose she came to see whether she could not announce that there is no hope for me, and I am bound to die."

"Oh, brother," replied Bel, "you are too severe upon Mrs. Ruggles. I'm sure she would grieve heartily if you were to die. But it was not she who was here; it was a young lady, and she has been here frequently in your absence, and we have been to see her too, and oh! she is so sweet!"

"Pshaw!" I answered gruffly, "I don't like sweet young ladies. They are generally nobodies. But who was she?"

"Oh, I thought perhaps you might like to hear of

this one's coming.   But it was no one but Mary Mc-
Intyre, who called to ask us to come out to her house
next week."

"Mary who ?   Mary McIntyre ?   Why, bless my
soul, why didn't you tell me that in the first place ?"
I exclaimed in some excitement!   "I suppose you told
her you would come.   Of course you must go, and so
must I.   I'll be perfectly well by that time, certain."

"But, brother," suggested Bel, "you must not expose yourself too soon."

"Expose myself! Oh, no, I'll not expose myself,"
said I, and I added to myself: "as though I hadn't
swam creeks, and ridden through sun and rain, and
night and day, as hard as Bango could stand it to get
to see her; or, as if my fever, or anything but my own
ugly looks, could have kept me from seeing her before
now !"

I got well speedily, and when the day came I was
all ready, and we paid the visit.   And two days after
I went there again alone, and Mary and I took a ram-
ble in the garden together, and when we returned she
had promised to be my wife.   And when we got into
the house we found quite a number of lady visitors in
the parlor, several of them strangers to me, and, after
sitting awhile, I rose and said I must go, and went up
and shook hands with Mrs. McIntyre, and Miss Sarah,
and Miss Lucy, and Tom Merriweather, and Hopkins—
confound him, he couldn't hurt me now—and then, my
embarrassment increasing with the magnitude of the
hand-shaking operation, I went all around and shook
hands affectionately with every lady in the room, to
the intense amusement of Mary's sisters and mother—

though she herself was rather too preoccupied to see the fun of it.

There are some things a gentleman naturally conceals, not because they are ugly, or paltry, but because they are too delicate and precious to be exposed to the careless glance, or to the unappreciative or the vulgar, who would distort them and destroy their symmetry even by an unhallowed look. The very regards of some men and women are a shock to delicacy and purity.

One of the very earliest lessons my father taught me was that the man who kisses and tells is a ruffian, and it has always been my most rigid rule to heed the maxim in both letter and spirit. Much more shall I refrain from exposing the pure and precious love shown me by the woman, the memory of whose love has many a time and often been the only guarantee I have had to myself that I was not myself utterly worthless. The love of a pure and sensible woman is a support to self-respect which it is wonderful so many men forget or despise.

Ay, young ladies! toothless and babbling as the old man now is, he has once been loved with all the ardor of a heart as pure and loving as the best and warmest of yours; gray-headed and withered as he is now, eyes as bright as the brightest of yours, once looked upon him as a fine type of manhood, and hands as soft and beautiful as any you ever saw have toyed lovingly with his glossy hair, and gently patted his cheeks firm with youth and health; and when he grows so feeble with age that he can only support himself erect upon his stick, he will pat himself upon the breast, and say with exultant pride, "I have loved worthily, and been worthily loved!" And when he says so he thinks that he has said all a man need say to prove himself a man, and all that he can say to show that, though he may not have accomplished fame or fortune, he has accomplished the noblest aim of life—to approach the quality and joys of heaven.

(Loving and loved is all Heaven's history.)

CHAPTER XVI.

THIS, the third year of my professional life, I made and collected twenty-five hundred dollars by my practice and the surveying expedition. There was a great deal of litigation and the prospect of its continuance for some years longer—and though some other young lawyers of my acquaintance made more, it was by large fees in chance criminal cases, and floating practice, whereas I had secured a *clientelle* of solid men and men of influence, and could calculate with safety upon an increase rather than a diminution of paying business.

But I attended to my business simply as business, and as a matter of duty. I had no love for the practice of law, though I regarded the science as better fitted than any other for enlarging and liberalizing the mind. The sphere of the physician, the preacher, or the mechanician is noble and useful, but it is contracted, and with the two first, as at present constituted, is filled with doubts and contentions for which there is no judge to decide. There are rules in medicine, and so there are in chess; but in neither the one nor the other does success always follow a precise adherence to them —nay, a precise adherence is often the very cause of failure. The symptoms in both are apt to be mistaken.

There are great fundamental rules in theology also, and the great doctrine of Christianity—the atonement, with its essential accompaniments—cannot be mistaken. But so soon as man begins to be a theologian, and to speculate about what is not clearly and unmistakably revealed in God's word, and attempts with his finite mind to judge God, the whole affair becomes a matter of temperament and the imagination, and he is certain to "darken counsel by words without knowledge."

Whence comes the confusion which has for ages existed and torn in pieces the Christian world, setting brother against brother, father against son, but from this very darkening of counsel by words without knowledge? Instead of humbly receiving the truth as clearly revealed, and humbly using charity toward opinions upon minor questions about which men may differ and yet be true Christians, they presumptuously judge God with regard to those questions, exalt those questions to the highest place of importance, and call upon all men—learned and ignorant, whatever the capacity and bias of each—to bow down to their judgment.

The science of law embraces within it all moral relations, and therefore the whole system of the moral laws of nature, from which no living man is exempt, and it is, therefore, the vastest and most varied of all sciences.

To liken it to Nature herself—it has its shady groves, where all is beauty and peace; its flowery meads, in which the mind may revel in pleasure; its arid deserts, its roaring cataracts, and its cloud-piercing mountains, which one ascends to look upward and upward to the throne of God, with nothing but the limit of his own power of vision to obstruct the view. And one lawyer cannot contend, and say to another, "I see further than you do."

I therefore have always loved the noble science to which I chose to apply my energies—but the practice of the lawyer and advocate has never been agreeable. My soul naturally revolts at discord and confusion; and to see, much more to handle and dissect, the follies and vices of my fellow-men has always given me pain. I never yet took pleasure in the antics or the humor of a drunken man, and though, if I know myself, I am not deficient in the combativeness which becomes a man, I have always had a nervous horror of a quarrel, and, unless compelled by special duty, have always avoided even looking at a brawl.

About this time I was temporarily appointed State's Attorney of my District, and it came into my way to investigate a case of murder, which, with its accompaniments, disgusted me thoroughly.

News was brought into town one day that a man by the name of Glass had been murdered in the northwestern corner of the county, and the coroner summoned a jury, and, accompanied by the sheriff and myself,—whom he overpersuaded to go,—proceded to the place.

It was a rough and barren country—the rural district

of the county—inhabited almost entirely by very poor whites, who among them all hardly owned a dozen slaves, and those almost as far below the slaves of the rich as their owners were below the rich themselves. Small one and two-roomed log-cabins, with a corn-crib and shed for horses, and two or three small out-houses attached, were dotted about on the hills and in the hollows every half mile or so over the district, and in these the families lived. Their fields adjoining were not much larger than patches, and generally extended from near the house down into and along a bottom through which ran one of the very numerous spring branches or small creeks which came together some distance below, and formed Brown's Creek.

Glass's cabin was one of the meanest in the district —consisting of a narrow front gallery, one principal room, and a very small cuddy or shed-room made by the extension of part of the back roof. The roof was of oak-boards hung on to the sheathing-slats by pegs, and confined to their places by heavy poles laid lengthwise across. A low rail-fence, about fifteen feet in front of the house, formed the yard and kept out the hogs and cattle.

When we rode up, we found the wife of the deceased —a sallow-faced young woman, dressed in striped homespun—seated on a low chair in the gallery, with a pipe in her mouth and a young infant tugging at her breast. A white-headed and almost naked little girl, about two years of age, was seated near her on the puncheon-floor staring at the strange assemblage. Another young woman, dressed like Mrs. Glass, and who, I found, was her younger sister, moved about apparently

17*

not ashamed that she was herself very soon to become
a mother.   Old Burdick, their father, and his son Jim
Burdick, were also present, having come from their
home, about six miles off, that morning, upon hearing
of the murder; and five or six of the neighbors, all
dressed in white homespun shirts and pants with knit-
suspenders, and without coats, were lounging about or
seated on the front fence.

The body of the deceased was not at the house, but
had been left lying where it was found, in the path
back of the field, about three hundred yards from the
house.   It is considered in the country to be illegal to
remove or even to turn over the body of one found
killed, until the coroner shall have held his inquest.

After the coroner had sworn in the jury, and all present he thought might be witnesses, we proceeded to
the spot where the body lay in its blood—guarded by
an old negro man, while a neighbor was seated on the
fence some yards off.   After viewing the position of
the body,—which lay on its face diagonally across the
path,—and carefully noting the surroundings, and examining the position and direction of the bullet-hole in
the back, just below the right shoulder-blade, which
caused the death, the body was removed and placed
under a beech-tree in front of the house, and covered
with a blanket.   The coroner then took his place upon
the gallery, and called up the witnesses one by one—
first the old negro, then the wife, two of the neighbors,
old Burdick and his son, and, finally, the sister-in-law
of the deceased.

The negro testified that about sunrise the deceased
left him in the patch near the house, saying that he

would go and look at his coon traps back of the field, and that, about twenty minutes after he left, he had heard him whoop, as though in answer to a call, and presently had heard loud voices, one of which was that of the deceased, and the other unknown; and then, after a moment of silence, had heard a rifle go off; that Glass was unarmed when he left him; that the breakfast-horn blew, and that Glass not coming, it was blown again, and that he was then presently sent to see what had become of him, and he found him lying dead as he was found.

Mrs. Glass had been back of the house, and heard the voices and the rifle shot. She did not recognize the voices, though one of them, she said, sounded like his (Glass's), and the other—well, she did not know, and didn't like to say. Upon being pressed, she said it reminded her of Joe Harlip's voice, but she could not say it was his. She showed little or no emotion, spoke of the dead man as "he" and "him," and never mentioned him as "husband," or Mr. Glass, or by any name of endearment.

Neither of the neighbors knew anything about the circumstances. Glass had been only about four years in the neighborhood. There had lately been some bad talk about him and a certain person—it was best not to name names. He was not a quarrelsome man, and didn't drink more than was general in the neighborhood—they all drank more or less; but he was apt to be mighty reckless when he got to going. One of them saw a man riding through the woods about a half hour by sun, going in the opposite direction from Glass's, and thought he looked like Joe Harlip, but he was not close enough to tell. The man had no gun that he could see, and was not riding very fast.

Old man Burdick was very stolid. He said he knew nothing, and did not wish to know anything about it. He had had a heap of trouble, and his trouble was on him now.   Glass was the cause of it, but killing him did not relieve it.   He did not wish to say anything which might get an innocent man into trouble. Mrs. Glass and Jane were both his daughters. Jane had never been married.   Glass had been mighty anxious to get Jane to come up and stay with her sister, and she had come about eight months before, and had been staying there ever since.   Joe Harlip had been courting her at his house and at Glass's up to about a month before, when he had quit, mighty mad about something, and he hadn't seen him since.

Jim Burdick's testimony was to the same effect. Joe Harlip, he said, had got mighty mad with Glass about something or other, and had not been about lately. He had seen him two or three days before, and he looked mighty grum.   Had not seen him since, and did not know where he was; supposed he was at home.

Jane, the younger woman, was now called.   At the request of the coroner, I had conducted the examinations thus far, and when she was called, he insisted that I should go on.

I do not care to give a detail of her statement, which showed she was shameless. Her sister had for some months been very jealous of her, but with Glass to up- hold her, she didn't care—not she.   Glass and her sis- ter had not been on good terms lately. They all drank whisky sometimes; she herself had taken her toddy with Glass that morning before he started out. She slept in the shed-room, and the jug was kept in there. She had taken two or three other drinks during the day on account of the trouble. She had not seen Joe Harlip for several weeks, and she didn't care that (snapping her finger) for him. When she saw him last he was mighty mad with Glass about her, and swore he would kill him. Glass had been a good man to her —and here she began to cry, and soon got into hysterics, caused by the excitement of the circumstances and the liquor she had drank acting upon her condition.

An examination of the ground around the spot of the killing showed that a horse had been hitched near there, and the print of the butt of a rifle was found at the root of a tree about twenty steps from where Glass had fallen. The murderer had evidently got into a quarrel with Glass, and had got his rifle and shot him as he was moving off.

The coroner issued a warrant for Joe Harlip, but he had left home, and as he was never afterward seen in the county, the case had dropped after the grand jury had found a true bill. Whatever became of Jane and Mrs. Glass, I do not know. I heard that Jane had taken up with a man named Gleeson who soon after came to the neighborhood, but gradually the whole affair, and all the persons concerned, passed off the stage of life.

I have mentioned this affair for two reasons. The first, to show the state of society and morals in the rural districts; and it is a true picture of all the other rural districts on this continent—in the North even worse than in the South—in Europe, and all over the world. The other, to exhibit one of the many causes why I did not like to practice law. Who would like to handle such affairs as this? It is bad enough to hear of such things, and, for my own part, I prefer neither to hear nor see them.

Now I am well aware that in saying this I lay myself liable to the charge of taking a narrow view of life, and giving a weak preference to its pleasures. I shall be told that the true man chooses an object and goes at it as into a battle, fights bravely, takes its pleasures of victory, or, if beaten, never submits.

It is correct to say that the true man always does his duty, whether it be agreeable or disagreeable; and I trust that I have proved myself a true man. Although I have done many things I ought not to have done, I cannot conscientiously reproach myself for ever lacking in my duty of doing what ought to be done. In spite of my dislike to the practice of the law, and, above all, of my impatience of its slowness and uncertainty, I attended to it faithfully during all this period of my life as a solemn duty I owed to my own happiness, and the welfare of my younger brothers and sisters, and the dear one who was so soon to be dependent upon me. The motive was superior to the disgust and impatience, and I worked hard early and late, and all the world said: behold a man who is bound to rise high in fame and fortune! Whether or not I am to be censured for not in after-life fulfilling this prognostication of the world, is a question I will discuss in its proper place. For the present it is sufficient to state that my labors met with such results, both present and prospective, that I was justified in my own mind and in the opinions of my friends in hastening my marriage.

Not many weeks after our engagement, Lucy married Merriweather, and Mr. McIntyre gave her as a dowry the value, in money and negroes, of $25,000. It was to be supposed that, as he could well afford it, he would give Mary no less, for he agreed without difficulty to our marriage—as indeed did Mrs. McIntyre and the sisters. My calculation, then, was that we would start in our joint fortunes with a capital of fifty thousand dollars—for my profession was at least equal in value to Mary's capital. Even allowing that my professional income did not increase, as it undoubtedly must, and Mary's capital only produced five per cent., we would have a yearly income of $3750, which would be amply sufficient to support us handsomely in all events, and, with prudence, by the time I became, in the ordinary course of nature, unable to work, we should be able to provide for our children if we should be so fortunate, or unfortunate, as to have any.

About two miles east of Yatton, on Brown's Creek, was a tract of three hundred and sixty acres of fine land, owned by Mr. James Yandle, who had built upon it a neat and roomy residence with all the necessary out-houses, gardens, and improvements, and had opened about one hundred and fifty acres of the bottom land for a sort of home farm. His plantation was in the lower part of the county on the river, but he lived here so as to give his family the advantages of church and school, and also on account of the superior healthiness of the location. But he was one of the gentlemen for whom I had gone to Alabama, and his ideas had become so elated by the descriptions he had heard (not from me, however) of the new country of El Dorado, that he determined to remove his family there with him as soon as, by making a visit first himself, he could prepare for them. He wished therefore, though I did not know it, to sell his residence, which he called The Holt; and as such a sale could not always be made at a time to suit one's convenience, he was willing to sell at the first opportunity, and remove his family, in the interim, to his plantation.

I had often admired the beauty and convenience of the place, and knew that the bottom land was fertile; but of course though I now desired to own it, I could not propose to Mr. Yandle to sell me what I knew his wife and children loved and had improved with such labor and taste. The man who goes through the world with the opinion that everything has its price, and is but a matter of dollars and cents, is a cold-blooded vulgarian.

Mr. Yandle seemed to appreciate my wants and his own opportunity; and meeting me one day on the street, proposed that I should take the place off his hands. He said that he had no need of ready money, and would give me plenty of time to make the payments, and that as he knew that I and my wife could appreciate and care for the place, he would even let me have it cheaper than he would a stranger, or one who had no taste. After some further conversation we agreed that if Mary consented I would take the place at seven thousand dollars, payable in equal installments in five years, and that I should have possession by the first of December. It was now early in September, and that would give him time to remove and settle his family, and give me time also to get settled on the place and commence with January to prepare for a crop. I had till the next Tuesday to give an answer.

That, Wednesday evening, I went out to Mr. McIntyre's and told Mary my arrangement, and asked her consent to it. Her father was sitting near us, and she appealed to him. "What does he ask, Page?" said he. I told him the terms, and he said they were very fair, and that if Mary liked the place he could see no objection to the purchase. The next day, however, Mr. McIntyre was in town, and when I went to his house Friday evening, Mary handed me the title to the place, made in her name, and paid for cash.

To cut a long story short, Mr. and Mrs. McIntyre also furnished the house and kitchen completely and well, and assigned to Mary a good cook and house girl—both trained under Mrs. McIntyre's eye. Of course I could make a volume of these arrangements by telling how Mary got my opinion about furniture without letting me know why she wished it, how she made me promise to buy no furniture until she should ask me, and how I was slyly consulted with a "suppose this," and "suppose that," about every domestic arrangement, and how, when all was completed, she enjoyed my surprise and pleasure at seeing it; and then about who were the bridesmaids and who the groomsmen, and how it happened that Jenny Preston had taken sick before the time, and Mary Forsyth was chosen in her place, etc. etc. etc.,—all the talk and feelings and arrangements of a young couple about to be married and go to housekeeping—but it would make my "Life" as trashy to read as all of those things are unimportant and common in their occurrence.

I took the trouble a short time ago to analyze the material facts contained in a voluminous book written by a living fashionable novel writer, and actually, except that in the last chapter the parties got married and lived happily ever after, there was not a fact or a reflection in the whole book worth remembering. I can enjoy to follow a rambling writer who always talks sense or pleasant nonsense, but one whose aim seems to have been quantity, and whose book I can close without having a single suggestive thought, or amusing or important fact to remember, is unbearable, however artistic may be the construction of his plot, or however glib and correct may be his style and language.

————

CHAPTER XVII.

SO Mary and I were married.

When a man marries, the mother of his wife, if she be a good and sensible woman, generally weeps, while every one else is madly gay. When a healthy child is born, it is Hip! Hip!! Huzza!!! and all is merriment.

For my own part, I think the weeping mother reasonable, and the careless merriment on both occasions

unreasonable and mistimed. I never yet have had a
great joy but that my soul seemed to shrink with ap-
prehension of sorrow. We often speak of "tears of
thankfulness," or write the fact that one "wept for
joy," without ever reflecting upon the profound meaning and pathos of the expressions.

That a bridegroom should rejoice, or that a father
should be joyful, is most becoming a man; but if he
rejoice without reflection, he is little better than a
mocking-bird or an idiot. The bridegroom who has
due respect and tenderness for his bride; the husband
who really loves his wife, and sympathizes with her
pain and danger; the father who really feels the responsibility of parentage; the man who in sober truth
and earnestness appreciates the sorrows and frailties
and uncertainty of life, must "rejoice with trembling."

To say, then, that I rejoiced at my marriage is
simply to say that I was a man; to say that I was
also thoughtful, is to affirm that I was a sensible man
—which means a man of feeling, quite as much as it
means a man of discretion. Now although I am old,
and perhaps trivial and erroneous in some of my talk,
I never, in my manhood at least, gave cause for being
called either gloomy or weakly sentimental in my feelings, opinions, or conduct. I have met all current
opinions of matters and things in a sturdy paradoxical
spirit, as willing to be convinced one way as another;
just as I have, when duty called me, met the obstacles
of life with a fair stand-up determination to accomplish
the right, if it could be done. I may therefore repeat,
with some degree of assurance that I am correct, a remark I have heretofore made—that the events of hu-

man life, except as they affect the immortal soul, are of all things the most trivial.

Except for this, the death of an ox is of more importance than the death of any man not the property of another; a timely shower of rain is of more real moment than a nation's mourning; and the accurate fit of a young lady's ball-dress of quite as real cause for concern as the adjustment of the balance of power in Europe. Birth is important because it brings a soul into being, to act and suffer. Life and death are of importance because of the manner in which the soul is employed during life, and the time and circumstances of its fate being sealed by death.

Where are the friends of my youth? Dead. Where are the friends of my early manhood? Dead. Where those of my prime? Dead. And their fathers are dead, and their children must all die. Of what importance is it to them whether they have been wise or foolish, rich or poor, good or bad, loved or hated? Their works live after them; the trees they planted flourish, the houses they builded are a pleasant shelter, the examples they set and the lessons they taught still affect others; but their hopes, and joys, and sorrows, their disappointments and pleasures and pains, which made life all in all to them,—where are they?

Does all this sound trite? Know then, oh man, that religion and politics, and all moral relations center in this fact you call trite. Except the plan of salvation, it is the greatest fact you ever knew or can know on earth. If it be trite to you, show by your conduct that you know and appreciate it. You will then be unreasonable in neither your desires nor your disappointments. You shall then perhaps be better able to understand and humbly submit to the government of God; and may possibly see a fitness and propriety in the slaughter of the Canaanites, and in the ravages permitted to conquerors, and committed to pestilences, which shall lead you to admit that at least the Ruler of the world may be just and good as well as powerful and wise.

I may be pardoned these grave reflections when it is remembered that I am writing as a duty which will be ill performed if it do not lead to serious benefit. That I should have married is certainly none of your business. Nor, if my object were to amuse you, would I mention it—for there was nothing funny about it either to myself or my wife. Like every other event worth rejoicing over, it was worth being thoughtful about; and when it is considered that I have been left alone of all who rejoiced at my wedding, the connection between the narration of my marriage and what I have here said will be admitted to be natural.

But of course my feelings, when I pronounced my vows, did not dwell on death and sorrow. They were tender and compassionate, as must be those of every gentleman upon such an occasion.

What a beast the man is who regards his wife as but the morsel for his appetite, or the slave for his comfort! I thank God that I have all my life had a profound respect and tender solicitude for woman, old and young, gentle and simple, for now, in my old age, I am not disposed to retire from the herd to some solitary spot, but can still find rational and pure pleasure in her society.

18*   o

CHAPTER XVIII.

IT was then the usual fashion to marry on Thursday, which gave two or three days to prepare and two days to right-up after the festivities; but whenever it was, for any cause, more convenient, it was in rule to marry on Tuesday. We were married a Tuesday, and moved to our new house on Thursday morning—in the lumbering family carriage, surnamed by the young men in town "The Swan."

The common mode of conveyance at that time, both for ladies and gentlemen, was on horseback, or in gigs, or sulkies hung high on leather and wooden springs. Some few of the wealthiest families had carriages—great unwieldy machines which could run only on the main roads. But these vehicles were so few in number, and therefore so remarkable, that each was named by the young men in town from some fancied resemblance or association. Colonel Stewart's, on account of its rotund capacity, was called "The Globe;" Mr. McIntyre's, from the distance in front at which the driver's seat was placed, "The Swan;" that of Mr. Harkness was "The Mortgage," from its weightiness and the manner in which it had been obtained—and so on.

The negroes given to Mary by her father had been already, the week before, settled by him in their quarters, and put to work repairing fences, cutting briers, and getting fire-wood—under the superintendence of a young man named Tomlinson, who was a good manager; and, by-the-by, became afterward, by luck and economy, a very rich man. There were ten hands—four of them women, with their four husbands, and their children, and the other two young single men.

The yard had been stocked by Mrs. McIntyre with chickens—among which were all Mary's favorites she had raised and taught to love her as their providence—and turkeys, ducks, and guinea-chickens; which, as the first-comers and already habituated, gave their fair mistress a noisy welcome as the carriage drove up.

The house was a frame building, fronting to the south, and built, about six years before, of lumber sawed at Brown's saw-mill, about two miles above us on the creek. It was raised on brick-pillars about four feet from the ground, and had a broad gallery both in front and in the rear. A wide hall divided it in the center, and into it two rooms opened on each side. The two on the west were the parlor and dining-room; the front room on the east we chose as our bed-room, because it gave us the first rays of the morning sun through the screen of forest trees around the house, and was sheltered from the fierce heat of the summer afternoons. The room adjoining was also a bed-room, and with another neat room, which had been added as a wing to the eastern side of the house, at the rear, and opened both into our back room and on the back gallery, and an office in the front yard, about twenty yards from the house, into which I could stow my brothers and their boy friends, gave us plenty of accommodation for all the visitors we were likely to have, for some years at least.

Although I was quite as hopeful a man as my father, I did not have to build my house, and could put off additions to a more convenient or necessary time. For the present, even to the kitchen, which was in the yard at the northwest corner of the house, all was large enough, and in good order.

East of the house, and coming up to within twenty yards of it, was Mary's flower-garden; in which were also fifteen hives of bees I had taken, with the place, from Mr. Yandle. On the northern side of the flower-garden was the carriage-house, as we called it, which contained the bran-new gig I had purchased for our use; and beyond that were the barn and stable, and then came a strip of wood on the side of the declivity, from the foot of which the field stretched to the east and southeast down to the creek. West of the house, and also near it, was my vegetable-garden, in which I soon took great pride and pleasure; and near that on the northwest of the house, about three hundred yards off, was the quarters—behind which were the gardens and little patches of the negroes.

The public road, about three hundred yards in front of the house, ran east from Yatton until it came to my field, which it skirted for a mile to the southeast, where it crossed the creek on a puncheon bridge. There was no fence between the house and the lane through which the road ran, and which was formed by the yard inclosure and the fence of the woods pasture beyond. This land in front of the house was level for about seventy-five yards, and then declined gently to the lane, its surface broken only by several swells and shallow hollows, except on the west, where a deeper hollow ran almost up to the quarters, and gave exit to the water from the spring which supplied my whole family with drinking water. Many of the original forest trees had been left on this expanse, and it was dotted—just far enough apart to allow a luxuriant sward of grass to grow—with oaks and magnolias, poplars and elms, with here and there a sweet-gum in the bottom.

If you should think that I have been too minute in this description of our place, remember, if you please, that it may some day arrive to you, too, that memory, and not fancy, shall bring your paradise to view. Fond recollection is all the old man has of the comfort and happiness of his youth. The house is here still, and I sit, lonely, and write in the bed-room to which, fifty-one years ago, I brought my bride—and with her brought light, and life, and joyful hope. My feeble footsteps take me through the rooms where once the gentle mistress dispensed order and comfort; and along the paths in wood and garden, where she stepped lightly at my side, and ever and anon looked lovingly in my face, as we talked with serious gayety of the improvements we should make to form our home an Eden. The trees which shaded us are here, the roses bloom in the spots she planted roses, and nature is vigorous and smiling as it was when she made it all so lovely to me—but my Love is not here! My Darling! oh, my Darling! where are you? Does your spirit lie unconscious in God's secret place? or does it live happy and hopeful in the plains of heaven? or does it hover near me now, and sympathize with the yearning heart, and long to wipe away the tears which flow down the cheeks of your poor husband? Oh, my precious one! God was good to give us to each other; and I shall not cavil that he took you from me; but it was hard to bear. These many years have I been lonely, oh, so lonely! waiting to join you; and I have feared unholy thoughts, and tried to live an humble, Christian life, lest in the end I should be separated from you; and am so weary! My Love! my Love! my heart is breaking!

CHAPTER XIX.

THE following week came our infair, a grand occasion, at my father's; and then a round of parties in our honor given by our friends in the county, all of which we attended—I, dressed as a bridegroom, in my blue cloth dress-coat with metal buttons, my buff small clothes, buckled pumps, white vest, and ruffled shirt, driving my wife in our gig as proudly as the charioteer of the goddess Diana.

The spring came on open and fair, and under Tomlinson's superintendence, the negroes worked well and quietly. My crop was pitched in season, and came up well. When the spring term of the court came on, I appeared at the bar, and among my fellow-citizens, with the more assured air of a man. It seemed to me I felt a greater breadth and precision of mind than I had ever felt before, and all my business was happily transacted. The practice almost began to be agreeable, as it was for the comfort and happiness of Mary I worked. The familiar tone of my acquaintances and former schoolmates was more respectful, for I was no longer "Abraham Page, the good old fellow, who has nothing better to do than to enter into your pranks, or keep them concealed." I was Mr. Abraham Page, who had a wife, and had become a settled pillar of the State. Even Stanley Ruggles, though he was Mary's relative, became more friendly than familiar, and was alert to sell me ribbons and laces, measure off cloth and cambric, and show a solicitude for my custom; whereas, before, it was, "You Abe, you don't want to buy anything. Where are you going this evening? Let's go around to Squire Carter's!"

My father, too, and my mother and sisters, seemed to feel at last that I was a grown man, and tacitly to acknowledge that I had other cares and other duties than those which clustered around our dear old home.

Every day of my married life I had reason to admire more exactly and to love more tenderly the woman God had given me. Her gentleness was a continual rebuke to my hastiness of opinion and speech; her thoughtful kindness for others kept my selfishness always in shame; her uncomplaining spirit hushed my restless discontent at the little annoyances to which nature and a household are subject; and the sweet sprightliness of her wit, and the delicate playfulness of her humor, were a constant surprise and delight.

In the long hot summer afternoons to lie upon a pallet in the wide, cool hall, and hear the cocks flapping their wings and crowing around the house, and the guineas going about leisurely, or chasing each other here and there in the yard, vociferating po-track! pot-rack! and the English ducks whispering and quacking about the steps, and the pigeons cooing upon the house-top, was almost like a dream of peace and content-ment; and then to have her near me busily engaged at some housewifely sewing, and as her nimble fingers deftly stitched, and snipped, and turned and stitched again, to hear her describe perhaps some visit she had made in her girlhood among her friends, and the grav-ity of this one, the affectation of that, and the offended dignity of the other, until realizing fully how ridiculous the scene was as it came again vividly before her, her merry girlish laughter would fill my soul with tender-ness and pride rather than with mirth, and I would wish in my heart that all the world could see and ad-mire her beauty, and wit, and goodness. Or if she spoke of some quarrel of her girlhood, or we discussed some wrong which had been done her (except what Mrs. Snow had said against me, which she appropri-ated to her own account), to hear her find a good reason for her enemy, and an excuse for the wrong done, was worth a thousand sermons on charity, and did more to soften my asperities than all my reading, prudence, and reflection put together.

Often my sister-in-law, Sarah, would stay with us for a week or two, and either she, or one, or both of my own sisters (and sometimes all three at once), were there always; for I had to be in my office in town every day until about four o'clock in the afternoon, and it would not have done for Mary to have remained alone and unprotected. Lucy Merriweather stayed over-night with us frequently when she came up from her husband's place to shop in town; and every Sunday

that the weather was fair Mrs., and often Mr. McIntyre,
would take with us an early dinner, so as to get home
before night. My two brothers also used to come out
nearly every Friday evening after school, so as to start
early Saturday morning fishing or hunting.

These, with my father and mother, who often came,
and some few intimate friends, were all of our visitors, except those who came to make fashionable
calls.

And so the summer wore on into fall. The rain
had come just when my corn needed it most. My
cotton had escaped blight, and rust, and worms, and
sore-shin, and shedding, and all the enemies and diseases to which cotton is subject, and the hands were
picking full weight all through November. The fall
term of the court showed, too, that I was a thriving
man, for my docket was almost double what it was before, and with paying cases too. But in the midst of
all this prosperity, I had care on my heart. My Mary
had to pass through her first ordeal of maternity; and
when, early in December, I found myself the father of
a perfect and healthy boy, my joy and gratitude knew
no bounds—not so much for the gift as for the safety
of the beloved sufferer.

The desire of man to have posterity is nigh akin to
his instinctive aspiration for immortality, and his
trouble at not having a successor from his own loins
is nothing but a modification of his natural dread of
annihilation. And yet, it is my opinion, there is too
much certain pain, and probable danger, accompanying
the gratification of his desire, to warrant his praying
for it as though he would take no refusal. Whatever

may be his course with regard to other earthly blessings, it seems to me that in view of the safety of the mother and the life, and conduct of the child during its life,—all of which must be taken into count in estimating whether it be a blessing or no—it is good policy in this case to add to his prayer the clauses "if it be best," and " Thy will be done."

I could think at first but little of the child; my thoughts were with the mother, the proud and happy mother, whose greatest joy seemed to be that, though at such risk and pain, she had added to my happiness.

Ah, how little do men comprehend of the love of their wives! How little did I, who loved so well, and, as I thought, so sensibly, appreciate the nature and intensity of Mary's love for me! She would willingly have borne all my pains and aches to have me escape them—as she bravely suffered her own because she thought it was to give me pleasure. If a day were fair, it was well because I could prosecute my plans, or not be exposed to get wet as I rode to and from my business; if it were foul, it was ill because my schemes were thwarted, or my comfort lessened. If she thought I desired a thing it was as though I had ordered it; if she imagined I disapproved an action it was as impossible to be done as though it could not be done. Present or absent from her, my comfort, my likes and dislikes, and my welfare were always in her thoughts to shape her actions.

And yet, if I ever saw a woman capable of discretion—yea, and able to assert her own will upon proper occasions; if I ever knew a woman fitted to guide a man or her child through the snares of life, and even of business, she was that woman. Many a time she seemed to know intuitively what I had not yet discovered, warned me of what I, a business man, had not even suspected, and suggested to me what I just then most needed to know.

In a few weeks she had fully recovered her strength, and her beauty assumed that indefinable gentleness of perfection added by the tender joy and solicitude of motherhood. The child grew to be a plump, good-natured, rosy little fellow, and nestled in my heart, all the dearer that he was my Mary's flesh and blood and pain, and resembled her; while to the inexpressible tenderness of my love to her was added the thought that she was the mother of my child.

There can be nothing more charming than the sight of a young mother with her child where both are bright and healthy. Even when both, or either, shall be sickly there is a sad pathos about it which nothing else presents; but when there is no such cloud to mar the picture, it is simply charming. Her alarmed ignorance of how it should be handled or should be treated for its little ailments, is charming; her brooding love when it is quieted, or when it sleeps, her little jealousies of the attentions of others to the precious object, her offended pride at any seeming lack of attention to it, or of admiration of it, her loving talk, and her grave instructions to it, its helplessness, and often its pleading smiles,—all, can be fitly expressed by no other word than charming.

There was another thing, I well remember, which puts the crowning touch of holiness to this picture of my married life. Mary, though a sprightly, spirited woman, was at all times very humble and trustful in her religious impressions and belief, but now that she felt the destiny of her little one committed to her, she became even more humble and more trustful.

She had said to me one day, soon after our marriage, when she had become sufficiently familiar with me to make such a suggestion : "Don't you think, husband,"—she called me husband, the sweetest word which ever came from beloved lips!—"don't you think, husband, that we ought to say our prayers together? We have so much to be thankful and hopeful for!" And as she persuasively put her arms about my neck, I felt so grateful to the Author of all good, and so dependent upon Him for a continuance of my blessings, that I assented at once. It was embarrassing at first to pray aloud, even with my wife; but that soon wore off, and we ever after kept up the custom. The expression, "O Thou that hearest prayer!" is to me the most touching appeal to God in the whole Bible. Unless man could pray, and knew that God heard and answered prayer, he would be the most unutterably wretched of created beings. Surely, the chiefest torment of hell must be that the damned cannot pray with hope!

But one day,—it was the Sunday our little David was baptized,—when we had come from church, I noticed that she was unusually thoughtful, and sometimes looked at me wistfully; so I asked her what she wished me to do, and she answered with a pleading, and but half-assured air : "Husband, why don't you join the Church?"

As my answer to this question was rather long, and may seem very dry, I will give it in a separate chap-

ter, so that it may be the more readily skipped,—
though it is in reality the most important answer to a
question I ever made in my life.

CHAPTER XX.

"HUSBAND, why don't you join the Church?"
"What Church, my dear?" I asked.

"Why, of course," said she, "I would prefer you
should join the Presbyterian Church, as I am a member of it; but if that does not suit you, join any other
Church you please, so you join some."

"But, my darling," asked I, "why should I join a
Church?"

"That you may obey the command," she replied,
"and acknowledge Christ before men."

"But I do acknowledge Christ before men, my dear,"
said I; "I have repeatedly done so in my speeches and
my published communications to the Yatton Gazette,
and always do so in my conversation when it is proper
or necessary. All who know me know that I have no
other hope of salvation than Christ our Saviour. Why
then should I join a Church?"

"I, for one, believe that you are a Christian, husband; and if you be, why should you *not* join a
Church?" she replied.

"I will tell you, Mrs. Page," said I, assuming a tone
and gesture of mock gravity, for I knew I was about
to shock her life-long prejudices, and instinctively acted

19*

as though I were a little in jest, so as to ease the blow. "I will tell you, Mrs. Page, if you will lend me your ears, which, by-the-by, are very pretty ears, my dear, almost too precious to lend; but let me whisper my reason into one of them. The reason is—because—I—am—a—Christian."

"Oh, husband!" exclaimed she.

"Yes, my dear," I went on, "the reason why I do not join the Presbyterian, or the Methodist, or Baptist, or Episcopal, or Catholic Church, or any other of the so-called Churches, is that I am a Christian, and can not conscientiously do so."

"Oh, husband, how you grieve me!" said she.

"Have a little patience, my love, and do not grieve, but try to understand me. I often talk solemn nonsense or jesting wisdom to you; but I am now in serious earnest, and am giving you my profoundest convictions.

"Do you love me, Mary?"

"Why, you know that I do!" she answered.

"Save me, then, from the penalties of my sins!" I exclaimed. "Please to save me!"

"But I cannot do that, husband. You must work out your own salvation."

"What! can't you interpose in some way for me? have faith for me? be holy for me? Then, upon my word, I think I should be unwise to trust a gross, and, perhaps, a very impure man, young or old, when a refined and innocent woman, with perhaps tenfold his intellect, cannot help me."

"Ah, husband, I knew you were jesting," said she, relieved, and smiling.

"Indeed, and I am very far from jesting, my love. You will admit that you cannot save me; though you should have all faith, all holiness, and should pray unceasingly. Perhaps my baptism may save me? No? Or the Eucharist? No! Well, will joining the Church, and praying and singing, and being preached to, and blessed, and absolved, by priests or preachers in vestments or without them, with lighted tapers and with crucifixes all about, or in bare walls, and with a deal-board pulpit save me?"

"Certainly not," she answered; "nothing can save you but the Spirit of God working faith in you. Christ Jesus is the only Saviour."

"Ah, my wife, you have hit the truth exactly. If I be saved at all it must be by faith in the atonement made by Jesus Christ, and I must have that faith for myself. I stand perfectly independent of every and all other men in the matter, which is purely personal to myself. I answer for my own sins, and am answerable for my own righteousness. Suppose, then, that I have saving faith, and am a true Christian, 'an heir of God, and a joint-heir with Christ,' can the Rev. Mr. Snow or Father Geoghagan be any more justified and more privileged than I? Am I not a Priest and a King? and who can be more a Priest and a King?

"Why then should I lay aside my Priesthood and join a Church as a mere Layman? Why should I lay aside my heirship and become a slave? If I be a King, what man can be my Spiritual Lord?

"It is a contradiction of terms, my dear, to say Methodist Christian, or Roman Catholic Christian— for in so far as one is a Christian he is neither Roman Catholic nor Protestant.

"The grand, fundamental doctrine of Christianity, and that which adapts it to all humanity of every nation and degree, and by which alone it can be expected to conquer the kingdom for Christ, is the Atonement—that Jesus Christ, the Son of God, lived, and vicariously suffered, and died, and rose again, to save men. The Roman Catholics believe this, and so do all men who call themselves Christians, and it is this alone which makes them Christians rather than moral men, to be saved by their own good deeds. If anything besides, though ever so slightly besides, the atonement of Christ, be necessary for man's salvation, then Christ is only partially the Mediator and Saviour. If, in addition to faith in Christ Jesus, I am to believe in Transubstantiation, or Election, or Falling from Grace, or if, in addition to proving my faith by my works, I am to practice certain genuflexions, and prayers, and certain rites and ceremonies; if I am necessarily to have taken the Eucharist, or to have been baptized—then the atonement of Christ is not sufficient!"

"But, husband," she interposed. "Do you not think we should be baptized and should take the Lord's supper?"

"Certainly I do, my love, and every true Christian, if he have the opportunity, will do both. But he will do so because he will love to obey his Lord, and well knows the spiritual benefits he receives by such obedience,—and not because he expects to be saved by either ceremony. He will also obey all the other commands of his Lord, for the same reason, and because if he have faith, it naturally manifests itself by good works. But if he obey with the hope of saving himself by that obedience, he is a slave, and not a true son.

"Now, my dear, if my salvation be purely personal to myself, and if I am to be saved not by my own works, or the works of any other man or men, but only through the atonement of Christ Jesus, why should I join a Church?

"Faith in Jesus Christ alone makes the Christian; and as none are his who have not that faith, and all are his who have that faith, Christ's kingdom is a unit, and his kingdom is entirely a spiritual kingdom. It is a gross error, my dear wife, to suppose that there has to be a temporal organization corresponding with this spiritual kingdom. Nay, it is *the* gross error from which all the rest have sprung. It is the Image set up in the plain of Dura. Here is the Bible, I will turn to the seventeenth chapter of Revelations, the third verse:

"'So he carried me away in the spirit into the wilderness: and I saw a woman sit upon a scarlet-colored beast, full of names of blasphemy, having seven heads and ten horns. And the woman was arrayed in purple and scarlet-color, and decked with gold and precious stones and pearls, having a golden cup in her hand full of abominations and filthiness of her fornication: and upon her forehead was a name written, MYSTERY, BABYLON THE GREAT, THE MOTHER OF HARLOTS AND ABOMINATIONS OF THE EARTH. And I saw the woman drunken with the blood of the saints, and with the blood of the martyrs of Jesus: and when I saw her I wondered with great admiration.'

"Now you know, my dear, that I do not pretend to be wiser than the pious and learned men who have tried to interpret the Revelations; but when I know that these visions seen in the spirit must be taken spiritually, and when I see so many facts bearing out this interpretation. I may, at least, be pardoned for thinking that this error is Babylon 'drunken with the blood of the saints and with the blood of the martyrs of Jesus,' supporting itself upon the civil authority of the State; for certainly the efforts, with the Roman, the Grecian, and the Protestant Churches to establish and maintain this temporal organization, have been in the spirit with which the Image was set up at Babylon, and have been the fruitful cause of all the spiritual and most of the temporal woes which have distracted Christendom in all its ages.

"Look at the progress of Christianity, my love. At first there were churches established at Jerusalem, at Corinth, Laodicea, Rome, Athens, and many other places. These *churches* were simply associations of those who believed in the atonement of Christ for the purposes of mutual encouragement and benefit, spiritual and temporal. They all had unity of faith in Christ, and each had its own internal regulations independent of the others. There were diversities of gifts, but the same spirit. Read what Paul says on the subject in the twelfth chapter of the first Epistle to the Corinthians.

"All the members of these churches, and all other Christians, if any other there then were, were the subjects of Christ's spiritual kingdom on earth. And when the Apostles died, they died without delegating to others their spiritual authority—which was confined to preaching the gospel, and, as the immediate Ambassadors of Christ, and guided by the Spirit, determining questions of faith and practice in order to the establishment of their Master's spiritual kingdom—and they left no prescribed form of government. Had the genius of their religion either allowed or demanded a temporal organization corresponding with the spiritual constitution of Christ's kingdom, do you suppose a matter of such vast importance would not have been carefully provided for by the Master and his Ambassadors? Had it been possible or proper, with regard to the spiritual priesthood in Christ's kingdom, to have designated and qualified successors in authority, do you think they would not have been most unmistakably designated, and most infallibly qualified ? But it was never intended that such an organization or such a hierarchy should exist. Both systems are opposed to the doctrine of personal and individual salvation, besides being the fountains of errors innumerable.

"These different associations of Christ's subjects, then, were a unit in the matters of faith in Christ and love for Christ and each other, though they were far apart and solitary among heathen. But by degrees the gospel spread, the associations became more numerous; those near each other began to form themselves, for convenience and for the strength of union, into confederacies, and that plan working with surprising effects, larger confederacies were formed, embracing all the associations of a State or province, and Rome, Antioch, and Alexandria became the three federal representatives of the church on earth; and other matters than Christ and him crucified were set up as matters for faith, and embraced and denied according to temperament, capacity, or education; and sanguinary as well as spiritual strife was engendered.

"I hope you are not tired, my dear?"

"No, husband; go on, I am interested," she answered.

"In Christ's spiritual kingdom, my dear, there is but one Head—Christ himself. If there be a corresponding temporal organization, there must be also only one head, to preserve order and unity, and from whom shall emanate all power to preach, baptize, etc. Now, who is that to be? The Catholics say the Pope. The Presbyterians say the General Assembly. Some say this, some say that—as they all must say something when they attempt to establish this organization.

"Now, let us see how the scheme has worked, and is working. Men have taken—and when I say *men*, just reflect for a moment what the word involves: a set of creatures weak at their strongest, foolish at their wisest, selfish at their best; creatures who may be actuated by ambition, by pride, by love of money, by every conceivable base motive! Men, according to their temperaments, their learning, their capacities, and the dictates of their selfishness, have taken certain matters of doctrine, some from the Bible, some from tradition, some for convenience, and have elevated them into matters of faith and practice far above the gospel of glad tidings—the doctrine of Christ and him crucified—and thus formed separate churches. This is what was done in ancient days in the formation of the Greek and Latin Churches, and what has been done in more modern times in the establishment of the Protestant Churches;—a vast and necessary improvement in many things, but in the one great point I am speaking of, an insufficient reformation, or rather a change than a reformation. Taking these tenets, in accordance with which they instituted government and forms, they have set them up, styled each of them THE CHURCH, and called upon the world to fall down and worship. The spirit which has actuated them has been one and the same, and it is the spirit of Babylon.

"Now, how does it work? There are hundreds of thousands of men living this day who are inclined to be numbered among nominal Christians, and yet who cannot conscientiously bow down and worship, and are therefore kept from the real spiritual benefits of Christ's spiritual kingdom so far as contained in the ordinances of baptism and the Lord's supper and in 'the communion of saints.' They cannot see the sense of many of these dogmas, and many others of them are repugnant to their reason or prejudices. They cannot become Catholics or Methodists, Episcopalians or Baptists, for the simple reason that they cannot conscientiously subscribe to the dogmas and forms of government which constitute these different and vastly differing sects. Is it to be supposed that the great Head of the Church does not know his own sheep unless they have the mark of some human branding-iron?

"I conclude then that a man may be a Christian without belonging to a sect, and that in view of the tremendous evils accompanying all sects—which means *heresies*—he is the better Christian by holding aloof from them."

"But, husband, how are we to have preaching, and the administration of the Lord's supper, and baptism, and Bible and tract and mission societies, and hospital associations, and all those things, without organization?"

"I did not say, my dear, that there was to be no organization, but merely that the organization should be very different from what it is, and for a very different purpose.

"What do Mr. Snow, and Father Geoghagan, and Mr. Surplice say induced them to preach ? They pretend that they were called of God to that service—nor do I doubt it. But He called them to preach the gospel, which is a unit. They were not called to preach Presbyterianism, Catholicism, or Episcopalianism, which are wholly antagonistic—though the two latter are suspiciously close of kin, from their looks—and if they pretend that they were called for that purpose, I pretend that they were not called of God, and are pseudo-Christians. If they were called of God, the Spirit of God put it into their hearts to seek and to save that which was lost by the only means by which such can be sought and saved ; and if they joined their sects, it was because it was the only means they knew, or had the courage to practice, by which they could obey the call. In so far as they preach the gospel, they cannot differ. In so far as they preach anything else, they go beyond their call, and it is of no material difference to the salvation of their hearers whether they hear and believe them, or disbelieve them, and refuse to hear.

"Suppose, my dear, that every ordained priest and preacher were to die to-night, do you think that Christ's kingdom on earth would have to be abandoned by Him ? Could he not raise up others by his Spirit and providence to preach the gospel of salvation? Ask one of your three reverend friends this question; and if he answer No ! you know that he blasphemes by limiting the Holy One of Israel; and if he answer Yes ! then ask him if the new preachers would all start out preaching Catholicism or Methodism, or any of the other isms; and if they would, which of them they would choose!

"I suppose you have read, my dear, how some wise men once determined to find out which was the original language of the earth, and shut up an infant where he could hear no sound of speech, until he arrived at the full age of speech, and how, one day, when his attendant went in to carry him his food, he exclaimed Bac! which being the Phœnician (or some other language) for bread, the wise men concluded that the Phœnician, or the other, was the original language. It would hardly be worth while to kill all the preachers in order to try a like experiment as to which is the right sect—since they are all wrong.

"When this great error of a temporal organization to correspond with the spiritual organization of the church, together with all the evils which spring from it, is put down, and Christ and him crucified is preached, and his spiritual kingdom is alone aspired to, there will be an end to Jesuitism, Abolitionism, Arminianism, and all the other 'isms' which exist, and are powerful by means of the error.

"The same Spirit which now calls men to the ministry would then call them, and make the call effectual.

"But with regard to the administration of baptism and the Lord's supper, where do you find in the Bible that one has to be ordained Priest, Bishop, Elder, or Deacon to administer either? According to the very genius of Christianity, as I have already shown, and as is as clearly taught as any other thing in the Bible, every true disciple of Christ is an heir of God, a member of the spiritual priesthood—which is the only kind of priesthood recognized under the new covenant dispensation—and if the disciples of Christ, laying aside their differences, and actuated by the spirit of Christian charity, should organize in every village and neighborhood, as the original Christians did, for mutual encouragement and growth in grace, and should select those among them best fitted by grace to preach and attend to the internal concerns and charities of the association, they could have the commands of our Saviour about baptism and the Eucharist performed in decency and with unquestionable and unquestioned authority and propriety.

"As for your Tract Society, and all that sort of joint-stock commercial speculation, it has not half so much to do with Christianity as it has with keeping down the prices of books and printing, and not nearly so much to do with the Church of Christ as it has with Printers' Unions, and the spread over the earth of Yankee and English calicoes and flannels. If the Christian people of the land wish to print Bibles, let them individually contribute to do so, or form joint-stock commercial companies for that purpose. And if they wish to send missionaries to foreign lands, let them send those who will preach Christ alone and him crucified. The Presbyterians and Catholics, and others interpret very liberally when they send propagandists of their peculiar doctrines of faith and church government instead of propagandists of the gospel."

CHAPTER XXI.

IT was not many days after this "talk," that Mary said to me: "How sorry I am, husband, that you dislike preachers so much!"

"Dislike preachers! Why, my darling, what put such an idea into your head?"

"I thought," said she, "from your remarks the other day, that you disliked them."

"Then you greatly misunderstood me, my dear," said I; "and there is one of the evils incident to attacking a class or system. If you attack a class, say of priests or preachers, for flagrant errors, you are pounced upon as an infidel—witness Gibbon, the historian—and if you attack a system, you are accused of hating some one or all of its disciples.

"Now, my dear, while no one fears and dislikes any form of hierarchy more than I do, there is no one who more respects a gentleman, or an earnest man, however he may be mistaken, particularly if he be earnest in a desire to do good. I confess that I do not like your acquaintance old Pisgah Barnes."

"Do not call him my acquaintance, husband, I did not invite him here."

"Nor did I, my dear. I found him here when I came from town, very much at home on the gallery quarreling with Jack about the manner in which he had curried his horse. Upon inquiry, I found that he had arrived and taken possession about noon, ordered his horse to be fed and curried, hurried up dinner, and refused to have you disturbed, as he said you were not perhaps——"

"Oh, husband, you ought to be ashamed of yourself; that was months ago, and——"

"I know it was, my dear, and I understand that the man is as great an old gossip about——"

"Do hush about that, Mr. Page," said she, blushing and annoyed.

"Certainly I'll hush, Mrs. Page, though I see nothing for you to be ashamed of. But the man is no gentleman who concerns himself about the affairs of other people, or who takes advantage of his position to thrust himself upon them, or to lecture them as he did me for saying that I thought the English laws of Mortmain ought to be the law in every country, and, besides, that no one should be allowed to leave money or property by will, either absolutely or in trust, to any religious body. To have heard him, one would have thought I was worse than an infidel. Then the manner in which he persecuted me to subscribe to the Pisgah Seminary was ungentlemanly. He had evidently taken stock of my means, and he prescribed how much I ought to give, and when I told him I could not give so much, he pooh-poohed me, and sneered at me in a most savage way, and actually treated me as though I intended to swindle him. Really, my dear, it is rather too much to ask me to like or respect a man who ought to be kicked into good manners! But, to show you how very liberal I am in my sentiments, I will acknowledge that I respect the man's energy and earnestness, and have very little doubt of his honesty

and of his ability to do much good in the way he pro-
poses, though he be such a fool, and so unchristian in
the ordinary courtesies of humanity."

"But, husband, Mr. Barnes—old Pisgah, as you call
him, is only one man——"

"True for you, my dear. He is fortunately only one
man, though he has already had four wives. A few
more such would ruin any sect in the country. He
differs materially from your other acquaintance, the
Reverend Jimpson, who seems earnest about nothing
except eating and drinking; and Parson Elvin, who
is a perfect Boanerges on the stump, and the very Reverend Mr. Sikes——"

"You select those men who are very much disliked,"
said she.

"Certainly, Mary, and I select them for a purpose,
to show you that even if there be any virtue in the
laying on of 'prelatical fingers,' it is very often most
mistakingly applied. Merely to be a preacher is no
passport to heaven, nor should it be to privileges in
society not allowed to other men, however pious and
earnest may be the preacher. In so far as a man is a
Christian he is a gentleman, for he has the humility
and respect for others, and the charity toward others
which Christianity inculcates, and true gentlemen
practice.

"Now I do not know any better Christian or gentleman than the Rev. Dr. Hatton. He is no busybody
in other men's matters. He shows deference with self-
respect, charity without ostentation, piety with cheerfulness. If he can speak well of a man he does so
without the air of patronizing; and if he be forced to

speak ill of him, he does so as gently but firmly as possible, and, while he is just, almost exhausts charity to excuse him. He is one of those who are in season and out of season (if there be any such thing) in doing good, and may be found, modest but energetic, wherever good is to be done to the sick and suffering in soul or body. In the pulpit he is grave and earnest, and brings forth things, both new and old, out of the treasury of his learning, to assist him in expounding the gospel. And, if you will notice, my dear, he always preaches the gospel. Whatever the text, the gospel is made to expound it, or it is made to expound the gospel. And with all his goodness, such is his quiet dignity that I have yet to see the man who would willingly insult him.

"He is my model preacher, my dear, and I will even acknowledge that there are some like him in all denominations of Christians (am I not charitable?); but how does that mend the matter so far as my argument of the other day is concerned?

"You never heard Dr. Hatton, nor shall you hear any of those like him, preach anything but the gospel. And here, my dear, I wish you to note one thing: the more earnest, learned, and experienced the preacher the more he confines himself to the gospel, pure and simple. It is your fledgling youngsters, your boobies, or your hypocrites who dwell upon controversial points as a practice.

"Now, Mrs. Page, will you be so kind as to tell me what good it does Dr. Hatton and the others like him to be Presbyterians or Methodists, Catholics or Protestants—except that they have thereby been ordained to preach, and have been put in a position to receive a call or an appointment, and make a living? Is it not rather a hinderance to them? The peculiar tenets of their different churches might as well not exist for all the illustration they get from them in the pulpit. They are held merely as matters of personal opinion which have nothing to do with that preaching which saves souls—the preaching of Christ and him crucified, which is above all earthly wisdom, and surpasses in importance and interest all metaphysical learning and distinctions.

"And do you suppose that if there were no Methodist, Presbyterian, or Catholic Churches, or if Dr. Hatton and his peers were excommunicated from them for heresy, they would not still preach the gospel? And is it not certain to your mind that if the barriers of the sects (their foisting of rites, ceremonies, dogmas of faith, and peculiarities of church government, as though they were matters of importance) were thrown down, and the fold was turned into one, just as there is one Spirit, and one calling, "one Lord, one faith, one baptism, one God and Father of all who is above all and through all and in all,"—I say, is it not certain that if this were the case, and all men were told : You need not believe in the Pope, the Mass, or go to the Confessional; you need not subscribe to the doctrines of Election and Predestination ; you need not believe in the Apostolic Succession, or in surplices, or wax tapers, or genuflexions; you may believe or not that you can fall from grace, or that infants should or should not be baptized ; you may believe just what a conscientious study of the Bible leads you with your differing temperaments, educations, and capacities to believe; all that is required of you is to believe truly in the Lord Jesus Christ as the only Saviour of sinners, and ye shall be taken into the Church militant, with a fair prospect of being hereafter received into the Church triumphant,—is it not absolutely certain, I say, that in this case thousands would volunteer as the subjects of Christ, and would obey the commands of Christ and be baptized, and partake of the communion of his body and blood with all the spiritual benefits which flow from an intelligent compliance with these commands, who now stand without, unable conscientiously to enter the visible fold, and consequently unable to obey these commands?

"This is a long question, my dear, but is it not a very pertinent one?

"You, in common with most Christians, have a strong belief in a Millennium to come; and all Christians have a strong desire to see the universal spread of Christianity. (How can there be a Millennium (I use the ordinary expression), so long as the kingdom of Christ upon earth is so split up into little provinces at desperate war with each other?) Do you not know that a Protestant Christian regards a Catholic Christian with suspicion, to be regarded in turn by the Catholic with pity and contempt? Do not Parson Surplice and Father Geoghagan think in their hearts that Mr. Snow's baptism of our son the other day was unauthorized and void? whereas every man, who exercises his own common sense and takes the Christian religion in its essence as his only criterion, knows that baptism is a mere form, which may be authoritatively and effectually administered just as well by my father or any other true believer as by Pope, Prelate, or Presbyter? Does not Father Geoghagan believe—or, at any rate, does not his church teach—that our marriage, though legal according to the laws of the land as a civil contract, still lacks that binding spirituality the church can alone confer? and that therefore—for it is the necessary consequence—our son is a sort of bastard?"

"Oh, husband, they can't think that! You are always following consequences, as you call them, to some ridiculous conclusion, which puts you in a high glee."

"Ah, my dear, the *reductio ad absurdam* is the fate of every religious tenet of human invention. Men who build of wood, hay, and stubble, though it be upon the sure foundation, must expect their work destroyed, and laughed at in its destruction.

"The safest criterion that I know by which a Christian can determine whether an article of faith or practice be correct, is to ask himself: does it in any degree militate against my personal responsibility to God? or does it in any degree militate against the perfect sufficiency of the atonement of Christ for my salvation? and if it do either,—if it imply that some other can do for you (that is, be holy, or faithful, or prayerful, or energetic for you) what you must do for yourself—or that some other thought, word, or deed is to be added to the atonement of Christ for your salvation,—you may set it down as a hurtful error. And though it militate against neither, if it be a matter indifferent to either, and be not an express command of the Master, it is a nonsensical error.

"This is the true meaning of the saying, that 'a man should believe only what his reason approves.'

"If a man should tell me that I must repent as well as believe, I try the doctrine, and find that it is correct; because my reason tells me that, though it appears that some additional act is demanded upon my part, the repentance is not an act which saves me but an act which enters necessarily into the acceptance of an offered salvation in which I believe. It is only another form of saying, by faith you shall be saved—for faith involves the repentance as well as the belief.

"And so, my dear, of everything else in religion. The first principles must be always borne in mind. If you lose sight of your premises, your conclusions must be either ridiculous or monstrous."

"There is one thing I wish to ask you, husband; you do not object to my being a member of the church, do you ?"

"Certainly I do not, my darling. On the contrary, I am glad of it for several reasons. I do not see how a woman, with her peculiar affections and trials, can get along without religion to support her; and I do not know how, as matters stand, she can gratify her religious longings and necessities without being a member of some sect—for the sects have a monopoly of religious exercises."

"Well, but, husband, Mr. Snow would allow you to commune, if your conscience impelled you to do so; and you could also join his church without any profession, save of your faith in Jesus Christ."

"Indeed ? Then Mr. Snow must have been copying after Dr. Hatton, or some of the old and really spiritual fathers of his sect; for, unless I be very much mistaken, the invitation to commune given from the most liberal pulpits includes only those who belong to that sect, or who are of good and regular standing in some sister sect. And, besides, suppose that he would not require me to subscribe specifically to the peculiar tenets of his sect in all matters of doctrine, would I not, to all intents and purposes, subscribe to them if I joined the sect?"

"Why, no, you would not. You could believe what you chose about them."

"If I did, my dear, I should have to do so as a hypocrite or a coward; for, if I attacked any one of them, I should be under authority, and should be pretty apt presently to find myself disciplined, as they call it, and expelled from my membership, as an outcast from the fold as well as from the sect.

"Now, Mary, there is one final suggestion I wish to make. Hereafter, when you read your Bible, the epistles especially, read in the light of what I have been saying about sects, personal accountability, and faith; and about the only *peculiar* doctrine upon which Christianity is founded, the atonement of Jesus Christ; and you will not only agree with most that I have said, but will find a unity and comprehensibility you did not find before."

CHAPTER XXII.

WE spent our lives in home-work, home-pleasures, and homesome talk. Although Mary, with her beauty, intelligence, and amiability was one a husband would be naturally proud to present in the world, we, neither of us, cared for the company of strangers, or to go any more in public than the very necessities of sociability demanded. We belonged to a coterie of estimable friends with whom there was a constant interchange of sociabilities and friendly offices, but although fashionable society was so much more modest and quiet in its exigencies then than now, we, neither of us, fancied it.

Mary, of course, always dressed as near the reigning fashion as good taste would allow. Her taste was exquisite, and, like all true women, she had an instinctive horror of the odd and *outrée.* I have always thought that it was a woman's duty to follow the fashions as far as she can with decency and honesty. There are some fashions which are not decent, and some which a woman cannot follow with an honest regard for her means; but, otherwise, she should be fashionable, even if it led to muffling her face, or wearing nose-rings. You will rarely find a fashion which, either strictly followed, or slightly modified, does not add to a woman's beauty or gracefulness, and it is just as much her nature and her duty to make herself pleasing to the eye of man, for whom she was created, and, particularly, that of her husband, if she belong to one, as it is to refrain from making herself positively disagreeable in appearance. In the name of nature, then, let her beautify herself, so she restrict herself to the rules of decency and honesty; I do not say the rules of modesty, for fashion seems to set the rules for that among the fashionables.

For my own part, when I was a young man, what other men's sisters and wives chose to add or leave off in the way of dress or ornament, never concerned me disagreeably; and I never saw a healthy young woman who had not some beauty, either natural or artificial. But still I think that decency is the best guide. (The "beauty unadorned" doctrine is an æsthetic heresy.)

I concerned myself very little, however, with society, or fashion. My books and practice, my farm and farm-yard, and my wife and little boy, gave me plenty of occupation and amusement.

The little fellow seemed, from his first beginning to notice, to regard me with peculiar complacency and a rare degree of faith—as though I were some pet giant who had to be ruled gently, and without any manifestation of fear. Even before he could talk, he and I were great cronies, and fully sympathized with each other in all our pleasures and troubles.

I may be called childish and silly, but the three objects which from my earliest years I have found most comical, have been: a hen, in anxious indecision stretching out her neck and stepping backward and forward and sideways, and then at last flying shrieking up to her roost; a duck, in a like state of indecision about jumping down from a step, or other elevation; and a little child, trying in vain to insert the point of a stick in a somewhat smaller hole in a piece of bark or pasteboard.

It is really not worth the while to try and analyze the whys and wherefores of this, but no scene on the stage has the power so to tickle my soul as either of these sights; and the busy, patient earnestness with which my little son, seated on the floor, would pursue this occupation in vain, often served to amuse me and to keep him quiet for an hour or two at a time. It was only necessary to show him how I could perform the operation with a smaller stick, and then to give him a larger, and at it he would go. Then I could discourse to his mother about him.

"My dear," I would say, "that boy of ours is bound to be a great man. He has the sound mind in the sound body. Look at his patience! see the energy of that movement to force the stick through the bark whether or no! I think he will become a great engineer. He already shows genius for the business. Why, my dear, in a few years he will be positively dangerous. As sure as can be we shall wake up some morning to find our house moved over to yonder hill, or elsewhere, as the notion takes him. I don't know, either. That examination he is giving looks very like a doctor's. What do you say to his studying medicine? It runs in my family, you know. There, he has turned his stick end for end. I'm afraid my dear he will be a lawyer after all."

This, I think was the happiest era of my life. I presume that every man who has passed the age for active pleasures, can look back at some particular period and say: then, I was happy. Happiness is like a swift rolling river; most beautiful when it is before you, and after you have passed it. At least, the sense of insecurity in its passage has always made it seem so to me. Here was I, a young and healthy man, with no vice to trouble me, prospering in the good opinion and wealth of the world, with a lovely and loving wife, and a healthy and perfect boy. What can any man hope for on earth nearer perfect happiness than this?

And yet, in the short summer evenings, when my fat and rosy little boy, tired with the heat and activity of the long day, was laid in his little crib beside our bed, and his mother busied herself about the closing duties of housekeeping, I would go and sit upon the front steps alone, and the old vague melancholy of my childhood would come upon me, and settle and darken like the coming night. As the last tint of day would fade in the west, the whippoorwills commenced their cries from valley and hillside; the bleating of the calves and the lowing of their mothers would cease; the chickens and turkeys would quiet themselves upon their roosts, some little chick now and then by a faint peep betraying its annoyance at being disturbed by some restless neighbor; the geese, squatted in company upon the grass lawn, would betray their presence and life by occasional low-toned questions and answers, or by the moving of some restless one to another spot; and as the darkness became deeper, the watch-dogs' bark would ring faint from distant farms; and with the shimmering light of the stars faintly shadowing the earth, and trees, and hills, the jarring crickets and katydids from the surrounding hedges and bushes would fill the ear with sound, which by its monotony would soon become unnoticed, and the mellow light of the glow-worm would here and there illumine the dewy grass; and then I would sit all alone and abstracted, brooding over myself. I would seem to myself to be in a great void in company with my thoughts, and fears, and cares, and hopes, and happiness, which would all present themselves for analysis and comment; and the void was dark, and I was helpless.

I would fain linger all my life in the memory of these days of my life. Even the melancholy which would sometimes overwhelm me has now a pleasant airiness about it like the faint discords which occasionally heighten and make strange the sweetness of a strain of music. I would all the rather linger here, that these days passed so quickly, and were followed by a woe to which all other misery must be as a sorry tale soon told.

As I have been writing a true history of the past, and not a fiction, I have naturally rejected the arts by which interest is held in suspense, and sorrow is surprised and taken captive. The fearful thought has been constant with me, since I first began to write, that I should have to renew my great grief by telling it, and I have cast about for some way to avoid it; but man can never shun his calamities, nor avoid the memory of them. At any rate, it cannot injure me, an old man, to recall once more a sorrow which must soon be laid with me in the grave, but never, like me, to rise again. But though I recall it, what language shall I use to describe it? Language cannot describe the supreme agony of grief, for the human mind cannot contain and realize it. Upon the Mount of Olives our Saviour found his disciples "sleeping for sorrow." Man dies of grief, goes crazed of grief, and sleeps of grief, because his mind and body cannot bear its full load; how, then, can he describe it in adequate terms? If perchance he survive it, and "go softly all his years in the bitterness of his soul," he does not willingly renew its agony, nor attempt to expose to others its particulars. It seems like sacrilege.

I had rather think of my Mary in heaven, or blooming with health and radiant with goodness here on earth, than think of her sweet face as it lay pallid and cold in death before me. I had rather try to imagine her voice joining in the glorious songs above, or in my fancy hear its loving accents again, and its sweet tones singing her favorite hymns in the evening dusk or humming a lullaby to her baby, than try to recall the feeble whispers of her sickness, the wandering wildness of her delirium, and the last sighs in which her life expired. Her words, her delirium, her last sighs, her pallid face, and her grave, are ever before me. I can still hear the first clods of earth jarring my very soul as they fall upon her coffin. I can still see my house all desolate as when I returned from the grave, with the funeral confusion not yet removed, the half-empty medicine bottles, the spoons, the cups, the basins still upon the shelves and tables. I can still see in yonder bed the last impress of her form after she was removed from it to be shrouded and laid in her coffin. I cannot escape these sights and sounds. As I carry my food to my lips, one or the other will strike my heart with a pang so sharp I wish to cry out. As I go along the street, or am conversing upon business, or am in the midst of social pleasures, they come upon me like an avalanche, and I would fain rise and rush away. And in the deepest sleep of the night they rouse me suddenly with alarm, and I fall back upon my pillow with groans and stifled shrieks, almost fainting.

No, my Darling, I cannot describe the sorrow I have felt, nor shall my memory ever again seek to recall the precious wreck of your fair body. Sleep on, my Love. If there be sweetness in the grave, I shall find it at your side, and if there be happiness in heaven, it shall be doubly blessed when shared with you.

CHAPTER XXIII.

THE light of my life was gone, and thenceforward I have walked in shadow. Like one who passes through a long covered bridge, the brightness of the past with the beautiful objects it shone upon still exist only in my memory, and away before me a faint spot of light has been growing larger and brighter, until I know I shall soon enter into the perfect day. Or, rather, like one whose sight has been weakened by disease, although the scorching sun has beamed upon me, the present has seemed confused and blurred with everfitful spots of light and gloom, while the past and future have alone shone with steady, natural light.

I do not know that I became insane, or that I am not so now. Nature has still to me its just proportions and true colors. I have forgotten nothing. I can still read and understand and enjoy the ideas of others. My powers of analysis and synthesis seem to be unimpaired, and I can investigate the relations of truth and of all narrated facts and ideas as clearly and conclusively as I ever did. My affections have been as warm as ever, and my conduct has been such as at least conveyed no idea of insanity to those who knew it best. And yet that I am not insane now, or that I was not insane before my great sorrow, is more than I can say; for certainly a great change took place, though why it took place, and in what it consisted, would be hard to determine.

Insanity is, after all, only a relative term. If a man persistently cultivate, for the amusement of himself and others, blasphemy of speech and imagination, he is not called insane; yet if he be flighty about business matters, a guardian may be appointed for him, or he may find himself in a mad-house. Now, the fact is that the wicked man is the more insane of the two. One man is always in a fever of ambition in his trade, his profession, his pursuit of some object which inspires fame; another is utterly careless and stupid in his interest in his trade or pursuit. Which is the more insane? Do not both manifest unsoundness of mind—real derangement of what reason shows to be a healthy condition of mind?

It is not a mere extravagant proposition, made to excite surprise or admiration, to say that every man is insane to some degree. The man whose judgment was always just, whose passions and affections were always equable, whose appetites were never rebellious, whose will was always to do what was best for others as well as for himself, and who had no hobby of faith or practice—if he had any judgment, passions, appetites, and will—would be the greatest wonder that has yet appeared as a mere man.

But though the proposition be not false, it belongs to a species of metaphysical or psychological hair-splitting which is much resorted to in modern days, which cannot possibly do any good, and which rather shows that the man who indulges it may have good personal reasons for his belief.

Since I arrived at a knowledge of the true value of facts, great rugged facts, in morals, I have had little patience with the arts which pry into them with microscopic designs, or seek to polish laboriously some rough corner of them. Eternity, and not Time, is the place to cultivate those arts. Truth has no need of ingenuity for its support, and casuistry on earth is the devil's work; as in heaven, it may be the work of saints throughout eternity.

The change which took place in me was, I am inclined to think, rather a modification than a derangement of the constitution of my mind. What was before most desirable, lost its allurements; and some things which were formerly very disagreeable, became best suited to my state of mind.

The fact is, that, although I have set myself the task of displaying my life as it actually existed and acted, there is a period of six years from the beginning of the last illness of my wife, so filled with numbing sorrows, that I must, for my own sake at least, pass over it as speedily as possible.

My dear old father died, Mr. McIntyre died, my noble little boy, who, from the death of his mother, was inseparable from me, took scarlet fever—that most dreadful of diseases—and died; and my elder sister, who watched over and nursed him, and my younger brother, Joseph, caught it and died.

And I took my journey through all that outskirt of the realms of woe, clad in its sombre livery, like one whose home was there. Even the last accents of my son, who in his delirium said: Papa come! and sighed and died, could bring but a woeful, wistful smile upon my lips.

Let me illustrate what I say by an incident which took place in Yatton some years afterward.

A terrible epidemic fever was raging, and numbers, of all ages and classes, were dying every day. The physician of the town, who had by far the largest practice, and was deservedly one of the most esteemed citizens of the county, was kept going night and day. He was a man of prodigious powers of physical and mental endurance, yet even he was so worn down he would fall asleep on his horse or in his buggy while going only a few hundred yards, or even while feeling the pulses of his patients. His own wife and his two children presently also took the disease, and then he had no rest. I have actually seen him have to rub red pepper in his eyes to stimulate the lids to open when it was necessary to measure out medicine, for otherwise he would feel his way about the room for what he wished. At last his youngest child died, and I, assisted by three or four others, buried it. He was present at the grave, but, though I knew he was devotedly attached to the child, he showed no feeling. When the grave was filled, I went up to him, and took his hand,

and said: "Doctor, I sympathize very thoroughly with you."

"I know you do, Page," said he, "but I can't feel. I lost all feeling some days ago."

And he went about his toil again as though sickness and death were the sole task of life, and too much of course, to call for sorrow or comment. When the epidemic and its excitement were withdrawn, which was the case, in a great degree, a very few days after, he was prostrated—that is the word—for several months. The wonder to me was that he ever rose again.

His expression, "I can't feel," has often recurred to me. (Numbness of feeling is nature's refuge from the sirocco of grief, and the pangs of death. Blessed be God for his goodness to his poor creatures even in the extremity of his wrath.)

I will then leave these six years of my life to their gloom, merely adding two facts which may be necessary to the full understanding of what I have subsequently done, or may yet do.

The first is the only pleasant thing I can recall in all that time. My sister Bel, who was engaged to Joseph Preston at the time of our father's death, married him, quietly, some six or eight months afterward, and in about a year presented her husband with a fine girl, who, I may here say, lived, and became the mother of my present and only grandniece, Miss Perkins.

The other fact concerns my property and affairs. So long as my son lived he was his mother's heir, and I preserved and tried to improve her property for his sake; but when he died, just after his Grandfather McIntyre's death,—although the property was mine,—it was irksome to me to keep that which others might think was but a slice out of their own loaf. I do not say that Tom Merriweather or his wife, or Mrs. McIntyre, or Sarah—who had married Carter Brooks—had any such thought; for they were, and I wish their descendants to know it, at all times as kind and even affectionate to me as though I was of their own blood; but I knew that Mrs. Ruggles had suggested, in her way, that "with Mary's property, Mr. Page is very well off; and is already fitted up, and in a position to take another wife." Besides this, my love for Mary had been so unselfish that it was rather a matter of pride and devotion with me to show that I had no desire to profit in my estate by what she brought me. But to give up to strangers the house she had hallowed and beautified, was more than I could consent to do; so I returned to Mr. McIntyre's estate the amount of the purchase money of the place, and all of the hands who were willing to leave me. Martha, the cook, and her husband, Jack, who was my hostler and man-of-all-work, three of the men and two of their wives did not wish to go, and I had their value assessed and paid it also into the estate—not all at once, but in two installments. As to the increased value of the place, I justly considered that it was the result of my own exertions and Mary's taste; and as to the furniture of the house, which had been presented to Mary, I returned its value in presents of the like kind to the different members of her family.

Of course I could not make all this restitution without remonstrance and opposition from Mary's family, who, I am sure, did not desire it—and rather feared that it should place them in a somewhat delicate position; yet who, I am equally sure, from my knowledge of human nature, could not really regret to see their means increased, and secretly thought, after awhile, that they were under no obligations. Even Mrs. Ruggles allied herself to the spirit of the family, and concerned herself vastly about what "my (her) family" wished and did not wish.

Whether she thought that I was performing an act of such superhuman virtue that her Stanley could never rival it, is more than I know. But I do know that she very adroitly manœuvred to checkmate my move, if it were so, by hinting, with much solicitude, that perhaps I was deranged.

The good woman made a mistake, if her idea was that my act was an effort of virtue. After thoroughly analyzing my motives, I long ago came to the conclusion that they were all selfish. I have stated some of them; but there was one which lay deeper still, in the constitution of my mind, which perhaps had more to do with my act than any other.

I declare that if I had a million pounds sterling, and had to take the trouble and anxiety of its safe investment and judicious management, I would willingly relinquish it for a stipend secure in its source, and giving no trouble about its collection; or, rather, I would speedily and purposely spend it until I could reduce a portion, however small, to as perfect security in its preservation and yield as is compatible with human affairs.

I had no one dependent upon me; for my mother and brother Eldred had a sufficient support, and my only sister was married to a man of considerable property. With my home, I could, by my own exertions, provide the little I needed; and the annoyances of managing a lot of negroes—having to settle their disputes with each other, and their infractions of law; to be, in fact, responsible toward God and man for their health, conduct, and morals—was more than I was at all inclined to undergo merely for my own benefit. I have always thought that wealth was dearly purchased by the loss of content and quiet, and I never have been able to sympathize with those who make wealth, considered as wealth, a good thing in any degree. Why should I toil, and torment myself for myself?

It does very well to talk about philanthropy and public spirit and exerting natural talents for philanthropic and public objects, and I agree that a man does owe to his fellows a just return for the benefits he receives from them. But is it to be pretended that because a man should not bury his talents he should therefore make himself miserable? Now, a man, whatever his talents, owes before God his first duty to himself; and the manner in which he has exerted his talents for his own moral benefit is what he shall be required to answer for. It will be vain for him to plead that he has done great things in music, painting, oratory, medicine, law, architecture, or any other branch of art or science, when he is brought to account for the faith, charity, and justice in his own heart toward God and his fellow-men. He will be answered: "These ought you to have done, and not to leave the other undone."

No universal rule can be laid down as to what is the proper degree of exerting one's talents, except that founded upon common sense: that he should cultivate and exert them with due reference to more important duties to himself and others. I know one who has a very extraordinary talent for painting; but to cultivate and exert it to the utmost would be to the injury of her eyesight, and the neglect of her duties to her family. I, myself, have had good talents which would have made me an eminent lawyer, a wealthy man, or a successful politician; but it would have been at the expense of my peace of mind, and my good feelings to my fellow-men. If I thought it best to content myself with a very moderate fortune, and the exercise of my abilities only so far as was necessary to secure that fortune, and for the performance of my engagements or obligations to others, who can blame me? I have no child, and no man can say that I have wronged him to the value of a cent by my choice of conduct, or that by it I have been lacking in charity toward him; and I certainly cannot say that I have done myself an injury, for I have in consequence of it been a comparatively contented man.

There was still another motive which, though it may appear trivial, yet I know exerted a strong influence in determining me not to reserve Mary's fortune. I was actually afraid that I would marry again, and was jealous that any other woman should profit in property by her death, and jealous also lest any other woman should be allowed by my weakness to interfere with the sacred memories associated with every object her beloved hands had arranged or adorned. Though I had been almost perfectly happy in my marriage, I had a reasonable fear that it might not be so a second time;

had a natural dread of undergoing the suffering of losing a second wife, if she should be a good one; and knew that I was still a young man, and that I had rather a facility for falling in love. In fine, I distrusted myself.

When a man says that he distrusts himself it may be set down that he has had sad reason for his distrust. It is only the fool, the madman, or the wholly inexperienced who has perfect self-confidence. For my own part, the experience of three or four drinking bouts during these six years taught me that my only safety from the dominion of my appetites and passions was that they should be preserved from temptation. (I am inclined to believe that with most men, in a thousand cases to one, to be preserved from temptation is to be delivered from evil. Blood and education are of great assistance, but the absence of temptation is the only safety.

But to resume my narrative: passing over these six years I found myself thirty-two years old, living alone at my residence, The Holt, occupying myself with my books and farm, and practicing my profession only so far as my duties to others, and the necessities for my own support required me. The activity of my life was over; and from that time to this I have led a sort of passive existence; like one condemned to death who saunters along the road amusing himself by looking at this or that trivial object until the place is reached and his turn shall come.

22*

R

CHAPTER XXIV.

IN spite of my books and my farming occupations I was lonely at The Holt. I have never thought myself very social, on the contrary, most of my time I have sought to spend in solitude, but the solitude I most liked has been one from which I could emerge at once whenever it suited me. To have to visit the houses of others to find pleasant company is a sad fate for any man, and I have always therefore preferred to have some one under my own roof with whom I could exchange ideas; or rather, as some of my friends think, I fear, to whom I can be dogmatic or sentimental at my pleasure. In this respect a good wife who knows her duties and has a woman's eye to her own peace and influence, is the best companion man can have; for the wisest of us like sometimes to babble, and the most amiable of us who really think at all have some fixed and favorite ideas we are fond of imparting.

Being lonely I invited Mr. Thomas J. Marlow to bring his young wife, and her infant and little step-daughter, and stay at my house as long as was convenient for all parties.

I had been acquainted with Mr. Marlow, who was a Northerner, for many years while he was a book-keeper in Yatton, and knew him to be very amiable, industrious, and intelligent—a really good man. His first wife, Priscilla Hunter, I had never liked much, on account of her quick temper and violent prejudices, but she had made him a good wife—had kept his clothes and house in order, and preserved his spirit from stagnation, had borne him two children, a girl and a boy, and just after the birth of the latter had pestered herself into a fever, and died. He bore his loss meekly; put his infant boy, who died afterward in teething, out to nurse, and took the girl off with him to the North, where the next I heard of him he was a book-keeper in a banking establishment to which his proficiency and known integrity commended him. Priscilla's father, Old Johnny Hunter, a particularly hard old man, died in a year or two, and left his little granddaughter Jane a legacy of quite a fine tract of eight hundred acres of land in the northeastern corner of the county on the river, which the old man had commenced to improve by putting up two or three cabins and making a small clearing.

The next I heard of Marlow he had married a Miss Mehetabel Crosby, a second-cousin of Mrs. Snow, and intended in the fall of the next year removing with her and his child back to Yatton. Unless he had been extraordinarily successful, or his new wife had money, which was not very likely, I knew he had no capital to start as a merchant, and I could not imagine his reason for coming back to Yatton to take up again his work as a book-keeper. Nor do I yet know the exact reason, unless the poor man found some comfort in being near the bones of his first wife, for even he, if he had no other motive for coming, must have had firmness enough to resist the vehement desire of his second wife to enter upon the enjoyment of paradise as a Southern planteress, which I found she had prepared herself to do upon Jenny's cotton plantation (!).

They arrived at Yatton in the fall of the year, and found temporary board and lodging at Squire Carter's, where, her mother being in feeble health, Jane (still Miss Jane) presided. Mrs. Marlow had an infant about four months old, and when I called with Marlow to be introduced to her, I attributed to it her dowdy appearance, and to the negro girl she had as nurse, the cross, discontented expression upon her otherwise rather pretty countenance. A negro girl nurse is a great trial to the patience of Southern mothers, and must be dreadful to a Northern woman who is ignorant of and unaccustomed to the peculiar carelessness and filthy untidiness of the black race.

Spring came, and Marlow had not succeeded in getting a permanent situation. He had found occasional employment in posting books, and doing copying for lawyers and others, but it did not afford a support, and his money, I judged, was nearly gone. Besides this, it came to my knowledge that he was uncomfortably situated at Squire Carter's, where his wife had had some sort of falling out with Miss Jane, who, however, was a prudent girl, and never said about others or herself more than was necessary. So I invited him to make my house his home for awhile.

It was with difficulty that I prevailed upon him to accept what his wife seemed eager for upon its first proposal. She had fallen out with the Carters, and from some cause was out of the good graces of her cousin, Mrs. Snow, who, upon her first arrival, had welcomed her with effusion, and had seemed overwhelmed with the privilege of indulging herself once more in Yankee talk to her heart's content; and I did not wonder that the poor woman should feel desolate, and be glad of the opportunity of a quiet home. If I had known that after Mrs. Snow had heard from her everything everybody in and about their native place had thought, done, suffered, and hoped for the last eight or ten years, she had in her turn communicated to the eager ears and retentive memory of the new-comer all the history, past, present, and, as far as possible, to come, of at least every member of Mr. Snow's congregation, and especially all the particulars about me, Mr. Marlow's special friend, and my history, I would not, I presume, have been so pressing in my invitation. But I did not know it; which is perhaps well, as I should have lost the knowledge of human nature obtained by my experience and observation of Mrs. Marlow.

Marlow protested that he feared to give trouble, but I insisted that far from it he and his family would be doing a good deed to relieve me of my loneliness. He also insisted upon paying board as he did at Squire Carter's, but I was firm that the little he and his would eat would only be wasted if they did not consume it, and I pointed out, what was true, that the little oversight his wife might occasionally give the proverbially wasteful negroes, would perhaps save me twice the amount of their actual expenses: I told him, what was also true, that if Mrs. Marlow would only see sometimes that the chickens and turkeys were attended to, she would do a real gainful service to me. The only expense I wished them to be at was for their washing, which I could not have done on the place. Martha, my cook, of her own free will, did my washing, but she had not time to do that of a family, nor did I feel disposed to require more than her mistress had required of her.

One Monday morning in May my gig and wagon moved them out, bag and baggage, and Mrs. Marlow took possession of the wing bed-room because I thought it would give her more privacy and more freedom in her domestic arrangements. There was also another reason, which I kept to myself, that I did not wish my rest disturbed by her baby if it should be colicky or otherwise noisy. Little Jenny, who was about seven years old, was to sleep in a trundle-bed in the back bed-room which adjoined mine, and opened into her step-mother's, and Eliza, the little negro girl, was to sleep on a pallet in the same room, near the door.

My end accomplished, I felt greatly relieved. Here have I at last, said I to myself, and that without the trouble of marrying her, a lady in the house to relieve me of household duties and cares. No longer shall I have to sit alone at my table, but a woman's pleasant face shall be seen at its head, and her pleasant voice shall be heard—the sweetest sound which from Adam's time has ever broken solitude. The merry laughter of a child shall again echo in the house, and I shall watch its play catching fireflies in the summer dusk before the candles are lit, and no longer shall I have to light the candles in the dusk to relieve myself from gloom.

The next morning Martha gave us a nice breakfast, and Marlow and I walked into town to our respective labors, and late in the afternoon walked out again together, I chatting gayly about what should be done and left undone about the establishment, he barely assenting, and seeming dubious and dull. About a week afterward, when Mrs. Marlow had become, as I thought, sufficiently domesticated and at leisure, I accosted her just after breakfast, and delivered to her the keys of the pantry, store-room, and safe, asking her to do me the favor to take charge of them, and to superintend the giving out of the necessary articles to cook. I told her she should find in the store-room sweetmeats and pickles, jellies and jams, with which my mother and Bel had continued to keep me supplied, and also the flour, meal, and meat, and all the other usual articles kept on hand for the table; that in the pantry were the crockery, napkins, and all such things; and in the safe in the dining-room were also butter, cheese, and what she should find; I did not know all myself in either place, but she could soon examine for herself.

'Martha," said I, "will take a great deal of the trouble off your hands, madam, for she is a good cook, and a faithful negro, and I don't think you shall find her either impertinent or dishonest, though she may occasionally need direction when you wish a little variety. Jack has the key of the smoke-house, and gives out the allowance to the quarter negroes every week, so you shall not be troubled with them."

"But, Mr. Page," said she, "do you let Jack, a negro man, have the key of your smoke-house, where you must have a great deal of meat and other valuable articles?"

" Why not, madam?" answered I. " He knows how to weigh out the allowance quite as well as I do."

"But I don't see," said she doubtfully, "how you can trust him."

Trust him!" said I. "Why, my dear madam, he is as honest as most white people at least, and even if he were inclined to be otherwise, he knows that I know just what quantities of articles are in the smoke-house, and that if they should fall short, he will be held responsible."

"I'll not mind the trouble," said Mrs. Marlow, "and if you will give me the key of the smoke-house also, I will see to Jack's measurement—that is to say, if it will be of any accommodation to you. To home my mamma always saw to those things herself."

"No doubt, madam," said I; "but your mother did not have a lot of plantation negroes to deal with, or she would have found it no very agreeable task. I find that Jack gets along very well, so I'll not trouble you in that matter."

And so I left, having first told Martha, when she came to me to get out the dinner, that Mrs. Marlow would attend to it thereafter,—a piece of information which Martha did not seem to be greatly rejoiced at, though she said nothing.

Mrs. Marlow, I had found, was, after all, a really nice little body, rather too prim and starchy, but quite smiling, and very willing to take trouble off my hands; and I congratulated myself for three or four months upon the good fortune which had brought her to my house.

A special term of court was coming on, and I was kept very busy preparing for it, and, in consequence, was not always able to get out to my dinner at the fixed hour. For a week or two this passed without remark, but one day at the usual hour I was at home, and dinner was announced, and Marlow had not yet come, and I suggested to the lady that she had perhaps better delay the meal a little until he should come. "Oh, no," said she; "Mr. Marlow is not used to having his dinner so late, and I thought he had better take the meal at his usual hour in town, and come out to tea."

"I have always been accustomed, Mrs. Marlow, to have my dinner at this hour, but I really dislike that Mr. Marlow should be put to inconvenience——"

"Oh, as for that," interrupted she pertly, "beggars must not be choosers, and I am sure Mr. Marlow and I are only too happy to——"

"My dear madam," interrupted I, in my turn, "please do not talk in that manner. I really do not see what other arrangement I can make to suit myself; but if you and Mr. Marlow wish your dinner at an earlier hour, it will be easy for you to have it, and I can take mine when I come home."

The next morning as we walked to town after breakfast, I told Marlow what I had told his wife, and it came out that he had not found the least objection to the dinner hour: "But," said he, "Mrs. Marlow has peculiar ideas upon such subjects, and though I always find it best to humor her, I am mortified to think that she may have interfered with your comfort."

"Not at all," said I. "The matter can be arranged to suit all parties."

Pretty soon I began to notice, day after day, that only two biscuits and a small piece of corn bread were reserved for my dinner, and though it was quite as much as I wished to eat, I rather disliked to be so allowanced. So I took occasion to speak to Martha on the subject, and when I remonstrated, she said :

"The Lord bless you, master, it ain't my fault. That there woman don't even seem to want to give out enough to go all around once; and she is always a lecturin' and scoldin' me about wastin', and a tellin' me that me and Jack don't earn our salt."

"Don't speak of Mrs. Marlow in that manner, Martha," said I.

"But it's the Lord's truth, master," said Martha, emphatically. "You dun know that Mrs. Marlow. Arter awhile she run you wild if she go on as she's been gwine "

"You don't like Mrs. Marlow, Aunt Martha," said I.

"Like her?" said she. "Did you ever hear what she done at Squire Carter's?   She wanted ole Miss Carter to be moved out of her room for her to take it, and got mighty mad, and said as how Mr. Marlow paid for the best, and she was gwine to have it; and her and Miss Jane had it high and low. And Miss Carter's cook say as how she runs Mr. Marlow ravin' distracted for all he seem so quiet; and she beats that poor little Jenny till she done cow her down worse'n a dog."

"Never mind, Martha," said I. "Old Phyllis has been exaggerating, I expect. You mind your work, and I'll speak to Mrs. Marlow about giving out plenty."

And so I intended to do, but I found it was a delicate matter at best, and with the new light old Martha had, truly or untruly, thrown upon the disposition of Mrs. Marlow, there were fresh complications of difficulty. How I managed to suggest my desire that more liberal issues of provisions should be made, I do not remember, though I know it was with many a hem and haw; but I recollect full well how Mrs. Marlow pursed her lips and said: "Very well, sir. But I thought it was your desire to save."

"So it is, Mrs. Marlow," I replied, "and you are perfectly right, madam; but don't you think it is always less trouble to give out a little too much, than to have too little? For my own part, I have always found that I gained in comfort by letting a moderate degree of waste pass unnoticed."

"Very well, Mr. Page. It was at your desire that I took the keys, and I am sure I don't wish to keep them one minute longer than I give perfect satisfaction." And with that she laid the keys on the table, near me.

What was I to do? I could not see my servants suffer, nor did I wish to be made uncomfortable myself; and, on the other hand, I could not bear to have even the appearance of hurting a lady's feelings—particularly in my own house. Therefore I handed her back the keys, and said:

"Do not mistake me, my dear madam. I had not the slightest idea of taking the keys from you. I only suggested what I thought would add to the comfort of yourself as well as that of the rest of us; and I am glad I have had the opportunity of telling you that my desire to save only meant that I did not like extravagant waste. You will oblige me by taking the keys again, and going on as I am sure your own good sense will direct you."

She took the keys again, without a word, and I had no more trouble on that particular score again very soon.

But in a few months Mrs. Marlow was more at home in my house than I was, and she began to suggest improvements. She had been to town one day, in my gig, of course, and had looked over the stock in Bright & Robbins's new furniture store. In the evening she brought the subject of bedsteads into the conversation, and talked in such a way that I had to ask her if her own bedstead (which I knew was a fine and costly one, though then, may be, a little old-fashioned) was uncomfortable, and if it would please her that I should get a new one.

"Oh no," said she; "I was not thinking about myself. It is true that the old bedstead creaks a good deal, and looks as though it used to have bugs in it; but it will do. I was thinking about the one in Jenny's room."

"But Jenny sleeps on her trundle-bed, Mrs. Marlow," said I.

"That is true," said she; "but suppose company should come!"

"Mrs. Marlow, the bedstead in Jenny's room is a fine and substantial piece of furniture, and fit for any company."

"So it is, Mr. Page; but then it is so heavy that it is hard to manage, and, besides, does not suit the other furniture. Now one of those new-fashioned, light fourposters, with a cornish on top, and a rich valance, such as mamma has, would suit exactly—and Bright & Robbins have just received a number of them from Boston."

Now there were many offensive things in Mrs. Marlow's conversation besides its tone and spirit. The imputation of bugs was very peculiarly offensive; for, besides that I knew it was wholly false, it was intended as a slur upon my former housekeeping, if not even upon the neatness of my dead wife. Moreover, Mrs. Marlow's evident desire to be mistress, and displace and upturn what Mary's correct taste and careful hands had arranged, and what had been religiously kept just as she had arranged it, outraged my feelings, and I would have seen Mrs. Marlow—— Well, there is no use in writing hard things; but it makes me angry even to remember the design and spirit of the woman.

I was already getting disenchanted of the pleasure of having strangers about my house, even for sociability; but two incidents which followed in close succession, just after this, showed me Mrs. Marlow in her true and odious character, and showed the true cause for poor Marlow's habitual silence and lowness of spirits. When he had formerly lived in Yatton, he was noted for his genial disposition and gentle, playful humor; but on his return I had noticed that he was silent and reserved, and rarely smiled. I had attributed it to his want of success in business, and had wondered how one naturally so hopeful and cheerful should be so habitually cast down by such a cause. I now discovered that his wife gave him good cause for lowness of spirits; and I actually think he was the most miserable man I have ever known—more miserable than Fitzroy, because he had more feeling. His misery was not only active, but also passive. He had to bear the torture in silence. It was his only comfort that he thought no one knew his misery.

23*

Here is how it was.

I have already mentioned the property left little Jenny by her grandfather; and I have spoken of the child only incidentally, because I knew I should have occasion so describe her in order to present her especial sorrows in their true light.

She was by nature a bright blue-eyed little thing, who had inherited her mother's spirit, tempered with her father's calmness and mildness of disposition. I had noticed, ever since she had been at my house, that she was not gay and confident as were other children of her age; and that even when she was surprised into some expression of delight or playfulness, it was but a flash, and left her confused and embarrassed. Even when she would be tripping about the yard among the shrubbery, she never pulled a flower—and was always stopping and looking toward the house, as though to hear a call.

Well, one morning when I had got about half way to town, I remembered that I had left on the table in my room some important papers, which I had to use that day, and told Marlow to walk on, and I would return and get them. When I arrived at the house, I had hardly put my foot in my room when I heard Mrs. Marlow, in the next room, exclaim, in a shrill, angry voice, to some one: "Come here, you nasty little wretch! Why can't I kill you! There! and there! and there!" and her blows with a heavy switch fell fast and furious, and she trampled about the room as though dragging a screaming child over the floor, and continued to beat her; and the screams were so heart-rending that, after knocking in vain at the door, I opened it and saw Mrs. Marlow, livid with passion, holding little Jenny by the hair and belaboring her with a switch even too large to whip a ten-year old boy with. When she saw me she let the child go, and retreated to her own room, putting up her hair as she went, and casting back at me a glance of mingled rage and fear.

Good heavens! And was this Marlow's wife? the daughter of a preacher? and a lineal offshoot of the Pilgrim Fathers?

I raised the little girl from the floor, and took her in my arms and tried to console her; but she would not be comforted. Terror was on every feature of her face, and she tried to push me away, saying faintly: "Do go away, Mr. Page; please do go away. She will whip me worse. Oh, she says she wants to kill me! and she beats me every day—and she will beat me worse now!" and the poor little creature sobbed, and shivered, and seemed to try to resign herself to the fate she feared.

To say that I was indignant, would be too mild an expression. But what was I to do? I really feared to leave the child there without a protector. After some cogitation, I hit upon a plan. I asked Jenny if she wouldn't like to go to town with me, and spend the day with Mrs. Diggory's grandchildren? and when she assented, I knocked at Mrs. Marlow's door, and said to her, inside, as calmly as I could: "Mrs. Marlow, Jenny is quiet now. Will you let her go with me to town to spend the day at Mrs. Diggory's?"

"Yes, sir," said Mrs. Marlow, "she can go with you to town——" and she added something I could not catch, in an undertone.

I told the little thing to get her sun-bonnet, ordered Jack to harness up my gig, and took her to Mrs. Diggory's, where, when I called for her in the afternoon, I found her playing with the other children, but awkwardly and a little reserved, and, from her movements, evidently quite sore.

During the day, Marlow had occasion to call at my office, and I took the opportunity to tell him what I feared he did not know; but I did so as cautiously and gently as I could. I told him that on my return to the house in the morning I had found Mrs. Marlow whipping Jenny with a very large switch, and that, from what I learned, it was a common occurrence, and I asked him if he did not think it would be well to advise with her on the subject.

"Advise with her!" said he; then rising and coming up to me, he placed his hand on my shoulder, and, looking at me with a world of sorrow and perplexity in his eyes, he said: "So you have found it out at last! Page, I am the most wretched of men!" and casting a wistful look at me, he turned and left the office.

That night I heard the first of a series of tirades which were soon to make the place too hot for me and Mrs. Marlow. She had lost all shame and desire for concealment when I had discovered her violent character, and seemed rather to wish to display what she could do in the way of vituperation and malice.

Her windows were up, as were mine, for the weather was warm. About nine o'clock, as I was busily engaged in drawing up an important bill in chancery, my attention was attracted by the loud and excited tones of her voice. I looked, and saw her standing near a window, and, occasionally, as she talked, glancing over at me, whom she could see with perfect distinctness. As it was evident she wished me to hear what she had to say, I did not rise, as I might have done, and close the window; for, as I saw that the woman was bent upon having her spite out for my benefit at some time, I thought the sooner it was over the better.

"Yes, sir," exclaimed she, in a rage, to her husband, "where is the fine plantation and the paradise you were to take me to?   You have no plantation, sir!"

"I never told, or even intimated to you, that I had one, my dear," said Marlow, mildly.

"You didn't?   Well, sir, if you want to get out of it that way you may do so.   That nasty little brat has some land, and you are too tender to her to make use of it, but will let me and my child starve.   When you courted me——"

"Stop, my dear," interrupted Marlow, "I rather think the boot is on the other leg.   If you had not been so very kind and motherly to Jenny, I never——"

"No, of course you would never," exclaimed she. "You married me, for what?   Because you loved me? No; I knew it; you never did love me, and you dare now to acknowledge it!   You married me to take care of that little chit!   Ah, I thank God, who sees and hears me now, at this very moment;" and she clasped her hands and looked upward almost ecstatically, as though she was really glad that God had an opportunity to look upon such persecuted meekness. "I thank God that not one drop of my blood is in the muddy, stinking stream in her veins, the deceitful little brat! She got that from another woman, your first love, who from what I hear was a mean and deceitful——"

"By God, madam!" exclaimed Marlow, much agitated, "that is too much! You shan't stand there and insult my dead wife! You——"

"Your dead wife!" interrupted she with a sneer. "Your dead wife! Oh yes! you are mighty touchy about your dead wife, but when do you ever think of your living wife? What have you ever done for me, I would like to know? When you first married me, you lived at my papa's house, and now——"

"Stop again, madam!" said Marlow. "I did live at your father's, but it was because you would have it so, and I paid all the expenses of the whole family while I did so, and loaned your father money into the bargain."

"Paid all the expenses! Loaned money! *You* say so! 'I paid, I paid!' That's what you always throw up to me! It was an honor to you, sir, to be admitted into my papa's house! The Reverend Jeremiah Crosby is as far above you as a man well can be above another, and you throw up to me that you paid! you paid! You have taken me away from my home and parents, but, you paid! You are permitting me and my child to live upon a stingy fool who begrudges——"

"Mrs. Marlow," said Marlow, in a mournful, pleading tone, "don't abuse Mr. Page. For God's sake have at least a little decency. For the Lord's sake let me alone, and do not torment me. You know that I am obliged to submit to your abuse. (I can't whip you as I would a man, and I cannot commit suicide even for all the misery you make me suffer.) Have a little mercy on me!"

"Whip me! You brute, whip me! I'd—like—to

— see — you — lay—the—weight—of—your—finger—
on—me! Commit suicide! No! you coward! A man
who will let another insult his wife as that Page of
yours did me to-day, by bursting into the room where
he knew I was, hasn't got spirit enough to ,kill himself!
Suicide! You try to frighten me by threatening to
kill yourself—me, a poor lone woman——"

"You are mistaken, madam," said he, "I did not
threaten to commit suicide."

But why should I continue all this scene! It can
easily be imagined by any one who has ever seen a
violent woman in a rage with a man she does not fear.

Poor Marlow! This was not the first or the last
trial of the poor inoffensive well-meaning fellow, who
in the fullness of his affection had married the woman
really because she was kind to his little motherless
daughter, and he had persuaded himself to love her
for it.

There is no creature on earth more spiteful and cowardly than an ill-tempered woman with a husband for
whom she has no fear; and there is no creature more
to be pitied than her victim; particularly if he honestly
love her, as most such unfeared, unrespected husbands
do love their wives—only too much.

One of the most touching expressions in the whole
Bible is that of David. "It was not an enemy who
reproached me; then I could have borne it."

This woman hated little Jenny, and hated her husband on Jenny's account. If Jenny had died, Marlow
would have inherited the property, which would consequently then be the property of Mrs. Marlow and her
child or children, and Mrs. Marlow wished her out of

the way. I verily believe that but for the law she would have murdered her outright. The idea of having her own delicate neck stretched alone restrained her. As it was, she was trying to kill her spirit, and would soon have killed her body, too, by slow degrees the law could not notice.

Although the tirade I have attempted to narrate was private, and treated as if it were unheard by me, Mrs. Marlow's aversion to me soon became too open and violent to pass unnoticed, and, not to prolong a disagreeable subject, I need not say they presently left my house. Marlow himself proposed it, and I did not oppose. They all in a short while moved back to the North, and I never afterward heard of them, except through an advertisement of the sale of Jenny's patrimony—an order for which Marlow procured from the Probate Court by his attorney two years afterward. He seemed to wish to sever every connection with those who had known him in his earlier and happier days.

I thought it was very weak in him to refuse the offer I made to take the little girl and raise and educate her, but he seemed to think that he might thereby expose to the world the wretchedness of his life, or, at any rate, set the world to inquire into the reasons why he had parted with his child to a stranger.

CHAPTER XXV.

I HAVE purposely omitted several scenes with Mrs. Marlow, in which she abused me roundly, and brought up my past failings, so far as they had been imparted to her by her cousin, with an accuracy of detail and a power of comment, which argued well for the soundness of her reasoning faculties and the brilliancy of her imagination. My frolic at Colonel Stewart's party and my frolics of the past seven years were magnified until even I, who knew the facts, was convinced that I was, almost, if not quite, a lost man; and my restitution of my wife's property to her family fitted me for hell as a hypocrite, or for an asylum and straightjacket as a lunatic—and I might take my choice.

I have purposely omitted all this because I would not be thought to take pleasure in detailing the follies and wickedness of my fellow-creatures, much less those of a woman. Indeed I would not have mentioned Mrs. Marlow at all had I not been convinced that though she was the only woman of her vileness I ever met to know well, her peculiarities are by no means uncommon, though manifested, generally, in a milder degree. Ill temper, selfishness, and a narrow mind are not uncommon, and together they make vulgar malice. Add to them that nervous excitability which moves the female tongue, and you have a Mrs. Marlow. Will any one tell me that there are not many Mrs. Marlows in the world? and many men just like her?

But my experience with her taught me, as I have before observed, that it was not pleasant, unless in very rare cases, to have strangers as regular inmates of one's house. Solomon says: "Withdraw thy foot from thy neighbor's house; lest he be weary of thee, and so hate thee." If it be not well, then, for either party to visit too frequently, much worse is it to take up abode with "thy neighbor"—unless he keep a boarding-house; that most wretched of all human institutions; that most pitiable, in cause and effect, of all the disasters of this estate of sin and misery.

I know of no classes of human creatures in each of which there is so much similarity in variety as in boarding-house keepers and habitual boarders. The latter I can dispose of in three words: they are selfish *ad nauseam.* The boarding-house keepers, however, are, as a general rule, infinitely superior to their customers. Nothing but the extreme of misery could force any man or woman, ordinarily constituted, to keep a boarding-house; and generally those who have the doubtful energy to appeal to that resort are good people, who have been reduced to poverty either by undue confidence in others, or by their own careless amiability. So far as my own observation extends, in nine out of ten cases a boarding-house keeper is very amiable, and very much troubled and imposed upon— just as his customers are very selfish, and very ill natured and exacting. The hotel-keeper has his office, and book-keepers, and clerks, and porters, and army of waiters, and place before the public, and all the imposing array which speaks out boldly and says: Pay, or quit!—be contented, or leave! Whereas the poor boarding-house keeper who, may be, has his office in his hat, and who has only two or three waiters and one dilapidated cook, is fair game for the bullying spirit of this wicked world, in which the rule is to bully or be bullied in one's dealings with the public.

Not that I by any means justify the boarding-house keeper for his half-raw mutton and overdone beef, with the same sauce for both; not that he is to be excused for his weak and muddy coffee, and his strong and oily butter, his soups that disappoint one's digestive organs, and his pastries that make a mock of them! I abominate his loud and turbulent dinner-bell, and his creaking bedsteads; and I hold him responsible for his bugs, and scant towels, the small number of his waiters, and his inches of candle, and smoky lamps, quite as much as any other selfish man (the word "selfish" is rather a redundancy); but when I reflect upon his present and what he must have been in his past sorrows—upon the nervous organization of his wife, and the natural stupidity and wayward fancies of his servants—I find in my heart a sentiment of pity which makes me long never to witness his troubles or their causes again. In fine, the hotel-keeper (I speak of the class) is a bullying, swindling humbug, and the boarding-house keeper is a bullied, swindled humbug—and that is about the difference between them.

But to return to private life. An old bachelor uncle, cousin, or brother is the only habitual strange inmate in a family who is at all tolerable, and he may be the most handy of all men, and the greatest convenience. You never have to wait breakfast, dinner, or supper for him, unless you are rather superhumanly amiable or affectionate. He can run errands, trim rose-bushes, keep you in game, arrange fishing tackle, sit up with the sick or fetch the doctor, see that your horses, cows, pigs, and chickens are properly fed, salted, watered, and doctored, stop out pigs, train dogs, watch the baby or the soap, pick fruit, keep the children out of mischief, and do a thousand other things better than you can yourself. He is the factotum of your wife, the wonder and delight of your children, and your very excellent friend and companion; and I have often thought that it would have been a happy fate had I, a childless, and possibly a childish man, been in his place from middle age until now.

It would have just suited me. I would have loved much, and done much, and given no trouble. The prices of meat, corn, and sugar should never have troubled me for myself. A few yards of cottonade, and a few yards of domestic, which my cousin, sister, or niece would have made up for me into coats, pants, drawers, and shirts, should have sufficed me for everyday clothes, and with but little labor, I could have made enough to keep me always with a nice Sunday suit and resplendent boots. I could have knitted my own socks in my leisure, and made my own pegged shoes, platted my own hats, spun my own thread, and made my own buttons. Always busy at just what I most liked to do, and always loving and performing loving offices, loved and having loving hands and hearts ministering to my comfort, I should have been a happy man.

It is no doubt best as it is. My sister Bel died and left one daughter, who married before her father left the world, so that I had no opportunity to have her with me; and I was not exactly in a position to live with her and her husband, who would have taken me, and all that I had, with a "thankye," as the negroes say, and wished then to dispose of me as Mrs. Marlow wished to settle poor little Jenny. I have never had the chance to be dear old Uncle Abe, or Cousin Abe. My niece's only child, my present grand-niece, has ideas which cannot tolerate old and old-fashioned uncles, and affections which are rather attracted by a man's title and what he possesses than by what he is.

It is somewhat out of place, but as I may not have occasion to refer to that young lady again, I will say a word or two about her here. It is painful to an old man to feel a dislike to his only surviving near relative, and even more painful to have to give his reasons for it; but as she expects to inherit my property, though, thank Heaven, she has not inherited my name, I must state why she shall be disappointed.

In the first place, her name is Sally Ann—Sally Ann Perkins—and a more disagreeable compound of names could not be invented. The "Perkins" is well enough by itself; that is to say, though it means "Little Peter," some folk like it, and some very good persons bear it; but with the Sally Ann, it does not suit my ear. Miss Sally Ann Perkins, I understand, likes my name quite as little as I do hers—so we are quits on that score.

If any one think I am foolish in this prejudice, perhaps he is right. I am old, and old men generally have weak fancies. But how would he be affected by the name of Aminidab Green or Habakuk Winslow, borne by a new acquaintance? There are associations attached to the sounds of different names and their collocations, and if the name of his new acquaintance would excite his organ of caution, I may be excused if another name excite disagreeable sensations in me. Why does the sound of the rustling of paper make some horses almost frantic with fright?

But in the second place, Miss Sally Ann Perkins is a snob.

There is no more expressive word in our language than snob; and no feeling more common to the American people than snobbery. It does not mean the mere desire for something better than we have; for that leads to improvement, and is laudable; but it means a mixture of abjectness and vanity, which meanly esteems something, of no importance in itself, as far above us, and if not to be obtained, at least to be aped. It leads poor people to dress and display far above their means, and leads rich people to assume aristocratic airs, and to think, oh, how near heaven they should be if they were only hereditary lords and ladies—strangely forgetting what they really should be if titles and trades were hereditary. It leads young men who have been to France a few days to forget English, and become *gastronomes* to an alarming degree. They will speak to you with horror of the *style barbare* of the *cuisine de ce pays ci* (and, by-the-by, they are more than half right, only they ought to take their view from a different *stand-point*—as is never said but by theologians) and discriminate between Pomard and Lafitte, groan at Port, and kiss the points of their fingers in ecstacy in describing the flavor of some French dish, as though you were not also tired of corn bread and hash, though you had never been to France.

If a man set out to be original in his extravagances, he is at once called crazy, though, perhaps, he only deserves to be called ignorant and foolish; for genius, in its most ecstatic frenzy, could not invent any fashion whatever, which has not already been tried by one or both sex. But generally, in this world (except by the envious who have the same feeling of inferiority, yet cannot possibly get up the imitation), persons are called neither crazy, ignorant, nor foolish, who only imitate the example of those they esteem their betters; for all the rest of us are hard at work, and emulating each other in our copying.

Have you not sometimes suddenly discovered a smirk or other affected look on the countenance of some damsel, and wondered where she could have got it? She was trying to imitate Miss Araminta, the unapproachable, who has herself copied just such a smirk from Lady Faddleday, of whom she caught a glimpse in New York last summer, who imitated it from the Duchess of Gadshill, who learned it from etc. etc. etc.

Mrs. X. dresses her daughters just like those of Mrs. A., who, in point of means also, is at the other end of the alphabet; and young Hoggins quits his old associates in pleasure and work to run with Sniffkins and his crowd of nice young men, to dress like them, talk like them, act like them; and Barkis, the shoemaker's boy, dresses, talks, and acts like them as nearly as is consistent with sole-leather; while the yellow boy around the corner regards them from across the great gulf as so many little angels in Abraham's bosom, or playing around him.

Let every one examine himself or herself, and see if there be not some one or more things in which he or she feels abject, and if there be not some other person whom they esteem far above them in point of style or social standing, and whom it is the most desirable thing in life to imitate. Don't you find yourself slyly boasting of your acquaintance or intimacy with those who you know are greatly honored or admired—on the principle that though not the rose you've been with the rose. (Well, all that is snobbery, and is mean. It is inconsistent with the dignity of character that becomes a man or woman, and leads besides to discontent, confusion, dishonesty, and toadyism.)

Have you not known many a man who made another man his model and authority, because he was to him the source of earthly good, and quoted his opinion·as definitive on all occasions great and small? who both lived and swore by him, and seemed to think he would go to him when he died? Have you not seen in him the gradual change from distant awe to familiarity, and at last to contempt, as the scales changed and he went up and his former patron came down?

That was all mean, very mean; and it was the legitimate result of snobbery. (He who is little-minded enough to be abject, will be little-minded enough to be vain, proud, and ungrateful.) Give me the man who, while he strives in this world for the best things, values what he has at present, and envies no man station or goods. (I had rather think I was the handsomest man, and had the best house, and the best horse, and the best dog, and the best land, and the best position in all the world, and value them at a thousand times their price,

than to esteem another desirably better looking or better off,—though I were very ugly, and my house leaked,
my dog were mangy, my horse were lame, my land should
not sprout cow-peas, and my position were that of a
piny-woods basket-maker. You may depend upon its
being the happiest and most dignified philosophy of life,
however humble the life may be.

My niece is not a disciple of this happy and dignified
philosophy. She is a snob. She laughs at the memory of my father and mother as a plodding old couple
who should have been vastly more worthy of her, Sally
Ann Perkins, had they been the first among the English nobility; while I can tell her that they were of a
nobility superior to that derived from human authority,
and that the most of the small drop of gentle blood she
has in her veins is derived from them. She, Miss Sally
Ann, thinks that her little noddle would vastly become
a coronet or crown, while I, her great-uncle, am reminded in that respect of what Sancho Panza said
about his wife: "I am verily persuaded that if God
were to rain down kingdoms upon the earth, none of
them would sit well upon the head of Maria Gutierrez;
for you must know, sir, she is not worth two farthings
for a queen."

I do not deny that she is a pretty girl, although her
nose is sharp, her lips thin, and she looks older than
she really is. She dresses, too, with taste; and though
her bonnet is of the smallest, and her hoop of the
largest, and her laces and silks of the finest, somehow
or other she looks vastly genteel, driving about in her
brette, and glancing with contemptuous indifference
upon the world and its vanities—as one would suppose

she esteemed other people's attempts at elegance. But how does she treat her two little, Perkins, orphan cousins? and how does she treat their old aunt, with whom she and they live? Do I not know that in her presence they hardly dare call their souls their own?   I have had experience with the young woman. She is not loud and unlady-like, but she is as silent and effective as a blister-plaster. One neither sees nor can touch the quality which hurts, but has to cry out for the pain, nevertheless.

Commend me to your silent scolds for malignant insults and running man, woman, and child desperate. How they manage it I cannot understand. Try to explain to one of them how she has insulted you, and you find yourself confused and ridiculous before her calm, innocent face, and perhaps doubly insulted by the very look and manner by which she shows her innocence. When I look at the beauty and serenity of Miss Sally Ann, and try to *precise* (that word is from the French verb *preciser*, and, like *approfound*, should be adopted in the English, as we have no single word its equivalent),—when I look at her, I say, and try to precise how she used, while she lived at my house, to insult me grossly and run me almost wild, and then humiliate me for being provoked, I sometimes almost think I have a waking nightmare. But the fact was real, though intangible, and I do hope she will marry a loyal duke. Finding that wealth and the highest title he aspires to do not secure happiness, he may perhaps turn his thoughts toward heaven. I am sure that is the only way in which my grand-niece will ever make a man try to secure the comforts of religion here on earth, and a final entrance to that blest abode.

What I have here said will explain to my executor, and to Miss Sally Ann, if she wish to know it, why I have not left my property to her—my natural heir. If these memoirs should ever be published, I trust that the discretion of my executor will lead him to omit this personal digression, or so to alter it in names and details as that it shall be understood only by the young lady herself.

[NOTE BY THE EXECUTOR.—Miss Perkins, now the Widow Lecompte, married in 1863 (after this was written) a stray music-teacher, exiled, as he said, in 1848, from his estates in France. Though not a Christian, he died a triumphant death in two years after marriage. Her property consisted chiefly in slaves, and has been, in every sense, rendered value-less by the event of the war. Having been fully advised by me of this part of the memoirs of my re-spected friend (I sent her, indeed, an authenticated copy), she refuses that it shall be omitted in publica-tion. She has commenced a suit to break Mr. Page's will on account of insanity and undue prejudice, and says that this shall serve as evidence in her cause. She denies that she ever treated her great-uncle with aught but the most perfect tenderness, and affirms that he was so insanely prejudiced against her that even her gentle manner of humoring his old-fashioned whims used to put him in a rage, which her quiet efforts to soothe only augmented. In an interview with Miss Bolling, the lovely residuary legatee of Mr. Page, I have it on the best authority that her intense calmness and simple words and gestures were so pro-voking, that the younger lady was at first indignant, and then so dissolved in tears of contrition (though what she had to be contrite for, unless it be that her own beauty and goodness made an old man love her, is more than she herself can see), that she wished to give up the estate at once to Mrs. Lecompte. She sent, wrote, and even—when I was last at Yatton—came to me herself to have it done; but as, by the terms of the will, that could not be, the suit is bound to progress. This will all be clear to the reader who has read the preface.]

CHAPTER XXVI.

I FIND that I have digressed greatly, in point of time, from the thread of my story. And yet I do not know but that by abandoning my design of narrating my life in the order of its events, and telling it as it occurs to my memory, I shall not be more natural, and therefore more engage the reader. I find, in fact, that after a certain period life began to fly so fast with me that the consecutive order of its events has become confused, and which is first of any two that occurred about the same period I cannot remember at all, or only with great difficulty by faint associations. For instance: Judge Dawson and Colonel Harper applied to me to become a candidate for Congress; and Miss Sophia Walker and I had a strategic attack and defense, she being the attacking party. Both events happened about the same period of my life, and I recollect that my brother, Dr. Eldred Page, was then living with me, but which of the two came first I cannot re-call—nor does it make the slightest difference either to me or to the reader, for they were not at all connected.

But before I speak of either, it is due to my own affection to say something about my brother Eldred.

He was six years younger than I was, and, I always thought, a great improvement upon me in every way. He was of larger stature, finer mind, and more unselfish soul than I, besides being greatly handsomer. I can make this confession without the slightest reserve, for to acknowledge the superior traits of one I love has always given me delight. Nor have my swans been geese, either; for mere friendship, however intense and holy, never blinds a sensible man, as love does, to defects, however trivial. When I was married he had just begun the study of medicine under our father, and was becoming greatly interested in bones and muscles, nerves, veins, and arteries, tissues and organs. His fancy inclined that way; and that alone was equivalent to talent; but he had talent too, and energy. Our father said he was naturally a doctor; and I verily believe it, for, added to his commanding presence and his taste, talent, and energy, he had a heart as sympathetic as ever beat in human bosom.

When he had sufficiently advanced, he went on to Philadelphia, where he graduated in 1819, at the University. Upon his return home he commenced the practice of his profession as the assistant to our father, to whom it was becoming too laborious, and succeeded even among those who had known him all his life.

Men usually dread commencing in their professions

where they were raised, but, unless they expect to succeed as charlatans, I am convinced that they are wrong. Real merit will succeed anywhere, and success is fixed upon the most profound basis where it has home pride, the vanity of locality, to support it.)

After the marriage of Bel, and the series of family calamities I have heretofore mentioned, brother Eldred continued to live at home with our mother, who, dear lady, constituted herself his housekeeper, and devoted herself to him. No young physician could have a better adviser than she, especially in those cases in which the experience and observation of an intelligent mother and wife are more peculiarly exercised, and he used often to say to me: Brother, our little mother is a better doctor than the whole College of Surgeons.

Ah, who knew her excellencies better than I? In all times of sickness and trouble she was the ministering spirit who came with relief. At the birth of my son, and at his death and the death of my wife, she was the person I most looked to for help, and when she herself was taken away, about ten years after my father's death, I felt that the last of the strong ties of affection which bound me to earth was severed. True, I had my brother and my sister Bel—but the latter was married, and had a husband to depend upon and love, and the former was a great strong man who did not need my assistance.

After our mother's death, both Bel and I considered the old place as Eldred's. We each had a pleasant home, and we hoped he would marry and make it his home. Until he should do so I persuaded him to rent it out to a careful tenant, and to come and live with me; and as my place was but little farther from town, where he had his office, he found it would not interfere with his business to do so.

He was no misogynist, and I never knew him to have any love scrape, or serious disappointment in love; therefore I could never account for his indisposition to marry. I am inclined to think, however, that though my sorrows and the fate of Marlow may have had some influence upon him, Miss Sophia Walker had a chief part in deterring him;—not that he was a man to form general rules from one or two particular instances, but the continued recurrence of obstacles will turn aside any man not fully bent upon an object.

Miss Sophia Walker was no longer in her first and freshest youth, nor was I, by any means, a young widower, when she manifested a design to change her name from Walker to Page at my expense. It was rather strange, to a casual observer, that she had never yet married, for she was still quite good looking, and in her youth must have been pretty. She had a fresh complexion, light blue eyes, flaxen hair with a dove-colored tinge, and a high-bridged nose; her lips were red, and the upper one beautifully arched. She was rather bony about the chest, but had a pretty foot and a handsome arm. Her fingers were long and bony, and the right thumb and index finger were well roughened by pricks of her needle. Her appearance was, in fine, that of one of those who are marked out by inexorable fate never to marry, do what they will. Every man has, no doubt, in his life remarked several of the class, and, though their appearance may have varied in its details, he has always been impressed with an undefinable similarity between them.

As a general rule, they are excellent women, these predestined old maids; are thoroughly contented with their lot, devote themselves to the good of their nieces and nephews, uncles and aunts, brothers and sisters; or, perhaps, if they have no such relatives, teach schools for little children; they are assiduous in their devotions, but more assiduous in their works of charity. I do love such an old maid as that, whether she be ugly or good looking, pleasant or brusque in her manners. When the great day of account shall come, she shall find laid up for her in heaven infinitely more than the love others may think she lacked here on earth. But sometimes these old maids are never contented with their lot, and never cease trying to change it while there is any possibility of hope. Miss Sophia was one of that kind. She always tried as genteelly as possible, it is true, but she tried, and I was one of her subjects for experiment.

I don't know why it is, but since I commenced to write about her, it has been with difficulty that I have kept my pen from writing French. My episode with her is just one of those subjects a spiritual Frenchman could best write about if he knew the facts—and there were any such old maids as Miss Walker in France. I am convinced, however, that though human nature is human nature all the world over, it takes parsons, and sewing societies, churches, and missionary societies, and sunday schools, and such like, to develop the peculiar traits of the Misses Walker.

What subject Miss Sophia abandoned as hopeless, to take me up, I do not know. I am inclined to think that her spirit was idly but incessantly searching the kingdom of nature to find her mate, when she espied me and thought she had discovered his peculiar marks.

She was a worshiper, I will not say of, but with Mr. Surplice, sang in his choir, and was one of his most faithful and active non-commissioned officers—a sort of female lance-corporal, to be put in function whenever the necessities of the case demanded it. To her Mr. Surplice was holy, and the church edifice was holy, the prayer books and Spiritual Harmonists, were sacred, and the tin sconces in the choir were consecrated; every object in, or about, or connected with the church, had about it some spiritual quality which was to her very imposing—nor do I hold her up to ridicule for it. The minds of a vast number of very good people are so constituted that superstition is a necessary ingredient of religion, and without it there is little of active interest in Bible truths. That a plasterer, engaged in repairing its ceiling, should whistle while at work in a consecrated church, strikes them as horribly profane. That a preacher, though he has flesh and blood, passions and appetites like other men, should be held to be mere man, seems to them to be a sort of sacrilege. However great a fool he may be, however complete a scoundrel, he is to be respected, outside of his folly or wickedness, as a holy man of God.

Ah, how much of this spirit has invaded the world, in and out of the Church! and what a tremendous injury it has done to true religion! When an insignificant little creature, such, for instance, as the Rev. Mr. Jabbers, shows his folly or hypocrisy, it hurts the cause of Christianity in his circle as though James the Less had been foolish or recreant; and if a bishop sin it is as

though Paul or John had fallen from his high estate.
And so long as there exist a hierarchy, or rather a
vast number of hierarchies, each of them pretending
to represent Christ's spiritual kingdom on earth, and
each assuming for its clerical caste a spiritual unction
which makes them holy and separate, and raises them
above other men, it must be so. What they assume,
they will, and must be held to. The character they
pretend to represent they must support with all its consequences, and it is utterly useless to tell the world that
they are men on the street, and superior to men in the
pulpit or confessional; that they can at once represent
Peter, and Simon of Samaria, whom he reproved.

The Misses Sophia Walker believe all this and much
more, and one of the very best evidences, to my mind,
of the divine truth of the fundamental doctrine of Christianity, is the fact that it has for so many ages existed
and spread in its intrinsic purity in spite of the egregious errors with which it has been burdened; and I
thank God for the Roman Church, and the Greek
Church, and all the churches; for having preserved by
their means, even though almost hid by canonicals and
ritualisms—the sacred truth of Christ and him crucified, burning with a pure and steady flame, like a taper
in a huge and gloomy vault beneath a massy cathedral.

What I have here said about church matters is no
digression, for it was my heterodoxy upon this subject
which seems first to have attracted Miss Sophia to me,
and excited a tender interest for me in her gentle bosom.
The result to her affections, and the process by which
it was reached need not be detailed, for since the world
began it has been known and felt of all men and women.

That she was earnest for my conversion to her faith, and, consequently, to the true and essential faith, I could not doubt, and though it was a bore (I am very ungallant, but I wish to be understood), if her attentions and pretensions had gone no further I could have endured it with philosophy; but it frets me to this day, on her account, not mine, when I think of the ridiculous position in which the good woman placed herself. The slippers she made me I received with thanks; her solicitation to hem my handkerchiefs I avoided by purchasing them already hemmed—but when I found she was in treaty with my washerwoman for a pattern of my shirts, so as to make me a dozen, I felt indignant, and ordered that, under pain of my highest displeasure, no pattern or even size should be given her.

Having described Miss Sophia's appearance, disposition, belief, and design, it is hardly necessary for me to enter into a detail of her actions, and talk, even though I could remember them. Most writers tell what a person says and does, and leave each reader to gather the particulars of disposition, appearance, and ruling ideas according to his or her astuteness and knowledge of human nature. My plan is, I think the best, as it is the most precise, and at the same time the most courteous to the reader. The exact appearance, ideas, and disposition of a character being given, the reader is left in no doubt, and is able freely and pleasantly to exercise an experienced imagination upon what the character shall say, or do, in any conceivable case; and I feel sure that an intelligent reader is just as well prepared now, as he would be if a whole volume of events and conversations were written on the subject, to hear my brother Eldred's exclamation to me one day: "Brother, if you don't take care, and go away, that woman will marry you in spite of yourself."

I took his warning, and did go away. I first went to M——, where I remained about two months in attendance on the Supreme Court. Thence I went to Charleston, and Richmond, and Baltimore. From there I took a trip by way of Havana to New Orleans, that most strange and delightful of all American cities for a gentleman bachelor who knows how to live and enjoy himself; and to Mississippi to see an old schoolmate. When I returned I found Miss Sophia's efforts manifestly enfeebled. They soon ceased, and with them almost ceased our acquaintance. At any rate, its gushing character was changed, and I found myself, to my great satisfaction, given over to hardness of heart.

Like Job, in all this I sinned not with my lips. My conduct toward Miss Sophia was always that which a gentleman's should be. I never spoke disrespectfully about her, and if I did not always talk to her sensibly, but sometimes answered according to her folly, I, at least, always spoke politely. And it is a great satisfaction to me to reflect that in all my dealings with the fair sex—even with Mrs. Marlow, yea, and even with my great-niece, I have been able to restrain my tongue, though it has sometimes terribly vexed my soul to do so.

CHAPTER XXVII.

THE appeal made to me by Judge Dawson and Colonel Harper took me by surprise for several reasons. It will not do for one of my age and position, who has spent much time and thought in honestly examining his heart and its motives, to pretend to any false modesty upon such an occasion. I by no means considered the place, or any place, as too high for me, as far as the honor was concerned, though I was but a country lawyer. What surprised me was the spirit manifested by the two political gentlemen, and the crude views they took of government.

One afternoon, about sundown, these gentlemen rode up to my house. Though never very intimate with me, they were old acquaintances, and when they dismounted, they brought in their saddle-bags, as though it was their intention to stay all night. I had their horses taken to the stable, and we seated ourselves upon the front gallery, and conversed about the weather and crops until supper was announced. After supper my brother left us to visit one of his patients, and pretty soon the conversation was brought about to politics. I noticed, from the drift of the talk and their mutual glances, that they had some proposition or other news to announce to me, but pretended to be unconscious of it until Judge Dawson, as spokesman, flatly requested me to run for Congress.

"When, judge?" asked I, in a jocular mood.

"This fall," answered he.

"Where, judge ?" said I.

"Why, in this district of course, Mr. Page!" answered the judge, as though surprised at my question.

"But this is a Whig district, sir, and has always been Federal, Republican, Whig, or whatever else it may be called, and I am a Democrat!" said I.

"True, Mr. Page," answered the judge, "but you are aware that at the last election the race was much closer than ever before, and we all think that with a really popular candidate, we may carry the district this fall; and we have settled upon you as the gentleman who will command the greatest personal influence in aid of our party. You have never aroused opposition as a politician, and your high talents and known integrity give you a commanding position."

"The majority against us at the last election," said I, "was two thousand four hundred and seven. Do you think, judge, that.my personal influence could overcome that ?"

"Perhaps it might," he answered, "for there is already a great change taking place in political sentiment. But even if it were not overcome at this election, the strong run you would make would discourage the opposite party, who have heretofore had it all their own way, and at the succeeding election you could certainly run in."

"That is," said I, "if I should then be alive, and disposed to run, and there were no other more available candidate to supplant me."

"Oh, as for that," said the judge hastily, "you need not fear that any one could supplant you. Common courtesy and gratitude, even if you had no higher claims, would secure you the nomination."

"Granted," said I. "But let us look at the case as it stands at present. To make even a fair race, I shall have to abandon my business, and traverse this large district making speeches for two months to come. To do this will put me to a considerable expense, besides what I shall necessarily lose by neglecting my business at home and in my profession. Besides that, it will throw me into collision with the opposite candidate, who has heretofore been one of my warmest personal friends. And all this for the almost certainty of defeat. I fear, judge, that I shall have to decline the honor."

"But the party, Mr. Page!" said Colonel Harper, speaking up hastily.

"Excuse me, colonel?" interposed Judge Dawson. "I think I know what you wish to say, and as we agreed that I shall do the talking, allow me to finish. Colonel Harper and I, Mr. Page, have talked over this matter earnestly, and with a view, believe me, to your interest. We think that in this case it matters very little with you if you be elected or defeated. To run will bring you prominently before the people, and place in your reach any office within their gift you may desire. But, apart from that, it gives you a claim upon the Administration. It will not be out of place for me to say that, two or three days before I left Washington City, your name was suggested in the highest quarters for the position of U. S. Attorney for this district, and you would have received the appointment if Colonel D., who is in the Cabinet, had not objected that, as the term of the Administration was so near out, you would not like to receive a place in which you might be superseded in five or six months. I thought it was interfering with your political prospects, but as he was known to be your personal friend, though not from this State, his objection was allowed to prevail, and the appointment was given to Mr. Miller."

Now, I had confidence enough in the friendship of Colonel D. to feel sure that if that or any other appointment would really be acceptable and beneficial to me, he would not oppose it, and I thoroughly understood Judge Dawson, who, though of the same party, was not on the best terms with Colonel D. who overshadowed him even here in his own State. The judge would not detach me from Colonel D. as a party man, but would put in a little private stroke at my personal friendship. However, I suffered him to proceed, and he said :

"We hope, Mr. Page, that you recognize the claims of your party."

"Certainly I do, judge,—as I understand them," I added. "I believe it to be a man's duty to his country to give an earnest support to that party the principles of which he thinks will best preserve and promote its interests. I regard it as a duty to the country, and the country alone ; and so far I recognize party claims. But you will pardon me, gentlemen, if I say that though, in my opinion, the Democratic party, with its fundamental principle of a strict construction to the Constitution, is the only party which offers any hope of safety, I do not believe that with the fundamental error on which this government is based, any party can save it from speedy destruction."

"Fundamental error in the government!" exclaimed the judge; and the colonel looked equally horror-struck. "I do not understand you, Mr. Page. To what do you refer? I thought our government, theoretically and practically, the most perfect monument of human wisdom ever erected."

"Certainly, judge," I replied, "it is a very perfect structure, and I cannot imagine one more stable and excellent, if it were only transferred from earth to heaven, or some other abode free of sin and folly. But as it is, it, in my opinion, is built upon sand. To be plain with you, gentlemen, I do not believe in universal suffrage, or in the stability of any government founded upon it."

"Why, Mr. Page, that is worse than Federalism!" said the judge.

"Not at all, sir," said I. "It has nothing in common with Federalism, which I detest and fear as much as you do. Universal suffrage will lead to Federalism, and will thereby destroy us. If you will allow me to give the reasons for my belief you will perhaps say that they are plausible, if not convincing. The idea is old, and I do not pretend that my course of reasoning is original; but where I picked it up, I do not know, and yet that it has not been wholly worked out by my own observation, I do not know, for it seems to me that I have always, and naturally, thought as I now do on the subject.

"The first great principle of human nature, overpowering justice and truth and honor, goodness and mercy, is selfishness. While it is the source of all energy, and private and public enterprise, it is also the prime cause of all the oppression, confusion, and decay of government, whatever be the form of government. The laborer tries to do as little work for as much money as possible, and the capitalist tries to give as little money for as much labor as possible. If you place men in power they will naturally try to benefit themselves by it regardless of the rights and feelings of others. The poor and ignorant being greatly in the majority will legislate themselves rich and into high position as far as possible, and as that can only be done by reducing the wealth and rank of those above them, you will have Agrarianism, Communism, Red-Republicanism, and all the anarchy which must come, as it always has come from the cry of 'Liberty and Equality!'

"I am no Coriolanus, gentlemen, but it seems to me that those who have dreamed these noble day-dreams of universal liberty and equality in political power, have not taken a sufficiently low estimate of human nature. Like all other day-dreamers in morals, they have not been practical. They have generally been educated philanthropists, and, actuated by their own noble and benevolent impulses, they have imagined a government of gentlemen and saints, whereas it should rather have had as its object the governing of ignorant plebeians and low sinners."

"It seems to me," said Colonel Harper, "that our government has worked very smoothly, so far."

"Do you call Mr. Clay's Compromise measure an evidence of smooth working?" said I. "Besides, no portion of this country is yet in a condition to experience fairly the evils I have suggested. The population, even in the North, is yet sparse, and is too busy subduing nature to be a Mobocracy; while here in the South the government is really an Aristocracy. The numerous class with us which represents labor has no political power. But look ahead at the time when the North and West shall teem with population, and consequently with active energetic selfishness; and imagine too what shall be our own position if slavery should be abolished, and our conservative Aristocracy should become a passionate Mobocracy.

"Besides, gentlemen, if the principle of universal suffrage, which is founded upon the idea that all affected by the government should have a voice in it, be a correct principle, I do not see by what right the suffrage is limited to males over the age of twenty-one years. Women and children have as many rights as men have, and very frequently have quite as much property. Idiots and lunatics have as many rights as sane men; the black and red as many as the white. There is no natural limit to the principle; if it be carried to its extreme it is destructive; therefore it is false.

"The object of government is order, which includes the full protection in the enjoyment of every personal right; and the best government is that which governs most strictly. The only natural government is the patriarchal rule, the very strictest man can invent. All other systems are purely conventional, and although it may be plausibly said that in their formation every man to be governed has a natural right to a voice, the assertion is not true in point of fact or practice. Those only have the natural right to govern who can best accomplish the ends of government."

"But, Mr. Page," said the judge, "you lose sight of

the Constitution. That is the supreme law which governs this country."

"Indeed I do not lose sight of it, sir," said I. "My whole argument is to show, that however perfect our Constitution may be, it is a mere experiment founded on an error: that it is a written instrument which has binding force just so long as it suits the selfish ends of a majority of the people—and not a moment longer. The question of the abolition of slavery has been lately started. Suppose the whole country were split into two great parties, and the Abolitionists were the stronger, do you suppose that the Constitution would stand as a permanent barrier? I tell you, gentlemen, that the pillar of fire by night, and of cloud by day could not check the selfish folly of the Israelites; and there is just as much human nature in the American people as was ever in the Jews. We may differ from them in personal appearance, but not one whit in nature. If it ever suit the views of a large factious majority to disregard or change the Constitution, you shall see that it is mere waste paper."

"What is to become of us then, Mr. Page?" asked the colonel. "What security can we have?"

"None at all, sir," I answered. "There is no such thing as security or stability in government. So long as you can succeed in preserving the Constitution as a holy instrument, to be regarded with superstitious respect, to be touched, as was the ark of the covenant, only by consecrated hands, and by even them only in accordance with express command, so long we shall be safe. But as that is impossible where every man in the country has an equal right to have his voice about it, to decide upon it, to treat it with contempt or as a hinderance, we never can be safe, for the reasons I have given."

"You then, Mr. Page, are not a republican at heart!" said the judge.

"As for that, sir," said I. "Let me ask you if you ever saw a gentleman who was? I am an aristocrat, or a monarchist, or an anything else which is opposed to universal suffrage; and am so wholly upon principle, for I neither wish to rule others myself, nor to be ruled by others. But for the existence of slavery, which makes our society and government in the South an aristocracy, and, therefore, conservative, I would not remain in this country one moment longer than was necessary to prepare and leave it. So long as that state of things exists, or, which is the same thing, so long as the Constitution is strictly construed, and the rights of the States are held sacred, we of the South are secure enough from actual injury. But with only a portion of the States thus conservative, and the power against them growing rapidly every day, it is impossible that such a condition should continue to exist. The selfishness of which I have been speaking will triumph in the end over the Constitution, and then we shall have either civil or sectional war.

"Have you ever reflected, gentlemen, upon the fact that the glorious people do not know the true meaning and importance of what they speak of so glibly, States Rights? Their preservation is the only chance for the preservation of the Constitution; for without them, and with universal suffrage, the people is a great mob."

"But, Mr. Page," said the judge, "granting that selfishness is the main-spring of human actions——"

"States Rights are the balance-wheel," interrupted I.

"Certainly, sir," said the judge, politely. "But, granting that selfishness is the main-spring, will it not lead our people to preserve rather than destroy the Constitution, which is so essential to their well-being?"

"A philanthropic philosopher may imagine such a thing in his closet, sir," answered I, "and I have no doubt but that such was the idea of the framers of our government; but to suppose that passion or a present benefit will be forborne for a future good, is to ascribe to the many-headed the wisdom and patience of the philosopher who imagines it. Besides, sir, what account shall you not make, in this matter, of party spirit, with its enthusiasm, its devotion, its inclination to carry its schemes as far as its power can reach, to disgrace its enemies as well as to overthrow them, to take continually a step further, and a step further, than where it first designed to go?"

"Ah, but, Mr. Page," said the colonel, "you cannot suppose that party spirit can move a majority of the people to destroy the government!"

"Can I not, sir?" I answered. "I will agree that it cannot lead them to designedly destroy themselves—their selfishness will prevent it—but it will lead them to their destruction by placing before them the allurements of a false good to be accomplished. Man's selfishness is governed by two potent masters, Hope and Fear. Place the good before him, and, however illusory it may be, he stickles at nothing to reach it. Place before him the fear, and he becomes cautious. A despot, who makes rigid laws, and enforces them inexorably, will keep men cautious by means of their fears.

Universal suffrage, with all the possibilities presented
by hope, will make them insolent in their desires, and
as fierce and ravenous as tigers when they come to
power."

Our conversation was long, and although I am aware
that what I have recounted of it sounds very much as
though I wished to read a lesson to the honorable gentlemen, I hold that I was perfectly excusable; and
when, in conclusion, the judge was trying to uphold
the excellence and harmlessness of party spirit, I said:

"Why, gentlemen, no one can charge either of you
with designedly doing anything not consistent with
perfect fairness, and yet even you wish me to abandon
my case and my prospects for fortune in order to take
up a more than doubtful contest for party—to sacrifice
me, in fact, for party—and even you, for party's sake,
would condescend to flatter me into it."

When I said this, both changed color a little, and
seemed disconcerted. I think I was justly offended,
but I preserved my courtesy, and they had to take the
lesson. We parted the next morning on friendly terms,
and I never heard any more of the project of running
me for Congress—for which mercy I am very thankful.

Alas! I have lived to see my prediction verified, and
a sectional war actually begun. God help us! If the
South should fail, and its conservative influence be destroyed, the whole structure of the government must
be swept away, because the rights of the States shall
be overthrown with the South. And when Peace shall
again smile upon the land, the inhabitants who shall
have been spared shall come out from their dens and
hiding-places to look upon the ruins, and remove the

rubbish, and with sad and discouraged hearts begin to build and improve again. This will be the case not in the South alone, though it may happen there first; it must be so in the North also. The principle of the government is wrong, and without the check of States Rights, can only entail anarchy until it is put down by the strong hand of a one-man power over an exhausted and dispirited remnant of the whole, or the feeble remnant in each State; and America shall be an Empire, or a congeries of Empires more or less despotic, instead of a powerful Confederacy of sovereign nationalities.

CHAPTER XXVIII.

I HAVE said that my brother, the doctor, was never, that I knew of, disappointed in love; but I do not wish it to be understood he never was in love. On the contrary, he had the family failing to a great degree, and his affections never seemed easy unless they were occupied with some fair object. His popularity with the young ladies was almost wonderful, for although he was too earnest and honest to pretend admiration, or to be fickle, he was perfectly self-contained and independent with them, and could laugh with them, or at them, as the occasion demanded.

In that he differed from me. From my earliest love-essay until now, the girl or woman for whom I have entertained either love, or a very particular liking, has had me as her slave, and the idea of offending her has distressed me beyond measure. I find myself propitiating the whims of my little pet, Kate Bolling, as though it were possible I could yet be loved, and sometimes the thought that my old-man's babble and attempts at gallantry annoy her, gives me as much uneasiness as though I were her young lover. If she has seemed abstracted and thoughtful during one of my visits, I am all anxiety to visit her again, and see if I have offended, and am never happy till I can see her smile, and show a merry, affectionate heart again. My reason tells me that in this matter I belong to the class of "Old Fools," and yet it gives me a great pang sometimes to think that she too may appreciate my folly. I dread to appear ridiculous to one I love.

When my son was born there were three things, besides health of mind and body, I most desired for him. The first was that he should have a hot temper; for I knew he could be whipped at home and abroad into governing it; whereas, if he did not have it naturally, he could never acquire it. The second was, that he should be obstinate; for I knew that if he had good sense the little harm his obstinacy might sometimes do him would be far more than counterbalanced by the thousand evils from which it would preserve him. The third was, that he should be almost totally void of the love of approbation, that most pitiable weakness with which poor man can be afflicted. It makes a man amiable to others, but a misery to himself. It accompanies an affectionate heart, but so governs all the acts of the most intelligent man as to oftentimes make him appear to have a weak head. For the approval of others he does what his good sense disapproves. In fine, his whole happiness depends upon the esteem in which others hold him, and he becomes an instrument to be jangled or made harmonious by every passer-by. A little child or an empty-headed fool can inflict upon him the most acute torments; by a look may cause him more pain than would a strong man's blow; by a word may make his soul shrink within him.

This love of approbation I have borne with me like a shirt of Nessus; or, rather, like a cruel sore to make me wince with pain for every pointed finger. My brother, on the contrary, although he had enough love of approbation to make him willing to accommodate and please, rather than show himself selfish and surly, never seemed to think it desirable to waive one whit of his manly dignity, or accurate sense of propriety. Therefore, being also handsome, he was popular with the ladies, and therefore he never got into love perplexities or had serious disappointments in love. He was always in love, however, after his fashion; and one little episode presents his character so perfectly, and also shows an amiable young lady in a situation so affecting that I must relate it. But as the story may be somewhat long I will give it a chapter to itself.

CHAPTER XXIX.

ABOUT three miles above The Holt, and just beyond the saw-mill on Brown's Creek, lived a man by the name of Allen, with his wife and daughter. They were very poor. Allen, a slender, weakly man of about fifty-five years of age, always cleanly dressed, however patched and coarse his clothes might be, bore upon his countenance the impress of weak good nature, and the traces of former good looks. In his youth he was, no doubt, a very handsome man; and indeed he must have been remarkably handsome and amiable to have won such a wife as he had. They had come from Virginia many years before and settled in the county, and their relative bearing and conversation were enough to make one suspect the history of their marriage. She was a ladylike woman, of good education, he was totally uneducated and had evidently led a life of manual labor. She had, no doubt, married him from pure love, and perhaps much against the wishes of her relatives. This was indeed the case, as I afterwards learned, and though she bore it with unflinching patience and cheerfulness, I often pitied the poor woman for the hard lot she had chosen. They had had several children, all of whom, except one daughter, had died in early youth by the diseases incident to a newly-settled country acting upon delicate constitutions. The daughter who was spared them was a healthy, merry child who, when I first began to notice her, was about ten years old, and already was of the greatest assistance to her mother. The little thing could read and write quite well, was a most industrious little sempstress, and never seemed better pleased than when exerting herself at the wash-tub with such articles as she could handle, or tripping to the spring with bare feet and head and fetching, with many a resting spell, pails of water she hardly seemed able to carry at all.

Mrs. Allen, from her first coming to the country, used to attend church regularly with her children and husband, and soon, by her intelligence and dignified demeanor, gained the acquaintance and good will of the ladies of the congregation and community. We all know how such friendships come about—sometimes the result of officious good nature; sometimes the effect of genuine charity. At any rate, Mrs. Allen soon numbered among her friends my mother, and Mrs. Ruggles (who in spite of what I have said of her had many generous impulses, and was a devout admirer of good manners), and all the other ladies of position about Yatton. When her children, one by one, sickened and died, she had their kindest sympathy and attentions; and when little Stephania (I do not know why she received such a name) was born a healthy, robust child, they rejoiced with her.

When Stephania was about twelve years old, by agreement of several of the ladies, who would share the expense, Mrs. Holywell invited Mrs. Allen to allow her to live at her house and go to school with her children during the week at the Academy in Yatton. After some hesitation the offer was accepted with the proviso that the child should return home every Friday evening to remain with her parents until the following Monday morning.

The Academy was a first-rate school, and Stephania was one of its best pupils, and one of the prettiest, and by means of unofficious presents from this and that person, always one of the most neatly and becomingly dressed; so that when she graduated at the head of her class, just after her seventeenth birthday, there was a no more accomplished and ladylike girl in the whole county. Her conduct upon her return home was so different from that of an affected, spoilt, vain girl, that she secured the admiration of the whole county. She tried at once to relieve her mother of her most burdensome duties, and her neat handiwork was manifested in house, kitchen, and wash-shed. Old Mr. Allen seemed, in her company, almost in heaven, looking at and hearing a choir of angels; and she was as fond of him as though he were the richest and most learned of the land. He was at the time, and indeed was to his end, occasionally employed at the saw-mill, and at other times in plying the trade of a basket-maker. He supplied the whole neighborhood with cotton-baskets for a number of years.

In the fall after her graduation, Mrs. Colonel Stewart—her husband was dead—projected a trip to the North, and perhaps to Europe, to be gone from home two or three years. She had two daughters—Emily, about Stephania's age, and Mary, two years younger; and as Stephania was a favorite with them, the old lady thought it would be a great convenience in every way to have her go along as their companion and Mary's preceptress. It was a fine opportunity for the young girl, whose fancy was profoundly moved by the prospect of travel; but it was with difficulty she could be persuaded to leave her parents. "Oh, dear ma," she would exclaim, when her mother would urge the acceptance of the offer, "what will you and dear old popsy do without your little daughter! I can't bear to be traveling about as a grand lady, while you two are living here so poor and helpless!"

"Poor!" exclaimed old Mr. Allen, on one occasion. "Why, gal, what are you talkin' about? Me and your ma aint poor. We're rich! Havin' such a sweet da'ter as you, is bein' rich; but, besides that, I have got the finest lot of white-oak basket-timber in soak I ever had yet, and more orders for baskets than I can fill in a year; and we don't owe a cent; and, please God, if I don't have the rheumatiz too bad this winter, I'll make money hand over fist!"

Mrs. Allen, however, answered her daughter more convincingly. "My dear," said she, "it is your father's duty and mine, and it is our happiness, to make you happy and useful. Although you would be a great assistance to me, as you always are, dear daughter, if you should remain at home, the fact that you missed the great advantages offered to you, only for our sake, would make us both unhappy. Why, daughter, we have only you to live for; and the hope of seeing you comfortably established and happy, is all the earthly hope we have left. It is your duty to do what you can to that end, and to take every advantage offered to you; for by doing so you assist us, and add to our comfort more than you could by remaining at home and working. We shall miss you, certainly we shall miss you," continued the good woman, with tears in her eyes, but a loving smile on her lips; "but it will not be for long, and it will be in the way of duty. You ought to know by this time, my love, how pleasant duty can make very disagreeable things sometimes!"

And so Stephania was overpersuaded—and with a sinking heart, and after many a warm and tearful embrace of her loved ones, she got into Mrs. Stewart's carriage one afternoon to go to Grassland (the Stewart residence), from which the family were to start, the next morning, on their travels. The old man, with trembling hands and humid eyes, kept fumbling at the cords which held the modest little trunk on the hind seat of the carriage, as though still to delay the parting; but at last mustered up the courage to slap his hand firmly upon the lid, and say, with choking voice: "All right! Drive ahead! Good-by, my dear!" "Stop!" she said to the driver; "one more kiss, dear old popsy!" and leaning out of the carriage window, she threw her arms around his neck, and held the old man close in her nervous embrace, as though she could never consent to leave him—and then, with a long farewell kiss, sank back in the carriage, and sobbed as though her heart would break, as it moved off; leaving the old man standing, with the tears rolling down his cheeks, whispering to himself, as though she were still present, "My dear! my darling child!"

When it became about time to hear from the absent one, who was to write from Charleston, and then from New York, the old man presented himself regularly at the post-office at the opening of the mail, which came twice a week; and his restless uneasiness if the mail were delayed, and his humble resignation if the postmaster said: "No letter for you, Mr. Allen!" showed at once the character of the man, and the intense anxiety he felt.

At last the first letter came, and then the second, from New York, then a third, from New York—a long, long epistle; and then in succession letters from Boston, and Niagara, and from this and that town at the North; and as each was handed to him, his brown and bony hand would grasp the treasure, and with eager step, and joy and pride in his eyes and bearing, he would hurry off to his home for his wife to read it to him. They were long, loving epistles, in each of which the writer seemed to try and convey to her loving readers the exact scenes she saw and as much as possible of the wonder and delight she felt. At last came one which announced that they would, the next day, take the swift-sailing A No. 1 copper-bottomed and fastened Liverpool and New York regular packet, the Sea Queen, A. J. Brown, Master, for Liverpool; and after the lapse of a month or two of great uneasiness came another, telling of a pleasant passage and safe arrival; and then others from London, and Paris, and Vienna, and Florence, and here and there in Europe.

Ah, it was a pleasant sight to see old Mr. Allen at this time, and hear him answer, when one asked him about Miss Stephania: "My da'ter was at Vienna on the 28th of June last, I thank you, sir; and expected to leave for Munich the next day. She was enjoying herself very much, and her health was good, sir, I thank you!" Even Mrs. Allen, who knew far better than he the locality of Vienna and Paris, and appreciated far more than he what her daughter was seeing and enjoying,—even she, with all her good sense and modesty, seemed to be rather over-elated with pride and awe, when she would recount to one how Stephania had seen the King of France, and had been in the Tuileries, and had danced at a State ball,—to which the American Minister had procured her party invitations,—and then how "My daughter Stephania was in Rome at our last advices, and expected to go to Naples in a few days, and thence by sea to Marseilles, in the south of France."

And then, after three long years, the news arrived that the party was coming home; and soon they did come, and Stephania—an elegant and beautiful young woman—took her place as naturally at home as though she was not a great traveler, whose eyes had been blessed with the sights of kings, and queens, and nobility, palaces and castles, famed cities, and famous rivers without number.

No young woman was ever placed in a more trying situation than she, and not one ever stood the trial more nobly. Work had prospered with the old man during her absence—perhaps the joy and pride he felt had lent effectiveness to his work. At any rate, Mrs. Allen was able to hire a woman to do the heavier household work, and many neat little articles had been added to the adornment and comfort of the modest parlor—which the old couple seemed to design as the special abode of their angel.

So far nothing had ever been said about any beau for Miss Stephania, and, but for meaning smiles and hints when she was with Mary and Emily Stewart, one would have supposed that she had not seen or spoken to a single young man during her travels. But one day our eyes were opened to the whole story. A fashionably dressed young man—a Northerner—arrived, in the A—— stage-coach, at the tavern, where he put on rather jauntily fashionable airs of the Northern type. After his toilet, from which he came forth resplendent, he inquired of the landlord, in an easy, careless way, if there was not a family by the name of Stewart living in the neighborhood; and when he was answered yes, he remarked that he believed an old gentleman by the name of Allen had a place near them, and learned to his apparent satisfaction that it was so; and thus the matter passed off that afternoon.

He had registered his name as Augustus Hotchkiss, Salem, Mass.; and much was the wonder why Mr. Augustus Hotchkiss, who was evidently neither traveling merchant nor mechanic, should have wandered away from Salem, Massachusetts, to such an out-of-the-way place as Yatton; and if any of our merchants had had dealings at Salem, they would have suspected him of coming on a tour of collection or espial. It came out afterward that Mr. Augustus Hotchkiss had met the Stewart party in Liverpool, and sought an introduction to them from persons they knew. As he was a young man of pleasant assurance and glib tongue, and was well connected, he was soon pronounced an agreeable acquaintance; and it was with pleasure that the party learned he was to return on the Flying Scud with them from Liverpool, whither he had gone with a consignment of his father's goods. As the Stewarts were rich, and Stephania was traveling with them as their equal in position,—as she was their superior in information and beauty,—and as he heard the girls speak to her once or twice, casually, about her father's "Place," he took it for granted old Mr. Allen was one of those wealthy Southern sheep who have always been sought as the choicest prey for Northern hunger; and when he learned that Stephania was an only child, he thought the gods were surely on his side. He had but little opportunity to make his court on the passage, which was unusually rough, and kept the ladies most of the time in their cabins; but he went sufficiently far to show that he was unmistakably a suitor for Stephania, and upon parting, hinted that he thought it likely he would soon visit the South as his father had business in A——, which might require his presence. So, after three or four months, here he was in Yatton.

The next morning Mr. Augustus Hotchkiss hired the landlord's gig—for he said he was not much accustomed to ride strange horses—and with the hostler's boy for a driver and guide, made his way to Mr. Allen's place. The road was very rough, as though but little used for wagons or carriages, and he repeatedly asked the boy Tom, if he was sure he was in the right road.

"Yes, sir," said Tom, "I's sartin I's gwine right. They aint no other road less'n you go 'round by Mr. Page's an' up the creek, an' dat's a mighty long road 'round!"

Mr. Hotchkiss no doubt began to think it "very strange! remarkably strange!" and perhaps mentally remarked that he would soon have a better road there—but when the gig drew up at the double log-cabin situated on the edge of a little clearing, and the boy told him: "Thar is Mr. Allen's, and yonder is ole Miss Allen in the passage," he was positively indignant, as he suspected that the negro wished to play a practical joke upon him.   Without showing his face beyond the gig-top, he questioned the boy closely:

"You say this is Mr. Allen's?"

"Yes, sir, 'tis!" said the boy emphatically.

"Is this the only place Mr. Allen has?"

"It's the only place I knows on," was the answer.

"What does Mr. Allen do?"

"Why, sir, he's a basket-maker, sir, an' sometimes works at the saw-mill," said Tom.

By this time Mrs. Allen, with a towel over her head, had come out of the house, and up to the fence, and asked the stranger if he would not alight and come in.

"No, I thank you, madam," said he.   "Does Mr. Allen live here?"

"Yes, sir," said she; "won't you come in?"

"I have not time just now, madam," said the unfortunate swindler,—I call him a swindler because he proposed to gain the pure and rich affections of a girl's heart in return for such a miserable, paltry piece of flesh as his own,—"not just now, madam.   Has Mr. Allen a daughter named Stephania, who was in Europe with the Stewarts?"

"Yes, sir," answered Mrs. Allen, "she is our daughter.   She will be at home presently.   Walk into the house."

"Excuse me, madam.   I am in a great hurry, as I

have to take the afternoon coach. I thought I would call by a moment and see Miss Stephania, if she was at home. Good-by, madam. Turn around, boy, and go back!"

"What name shall I say?" said Mrs. Allen, as the boy turned the gig, but Master Augustus pretended not to hear her, and rode back to town, paid his bill, and left in the afternoon coach as he proposed.

When old Mr. Allen, who had been in town on some business, came out by a nearer path through the woods, he began to joke with Stephania. "Oh, ho, Miss Stephy! so your grand beau has been to see you! They told me at the tavern that Mr. Augustus Hotchkiss had come to stay for a week or two as he said, and had come out to see you. What have you done with him, Miss Sly Boots? Eh?"

That told Stephania the whole story as well as though it had been written in black and white.

I do not think that her heart had been touched at all by Mr. Hotchkiss's charms, for she was, of all girls, difficult in her requirements of what one to love should be, and his manners were rather too much of the mercantile order to attract her at first sight. Indeed I do not think that with the most attentive and devoted wooing she ever would have accepted him, though he had been a millionaire. But what girl can regard without some emotion the intentions of her first lover; though he be ever so little to her taste, so long as he is not positively offensive? To think that she is loved will cause a flutter in every true heart; and she will say to herself: "I at least owe him some respect, since he loves me!" But here the false love was made naked at once, and Stephania found that the respect she had felt had been bestowed on the meanest of objects.

Of course I do not know what was in her heart. I only know that her heart was pure and sensitive, and that all of her ideas were elevated and refined. Of one thing I am certain, she never told the story to her parents, or breathed it even to her friends, Mary and Emily;—who did not see her until they had heard the whole truth, and were too much ladies and friends to hint of it to her.

Not many months after this, Stephania was inducted as Mistress of the Rose Hill School, about a half mile from her father's house, higher up the creek. It was a neighborhood school-house, delightfully situated on a high spot, a short distance from one of the main roads to Yatton, in a populous district; and she commenced her labors with twelve scholars. The path from her father's to the school-house was through the forest, so that she was but little exposed to the sun, or, except in very wet weather, to the rain; but one of the neighbors, when he thought of the distance she had to go in all weathers, loaned her a pony, which he had some difficulty in making her accept (she could not be induced to take it as a gift), and she and Sprightly—so was the pony named—were soon the best friends in the world. Her school gradually increased until she found her hands full with eighteen scholars, all of them devoted to their gentle mistress; and so it continued, old scholars leaving, and new ones coming, for about three years—which brings her to her twenty-fourth year, and me to the point of my story.

In the fall, I recollect the season, but not the year,

a neighbor came in haste one day for brother Eldred to go and see Mr. Allen, who was very ill. I think the old man was taken with congestive fever, then very common in the country, and his constitution received so great a shock, that he, for a long time, was confined to his bed. Brother Eldred's visits were at first necessarily frequent, but I noticed that even after he had told me the old man was convalescent, every day or two would find his horse traveling to the Allen place. He remarked to me one day during the severity of the attack, when I proposed to go and help nurse the old man, that it was unnecessary as he was very quiet, and needed little attention, and was annoyed by the presence of strangers; and when I asked him who were the nurses, he answered : "Mrs. Allen and Miss Stephania; and I tell you, brother, Miss Stephania is a noble woman, and reminds me more of our dear little mother than any woman I have met with yet."

This was the highest compliment I ever heard Eldred pay to any one, for he adored our dear mother; just as he reverenced our noble and wise old father. It used to make me feel very proud, when, in the fullness of the dear boy's affection, he would sometimes tell me that I resembled our father, who, I still think, was the most magnificent specimen of grand manhood, in mind, soul, and body, either of us ever saw. Alas ! my resemblance to him existed only in the love my dear brother bore us both.

One day, at the close of the winter, when Eldred came into the house after his morning round of visits, I noticed that he looked very much concerned, and he presently said to me: "Brother, you must look out another school for your pets" (I was sending a couple of orphans to the Rose Hill School), "for I have advised Miss Stephania to give up her school, and I am very much afraid it is even now too late." And presently he added, abruptly: "I've bought Mr. Allen's place."

I knew Eldred well enough to know that at a proper time he would explain to me what seemed so mysterious; but it was a long time before I learned the full particulars of the transaction.

It seems that when Mr. Allen was first taken sick, Eldred had remarked that Miss Stephania was a little troubled with a cough, but she had so many excuses for it—she had got her feet wet; or, she had sat up near the open window; or, it was a mere nothing, and would soon pass off—that his suspicions were allayed for a time, particularly as her father's case was so precarious; but the cough kept getting worse, and she lost her color, and he then began remonstrating with her, and advising her to give up her school—which she steadily refused to do. Eldred was so single-hearted himself, that he needed no hint to enable him to divine her reasons. Her father was sick, and she felt the whole duty of providing for the family to be on her. Here was now a difficulty. Had he been able to follow his own desires, he would have gladly supported the whole family, and even have moved them to the Virginia Springs if necessary; but he had too much delicacy to make a proposition which delicacy could not accept, and yet would be sorely wounded to decline. He was a gentleman *pur sang;* and I feel certain that he never in his life deliberately and unprovokedly hurt the feelings of man, woman, or child.

At last he solved the problem. The term of his tenant at the old home place was about to expire, and he was under no obligation to renew it. Mr. Allen was just then beginning to get about again, and Eldred finding him alone on the gallery, told him that he had been looking about his place, and found that it was a good mill-site, and he wished to purchase it, and put up a mill as soon as he conveniently could.

"If I sell you my place, doctor," said Mr. Allen, "what shall I do? for my living is here, as well as my home."

"As far as your living is concerned," answered Eldred, "it will be fully six months before you are able to do anything, and, in the mean time, your daughter's health is suffering severely from remaining in this low spot. To tell you the truth, Mr. Allen, although I do not wish to alarm you, your daughter must give up her school and remove from here, or I will not answer for the consequences. My house near town will be vacant at the end of this month, and I very much need a careful tenant for it. Sell me this place, and move there. You will do me a great favor by doing so. Speak to your wife about it, but say nothing to Miss Stephania. She is so much attached to her school children that she will oppose leaving them."

This was the conversation, in short, and it would be useless to recount all the difficulties which arose and were successively combated until Eldred's point was carried, and the first of the next month found the Allen family settled as his tenants, and the famous mill-site bought and paid for at a generous price. By-the-by, as I now own it, I would leave it to my grand-niece, if it were not that she might think I was adding insult to injury.

Stephania was too intelligent and sympathetic not to appreciate to its fullest degree my brother's plan and kindness; but she was ignorant of business, as indeed was her father, and had no idea but that he would make some profit by the transaction, though she knew he had not been moved by any such consideration. The excitement of moving and the change seemed to benefit her, but the improvement was only temporary, and she soon knew and began to realize that she was not long for this world.

Poor girl! while her health and strength had lasted, she had had little joy in living, but now that both were failing, life became very desirable. She saw the wealth of love in a strong man's noble heart ready to be lavished on her, but kept in check by prudence. How women know such things intuitively is more than I can understand, but they do know them, and it is the pure-hearted, not the cunning woman, who perceives it first. That she loved him I have no doubt, and that she loved with all the trustful love of the weak toward the strong, and the tender love of the holy and generous for the pure and great-souled, I have no doubt; and his gentle compassion must have been very sweet to her.

It was a hard fate—a very hard fate; but the Providence who had allotted the fate had fitted the soul to bear it. I do not think that Eldred knew of her love as I did. His humility blinded him. But even if he had known it, I doubt if he would have discouraged it, for he would have felt how precious it was to her, and in very pity would have spared her the treasure. She leaned upon his arm to take the daily walks he prescribed for her, and gained strength of soul; from his hands she received her medicines, and with them drank healthy draughts of love. Day by day she faded, and day by day her love grew more heavenly, until at last it was merged in the bliss of the saints, and her fair, fragile form was laid in the earth.

Many a rosy cheek was paled, and many beautiful eyes were dimmed with tears around the grave that day; and the voice of the preacher carried new impressions to the minds of the weeping girls when he read: "Blessed are the dead which die in the Lord from henceforth: yea, saith the spirit, that they may have rest from their labors; and their works do follow them."

Eldred was very serious, but showed no emotion. Her death was no shock to him. Whatever might have been the case under other circumstances, he had not felt for her the passion of love—only a warm friendship, and a very great and tender compassion. Her death was no doubt a relief to him, for he was too good a man even to think of what he might desire when another's sufferings were before him. She was simply the most admirable young woman he had ever known, and the most interesting patient he had ever had, and when he found that death alone could bring her relief, he welcomed death for one to whom it had no sting.

He was now forty-three years old, and knew that death was a great mercy. "Why, what a hell the earth would be but for death!" I have heard him say. "We often praise God for in his wrath remembering mercy

when he prescribed labor for man, and forget, in its re-
volting outward form, that death is the most precious
boon to sinful, woeful man. The thousand other blessings of life are but as flowers scattered along the path-
way to the Palace of Rest. When a child dies, what
has it lost? Nothing but a knowledge of sin, and
pain, and sorrow; for shall it not live again in pure
and unfading delights? And when a good man dies,
what has he not gained! The corrosion of sin could
not be arrested in any other way, and he rests in death,
to rise in incorruption at the Last Day. Even to the
wicked, death is a blessing, for without it this life would
eventually prove a hell whose torments would go on
ever increasing. Possibly his death puts an end to the
number of the sins which are to be his torments in
eternity. In fact, it must be so. The future state is
very different from what we imagine it if Mrs. Marlow,
for instance, is there to have another little Jenny to sin
upon. The little Jennies, it seems to me, shall all be
in heaven. But even admitting that it is not so, and
that the wicked go on committing sins, I cannot see
in what hell would differ to them from earth after a
lapse of a few thousand years. Even on earth they
often in a lifetime reach the point of despair, which is
but the seal of hell."

My poor dear boy! Only two years after this he
reached the period for his rest while far away from me.
He had gone to Alabama on an errand of mercy, to
reclaim, if possible, for a poor old widow, her son who
had there got into difficulty; and on his return, unsuc-
cessful, he stopped one hot June evening at the tavern
in Macon, shivering with cold. A doctor was called at

once, and several gentlemen of the town, brother Masons, came to wait upon him; but the congestive chill was too violent, and before day he was dead. I hastened there as soon as I heard of it, for how could I stay away, even though I were assured that he was dead and in his grave! Did I not have to see with my own eyes the room in which he died? and the place where they laid him? and gather with tender care, as precious relics, the clothes and papers he had left? and give my personal thanks, mingled with envy, to those who had seen him last, and had been kind to him?

They told me that while they were seated near his bed after all had been done which could be done, he said in a clear, sweet voice: "Good night, gentlemen!" and turned himself wearily on his side, and was dead.

Now I was truly alone in the world. Father and mother, wife and child, brothers and sisters, all were gone! and what had I left to live for? From that day to this I have lived for death. It has been the sweet term and fruition I have had appointed for my desires. Blessed be God, for Death! It will restore me to my loved ones, and I have the firm and glorious assurance that not one of them shall be lacking at our meeting.

"If in this life only we have hope in Christ we are of all men most miserable," says the apostle. "But now is Christ risen, and become the first fruits of them that slept. For since by man came death, by man came also the resurrection of the dead. For as in Adam all die even so in Christ shall all be made alive. But every man in his own order: Christ the first fruits: afterwards they that are Christ's at his coming."

Come quickly, Lord Jesus!

28*

CHAPTER XXX.

LET it not be thought that the old have no pleasures. I am sure that while I have been waiting these many years since brother Eldred's death, I have enjoyed myself far more than most of the young who have grown up and died around me while in the feverish pursuit of pleasure. My health has been perfect, and although I am feeble, nature lends herself with all her charms to beguile my way. The deep shade of the trees I planted as saplings under my Mary's direction afford me refreshing coolness in the burning heats of summer. The skies, whether in the brassy glare of August, or with their deep blue flecked with April clouds; whether darkened by tempest, or clothed in the fleecy dun of winter, are always beautiful to me; for they show the wisdom, power, and goodness of God, and I behold in my imagination, above and beyond them, the present abode of my blessed ones. The earth, with its hills and trees and flowers, its babbling rills and its grassy slopes, my imagination re-creates free from blemish, and from death, as our future eternal abode. Some spot like this I'll have in the suburbs of the Eternal City, and thither beneath unfading trees we'll gather, in the light which God gives us, to help each other toward perfection in all our faculties of mind and soul; and there shall be no night there. Mary's sad lullaby to her child shall be changed to sweeter, happier strains as she holds him in her arms; my mother's brow shall bear no brooding thought of care as she looks upon her loved ones around her; Eldred and our father shall discourse to us of the discoveries of wisdom, power, and love they shall find in their studies of the nature and works of God; and I, whatever may be my knowledge, shall be a loving little child in heart again. Except to do some pleasing task required by Heaven's polity, we'll never separate; and then the separation and the return will be but zest to our joy.

All this is not merely imaginative. Though there is no revelation upon the subject sufficiently definite to prevent the free exercise of the imagination, yet the revelation is sufficiently precise when taken with known facts, to guide the imagination with some degree of certainty.

It is revealed to us that there shall be a resurrection of our bodies, to which our souls shall be united, and that we shall thus dwell in our individuality throughout eternity. It is also revealed that there shall be a new earth upon which the saved shall live in eternal happiness. Now, God is the only source of happiness, for he is the source of all the attributes which constitute or add to happiness, and he is infinite in all his attributes. The finite can never become the infinite, though it increase throughout eternity.

From this it is to be induced that the blest shall spend their eternity in becoming more perfectly in the image of God in which they were created—that they shall become more perfect in being, wisdom, power, holiness, justice, goodness, and truth.

To be very plain, it is but a fair deduction from what is revealed, and from what we know of ourselves, that

we shall become more and more perfect in the knowledge and practice of the laws which govern human
actions, and in the laws of harmony and melody, of
color and light, and of all the other laws which govern
mechanics, mathematics, vegetable life, and whatever
else the attributes of man, made in God's image, are
fitted for learning.

All Christian philosophers are willing to admit that
the memory shall be perfect in the damned, and shall
constitute the basis of the torments of hell; and they
bring up evidences, both spiritual and material, to
prove it. For my part, I believe them without trouble,
and say, moreover, that in the future state of blessedness, I shall no doubt be able to whistle perfectly—
that is, if whistling be not offensive to glorified ears—
every tune I ever heard in my life here. Not a note
shall be lacking or untrue. And if any man have no
taste for music here, he shall acquire it there, and
during eternity become a first-rate musician. And so
with every other natural faculty and taste.

It is not at all philosophic to cry out upon this and
call it absurd, or say that it takes from the awe with
which we should regard the future state. Most men
never permit themselves to reflect upon the nature of
that state at all, except as something vague and dreadful; that is just the word—Dreadful! We are to be
happy, they all admit, but the happiness is to be altogether different from anything mortal beings can con-
ceive of, and of a character too dreadful to think about.

Let us be more reasonable. We shall be men still,
though glorified men, freed from sin and sorrow, pain and
death. Can you imagine myriads of glorified beings,

endowed with all the various faculties of human souls and bodies, spending an eternity in singing? which is not the best way to glorify God even here. Or shall they spend it in twiddling their thumbs? or in floating about hither and thither like birds, or like clouds endowed with volition?

As I approach nearer and nearer to my change, I take more and more reasonable views of what that change shall be. The contemplation of and trust in the attributes of God, as manifested in his works of Creation, Providence, and Redemption, are the basis of the happiness of the Christian here on earth, and the more fully he can understand and trust his God, the happier he is. His happiness in eternity shall be to fully trust, and to constantly increase in the knowledge of God.

The astronomer shall more and more fully understand the laws of matter and motion, and shall calculate with perfect certainty their action. The mathematician shall constantly find new and vast fields for the science of numbers. The musician shall make new operas, and make them more and more perfect. The mechanic shall discover new powers and new applications of the mechanical powers. The chemist, the botanist, the metallurgist, the microscopist shall each become continually more perfect in his art and science; and the chemist shall become also an astronomer; and the musician a mathematician; and the microscopist a mechanic; and all shall grow in the knowledge of the laws of moral relations, and all shall have common-sense. There shall be none of the vagaries and follies which have afflicted genius here.

Though I should write a volume on this subject, and should refer to all human learning about it, I could not make my idea more clear, however I might develop its details and consequences.   Let me return then to the point from which I started.

The old have many pleasures.   While writing this book, and the two or three others my executor will find in my desk, I have almost lived my life over again, and if at times it made my heart sad, the sadness had no sting.   The company of my young friends gives me more pleasure than it did when I too was young.   They little think that their health, and joys, and mirth impart more gladness to an old man's heart than they themselves can feel, and that their grace, innocence, and fresh beauty are dwelt upon in his mind as clear proofs of the eternal perfection he hopes for.

There is my little pet, Kate Bolling.   It makes my old heart smile to think of her, she is so bright and pure, and so loving to all around her.   Unlike poor Stephania Allen, though not more good or beautiful, she has no sorrowful story.   Her life has been one of mirth and sunshine, unclouded except sometimes by her own sad thoughts or gentle pity for others less blessed than she, or possibly—who knows?—by her little tempers which are inseparable from human nerves.

Her grandfather was my near neighbor and old friend—Isaac Davis; and the old place with an ample fortune had descended to Mrs. Bolling.   Kate had been born, when I had begun to think myself an old man, but she had been off to school and upon her travels so much that I scarcely ever saw her from her childhood, until she returned home to stay, nearly two years ago.

One afternoon just after she had arrived I called to make a neighborly visit, and when the beautiful girl came into the room to meet me, I almost thought her some lovely vision, and feared to take the delicate white hand put forth to welcome me. And when I thought of what I had heard of her intelligence and accomplishments, and remembered that she had traveled and been fêted and admired abroad, and the refinement she had been accustomed to everywhere, I felt embarrassed before so fine a lady, and hardly knew what topic I should touch upon not to betray my country breeding. And yet, when the conversation had become engaged, she seemed to think it so natural when in my old man's way of talking I called her my dear, and she entered so pleasantly into the playful vein our talk had taken—that I was encouraged soon to repeat my neighborly visit, and my visits became habitual and frequent.

Now, I am not going to pretend that in my old age I have found a non-such. I have seen more beautiful women, and women more wise and lovely. Had she been living in my youth, I should have had no hesitation in a choice between her and my Mary, and yet, for all that, she is a charming girl, and has very naturally taken a warm place in my affections.

She will no doubt at a future day marry some man she loves, and her life shall be merged in his; for him shall be her pride, her hope, and all her affectionate solicitude. I cannot say that I envy him; for if I could exchange my gray hairs for his youthful locks, or baldness—as the case may be—my old frame for his vigor, my memories for his hopes, my reflection for his passion, I would not do so. And yet I feel strangely jealous of him—and when I see a young man about her trying to make himself agreeable, I fear that he wishes to gain her affections also, and feel bitter toward him, and have an impulse of heart to think him a puppy, even though he be one I respect and have hitherto liked.

It would be easy enough to account for my hating a man who should be unkind to one I love; but whence comes this jealousy, which my reason tells me I must not indulge too far?

There can be nothing sinful in it, nor, since it is natural, will I call it foolish. Old men are even more tenacious of their love than young men; and well they may be. The young have life with all its buoyant hopes to look forward to; their love may be a rage, overwhelming while it lasts, but it is not all of life. An old man's love is all of the present he has to cling to, and his future is a blank unfilled by any hopes save those of heaven. He is jealous of the last lingering brightness of his life, and cannot bear to see it eclipsed. This is the true cause why old parents are so difficult to please in the choice their daughters make of husbands, and is, I suppose, the true reason why I feel such a pang when I think there is a chance my little Kate will marry. My heart says: God bless her! and my reason adds: and give her a good husband! But if I should let my heart alone speak, it would revolt against the husband, while I lived, unless, indeed, that husband should be one certain young gentleman whom I have long looked upon with the affection of a father. After thoroughly examining my heart, I can say conscientiously that although such an event as their marriage in my lifetime would give me a twinge, I would, after the first blow, rejoice at it. They are worthy of each other, and I sincerely hope they may, after this war is brought to a happy termination, love each other truly, and marry.

Miss Kate and I were talking about family names a few days ago, and she told me that she had never thought she could like the name of Abraham so well, and asked me how I happened to be called by that name. I told her that it was no family name, but that my father had given it to me for many good reasons. What those reasons were I will give here, though I did not inflict them at length upon her.

My father was a man who loved his Bible. From his youth he had carefully studied it, and he seemed to have a most intimate acquaintance with all the characters in it, and, no doubt, had formed in his own mind a distinct idea of even the personal appearance of each of them. Abraham is the first and almost the only gentleman whose history is given in the Bible. He is certainly the only one who came up to my father's idea of what a Southern gentleman should be; and if you will look at the facts, a Southerner is the only man who can come up to the noble type of gentleman presented to us in that Patriarch.

He was brave, hospitable, domestic, a just and kind master, a loving, patient husband, a generous neighbor, and a faithful servant of his God. But one reproach can be made him. "Ah, my son," my father used to say. "That trip down into Egypt was a dreadful one for Abraham's reputation. His fighting so bravely afterward confirms me in my belief that his conduct on this occasion must be looked at very narrowly to be properly judged. He started in the wrong by telling a lie, and that crippled his energies, as it would those of any gentleman. He could not cut Pharaoh's throat, because Pharaoh was not to blame, and, besides, his force was powerless in open war against the hosts of the king, and it was not likely the king would fight a duel with him, although he was a distinguished stranger. What was he to do? The plainest way I can think of would have been to go up and acknowledge that he had lied, and claim his wife again. But then the original cause of his lie would remain. Abraham, my son, was certainly in what we Southerners would call 'a fix,' and I presume that he thought it best to be very quiet and prudent, and to rely on God's promise and help for deliverance, and he no doubt went upon his knees and prayed with all his might that the matter should go no farther. God did deliver him, and he went away all safe, but crestfallen. Pharaoh's rebuke must have cut him to the heart, and he was, no doubt, glad to get away from among those who knew of his ridiculous disgrace; and the danger his honor had run must have made him tremble ever after when he thought of it." And my father, who had a keen sense of humor, would shake his head and declare that Abraham's accepting all those presents looked very badly, and that he did not at all understand him in the matter.

But, except in this one instance, where in all history can you find a nobler old gentleman than Abraham? He was the Master and Judge Supreme over his large household, and very courteous to his neighbors, and independent of them. His refusal to take the spoil offered him by the King of Sodom was as graceful an act as you shall find recorded anywhere; and his treatment of his very disagreeable relative, Lot, was far more generous and patient than could have reasonably been expected.

What other gentleman than a Southerner can be a Patriarch such as was Abraham? To be the master over hired servants does not call forth the qualities of mind and heart which distinguished him; for I contend that the justice, benevolence, independence of spirit toward equals, courtesy and kindness to inferiors; —in fine, the true dignity of man as he was made in the image of God with dominion, can be fully developed only in those who resemble him in the circumstance of being a master over slaves and responsible for them before God and man. The earth has never seen nobler gentlemen than Southern gentlemen.

The kind of gentleman made by universal equality is of a baser sort, and can only be called gentle in default of better. His is an ill-assured, shop-keeping gentility; an envious, contentious gentility; a discourteous, impertinent, assumptious gentility, which must result from the confused order of social position caused by the attempt to establish a factitious system of equality in defiance of nature. Under such a system the so-called gentleman is very likely not a gentleman at all; and even if he be a gentleman by birth, to be held as a gentleman he must necessarily be more or less of a snob, for the simple reason that his social position must depend upon his wealth and his assurance. This is the case even in countries where there are separate and well-defined orders. A family there, however noble, shall by loss of wealth after awhile become mere *roturiers,* and their remains of pride shall be very much mixed up with assumption. But with universal equality, the gentleman by birth has no chance at all unless he have wealth.

What I say does not result from pride of class, but from observation, and any man who has ever lived among the universal freedomites anywhere, or in any age, will confirm me in every particular. True, I am a gentleman, and so were my ancestors before me for ages. Why? Because, being gentlemen, their caste was assured in England, and since they have lived in this country, it has been in a section where the position has been equally assured. But if I had descendants, and universal equality should become the rule in this country, though my children might maintain their spirit and position, their children would be more or less snobbish, and in a generation or two more would be confirmed snobs, though they should be rich as so many Crœsuses. They would find themselves obliged to be very exclusive, very haughty, and very retired, to preserve their position—it would not be firm and unquestioned.

I have seen too much of the world not to understand this thoroughly, although I have never lived where this equality existed. The most exclusive, haughtiest, and most snobbish of all the Southern families I have ever known have been those which were *parvenues;* people of no former social standing, who have acquired great wealth, and consequently have taken this ill-assured position of gentility in society. They must needs put on airs of assumption to confirm what they felt was insecure. The same feeling of insecurity and spirit of assumption must needs produce the same conduct where wealth and assurance are all which can raise families above the surrounding dead level. As for virtue and talent without wealth, they are looked upon as impertinences.

I trust it will be ages before the changes in society in this country shall render the peculiar characteristics of the Southern gentleman impossible to be developed.

But enough of this. I have wandered far, but always in natural sequence of ideas, beyond the answer I gave to Miss Kate's question. Heaven forbid she should ever marry any but a Southern gentleman. A German Baron, or a French Marquis, or a Cotton-factory Lord would be but a poor substitute to a Southern lady—although my grand-niece thinks to the contrary, for herself.

CHAPTER XXXI.

ONE of the most singular of all the phenomena of old age, at any rate of my old age, is its barrenness of incident. I know that of late years very many things have occurred about which I could write—but they do not interest me. I find that I have forgotten them, or that my memory and feelings are sluggish about them. I do not speak, of course, of the great public events which I presume engulf almost all other incidents, even with the young. History will record them. I speak only of incidents in private life which affect me.   If I chose, I could fill volumes with little events of my earlier days which made profound impressions upon me.   My affections were then vigorous, and my relations in life were varied.   Now I am neither a father, a husband, a son, a brother, or a lawyer—I am nothing but an old man, living at peace, personally, with all the world.   Except Ben Eccles and my servants, there is not a soul dependent on me.   A visit to Miss Kate, or by her to me, is a marked event in my placid existence—because, I suppose, it is the only one which excites my affections pleasurably.

Yes, the only event; for my visits to John Mitchell, or to his sister Margaret, who now teaches the smaller children at the Academy, are seldom pleasant, except in a philanthropic point of view; and Ben Eccles, poor fellow, frequently bores me.

My executor will find among my manuscripts one which relates what I know of Ben Eccles, and I will therefore here say of him only that he is a good-hearted man, of good family, who used to be highly esteemed for intelligence, but who had at times, for many years, a singular derangement of mind which, while it lasted, unfitted him for any manner of business.   I took him to live with me not very long after the death of my brother Eldred, and he has given but little trouble, and often been of great convenience to me.

John Mitchell and his sister are, or rather were, orphans, and not very interesting orphans either—except, as I have said, in a philanthropic point of view.   Their father was an Englishman, a carpenter, who came to Yatton, some eighteen or twenty years ago, with his wife and two children.   He was a loose sort of char-

acter; frequently drank too much, and kept his wife
and children in hot water while he could drink, and in
utter misery while he had the consumption, from which
he speedily died. His wife soon took the disease, perhaps from him, as she had already got from him the
habit of drinking, and died also, leaving the two children destitute. John was a Jim Holmes sort of a boy
—just as sly, and far more reckless. His father had
whaled all feeling out of him; but after he had received
as good schooling as was possible in Yatton, he seemed
to be inspired with an ambition either to be genteel, or
to live without work, and, instead of becoming a carpenter or taking up some other trade, he must needs be
a doctor. He was gratified in that, sent to a medical
school, where he graduated, and returned here to Yatton three or four years ago, and commenced practice.

I have very little to say about him. His conduct,
so far as I know it, is irreproachable, but he is too
overwhelmingly grateful and shrinkingly humble to be
sincere, and he shows himself so selfish toward his
sister, who, as I have chanced to learn, has two or
three times had occasion to borrow a little money from
him, of which he has held her to the rigid repayment,
that I doubt if he will ever marry. He never will, unless he can benefit himself by marrying rich, and I do
not believe that any girl, in this part of the country,
above the class from which he sprung, will marry him.
However, we shall see. It is certain that if he live he
will be rich, and it is equally certain that he will not
be killed in the army. He has already been offered in
succession the posts of assistant surgeon and surgeon,
but he has his excuses, and no draft likely to be made

will include him. He has always a couple of fine fast horses which no press can take, because they are, or may be, necessary in his practice. I'll warrant that he keeps them fat, and keeps fat and nicely clad himself, whatever may betide.

If any one think that I am uncharitable in putting this on record, he is mistaken. The punishment is not commensurate with the offense. Add to it the pillory for life, and you should not be too severe, nor should you thereby add one stigma to the infamy which must descend to this man's remotest descendant. He deserves it all, and though he is but a poor little creature to be thus made notorious, he represents a class, on every one of whom the same remarks and sentence must be passed.

The truth is, that it as impossible to make a noble man out of an ignoble stock as it is to make a white man out of a negro. A great many good people have tried, and are trying of late days to make silk purses out of sow's ears; just as great masses of fanatics are trying to make the Ethiopian change his skin. Neither can succeed. The negro has been a negro for at least four thousand years, and will still be a negro four thousand years hence. The mean white has been mean for ages, and his blood will be mean for ages to come wherever it shows itself. But for all that, it is our duty to try and elevate the mean of each generation; for by doing so we improve in some degree, physically at least, the generations which succeed them. I have long since, however, found out that it is a foolish weakness to fall in love with the objects of our charity, and nurture them in our bosoms.

Nevertheless, there are orphans, and orphans. I have known some who could only be nurtured properly in one's heart of hearts.

About thirty years ago there came to Yatton a young lawyer and his wife. She had been a Miss Ellen O'Brien, of South Carolina, born and raised a lady, and had married Robert Harley, of Virginia, a young lawyer just getting into good practice in his native State. But the climate of Virginia had proved unfitted for her, it was thought, and the doctors advised her removal farther South. So they sold all their property except three or four family servants, and removed to Yatton, in a pretty cottage, in the suburbs of which they lived in quiet and elegant simplicity. He brought most flattering letters of introduction, but they were scarcely needed; his appearance and manners were sufficient to introduce him favorably anywhere.

His gentle and beautiful young wife loved him with perfect devotion—which was not at all wonderful, for he was in all respects as noble a young man as I have ever known—and he repaid her love by the most tender affection and solicitude.

His first appearance at the bar was in a criminal case of some notoriety, which he defended successfully with rare tact and splendid eloquence. Business flowed upon him—more than he could possibly attend to was offered; for he was as genial and bright in private life as he was learned and eloquent in his profession. As he never felt the want of money, he never cared enough for it to accumulate it. He seemed to continually put off to a future time the care of making provision for his family in his old age or in case of his death.

Mrs. Harley's health remained delicate for three or four years, and he would travel with her every summer to this and that springs, to the seashore, to the mountains,—wherever it was suggested she might receive benefit,—until at last little Robert, their first child, was born. Harley was almost perfectly happy, for the little fellow seemed to bring health with him to his mother, who became rosy and strong, and devoted herself with unfagging love and pride to his care and adornment.

I have never seen a man who could do so much business so thoroughly in so short a time as Harley. His powerful mind was perfectly under control, and he could direct all of its force upon each complication and dispose of it while most other men would be hesitating about its preliminaries. The new happiness which had come upon him seemed to give a grandeur to his mind and a gentleness to his feelings which made him even more attractive than before, though he had never seemed lacking in either grandeur or gentleness. He made a great deal of money, but he had a great facility for spending, also. He gave large and splendid dinners and evening parties. He insisted that his wife should dress splendidly—and as he was particularly fond of precious stones and jewelry, he continually made her presents of those things, which she did not wish to wear and did not know how to decline.

Three years after Robert's birth Alice was born, and two years after that Harley died suddenly of apoplexy —and within the year his wife followed him. When the estate came to be settled up, it was found that there were unpaid accounts, some of them very large, in almost every store in town; and when they were all paid, the children were almost penniless.

When, after Mrs. Harley's funeral, I saw Robert and his sister: he a manly little fellow, and not yet able to fully realize his loss; she´ a beautiful little curly-headed girl, already imperious, rigged out in her finery by her nurse, and seated on the floor playing with a book of plates, and calling: Mamma! mamma! and presently saying to her nurse: "Betty, tell mamma come!" I determined that not even an Orphan Asylum, blessed institution as it is, should have the management of them—and I took them to my house, where they remained until old enough to be sent to school. They were the two orphans Miss Stephania Allen was teaching; and they have repaid me by affection and by their own goodness and intelligence for all my care. Alice married a very excellent and wealthy gentleman, who is now colonel of one of our regiments; and Robert, a promising lawyer, is a captain in the same regiment.

People are so accustomed to hear charity sermons, and charity cant, and charity begging, and to see speculations for charity, and charity swindles, that nowadays the very name of charity has been suggestive of money, and causes a sinking of the heart and an involuntary grasp upon the pocket-book.

But let any one take a moment of solitude, and imagine himself an orphan child, or his children little orphans, with only strangers to look to for love and assistance if they are to have love and assistance at all, and if he have any imagination and heart he will find a feeling of sad compassion coming over him.

The source of most of the hard-heartedness in this world is thoughtlessness. There is no lack of sympathy when men allow themselves to imagine themselves in the place of those who are needy or suffering. The injunction, "Know thyself," means: know not only what you feel and think now, but also how you would feel, think, and act under any given circumstances. Compassion and sympathy are feeling just as the object presented feels. We have compassion upon the suffering, and sympathy with the poor or joyous, only when we can imagine that we feel just as the suffering, or the poor, or joyous feel.

Try, while by yourself to-day or to-night, and imagine yourself, or your child, an orphan. You will then be able to sympathize with an orphan. Many of the little children at the orphan asylums have had as good and loving parents as you or your parents, and as comfortable homes as yours; but the parents are dead, and the homes are desolate or occupied by others.

Shut your eyes now, and give the reins to your imagination. You are dead; your little boy and girl are parentless. They can be no longer clasped in your arms. Their tears are unheeded, or harshly reproved. Their wants, even if relatives supply them, are only half foreseen or provided for. Your anxious love no longer watches over them, and their joys and their sorrows must be imparted to strangers. But those to whom you or circumstances have intrusted the little ones deprived of your care, become weary of them and they are shifted off to other strangers, or allowed to run, half wild, upon the streets, until at last they are sent to an orphan asylum—if there be one in the community. Thank God for that! They have a refuge at last, and their most necessary wants may be supplied,

even though the supply be precarious. Charity is often
at a discount in the community, and sometimes bread
and meat and clothes are scarce with your little ones
and the other little ones congregated there; and you can
imagine your cherished children trying on the half
worn-out shoes, and out-grown jackets and frocks sent
in chance of a fit by some fortunate mother, and can
see their pride and comfort in wearing them, and can
see, too, the greed and joy they feel at the little treat
of a piece of cake or a bit of candy—those children you
now love so much, and who have everything they can
desire.   And you see them of a Sunday going to
church in the procession, two by two, with the ill-
assorted dresses, and shabby, well-brushed shoes, and
thread-bare pants (for charity, remember, is at a discount), and see them file in and take their seats to hear
a sermon upon Charity, which falls upon weary ears,
and excites no sympathy for your dear children. They
go back to their public home, and the matron, though
she be an angel upon earth, can work no miracle and
give them delicacies where there is a lack of even plain
food, and though she were endowed with all human
wisdom, and goodness, and patience, cannot indulge
them in all the childishness you would have tolerated.

All this is very sad.   Even though a bountiful fund
were provided for the public charity, it is sad to be dependent upon a public charity for love, and for food
and comfort. How much more grievous for matron,
and nurse, and children, where the fare is poor, and
scant, and precarious, and even rags, and old hats, and
bonnets, and shoes are acceptable gifts! How infinitely
worse is it when there is no public charity! I had al-

ready begun to think myself growing old when the first orphan asylum was established in any town near Yatton.   The population of our country was so sparse, comparatively, and the circumstances of the whites were generally so good that there was but little use for such institutions.   But I am convinced that, except in special instances like that I have narrated of Robert and Alice, it is best where children have to depend upon strangers for a support, to place them in orphan asylums.   My observation has taught me that, in nine cases out of ten, they are more apt to retain their self-respect when dependent upon the public, than when upon private charity—and not only so, they have less opportunity for ingratitude.

I made my little story about Alice and Robert as short as possible, because I only told it for illustration. But I may as well say here, in explanation, that I do not leave my property to Alice because she has enough without it; and I do not leave it to Robert for reasons which I will explain to him when I see him, and which I heartily—yes, fondly—hope shall prove satisfactory.

[NOTE BY THE EXECUTOR.—Captain Harley was killed at the battle of Seven Pines, while bravely leading his company.   It was Mr. Page's great desire that he should marry Miss Kate Bolling.   I knew Robert when he was quite a small boy, and he then bade fair to become the noble young gentleman Mr. Page considered him.   I suppose that Miss Kate was also acquainted with him, but from what Mr. Page has already said, I have no idea that anything more than a mere acquaintanceship had sprung up between them in the short time which elapsed between her return home and his starting off to the Virginia army.

Ben Eccles, who is mentioned in this chapter by Mr. Page, died in 1864.]

CHAPTER XXXII.

SINCE I wrote the last chapter the confusion of a great war has surged up all around me, and the events of my life, and my life itself, have become so dwarfed that I have no patience to task my memory with the one, and would feel ashamed of my unsympathetic egotism in writing about the other. What I have written is written, and I am glad that I wrote it before the present great excitement, for now I could not write it if I would; I cannot even revise it. If I should be alive and well when a glorious peace shall close our successful struggle, I will go over it again and correct its errors, if I shall discover them, and make its language more harmonious if I can, and add to it if I find it proper; but with the misery, and sorrow, and dread, and pain all about me, as it is all about in every part of my country, I have no heart to write or think of myself.

In reading over this paragraph I have just written, I find that I have three times repeated the same idea—the idea of a general trouble which absorbs all other interests. The earth, the air, fire and water, are full of that idea. The earth bears or withholds its fruits, and its minerals and metals, in relation to it; the rains descend and the waters rise and flow, for good or ill, with regard to it alone; the air vibrates with the wails of sorrow and pain and the mighty din of conflict, until the soft accents of peaceful love can no longer be distinguished; and fire lightens, hisses, and roars from the ends of the earth only to increase that trouble. All nature seems to act and torment itself alone for our safety or destruction; and man's individuality is as much swallowed up in the confusion of the physical contest as it shall be engulfed in the social amalgamation which must result from the moral and political maelstrom into which the triumph of the principles we oppose would plunge us. May God prolong and even intensify the present trouble rather than deliver us into the worser woe! The present trouble may end in peace, but the principles which war against us can only bring on continuing misery and renewed war, to end in destruction and a new creation.

I have perfect faith in the justice of our cause, and great confidence in most of those we have constituted our leaders. With the great man upon whom we have imposed the task of finding and organizing strength for our weakness, and accomplishing by all means our desires, I have a profound sympathy. No man has ever before borne such a responsibility against such odds; and yet I have a firm belief that if we be true to ourselves, and the agents he selects be faithful, he shall, by God's help, and without a thought for his own personal aggrandizement, bring us through the effort a free and prosperous people. I believe that he loves, more than he loves himself, the people who have of their own accord imposed the burden of their troubles upon him, and that he has the honest and firm conviction that strict constitutional government is the only safety of mankind from the evils of the selfishness of their own nature. If we succeed, he will rank the greatest of historical men in varied ability and virtue, and if we fail, and he survive the failure, his only care for his own fate shall be to preserve in it his own integrity, and illustrate by his life or death the brave and honest people who have made him their head, the class of Southern gentlemen from whom he has sprung, and the Christian fortitude he professes.

It may be that I shall not live to see the end of our contest. I am a very old man. I have passed my threescore years and ten, and can truly say that my strength is now "labor and sorrow." The rest by Mary's side shall be sweet, and I will be glad when the time comes for me to be gathered there, for I am very weary.

I wish now, and here, to lay aside the past, with all its joys and sorrows, its right things and its errors, its approvals and condemnations, as they exist in my memory, retaining only the hopes and feelings my experience and observation of the goodness of God has engendered. To hope, to love, and to weep are the only results of all the learning of my life worth a thought. I have learned to love my fellow-men, to weep for the miseries of humanity, and to hope for a better future for it on earth, and the blessedness of heaven for many more of my race than I once thought could be received there. The hopes must end with life or fruition; the tears shall be changed to admiration in contemplating the justice and goodness of God; the love alone shall remain suffusing my being throughout eternity.

At early dawn this morning I walked in Mary's garden. The birds sang to me of her, and the soft, perfumed breeze whispered to me that in all its wanderings, it had not met her since she stood there at my side. But I have no fear that I shall not find my Mary. Before my body shall be laid by hers my love shall have urged and guided me to her, waiting with eager patience to lead me in sweetest converse to the presence of our Lord.